Clochán

By Lawrence Patrick O'Brien

Mischief Makers
Swallowing the Muskellunge
Clochán

Clochán

A Novel

LAWRENCE P. O'BRIEN

2021

Clochán © 2021 by Lawrence P. O'Brien
www.lawrenceobrien.ca
LoonCE paperback edition 2021

LIBRARY AND ARCHIVES CANADA CATALOGUING IN   PUBLICATION DATA

Clochan
O'Brien, Lawrence

ISBN 978-1-7778155-2-3 (hardcover)
ISBN 978-1-7778155-0-9 (paperback)
ISBN 978-1-7778155-3-0 (EPUB)
ISBN 978-1-7778155-1-6 (PDF)

I. Ireland—History—Rebellion—Wexford—1797-1812—Fiction
I. O'Brien, Lawrence II. Title

Clochán is a work of fiction. Any resemblance to actual events or persons, living or dead, is entirely coincidental. The events occurring in the Irish rebellion, and the murder of John Colclough and animosity between the Colclough families is widely reported in historical documents. For the purpose of the story, the number of characters and their roles in bringing trouble to the brothers of Tintern Abbey was simplified. Although the Colcloughs and Denis Brien are historical characters, their story as written is purely fictional.

Cover design by Damonza.com
Wexford map by Lawrence P. O'Brien
Published in Canada by LoonCE

For my father—Patrick

The *Tuatha Dé Danann* (people of the goddess Danu) came to Ireland in a cloud of mist from the west. The Celts who arrived much later, went to war and took everything they saw. The *Tuatha* took everything else—they coveted the underground and the forests. The Celts in return named the land after one of the women killed. Her name was *Éirinn*.

Paraphrased from the Irish medieval manuscript *Book of Leinster.*

In early times a chieftain offered a knight a reward for getting rid of a fearsome monster in a deep lake at the foot of Mount Laighean. He was offered a large tract of meadow, forest and a river by the mountain, a noble title, and

the hand of the very beautiful dark-eyed *Banbha.*

The local chieftain neglected to mention that Banbha resided at the top of another mountain far away on the other side of the island. She was a defiant warrior princess who would not be moved and like her sister *Éirinn*, belonged to the *Tuatha Dé Danann.*

Paraphrased from

Evenings in the Duffry, Patrick Kennedy, (1869), p. 246 and

Legends of Mount Leinster, Harry Whitney, (1855), p. 17.

CONTENTS

PART 1: In a Bad Way (1798–1799)

You've learned to walk on your own. (Joseph Kavanagh)

Loki's Shadow

Thomas stepped up onto the stones and gave the top a firm stamp. The short dry-stone boundary wall didn't shake. "Laid before the damned landlords, I'll bet," he muttered with an eager rasp. He stood tall to take in the view ahead.

Aside from this spot, brambles, vines, and short bushes over-laid or replaced stones. The rest of the wall was wild-looking, like the rest of the property lines. The many boundaries ahead blocking his path to the mountain road were a mixture of light browns with light and dark greens and intermittent splodges of rust. The fields were tinted with yellow browns, and emerald, lime, and dark greens. Amongst such personality and wicked good looks in the landscape, he noticed the occasional run of vermin. Up on the mountain road, some of the landlord's riders disappeared behind a cover of trees.

Above the road, the dark green forest covered the slopes below the towering cliff face of the mountain. An orange glow lit across the summit.

Scratching his nose, he said to himself, "Yes, but maybe Denny was right."

The young storyteller wiped his brow, checked behind and then hopped off the wall.

When he got close to the mountain road, a red-orange sunset shone through breaks in the mountain's smooth line. An angled shadow stretched from the gash across the crag facing him into the thick woods he was trudging towards. He pushed his long, sweaty brown curls back. "There's no understanding him," he ranted again.

A slip on wet horse dung almost caused him to fall. Skipping a step to maintain his balance, he continued with a "Well, how do you like that?"

"Gahd," he said after noticing the tear in his shoe had ripped some more. "Just until I get home, and that'll be grand." He bent down and retied the loose laces. "It'll be a terror if it doesn't last, won't it? Nothing more I can do about that, is there?" He gave the ground his spit.

He checked around before getting up.

"The first Irish sorrow is about the Children of Tuirenn. The children do impossible things… Loves his stories, doesn't he? Quoting that one will set him right, won't it?"

He proudly clenched the lapels of his well-worn tweed coat. When he fingered the coat's top button, he found it dangling loosely. Afraid it would come off, he let it go, pulled on his cap brim, and marched on to the Stua Laighean mountain road.

When he got there, he checked to his left where the landlord's men had gone and then the turn where he was headed. He didn't see a soul. When he checked back the way he had come, he recalled the conversation with his brother before leaving.

"So why are you going?" Denny asked.

"There's got to be a better way. Just because he's got a thick head doesn't mean I should give up, does it?"

"Do you listen to what you say half the time?" Denny asked.

"He'd go on for so many times," Thomas said. "how I hadn't got the other two right. Telling the old stories I mean. 'It's like this and that,' he'd say. But he was right—with those stories we got to fix their pots, didn't we? Good money until the Sheriff's men stole from us, wasn't it? I owe him. We owe him. Even when he's a touch off.

"You was the one that was always going on that you wished him dead, that he'd leave forever.

"Can you blame me? There was a real flare-up. He got really out of control, and it looked like he was going to do us serious harm.

"You see, the world was on fire—Captain Kelly trying to save us all and gahd—this one hides away; and all them listening…they're dead. He didn't like that a bit. And when I asked him—what about the orphans, Mr. Keane ordered me not to come back..

"And he who he is; my gahd—no arguing that. I tore out of there faster than if I sat on a hive of bees.

"Go on with yeh then. Just make up your mind."

Thomas ripped a leaf from a bush and flicked it away with his middle finger.

"No, Denny, I guess I don't listen."

Thomas walked sombrely in the grey gloom until he reached a darker patch in the road. Branches from thick rows of trees on both sides interlocked over the road.

Maybe we can start again. It's all about trust, isn't it? Time enough, isn't it?

Thomas, with closed fists, walked on. Eerie web-like shadows felt like they were closing in.

"And he told me not to come back," he whispered.

He heard a light sound of branches stretching and grabbing. Thomas grabbed his lapels and focused back on the road.

"And if he asks why am I here? Well, I've had my chores, I'll tell him. And as my brother tells me, I sometimes forget.

"And if he doesn't like that, I'll say I'm here because it's Denny's fault. 'Two farts in the wind,' he calls us."

Thomas followed the turnoff from the main road. It was bound by a hedged line of trees on the left side and thick bushes behind. There were still open pastures behind a line of trees on the right. He felt he was being followed but didn't see anything behind him. Scratching the back of his neck didn't help.

He followed a fork to the left that would lead him deep into the forest.

"If I say I'm sorry, is that going to be enough?" Thomas muttered. A snap came from the forest. Nothing moved on his left. Frozen, he clenched his fists again.

Got to get this over with before the light goes. He picked up his pace to a light trot. He stumbled over a thick branch hidden in the shadows. When he tried to get up, he noticed that his shoe was in a bad state. The rip stretched from the side to the front, showing a bare toe. *That's the last thing I need right now.* He heaved the branch into the brush and walked on.

He arrived at an open spot where he usually met Mr. Keane. Thomas called out his name a few times, but no-one called back, which was odd because Mr. Keane had unusually good hearing.

Although the light was weak, a swathe of changing shadows encircled him. The figures on the evergreens shifted like tall giants hovering over prey. Flailing motions scared him back to the path he had come from. The trees towered around him. In the break between two bushes directly in front, he faced the darkest of the dark.

He refused to give up his position but kept scratching an upper arm incessantly. Ten minutes of relative quiet passed. Thomas debated whether to go back or start walking uphill. He waited some more and then called again.

If he wanted to talk to me, it wouldn't be difficult to find me, would it? Nothing gets by him.

Scuttering sounds came from somewhere ahead but deep inside the forest.

"Wolves," said Thomas. *Giant wolves. 'No way,' says Da. Killed off a long time ago. But all those terrible piercing eyes and all that ripping apart business.*

Whatever was in the forest stopped. There was only the light sound of wind shaking the tops of trees.

Just a field mouse. That's what it was. Heaven's name—field mice is what it is. Well maybe a small fox.

Mister Keane must be here somewhere. He's just busy. He scratched the stubble on his cheek. His stomach growled.

With all this trouble and this late hour it would be appreciated if he could give us something to eat. Well, either that or I'm going home. He slapped his leg and rubbed his hands together and took another deep breath.

With another "Lord forgive me," he marched right on through the bushes and into the opening in the forest.

Something scraped at the tear on his boot. "Not again," he said and froze. It was quiet, but hairs rose on the back of his neck. He couldn't see anything, but he was convinced something was in there and that it was bigger than a mouse.

"My," he muttered, and slowly hobbled back out.

In the clearing, he heard only the wind. "In the name of the Almighty, what am I going to do?"

Something rushed deep in the forest. It slowed, and then it seemed to meander as it rushed downhill. It sounded heavy, swift, and powerful.

"Heavens," he moaned. "What's happened to Mr. Keane? This isn't right."

Thomas continued moving backwards on the path that led to the main road. He stopped to listen.

Whatever was in the forest stopped.

He removed his cap and clenched it in his fist. Fear that started in the pit of his stomach was rising. Thomas didn't care about trying to figure out what it was; he had heard enough. He pivoted on his foot and raised the other to turn. Three toes protruded from the end of the torn boot.

Thomas knew that if it wanted him, it would get him. Seeing the open road, he lunged forward for a powerful run. Dim twilight lit the way. The young man leapt over rocks and shadows, desperate not to slip on fresh horseshit. Ignoring the racing steps behind, he ran faster, faster than he thought possible. Thomas didn't care that he was about to lose his boot. Breathing so hard he didn't hear it come alongside. Before responding to the musky breath at the back of his neck, he overheard the most frightening thing he had ever heard in the whole of his life—his own voice screaming as his body was ripped apart.

Crossings

The phrase, *Isn't there something you're forgetting?* took form. The dark of the dark floats on the infinite. An existence oozes into ether from a determining virtual still point warding off forgetfulness. He is succumbing to a drowning numbness with an inevitability of fading dreams. The phrase within the bubble is nurtured within.

Alone and almost without projection or sense, an existence referred to as Kevin Neal accepts the question.

Only bad memories, came an answer.

From blackness came a glimmer of story. Within that light smouldered.

Kevin realized at the end of times that he was older because there was a life before. Slipping into darkness, he waited in disbelief for the next memory.

The word "find" was within.

What? was his answer.

Remember when you were young?

Remember? He was hesitant to define that word. It meant direction, but where he was—there wasn't any.

Remember, he repeated.

I remember grabbing the stick. In his mind, he closed his hand into a fist.

"Find," repeated the voice.

The beast, added Kevin, as his body kept sinking in the water's deathly embrace.

The twenty-one-year-old was in a tight spot.

From within a mist-like smouldering flicker was a vision of the first of his many troubles. Kevin Neal was seven, which was five years before Thomas had been killed.

To reach him, you followed the mountain road for a mile after Kiltealy village to his neighbours, the Kellys. Their small cottage was turned away from the road. Its rolling fields stretched away from the trees at the base of County Wexford's tallest mountain to an openness that extended towards a misty horizon.

On the path to the cottage, a pair of women and two girls rushed back and forth in half circles around a motionless little boy, like a flock of birds preparing for migration. The women were sorting out who was going to take flight first. The motionless one next to the dropped coat was Kevin Neal.

Kevin's sister, as she paced towards the Kelly's cottage, yelled, "I *am* going." She wiped sweat from her brow with her sleeve.

"Heaven help us. No, you're not, Kathleen," replied Mrs. Neal. "I've got to bring Seamus home. I don't have time…"

Kathleen picked up her ankle-length dark-brown dress, revealing matching socks and brogues. Without looking back, she ran to the road.

"But, Mam…" said little Kevin as his mother passed him by.

On the other side of Kevin, Mary Kelly said, "Don't you dare."

"I've got to go," said Mrs. Margaret Kelly as she paced nervously to and from the cottage. "…and you're not to see that Stephens boy, do yeh hear me? No, you're not. And you'll watch over Anty. Do yeh hear?"

"But...?"

"Do you hear?" Mrs. Kelly repeated. "That's the last of it. Don't start on me. Your sister's inside—by herself."

"No."

Mrs. Kelly stopped and gave Mary a terrible mad glare.

"I hope they run away from you," Mary said as she rushed towards the cottage.

"That's awful. You don't really..." Her mother let go of her skirt to swat locks from her face. "Anyway, we'll talk about this when I get home. I've got to go." She turned and saw Mrs. Neal running after her daughter, who already was already well ahead of them on the mountain road. She noticed that Kevin was staring at her.

"Mr. Murtagh will be fine," Mrs. Kelly said. She pulled her kerchief up over her hair and wiped her hands on her apron. "Kevin, Anty's inside. Sorry, but it's really important. I have to go." She picked up her skirt and ran after the other two.

As Kevin stared at Mrs. Kelly, his mother, and his sister hurrying down the road, there was the sound behind him of Mary Kelly slamming the cottage door. The noise of minutes ago was replaced with an unnerving quiet.

The boy wore a long-sleeved linen shirt, with coarse woollen knee-breeches, and bare feet. His hair was cut short like his father's. He dragged his toes across in front to make a mark in the dirt.

Mary Kelly came rushing back out of the cottage and told him, "Kevin, you can't stay there. You've got to go inside."

Unmoving, he stared at the line in the dirt.

"Anty's inside. I've got to go. She'll stay with you until I get back," she told him.

"Kevin Neal, look at me."

When Kevin raised his eyes, young Mary repeated, "I want you to go in with her 'til I'm back, do you hear me?"

Kevin nodded. He watched her climb over the short boundary wall and hurry away.

"Should go in," he said as he looked back at the cottage. Putting his finger to his lip, he considered trying to get Anty to give him some food from the kitchen. Her name was common in the Wexford mountains. It was short for Anastasia.

"Bossy," he said.

He wiped his snotty nose with his sleeve.

A strong, chilling wind made Kevin pick up his coat. As he tried to put it on, he noticed that sheep and lambs were trying to escape through the open gate.

"No, no, you bad sheep," he yelled.

As he tried to pull on the other sleeve, he ran to stop them from getting out. He reflexively hopped back after his bare foot almost stepped on a soggy sheep dropping. While stopped, he pulled his sleeve up again. In front of him, another sheep sauntered out through the gate.

The young lad hurried over, shooed the others away, and started to close the gate. He saw animals loose on the other side, so he stopped and slipped through instead. Kevin picked up a stick that was leaning against the fence. His brother Seamus had shown him how to use it to loop the rope, over the post. He reached to touch the rope but a lamb sneaked out by running around his feet. "Hey," Kevin warned.

Facing the escapees on the other side of the road, he said, "Bad sheep. You have to come home. I count oooo-n-e, two, three, f o u r, five..."

He pointed to the last one but didn't know the number. "I see you," he warned. He shook a finger but looked wistfully up at a trail that led up to Cloroge More hill.

"Kevin, you can't do that. Get back here."

He turned and saw nine-year-old Anty running towards him. *She's a girl. She's going to squeal,* he thought. *I'll get in trouble.* He looked back at the path that led up the hill.

Anty opened the gate and closed it behind her. Her hair was tied back in a bun like her mother. She wore a knee-length woollen dress, long stockings, and shoes.

"Kevin Neal! You're not supposed to be here. What are you doing?" she asked.

"Sheep got out."

"But you're supposed to be on the other side," she said as she put her hands on her hips. She took a deep breath and looked at the loose sheep and said, "Never mind. Let's get them in."

When Anty brought the last lamb towards him, he opened the gate again and told her, "You always say you want to climb the mountain…"

She looked up and then back at the open gate.

"They did leave it open, didn't they? We do have an excuse," she said.

"An adventure," he said. He remembered that Seamus had repeated that to his older brother, Aiden. Besides, Anty had told him that less than a week ago.

Anty stared at the trail and said, "Maybe we could go a little way."

"Will we see my da?" asked Kevin.

"Coming?" she replied, as she passed him.

Kevin took the stick leaning against the fence, ran after and passed her.

"Hey," she yelled. She raced past him towards the stream. When Anty got there, she ran across the stones and jumped to the other side.

Kevin hopped from one stepping stone—one clochán—to another. Before hopping to the fourth one, he crouched and smashed the surface of the water a couple of times with his stick.

"Are you coming?" Anty yelled.

Kevin tried to get up but wavered when he was almost up. He dropped his stick and screamed, "Yeaaagh!" He stepped back but missed the stone and landed in the stream. The water reached his knee. He was about to fall sideways but spun and landed on the other foot which got wet just above the ankle. He managed to twirl and flopped onto the beach.

"Wow, that's cold," he yelled.

"Well, look at you." She put her hands on her hips. "And you threw away your stick. What if we get attacked by monsters? Well, I'm going. Catch up, if you can."

As his stick floated away downstream, he watched Anty disappear into a line of trees. He got up, and as he brushed the dirt off, he sensed a presence on the other side of the stream, beyond the trees. He didn't see anything. Other than the steady gurgling from the stream, it was quiet. He stared back at where Anty had gone. *It's there because she's not here*, he thought.

Tree branches on the other side ruffled. For an instant, Kevin froze. They started shaking again. Without further hesitation, he raced to the place where Anty had disappeared.

As he raised his bare foot to run, he wondered, *was it the breath of the faeries in the wind or were bad men speaking?* He remembered that the last time his family was together was at Mass at the top of the hill and he and Anty had been looking up at the mountain.

A week and a half earlier, Kevin had come to the crossing with his mother, and old man Kavanagh had been there to stop him. "Joseph Kavanagh, don't let Kevin cross before I get there," she yelled. "Joseph, do you hear me?"

Old Mr. Kavanagh waved in acknowledgement.

Kevin stopped, turned back and saw his mother's eagle-like eyes staring at him.

The man sat on the grass, a few feet to the boy's right. His feet dangled over the small bank.

The stream was only about five feet across, and Kevin didn't think it was deep because grass grew in the middle. It was lined with tall trees and spotted with tall grasses and plants. His father and brothers had already crossed and gone beyond the trees on the other side.

"Do you like our eggs?" Kevin asked.

"Eggs?"

"I feed the chickens and my brother—"

"Seamus. Yes, it's nice of him to bring me some. I saw him and your brother go by with your da a few minutes ago."

"And I—"

"—and you feed them. I know. If they could talk, they'd say you're a good lad."

Kevin looked down at his Sunday shoes and kicked a rock into the creek. He paced around the path to the stream, while he looked for something else to say.

"Are you fishing?" Kevin asked.

"Do you see a rod?"

"No."

"Then, I guess that means I'm not fishing."

"Then what are you doing?"

"I'm thinking."

"Why?" asked Kevin.

"Why not?" Mr. Kavanagh replied.

"Are you thinking about fishing?"

"No."

"How come you're not going across?" asked Kevin.

"I'm weighing the cost of getting to the other side. Besides, there's lots to see here. There are birds, fish, plants—and nosy people like you."

Kevin watched his feet go back and forth, and then he looked back at his mother.

The old man smiled. "Have you ever been up there?"

"No, but my Mother's over there with those ladies and she'll tell you lots if you don't go to Mass up there."

"I suppose you're right, Kevin. One way or another, I'm in for it. Do you see that water there? That's the Urrin River."

"It doesn't look very big."

"Here it's small, but the mountain feeds lines of streams into it farther down and eventually it becomes a river. Little things can become bigger things in time. This water will go around Duffry Hall, into Enniscorthy town where it joins the wide, gentle Slaney River which meanders through the heart of the county. It goes a long way and it will force its' way into the Irish Sea. Do you know what a sea is?"

"No," Kevin answered. He looked back and he saw that the other ladies had finally reached where his mother was waiting for them.

"The water in the sea is like this water, but it's filled with lots and lots of salt. You wouldn't want to drink it. It has huge fish in it and they're bigger than both of us. They can eat you up. You'd be a nice tasty snack, don't you think?"

Kevin laughed.

"The thing about the sea is that there's so much water you can't see the other side. It's the biggest thing you can imagine, and there's more. There's lots more. It keeps going on and on."

"Mister, are you going to the sea?"

"No, I'm just thinking about going across."

"Mister, if you run fast, I bet you could probably jump over it."

"Kevin, Kevin, Kevin. And maybe not. You see, the clochán is there to guide your way across."

"Clochán?"

"You gotta find the right stepping stones—the clochán, and with their help, you'll get across as long as you step carefully."

The old man stared at the path through the trees and added, "Wherever you go, Kevin, choose wisely."

Mrs. Neal walked up behind Kevin with an entourage of women and said, "Thank you, Joseph, for minding my Kevin. Evelyn loves to talk."

"I heard that Bridget Neal," shouted Evelyn Scallan. "And who was it that was complaining about the price of eggs and the lack of good milk?"

"Hold on Kevin. Not without me, you're not," Kevin's mother said as she reached for his hand. Kevin withdrew his hand from her grip.

"Mister Kavanagh says he's not going to church."

"Kevin's got an artful imagination," responded Mr. Kavanagh.

"Now leave Mr. Kavanagh be. He'll move when he's ready."

She stared at the man sitting by the river and added, "And that won't be too long from now I hope." Kevin saw her give him a firm glare.

"Mr. Kavanagh told me to walk across the stones. I can do this on my own."

"No, you won't, dear boy," his mother said.

Kevin quickly scurried down and hopped to the first stone, and his mother quickly followed. He hopped to the second, the third. The last was much farther away than the rest.

"No," yelled his mother, but he jumped anyway.

His right foot touched the stone, but he started to fall back. Mrs. Neal grabbed his hand, spun him around her while she hopped to the stone and swung him around. She held him dangling over the water. "Should I let you go?" she asked. "Then what would you do?"

"No," he yelled as he wiggled and tried to swing to the stone.

His mother grabbed him with both hands, hopped to the other side, and let him go. He scurried up the bank. On the far side, Kevin stood tall and put his hands on his hips. Before he could say a word, his mother ordered, "Enough of that. You let Mr. Kavanagh be. He lost his wife and recently his son joined his brother in the fishery."

"Where?" asked Kevin.

"He's gone to the new found land."

Before running through the trees, Kevin watched his mother point a finger at Mr. Kavanagh and draw a line up and over the trees towards the open-air Mass. "Kevin," she said, "on your way up, tell me if you see any wild strawberries."

Beyond the trees, Kevin followed a goat path across a grassy field which led to the huge hill. Before him was a patchwork quilt of greys, rust reds, toasted browns, and fresh greens with the random spattering of colours of wildflowers. The white of wild goats and granite rocks salted the dark fields.

Kevin's long stockings protected his calves from the scratchy, dense bell heather, yellow gorse, and thorny blackberry bushes. It was a rugged hike and sometimes the vegetation scraped at him higher than his knees.

The pure mountain air, warm spring morning sun and his desire to get to the top fuelled his will to keep climbing.

Higher up off the path his Da waved to him. He was talking to Anty's father. Kevin saw some goats with kids munching on the prickly heather much farther to the left.

When Kevin reached his father, he was told, "You can take a rest if you want."

"It's fine, Da. There are flowers over there. Can I pick them?"

"I don't know, can you?"

Kevin picked a few and waved the flowers for his mother to see before his father carried him back to the path. When Kevin's mother joined them, she was accompanied by Anty Kelly.

When she asked if she could have them, Kevin pointed to where he got them. *Pretty scratchy for a girl*, he thought, as he stared at her bare legs. "Fine. Here," Kevin said, and he gave her the flowers.

With the flowers in hand, she walked back down the thin trail to her mother and her sister.

"Is it far to the top of the mountain?" Kevin asked his father.

"It's a lot farther than our walk to the top of this Cloroge More. The name means 'the mountain's big bend' because it's part of the mountain. It is not quite right because you really have to go down and walk up a far piece. Kevin, it's a ways and I am sorry to say we won't be able to do that today. Really. It's something you'll do when you're older. It's a long hike to climb Stua Laighean."

"How do you know that?"

"Thomas Brien the story-teller told me."

"I wonder what you could see up there," said Kevin. "Could you see the sea?"

"The sea? Who's been talking to about the sea? Maybe if you had better eyes than mine and it was really clear, maybe," said his father.

"Are there creatures up there? Will they hear us? Those people following the path look like a line of ants," added Kevin.

"Those are all very good questions," his father said, but before he could add anything Kevin started running ahead. He was trying to catch up with his two older brothers. They were almost at the top of the hill and that's where he wanted to be.

When Kevin reached the end of the climb, he was really tired. He was going to keep running after his brothers, but the mountain captured his attention. This top of the hill was a stepping stone to places of wonders.

If only I could fly to the top of that mountain, he thought. His eyes followed the pathways. It was difficult to figure out where the lines of the cliffs were. He looked back and saw his mother watching him. *They'll never let me go,* he thought.

He was going to sit down, but Mrs. Scallan came over and shooed him towards the rest of the crowd. Remembering the goats he had seen on the way up, he thought, *If I had some goats with me, then she'd stop that and leave me alone.*

He wandered into the crowd of people. A very tall man stepped aside, and there she was. *I'd recognize her even if she was on that mountain way up there,* he thought. *If she wants something, she'll just come and take it. It's Anty.*

She came towards him with a bunch of flowers. She had picked more of them since he last saw her.

I wish she'd brought me back some berries. I'm starving.

"Do you like the flowers?" he asked.

She moved her brown curls away from her face. "Yes, I think my mam will like them."

"Oh," he said. He turned back to the mountain. "Have you ever walked up there? What do you think you can see? Can you see the sea on the other side? To get there, do you think you'd starve? Do—"

"Kevin, are you asking me a question?"

"Yes, but…"

She stood there waiting for the rest.

"Yes, but…" he added.

"It would be an adventure. I think it would be grand to go way up there," she said. Her fingers fiddled with her wavy, dark brown hair above her ear. "We could go and leave this place, and we could go see what we can see."

"But…" added Kevin.

Kevin's mother intruded into the conversation and added, "Father

Barrett's Mass kit hasn't arrived. The Mass is going to be delayed. Father is going to give you your lessons now so I want you to hurry on over there. Hurry. Don't keep him waiting."

Kevin kept moving his legs, but he didn't see the priest. He made sure he walked ahead of Anty, but he kept listening for her voice to tell him where to go.

Father Barrett walked over to the children. He sat down on his heels and directed a stern gaze into Kevin's eyes. "If you don't practice reciting your prayers, your Lenten penances will be marked down by God as coming up short. Do you hear me?"

Kevin looked away, then down, and followed it with a nod.

The priest said some prayers with them and asked, "Do you have any questions?"

"Is it wrong to ask God for something that maybe some people think isn't right?" asked Kevin. He was thinking about getting God's permission to climb the mountain.

The priest looked at Kevin's father and the group of rebels he was with on the other end of the field. "Some people don't know what they pray for," he said. "Although they want something it might not turn out the way they want. It's a big world and God has a lot of responsibilities. It's not always clear what the right thing is. It's God's guidance we should be asking for." He hesitated.

"And young man, until you're older you'll ask me what's right. Do you hear me now, young Kevin?"

"Yes, Father."

"For your sins say another two 'Our Fathers' and three 'Hail Marys'. Now off with you. I see my kit has arrived and I have a Mass to prepare for."

On the walk down after Mass, Kevin and Anty took their time. Kevin gave his version of what he asked the priest. "Father told me that if we pray about climbing it, we can go on up," he said.

She looked up and away, and mumbled to herself, "I don't think that's exactly what he...Well, if you squint your eyes and ears a little." To Kevin, she replied, "You might be right."

After rushing out from the stream's forest cover, Kevin was abruptly stopped by the glare of bright sunlight. He rubbed his eyes and looked up. Anty was earnestly hiking up the hill. She must have heard him because she turned and waved. Kevin intended to remind her that the priest last time told them they could go to the mountain.

He stepped slowly and cautiously through the prickly and thinly spaced goat's trail that Anty followed, since he wasn't wearing the stockings or shoes that he had the last time.

When Kevin got closer, she meandered off the path to get some wildflowers. He got distracted and went in a different direction because he found something better—lots of juicy berries. There were lots of small wild strawberries.

He was impatient with eating them one at a time. He devoured them by the handful. He spilled more than he swallowed.

He heard Anty say something and saw her waving. He collected another handful of berries. He intended to give them to her but kept eating them as he walked.

When he reached her, he noticed that she was bent over and staring at the ground.

She looked back at him.

"Want some berries?" he asked.

"It's all over your face," she said.

Kevin wiped his sleeve across his mouth and saw that it was marked with berries.

"Did you get lost?" she asked.

"I saw the Púca."

"No, you didn't."

He hesitated for a moment and thoughtfully said, "Well. It could have…"

"Over here," she called.

He looked at the mushrooms and replied with "Can we eat them?"

"Faerie ring mushrooms?" she answered. "No, you can't just eat them. Mam says they have to be dried out."

"So, there are faeries around here."

"They were dancing last night. See the circle around it? That was them." She reached for the mushroom.

"No! No. Don't! They won't have any place to come back to and they'll curse you," Kevin demanded.

"And how do you know?" asked Anty.

"Mr. Kavanagh. He told my brother, Aiden. I heard him."

"I knew that, cause my mam told me," she said.

"Did you know that besides a curse, they'd follow us?" asked Kevin.

She looked at him and asked, "Why don't you pick it? Then they'll only bother you while I eat it."

"Shush. They might be listening," said Kevin.

"I don't see them."

"That's because they're hiding."

"My da told me that he knew someone who saw a faerie man cut wood down there up the road near old man Kavanagh's," said Anty. "He was talking to a raven, he said."

"Why?" she asked as she stood up.

"Well, everyone knows that old ravens know things about what's happening in far-away places," she said.

"What do you think he would tell us?"

"The raven or the faerie?"

"Birds? I don't understand what they say. Do you?" asked Kevin.

Anty brushed her dress away from a clump of heather that pulled on it.

"Besides, there are good faeries and bad ones," added Kevin.

She looked up, told him, "I'm going up there," and left.

Kevin saw a wild red grouse staring at him while following her up the hill. The thrusting, bobbing head with red eyebrows seemed to be warning him to "Go back, go back, go back."

Anty stopped to sit on some flat rocks about half-way up the hill. Kevin had to walk past her to get a seat and the heather scratched his leg again. He stared at her fist-full of flowers and as he ate another berry, she snatched a couple from him.

They were both tired and breathing hard after a long climb. There wasn't a damp wind to refresh them from the beating sun. The clouds were thin, very far away, and wispy.

In the landscape ahead of them, they saw white-washed cottages sparsely dotted across a gently rolling patchwork of colourful fields. The flat line at the horizon was interrupted by some distant peaks.

Anty had her thumb in front of her eye.

"That's Kiltealy," she told him.

The grey thatched roofs of the few stone cottages clustered in the village looked smaller than her thumbnail.

"They're down there," she said.

"Mam and Kathleen?" asked Kevin.

"Our das are there somewhere, but I don't see them."

"I see sheep," replied Kevin.

Anty gave him a quizzical look.

"I think I see my mam," she told him.

"Where?" he asked.

"By the street."

"What street?"

"She's carrying a basket. That's her—right there."

Kevin put his thumb in front of his eye like he had seen Anty do. "Doesn't help," he said.

"Your legs are bleeding—should have held onto your stick."

He flicked some dirt with his toes.

"I wonder what we could see from the top of the mountain," she said.

"There's a sea over there," Kevin told her. He didn't know where, but he pointed anyways.

"I don't see my mam anymore," she said.

"Where's my da?" Kevin asked.

"I don't see any of them anymore. What will happen if they don't bring them back?"

"Don't talk stupid," he replied.

"It's just… I heard my da and mam saying terrible things. I'm… Da said he had to take my brothers."

"Why wouldn't they come back?" Kevin asked.

"They're going to fight with my uncle. They're going to keep the bad people away."

"The Púca is there," Kevin said, as he pointed to the trees that reached the sides of the hill and the mountain. "He lives in the Duffry Forest. He's right there."

"You said he was down there," she said.

Kevin just scrunched his shoulders.

Anty looked at the Duffry forest and then pulled her shawl up around her neck.

"What?" asked Kevin.

"I thought I felt something staring at us. It's nothing."

"Thomas, the storyteller, said that nothing can stop him."

As she turned around, she adjusted her skirt and stared at the heather near her feet.

"The Captain can have him do the fighting and our das can come home. The Púca can become anything. He'll fight anything. He's better than Fionn McCool and even Cú Chulainn. Nothing can stop him."

"Have you ever seen him?" Anty asked.

"Well, no, but Thomas has and…"

"He just tells stories…"

"You're being stupid," Kevin yelled as he stood up, and the berries spilled to the ground. "I know things… It's…"

"There's nothing you can do about it," she yelled, as she dropped the wildflowers to the ground and walked away.

"You're just stupid," he repeated.

The mid-day sun was hot and bright.

He watched Anty hurry away from him. Kevin looked back at the thing that he sensed was staring at him through the trees. He stood tall and put his hands on his hips like he saw Anty do.

"Where's my Da?" he asked.

He sensed that something heavy and powerful was laughing at him. "Or is he stamping and growling?" he asked in a quieter voice.

He ran after Anty but the heather tore at his feet again. He hobbled and then rushed faster. He didn't heed the thing watching him. He just didn't want her to leave him alone.

The Fallen

nty's father, Patrick Kelly, stared at the Stua Laighean mountain that towered over the rooftops of Kiltealy village. It belonged to the Irish pagan god Lugh. The Vikings knew him as Loki. Patrick's farm was on a slope at the base of it. Folk, like his wife Margaret, referred to it as Mount Leinster. Patrick wondered if on top of it, wasn't where they should be.

He stood at the crossroads in the heart of town. From the main road, another led through Scullogue Gap. The break in the mountain enabled access to counties on the other side. It was a relatively dry day in north-western County Wexford. A gaggle of disconnected ramblings from hundreds of men and boys swirled around him.

"Will you quit your belly-aching, or I'll smash your head open?"

"…a taste of what you deserve"

"Would you ever g'way!"

"Give that back."

"Lort! Are you alright?"

From behind Patrick, a voice of experience said, "…and slap the English with the likes of this… better kiss your arse and tell it goodbye."

Patrick scratched his balls and wondered where his wife was.

Near him, he caught sight of his sons. Conor, the oldest, was looking up. He was watching a bird dropping a poop. He pushed his brother Seán into it and yelled, "Share the wealth."

"You arsehole. What the?"

"So Lizzie is it?" said Conor, as he paced back and forth waiting for his brother to smash back.

"She's here?" Seán asked as he quickly tried to brush it out of his hair.

Patrick shoved Conor's shoulders hard and demanded, "Now what was that?"

"Da, not here," Conor whined as he watched people around gawking at him.

"…and why's your coat on the ground?" his father asked the youngest.

"Because it's too hot," Seán replied as he grabbed it and gave a laugh.

Patrick, knowing he dropped it so he could return a punch, said, "yeh, right. You'll know what you're missing when you don't have it anymore. Won't you? There's no sense in either of yeh, is there? I mean, why can't you get along? What would your mother say? And…"

Before he completed the sentence, Seán interrupted with, "Lizzie, is she really here?"

His brother, Conor, shrugged. Seán ran off into the crowd.

"Your mother?" their father asked.

Conor shrugged again. "Haven't seen her."

"You know her. She's telling them what's right. And your sisters, they're not going to want to stay."

"Where's the Captain?" asked Conor.

"The Colonel, you mean?" said his father with a grin. "He'll be the last to speak."

"yeh. Sure," said Conor.

"Your uncle will be anything he wants to be."

"And it will be on us, won't it?"

Patrick stared at the enveloping crowd. He just shrugged and told them, "Your mother will be here soon and she'll have lots to say."

Taking the cue, Conor rolled his eyes and quickly slipped away.

Patrick caught sight of his neighbour John Neal as he weaseled through the crowd. "It's him. It's John Kelly. I saw him," yelled a man beside him. He wore a dark brown jacket and was waving a cap madly. "He's riding in," he added.

"Now we're going to hear how we're going to fight those outsiders," said another man while raising his pipe.

"Shut up and you'll learn something," an old man in a light brown waistcoat replied.

"Shore enough," echoed a voice somewhere in the crowd.

Margaret should be here soon, Patrick thought.

"…souped up with too much hope and unfettered dreams," he remembered Margaret telling him. "The likes of you. …forgetting the tempests that killed the French landing two years ago. You don't know what you're dealing with."

She was right, he thought. *She was the one that maintained order.* But he knew whatever the cost, he would be taking all of their boys to the fight.

Patrick returned John Neal's wave as he made his way through the crowd to join him.

Three weeks had passed since Kevin's sister Kathleen and his mother had marched to Kiltealy. Their attempts to bring home at least Seamus had failed.

In the early graveyard hours, Kevin's oldest brother Aiden Neal rode in formation with the rest of Captain John Kelly's cavalry. It was early June and for this time of night, it was warm. They were going to New Ross. Remembering the women trying to convince them to return home made Aiden give a mild laugh. The pain in his side quickly sobered him.

He was slightly hunched over and groaned as he stared at the passing ground. There was the beginning of an outline of a shadow. Aiden twisted back and saw an early glimmer on the horizon. When he looked forward, it was still difficult to see anything, except around the lantern holders who led the way.

He, like many of the others, wore a coarse dark woollen vest, coat and knickers. His long socks were black. His hair was short, straight, and dark brown like his father's, and unlike the others, he didn't wear a hat. Aiden wiped a hand across the rough stubble on his cheek. He was tired and was slipping out of line with the horsemen on his left.

About ten minutes later, Aiden was jarred back to consciousness. Something kicked his shoulder, and a voice yelled, "Hey! Wake up."

Aiden realized he was on the verge of falling off his horse. His body had been leaning towards the ground. He stopped his fall by holding his horse's neck. He pulled himself back up quickly. He was more than a horse length behind the others and saw the man next to him had put his foot back in his stirrup.

"Keep it together," the rider with the broken nose ordered. He was chewing on something. He pulled his Irish top hat down and then flicked up his chin as he said, "Get on with yeh, and stay alive."

Aiden gave him an embarrassed nod and nudged the horse with his heels to pick up its pace. When he got ahead, he saw Robert Johnson at his left shaking his head. "He should have let you go," he said. "A hit on the head and a nice run, that would wake you up, wouldn't it?"

Aiden held his reins tighter and tried to ignore his snickering. To keep alert, he focused on an exchange a couple of rows back. He heard a horseman who was a couple of lines behind ask, "Mick Murphy, isn't it?"

"Sergeant Murphy to you," came the reply. "Young Tadhg Roach, is it?"

"Right you are, but twenty-two's not young."

"We'll see. You up for the fight?" asked the Sergeant.

"Right as rain," answered Tadhg Roach. "You're from the north-east. Yeh must have seen the start of it."

"…first of it in Wexford…was a terrible thing. There's no fixing for what they've taken from me, and I'm just glad I have a way of showing them the errors of their ways."

"But…" said Tadhg Roach.

"The traitors burnt our houses, and flogged and tortured as they went," Sergeant Murphy interrupted. "On the north side of the Slaney river, they beat us real bad. The rest of Wexford wouldn't stand for it, and they pushed back hard. With the help of the clergy and some upright Protestant gentry, we stopped them in their tracks."

During the break in the conversation, Aiden continued to try to see through the darkness, but he still had no idea where he was or what was around them.

"Tadhg, where did you join up?" the Sergeant asked.

"Joined Captain Kelly when he brought his mountain people to Enniscorthy. That's where I'm from. We took it back and then we took back the town of Wexford.

"We were definitely in a time of grace, weren't we?" posited the Sergeant.

"There's a lot of us. …shouldn't be difficult to take New Ross."

"The Captain told me he expects between five and ten-thousand men will meet up to-day. Keep focused, my son. If we can take New Ross and the mountain pass at Newtownbarry before the English reinforcements come, the rest of Ireland will rise up.

"And if we fail, the Crown's army will put an end to us, won't they?" said a heavily bearded rider next to Tadhg.

"You're right there. Do you understand what we're up against, Tadhg?"

"Yes, I do, Sergeant."

"Young Tadhg Roach—good to know you're awake."

Aiden heard the Sergeant make a series of clicking sounds, and the horse advanced his way.

"Aiden Neal, is that you?" asked Sergeant Murphy as he came along his right side.

"It's himself." Aiden replied.

"Sergeant Mick Murphy—Captain Kelly told me to look in on yeh.

You don't look well. Straighten up. You're a soldier, so act like one. You're supposed to be joining the advance guard. Look the part." He looked ahead and added, "Damn, we'll see the outline of the town soon enough."

An awakening dawn reflected off the backs of men's coats in front of them.

Aiden didn't look at the man talking to him, but asked, "Why did we have to kill the farmers at Three Rocks? Not all of them could have been the enemy."

"Aiden, do what you're told. You think too much. We need to know we can rely on you to not get our boys killed."

"That's rubbish," Aiden replied.

"Destroying that village saved lives. Ambushing the redcoat's reinforcements won us the town of Wexford. Most of those people were just chased off, and you don't know what you saw. But when someone tries to swing a sword across your neck, you can't hesitate. War is a damn bloody thing—and doing nothing is a whole hell of a lot worse. We're going to liberate New Ross. You've got to be a man and do what you have to. Do you hear me?"

"Why did John Kelly stop me from going to see my da?" asked Aiden.

"He's Captain Kelly to you, and don't forget it. His uncle might live next to you, but…"

"How did you…?"

"Never you mind and don't interrupt. That doesn't give you the right to show him a lack of respect. Aside from that, I hear yeh. John Neal was a brave man."

"What do you mean 'was'? You don't know that. You don't know anything."

"Calm down, boy. He fell on the battlefield, and a branch punctured his chest."

"You don't know he died."

"It looked bad to me. I saw a lot of blood."

"Why couldn't I just talk with him?" he asked as he squeezed a curl of reins in a clenched fist.

"We have a war to fight, and the Captain won't give anyone special treatment. Straighten up. The Captain ordered us to be at the wall at the break of dawn. You're making me look bad. Your father had blood on his sword. He fought well, but for us, this is just the beginning. Now, if you don't mind, I have to take care of something."

Aiden straightened up and said, "My da died chasing a bunch of Wexford farmers from their homes."

The sergeant didn't pay attention. He moved out of formation and rode ahead. Aiden saw him stop and dismount by a tree.

When Aiden passed, he watched the man stab a body, that was seated next to a tree. He saw him being stabbed in the neck and chest repeatedly. The victim didn't move or make any noise.

"Not much interest in asking who they're fighting for, is there?" Aiden muttered. He straightened and advanced. The rider in front picked up his pace to maintain formation.

About twenty minutes later the rebel cavalry approached New Ross amidst a purple sunrise. Aiden's contingent waited to merge with the rest of the horsemen. The cavalry was becoming part of a second line of the advance guard. Long lines of men with pikes were lining up on their flank. He estimated that once they got into position, there would be about five hundred of them lining up facing a wall that wrapped the town in a half-circle along the Barrow River. An existing line of horsemen stopped in front of the open Bewley gate. The entrance gate was adjoined on one side by a two-storey tenement and on the other by a wall. A marksman hid behind a low defensive wall above the gate. A couple of muskets hung out of windows on the second floor of a residential tenement.

Aiden looked around but didn't see any sign of his younger brother, Seamus. He hadn't seen him since before he followed the charge into Three Rocks. The purple was surrendering to an advancing column of blue sky flowing from the east. He felt helpless as the sun dragged him into another day of dread.

A crowd, mostly of women and children, watched the preparations for the battle from about a quarter of a mile above and north-east of the Bewley Gate entrance. They stood on the crown of a plateau, which had a gentle slope that swept down to the town walls, through the town to the river beyond. The spectators watched the soldiers and cannons move around in the town streets. They stood in the open, to the north of the medical tent. A road that ran parallel to the town wall separated them from the wounded. The families had heard that the battle was going to be fierce and were collected there with the intent of bringing their wounded home.

Bridget Neal had a firm grasp on seven-year-old Kevin's shoulders. His fourteen-year-old sister Kathleen stood beside him and within her line of sight. Julia Sinnott, a close friend and neighbour, stood to her right, with her twelve-year-old daughter Fiona.

Kevin's Mam crouched down, turned him around, and as she rubbed his eyes, greeted him with "Maidin mhaith." When she didn't give him the food, she promised, Kevin stared up at his sister. Kathleen pointed to the food bag her mother was carrying.

"You must be starving," his mother told him as she caressed his curls. She gave each of them a chunk of bread. When Bridget Neal stood up, she nervously caressed her wavy hair. There was chaos in the curls, that couldn't be tamed by a bun at the back. She pushed up a rolled sleeve that persistently settled below the elbow but then held the edges of the shawl that hung loosely over her shoulders. As lines of men from many directions entered into formation in front of the wall. Bridget nervously paced back and forth in her space between Julia and an old man who moved into position to her left. He didn't look well, and he spat out a big gob of something unsightly.

"Are Aiden and Seamus here?" Kevin asked as he pulled on her skirt. "Where's da?"

"Just give me a minute," his mother replied.

He kicked at a small rock.

"Kevin, those are your Mass shoes. Don't." She took another look at the cavalry that was lining up in front of the town wall. The battlefield was still, except for a few officers scurrying back and forth behind the troops. In the distance, she saw men leading a herd of cattle.

She caressed his dark hair again, put both hands on his shoulders, drew him near without looking at him and told him, "They should be with the other horsemen in front of the wall, but I don't know. I don't see them."

"Yeh know, tis as fine a place, as they come," Julia said as she looked at Bridget Neal and with her finger mapped a half-circle in the air. She gave a side look to Kathleen, pointed with a thumb over her shoulder and said, "The infirmary, behind us there, is where they'll set them. Heaven on that." She returned her hands to clasp each other at her waist. Julia Sinnott was a solid build of a woman who was used to gruelling hard work. She hesitated to state anything as fact without seeing for herself. A white linen kerchief covered her hair. A light grey linen blouse was modestly covered with a woollen shawl which was securely wrapped and tucked into a belt. The sleeves were rolled up above the elbows, and a light linen apron covered a dark, calf-length skirt.

"Is it safe to be up here?" Kathleen asked. "I mean people in the town can see us looking at them," said Kathleen. The sleeves of her light linen blouse were rolled up below the elbows like her mother. Her uncovered light grey blouse was buttoned to the neck and the light grey skirt didn't have an apron. Her hair had the light brown colour of her brother Seamus's but was straight and manageable like Aiden's. Her mother was going to answer, but it was Julia Sinnott she was looking at.

"We're with the sick," Julia said. She turned and leaned closer to Kathleen and said, "Heavens, yes. D'hey wouldn't dare touch us."

"But have you ever seen…?"

"Kathleen, don't be rude," interrupted her mother.

"The people dey're are common daycent Wexford folk. You've got a point dough. Dey're all in a terrible state." She gave a stern stare to her daughter, Fiona, who pretended to ignore her. She bent closer and told her, "Don't yeh go leaving us, yeh hear, or I'll clobber yeh." Julia stood upright, giggled and gave Bridget a wink.

"Kathleen, you look out for Fiona," Bridget Neal added.

Kevin pulled on his mother's skirt and looked up at her with a persistent gaze.

His mother ignored him, and after staring at the lines of rebel cavalry, she reported, "I see some other groups of horsemen riding in to join the lines at the gate."

"Dat's dem," Julia added. "…don't see my Fredrick, but dere's Captain Kelly. Dat one is as fine as dey come, yeh know." She bent down and pointed out what she was looking at.

"Mrs. Sinnott, do you see my da?" Kevin asked again. "What's Seamus doing?"

"No, not yet," she replied.

When she stood up she leaned over to Bridget and added, "Dat's a special ting. She drew a small circle ahead of her, raised her hand upwards, circled again as she said," See the officers are going on about something with those lads with white flags. …A peaceful surrender—wouldn't that be something?"

"That just means no-one's going home," said Bridget Neal. "After this, they'll just go to the next battle. Winning here isn't going to end it. The English are sending an army of soldiers to fight farmers with pikes. How do you think that's going to go?"

"Hard to know what to pray for," Julia replied, as she watched representatives with white flags march from the officers' tent, towards the town wall gate.

"Well, will you look at that?" said Mrs. Neal.

"What's dat," asked Julia.

"I think I see Seamus," said Bridget. "He doesn't have a hat, and he's moving his arms while the rest aren't doing a thing, can you see him? He's lost his jacket…"

"Dat hair, da way he's not sitting and acting. Yeh, dat's your boy."

"And I see Aiden. There he is!" Bridget said. "He's near the gate." She meant to point them out to the children, but they were gone.

As Aiden's lines of horsemen merged into formation with the rest of the cavalry in front of the gate by the New Ross wall, he saw a big herd of cattle being positioned behind them.

The rider next to him was scratching his head.

"I hear yeh," said Aiden.

He watched Captain Kelly ride up front, where he gave a speech to the men.

"We will take New Ross as we did the towns of Enniscorthy and Wexford. You've all fought well beside me and have proven to naysayers that in the end, we can and will rule the day. Look at us! We're United Irishmen. Wexford's Protestant and Catholic finest are riding together to show the English crown that Ireland can and will manage its own affairs, thank you very much. Lads, our fight begins here in Wexford. When the rest of Ireland sees what we've done, the rest of the island will follow. Ireland has freed itself from the discrimination of the penal laws, and because of what we do today, I can see a day when, like the French, we'll have the rights and freedoms we deserve.

"Liberté, Égalité, Fraternité!" shouted an Irish rebel.

"Like the French," yelled a rider behind him.

"Away with land ownership of the few!" cried another.

"Vive la France," yelled another Irish man, who raised his hat in the air.

"Éireann go Brách," Captain Kelly shouted. "I see families in the distance. Men, make them proud. Stand fast and await my orders."

Captain Kelly and several other officers rode back to join the commanding officer.

Aiden saw long lines of pikemen march towards a side gate in the wall. On the other side up the hill, he saw a line of women but couldn't make them out well because they were too far away.

The battle at Three Rocks had left him disheartened, but he like the men next to him knew they had to take this town. If they couldn't take it from the locals this time, it was going to be much more difficult when the English sent in reinforcements.

"Who's that?" Aiden heard someone ask.

"The commander, you mean?" said a man who was a couple of horses away from him. "That's Bagenal Harvey of Bargy Castle. He's a Protestant barrister. He's trying to persuade the other side to surrender."

"How do you know?"

"Men with white flags have been going back and forth. We're just waiting for another white flag to come out and tell us if they're going to surrender. It worked at Wexford, maybe it'll work here too."

"So, we're going home," someone yelled from behind.

"Go tell that to Harvey and he'll string you up."

Aiden, along with the rest of the cavalry waited for what seemed an eternity. He watched a man with a white flag walk out from the entrance gate. Captain Kelly rode through the lines of cavalry to intercept him. A soldier from the wall shot the man with the flag. There was a cacophony of screaming and yelling. A few minutes later the chaos was followed by a herd of stampeding cattle which thundered around the cavalry's formation from their flank and ploughed towards the open Bewley gate.

Aiden heard someone screaming, "Halt, you fools!"

He heard Captain Kelly order, "Draw swords."

To Aiden's right, he saw the Captain with his raised sword, order something to the contingent at his far right. Aiden felt frozen with fear. What he was experiencing didn't seem real. He squeezed his raised sword tightly to feel something. He heard the Captain give the order "… CHARGE!" and he watched him slice his sword forward. The contingent on his right raced towards the noise of the thundering hooves coming from the dirt cloud emanating from the gate. The Captain raised his sword again.

It's time to face death, thought Aiden. *Da, I pray, I can do what I have to*. He wanted to bless himself but was afraid the others would consider him weak. He noticed that the hands of a boy ahead and to his left were shaking nervously. Aiden squeezed his sword and his reins more firmly.

Once the command to charge was given for their line, the riders raced towards the entrance in pairs. Aiden prepared to hold his breath as he passed through the dirt cloud, but he saw a spew of blood gush up by his left hand. The wind spewed some of it in his face. The horse's head twisted. His mount buckled and as Aiden spun off everything seemed to slow. The gates were so close. Aiden couldn't believe this is where he would die. He noticed that the rest of the cavalry was edging to race around him and leave him behind.

Mam doesn't know da's gone, he thought. *I'm not there… and this is it and for nothing. Dear God—no!*

Before hitting the ground he heard the bugle sound for the next line to charge. His body slammed and rolled across the ground. He lost consciousness when the back of his head hammered the ground.

⌖

"Kevin, what are you doing?" asked Kathleen, as she and Fiona came running up to him. "You can't be here without telling us."

"I'm still hungry." He was watching a grey-haired man who was on the road building a wooden table.

Kathleen noticed a breastfeeding woman was giving a girl that was about Kevin's age some bread.

"Mam's just worried. That's all," Kathleen told him, and she drew out a bit of dried bread that she had stored in her blouse. "You can have this," she said as she waved it in front of his nose.

He grabbed and ate it. Kevin looked at the young girl in front of him and said, "Some people are just stupid."

"Anty, is it? So what did she do?"

"Are the Kellys here?" he asked. "Is she?"

"No, they went to Enniscorthy," she replied.

"Why are people mean?"

"They don't know their head from their arse, I guess," she replied. "What's that got to do with Anty?"

"She said that da's wasn't coming back, and there's nothing I can do about it."

Kathleen noticed that the mother and little girl were gone and that the man was pulling the table off the road and yelling at women that were nearby. One of them brought over some saws and knives. *He must be a doctor,* she thought.

"But…" she added. She didn't know what to say. "What would you have liked to tell her?"

"That I told Captain Kelly. She didn't listen to me."

"What do you mean, you…?" but before she finished her thought, Fiona interrupted and told her that her Mam was waving at them. "Your mam must be upset because my mam was holding her hand," she added.

Kathleen looked back at Kevin asked, "What else is it?"

"Maybe she went away because she didn't believe me."

"Kevin, that's not true. Her mother just took them to a safe place. That's all. She's not going to…"

From the infirmary, a woman screamed, "Do what I asked. It's begun, and there's no time."

From the other side of Kathleen, someone else screamed, "Fiona, what'd I tell you 'bout walking off?" It was Julia.

"Do you know where we are?" she asked. "What are you doing here? Kathleen, you should know better."

"But it was Kevin."

"Don't blame…"

"Seamus?" Kevin asked.

"What? I don't know. You should ask your mam. Kathleen, take care of them please," Julia Sinnott ordered. "I've got to get back."

The boy watched Mrs. Sinnott run to the infirmary. She argued with a couple of boys and then rushed back to join his mother.

Kathleen crouched down, looked him in the eyes and told him, "Kevin, don't know exactly what it is between you two but the next time you meet, you tell her. You have to fix it. Do you understand?"

Kevin looked at her quizzically, nodded and put a hand out.

"After this, you'll have to get it from Mam," she said, as she gave him another small piece of bread. "I don't have anymore."

⸙

Aiden opened his eyes slowly. His head was pounding, and he was dizzy, out of breath, and ached all over.

Aiden remained still while he analyzed his situation. He was sprawled out on the ground on his side and faced the wall gate at an angle. He remembered falling and being shot at. Above him, he noticed that the barrels of two muskets stuck out from openings in the wall.

There is no doubt, one of them will get me if I move, thought Aiden. Where's my sword? He didn't see it anywhere. *Beyond the gate, there's a lot of fighting. If Captain Kelly routs the town, they'll come back for those two, won't they? Is that likely? I doubt it. God in heaven…can't stay here. I'm going to have to make a run for it.*

Not far from where he lay, he saw the body of a dead Loyalist. "Lord, he's the one that killed the man with the white flag. Not playing with a full deck, were yeh," he whispered. Aiden recognized the feather in the man's hat. He didn't see his musket anywhere.

Beyond the gate, he saw that the dust from the cattle and the cavalry had cleared. There was a lot of rifle fire in the background. Other members of the cavalry lay around him, some moaning, some ominously still.

A middle-aged rebel struggled to stand up. "Idiotic fools," he said to the wounded. "New Ross surrendered. Why didn't we wait for reinforcements?" Blood flowed down his cheek from an open cut on the side of his head. His hand covered a wound on his arm.

Aiden looked on with disbelief. *You fool. Don't you realize?*

Blasts of musket fire sounded from the wall above. There was a gush of blood up from the top of the man's head. He spun slightly, and Aiden barely caught the look of shock on the man's face as he toppled dead to the ground.

Aiden froze with fear. He rolled his eyes up and caught a glance of the face of the soldier, but he and the other musket-man quickly pulled back from the wall. *Something has got their attention.* He felt himself shivering. When he tried to move, he felt a sharp, stabbing pain in his left shoulder. *Lord, it feels ripped,* he thought as he stared at the bloodstain on his jacket. *My right leg feels sprained, and I really must have smashed my head. We're having a fine time of it, aren't we? The muskets are firing inside now,* he observed. *I'd better make a run for it while they're distracted. I wish I had the stamina of Seamus. If any of us is going to get through, sure enough, it will be him. Nothing is going to stop that one.*

Aiden tried to push himself up, but he felt dizzy. *Lord Almighty, it aches.* He stopped, but the pain in his head didn't go away. *If I could take a little rest,* he thought. He wanted so much to close his eyes.

⎯◦◉◦⎯

"Bridget, I spoke to the children. Dey'll stay close and don't worry, I'll keep a good eye on dem."

"He's trying to move," Bridget told her.

"Went to the infirmary and spoke to the boys who carry in the wounded. Dey won't go out unless the soldiers tell them it's safe. Aidan is too close to the wall, dey say. I'd pray that your boy doesn't let them know he's alive. If he lies still until they win the fight inside, we'll get him out. Save your prayers for dat."

Bridget looked around the medical tent for older and more capable men, other than the doctors, but there wasn't anyone else. She heard cannon and musket fire inside the town and at other gates. She watched clusters of men hack each other mercilessly throughout the town streets. The dust from the stampede receded, and the formation of the rebel cavalry was starting to disperse.

"Lort help us. If only, dey're were more soldiers," said Julia.

"Well, there aren't. That's all there is," said Mrs. Neal. She grabbed

Julia's hand and held it tightly.

⤙⊚⤚

Through the Bewley Gate, Aiden watched a wave of rebel pikemen run by the end of the entrance roadway. Although background gunfire was consistent, the amount of it lessened. *Dear Lord, we're running out of ammunition.*

At the end of the street, the fighting became chaotic. He saw loyalists with swords stabbing rebels without pikes. He watched three Loyalists turn a wagon over at the next intersection. A farmer hit one of them with a club and took his sword. He and some other men chased the remaining two down the roadway towards the entrance gate. *What fools they are. They think they have the loyalists on the run, but they're going to hit back.*

Muskets fired, and the farmers started to fall. When the musketeers stopped to reload, two men jumped up from under the bodies.

God Almighty, it's Seamus. That stupid fool. They're going to kill him.

Aiden pushed his hand towards him and muttered, "Go away. Go back, Seamus."

He looked up at the wall and didn't see the guns, but he knew they would hear him if he called. He dragged himself a few feet nearer to the gate, pulled some stones towards him and threw one as far as he could, but it only went as far as the gate entrance.

Aiden saw Seamus drive a pike into the face of one of the Loyalists.

"Have to do something to help…" whispered Aiden.

Seamus fell, twisted, ran, picked up another pike and used it to kill another combatant. From the fallen man he grabbed a sword, chopped at the arm of an older man and stabbed a younger one.

Aiden tried to stand and pointed upwards with two fingers. Seamus recognized him, and he froze for an instant. He stepped back, picked up a fallen musket, checked, prepared it and fired. He must have missed because a couple of shots were returned and one grazed his leg.

Aiden noticed that some men had set a fire in the middle of the crossroads far behind Seamus. Some men dragged the wooden wagon towards it.

Oh my God, thought Aiden. *We're losing. Damn it.* He realized Seamus's only chance for survival was to follow, so he beckoned his brother to join him.

Seamus kept loading his musket.

Aiden looked around for his sword, but he didn't see it. He could barely stand.

Seamus fired upwards at a musketman. Another shot him in the leg. Two New Ross men with swords and one with a pike ran towards him from the other end of the street, so he dropped the musket, picked up a sword and hobbled bravely towards them. He sliced the arm of one of them and blocked the blade of the other. With horror, Aiden saw two more soldiers enter the street with muskets.

Seamus stepped out of the way of a pike and managed, with his left hand, to pull the man towards him so he could stab him.

Far behind the soldiers, he saw men throw a body onto the bonfire behind them. It started moving madly when it burst into flames.

"The man's alive. They're animals!" Aiden choked.

Loyalists threw another wounded man on, and then another.

Aiden hobbled towards the gate, but Seamus waved him back.

Aiden flagged him to run to him and started shouting, "I'm here, you pagan, rat-infested bowl of swill. I'm over here you cowards." He quickly started hobbling away from the wall to get beyond the range of musket fire. As he backed away, he kept flagging his brother to follow.

Aiden saw the end of a musket appear on his side of the wall. As he prepared to turn, he saw Seamus start to run towards him, but he was too late. One of the men chasing him caught up to him and slashed his left arm. He saw his brother quickly cover the open, bleeding wound with his other hand, and he called something to him.

"Seamus," groaned Aiden as he turned and stumbled in a mad struggle to stay alive. He focused on the image of his brother's lips saying something about "Mam."

Something hit the ground beside Aiden. The next shot and the next were behind him. He looked back and saw three men slashing his brother's body with swords.

Aiden forced himself to keep moving away.

"Dear God, Seamus has fallen," he said under his breath. *We're going to lose New Ross. I have to tell someone. …and Mam needs to know.*

He took a last look back. Beyond the gate entrance, the pyre now looked like a blazing inferno. Above the gates, he now recognized the presence of other smoke plumes.

I'm looking at hell itself, he thought.

"Why is Aiden just standing there? Why doesn't he run?" asked Bridget Neal. "Get away from there!" she screamed.

"Bridget, if he can see you jumping, waving and screaming, don't you think they will too?"

They watched Aiden hobble beyond the range of musket fire.

Bridget stared at Julia and yelled, "He made it. He's done it."

Julia gave her hand a comforting squeeze.

Bridget looked around for the boys with the stretchers, but she didn't see any of them. She also didn't see the girls or Kevin.

She heard Julia say, "No. No, dear Lord."

"What?"

"The soldiers—dey're coming out of the gate."

Bridget heard musket fire and saw the form of her son Aiden fall to the ground holding his stomach.

Two men with muskets came out of the gate. After three attempts each, one of them managed to shoot him in the lower back. One of the two looked back inside and yelled something. The other followed him back inside.

"He might not be dead," Bridget moaned. "I'm going. Oh dear Lord, the children!"

Julia took a quick scan, but she didn't see them. She touched Bridget's hand and said, "Dear, if you have to… Yeh don't have to worry." Julia added a nod.

Bridget picked up her skirts and ran as fast as she could down the slope and across the open fields. The men who shot her son hadn't advanced beyond the town entrance gate. She got close enough to recognize the jacket his father had sewn for him. She got close enough to recognize the way Aiden parted his hair, the lines of his face, and finally the remaining life in his eyes.

She saw his lips say, "Mam?" with a look of utter disbelief.

"Your father?" she asked as she was running.

He pointed away with his right hand and lowered his eyes.

"Oh, good God," she said, as she fell on her knees. "Lord in Heaven. Aiden. I…" Aiden started crawling towards her.

She stopped about 200 feet from him.

"And Seamus?" she moaned.

He pointed with his left hand to the wall and lowered his eyes again.

"Oh, my God." She blessed herself and got up.

Bridget started to run to Aiden again, but she stopped. She stood frozen.

Responding to the expression on his mother's face, Aiden glanced back. A man on the wall was waving a pike with a decapitated head on it. Seconds later a charge of riders rushed out of the town gate.

"Mam, run. You have to go now!" yelled Aiden. He grabbed a handful of sand.

Bridget didn't know what to do.

"Go. You don't want to see this. Run!" With a scream, he stood up and took off his coat. He raised a palm to her in front of his chest and looked down.

She saw that his hand that was holding his stomach was covered in blood. His face was also spattered with blood.

"Why?" she screamed as she held out her arms. She saw the soldiers riding their horses hard, and every one of them had raised swords. All she wanted to do was stay with her boys and her husband John because it felt so right.

"Damn it, Mam. Go!" yelled Aiden as he threw his handful of sand at her. "For Kathleen, Kevin and me!"

She crossed herself, touched her lips, and turned away. She ran and ran because their world depended on it.

Julia Sinnott stood in shock. "The children," she gasped.

They weren't close. She looked and looked and still didn't see them. She stared around and into the crowd until she located the girls talking to some children.

After rushing to them, she raised her open hands wide above her shoulders and shouted, "Girl, what were you thinking?" and slapped Fiona's behind. She pointed to Kathleen and spun her finger like a little tornado in the air for emphasis and told her, "You're scaring us to death. Were you told to wander off? Well, were you?" She gave each of the girls a disappointed look, and pointed to her Fiona and told her, "You have no sense, don't yeh know?"

"Kathleen was helping that little girl. She was lost, and we found her mother and then we came back here to help these ladies."

"And where's Kevin?"

"Well, he was…Oh, he's just being stupid," said Fiona. "Now he's way over there. He's next to those shrubs. He's talking to a lady who has a boy that's his age. She's wearing a dark red shawl."

"I am going to get him and I want you girls to stay dey're until I get back."

"Where's my mam?" asked Kathleen.

"Stay dey're til I get back," ordered Mrs. Sinnott, and she hurried past the infirmary.

"What in heaven's name is he doing way over dey're?" she asked herself. "…not thinking of running away, is he?"

She found him talking to the son of a Biddy Greene. The boy was a couple of inches taller than he was. "Nothing to worry about, Julia. He's been good company for my son, Jack."

"Kevin, your mam, and I were worried," Julia said as she patted his hair. She bent down to look him in the eye, put her hand on the little boy's shoulder and asked, "Why did you run away?"

"It was smelly and people were screaming and acting mean."

"He's quite talkative," said Biddy, "and he really knows his stories, doesn't he?"

Julia gave her a cordial smile and a nod. "What's he been saying?"

"He was telling us about how Fionn McCool and his men would do such a fine job if they were here. He says, that the Púcaman is going to help Captain Kelly and that everyone else will be able to just sit back and watch. That would be grand, wouldn't it?" she said as she fiddled and wrapped her shawl more securely around her neck and drew nearer to the boys.

"That's just what we need," Julia said, and forced herself to give him a pleasant smile as she stood up. Her hands were clasped in a relaxed fashion at her waist. "…Just like his brother Seamus, isn't he? If only it was as simple, as all dat."

Julia looked back at New Ross. She saw the smoke from rising from raging pyres at street corners throughout the town. She walked about ten feet away, so she could get a clearer view.

She saw Bridget, getting off her knees. Julia was overtaken with horror when she understood what was happening.

Aiden was standing, and trying to flag his mother away. Loyalist cavalry with swords poured out from the town gate. Julia watched them stab the fallen as they moved across the field.

"Oh dear Lord. Dey're going to take you both," Julia gasped. She froze with guilt and disbelief at what she had just said. Bridget's son Kevin was behind her. She brought her knuckles to her chin.

Julia saw heads on sticks being raised along the top of the town wall. "…God forsaken heathens. How could dey?" she asked.

As she watched Bridget leave Aiden, the riders bore towards them. Aiden staved off the first blow by whipping back with his jacket. A second rider from behind slashed Aiden in the head.

"Dear girl, don't look back. Run," ordered Julia with her fists clenched by her chest like a boxer. "Just run. Keep running." She sensed that Mrs. Neal knew what had happened because she stretched out an arm to her even though Julia knew that her vision wasn't as good as hers. She returned a symbolic last small wave. Julia stood stunned, horrified, yet captivated as she watched the enemy continued to race towards her. She didn't wait to witness the murder of her friend as she turned and ran. She gave a quick check back and saw that the riders continued to ride towards the hill.

"Dey're coming to kill us," Julia gasped. "Dear Lord in heaven—the children. Where are the poor children?" she yelled after turning and not seeing anyone behind her.

"Oh my Lord, Kevin! Where are yeh?" There were clusters of women and children madly racing away from the lookout to the north-west towards the trees and mountains.

She caught sight of Kevin running with an elderly woman.

The boy has more sense than I do, she thought. She looked back to where she had left the girls. They were supposed to be on the far side of the infirmary. She didn't see them anywhere.

"Dear God, what do I do?"

She looked back at Kevin. He tripped, and the old woman kept running. Julia ran to him and found him crying. She grabbed him and hugged him, burying his face in her deep cleavage with her hand at the back of his head, and told him, "Kevin, I'm here." She let him go and stared him in the eye and said, "We're looking for Kathleen and Fiona." When she stood up, she noticed that everyone around them was running in a panic and that they were being left behind.

"Where's my mam?" Kevin asked as he stood looking up at her.

"The bad men were chasing her. Now they're after us," she replied. "We have to find Kathleen and Fiona." She firmly grabbed Kevin's hand.

"Kathleen," he said as he pointed behind her.

Julia looked back and saw her daughter Fiona next to Kathleen by the medical tent. A stampede of horsemen was rushing towards them.

"Dear God, dey came back. Dey did exactly what we asked of them," Julia gasped. "Oh dear, God."

—•©

Kevin pulled on her skirt and said, "I'm afraid."

As Julia picked him up, Kevin noticed that the solid bear of a woman had eyes that were filled with tears. As she held him, he heard her say, "Dear, dear Bridget. Why?" In an instant, she squeezed him so tight that Kevin didn't think he'd be able to breathe, but her grip loosened when she started running.

Kevin stared over her shoulder and watched the girls move away from the medic's tent. It looked like terrible men on horses were coming out of the ground on the horizon. People were terrified of them. They were running away and screaming. Kevin started crying. When the riders got near the people by the tent, they hurt them very badly. Kevin watched a rider chase Kathleen and when he reached her, her head shook, and there was a spray of red. Kevin watched her fall but lost sight of the girls because soldiers kept hurting people and breaking things.

"Mam?" Kevin screamed. "Mam!"

In the tears of big solid Mrs. Sinnott, in her touch and in the pronunciation of his mother's name, he felt his mother's tears. Kevin didn't know what to make of it, but he felt it.

In the bounce, bounce, rhythm of Julia Sinnott's running, he felt, heard, and saw the waving of many arms with swords, reaching from a clump of men and horses, cutting and torching wantonly. He watched the horses trample a young girl. Through his tears, he watched flames from tents spread to the clothes of the wounded and nurses.

Through his tears and the sounds of his own crying, he watched beasts slice people apart. A barefoot woman who was racing near them with a young girl in her arms was falling behind. He watched her trip, and the two of them tumbled across the ground. Kevin screamed louder and wet himself as he stared at eyes of men and horses that looked stressed, maddened and unnatural. The bad things were racing after them.

Kevin saw a big, single, thundering, mad beast. The monster of war was an evil thing, like nothing he could have imagined. It had many legs and arms, breathed fire and cut life from the living.

"They are coming for us," groaned Mrs. Sinnott. She held on to Kevin tightly, as she ran. Kevin could still hear his own screams when he put his hands over his ears.

Mrs. Sinnott stopped near a crowd of women and children. She put the boy down, stared back and saw soldiers riding towards them. She knelt, took his hands off his ears and told him, "The bad men are coming. Look at me," she said as she caressed his hair and put her hand at the back of his neck.

Kevin was crying uncontrollably and shaking. "Yeh have to stop." She slapped his behind and repeated, "Yeh have to stop. The bad men are coming and yeh can't let them hear yeh. Do yeh understand?" She glared at his eyes.

He still shivered uncontrollably but nodded. She grabbed him and gave him another powerful hug and kissed him and rested her forehead on his.

"Someday, you're going to make the monsters pay. Your mother will be proud of yeh," she said. Her face was covered in tears. She wiped her eyes and said, "Now, I want you to hide in the bush behind me and make yourself small. Whatever happens, don't move and they won't find you. Do you understand?" She waved him away. "Now, go," she ordered. "Hurry. Quickly. Dat's a good lad." After he slipped into the small bush, she stood up and turned to face the oncoming rage of beasts.

Although Kevin huddled up with his head between his knees and his hands over his ears, he could still see the back of big Mrs. Sinnott's dress through the leaves in front of him. As the sounds of horses' hooves got close, he heard a woman call out, "No, no you can't." Terrifying bouts of screaming followed.

Kevin heard Mrs. Sinnott in front of him choke, "In God's name, have you no mercy?" He heard the snort of a horse and then he watched Mrs. Sinnott raise her arms. She gave a terrifying scream like he heard, before as something smashed at her and smashed… There were sprays of red and she toppled to his right. He could only see the back of her dress when she landed on the ground. When the horseman rode out of the way, he saw that the circle of women and children was on the ground and had ugly gaping wounds. Kevin wanted so badly to scream with all his might, but he saw a woman on her knees screaming very loudly. A horsemen came back, got off his horse and cut her with his sword. Other horseman came back to the circle, dismounted and collected things from the bodies.

"Mamma," moaned Kevin very quietly as he rocked back and forth, back and forth…

He looked at the back of Mrs. Sinnott's dress. It had stopped twitching. She was unmoving.

After a few minutes, the horseman rode away out of sight. Kevin closed his eyes, but he still saw the bad things. Putting his hands over his ears didn't stop the sounds. They were still loud, awful, and terrifying. His pants were fouled with pee and poo and he shivered with fear. If anyone saw him move, he knew the bad men would cut him too. *No crying, or they'll hear me*, he thought. He tried to clear his tear-laden eyes.

From behind young Kevin, a pair of hands grabbed the back of his coat. The boy attempted to lean forward and reach Mrs. Sinnott. The hands on him were too strong. Kevin tried to slip out of his jacket, but the hands grabbed him by his armpits. He saw that a hand had fresh blood on it. Once Kevin got pulled out of the bush, he tried to kick the figure's shins.

Kevin twisted around and saw that he was fighting against a boy who looked like he was about Kathleen's age. He was about fourteen and had a bleeding cut along his neck and another across his shoulder.

"Quiet boy, we have to run for it. I'm trying to save your life."

"But…"

"Oh, good God, stand up," the boy said as he pulled him up by his bloody hand. He wiped the wound at his neck with the back of his sleeve and then grabbed and hefted young Kevin over his shoulder. "Damn it," said the boy as he started to run.

From the boy's shoulder, Kevin saw a man hit a boy with a stick. He kept hitting and hitting…

After a long run, the boy put Kevin down.

Kevin heard someone scream, "Douglas, Douglas. This way. Quickly. We're leaving."

The boy grabbed his hand and pulled him towards a crowd of people. He attempted to put Kevin's fist in the hand of an old lady, but Kevin pulled it away and slapped back. The old woman's hand was bleeding and dirty looking and Kevin didn't like the look of it.

"She will take care of you and I have to go," the boy said and ran away. Kevin heard him call, "Mammy, is that you? Wait for me."

Kevin backed away from the old lady. She pointed across an open field. "That's where I'm going," she said.

"No. I am going over there, toward the mountain," he replied and pointed in a different direction. Kevin ran toward the mountain and followed a line of people marching to the road that had led his family to this awful place. He didn't recognize anyone's faces. Most of the strangers were bleeding, moaning, or crying. He couldn't tell if any of them were good people. He felt guilty of leaving nice Mrs. Sinnott, but he was very afraid. He was very afraid.

A young girl took his hand for a long piece, but she got distracted and Kevin lost contact with her. A lady shuffled him along with her two boys and a crowd of a dozen others.

When he reached the main road after an hour of walking, he heard someone screaming, "They're coming. They're coming." Kevin ran from the clutter of strangers across the open fields towards the mountains. He managed to get away from people. He found a farmer's three-foot stone boundary wall similar to the one he curled up against with his mother and sister the night before. Although very tired, he dragged and leaned fallen branches against it as his mother and sister had shown him. They needed to be protected against the bad men his mother had told him. He crawled in under the cover and lay with his back against the stones.

Kevin kept seeing images of running feet, screaming faces and people letting go because they were being chased. "Mamma, where are you? Mamma? I miss you," he muttered to himself.

When he rested in Julia Sinnott's arms, he had felt like he was being told that he would never see her again.

"Where's Anty? Wherever you are Anty, don't come here!" he whispered.

Like all those hurt and frightened people, he was terrified. His body jolted whenever he heard something strange. He kept softly repeating, "Run. Anty run." He stopped making sounds for a minute. When he didn't hear anything in a louder voice, he told himself, "Someday the monster is going to pay."

With his blood-covered hands, he reached for the branch and broke a stick off it. He pulled it back to his chest and curled up. Yesterday, he had his mother and sister's embrace. Now, he lay alone and shivering.

After waking from a sleep, Kevin still felt tired. He looked around and remembered where he was. He wiped his eyes. The sun was starting to pass beyond the mountain so that it was almost dark. He was groggy. He called, "Mam," but he didn't see her. "Mam," he called again. All he saw was darkness, some trees around him, and some strange fields.

He remembered seeing his sister. He saw her strange, open eyes. There was just that stare.

That wasn't her. That wasn't Kathleen. "Mam? Da? Where are you?"

His tears, sobbing and shaking, eventually felt like someone else's. While waiting for morning, he watched for the monster. He had seen it. It had many heads and did very bad things. He held the stick tightly.

"Kathleen," he began.

Kevin startled and moved his head and looked up through the leaves to a dark blackness above. It wasn't a sound that surprised him. It was a feeling that there was a thing out there that was unseen and it was coming. Another gust of wind fluttered the leaves.

"Why?" he asked in a quieter voice. His feet shifted from the weeds. The cold, firm farmer's ground made him yearn for Mam, and neither she nor Kathleen was there for snuggling. "Sometimes she walks so fast. She doesn't wait," he scolded. In a louder voice came, "She could have stayed with me. And she yelled at Mr. Murtagh.

"And always leaving when she's not supposed to.

"She…"

Remembering things not supposed to be seen, stopped him. Closing his eyes didn't make it go away.

The torn oak saplings above him shook threateningly, and Kevin retracted his hand. He stopped breathing. Curling onto his side, he whispered, "…but he didn't save us."

Pushing back firmly against the cold stone boundary wall, he tried to control the shivering. He stilled for the sounds of monsters, waiting for the voices, but they didn't come.

"For good people, he'll do anything," he remembered Thomas say.

His little dirt-caked hand loosened its grip on the sticky, blood-stained weapon. The foil touched the rustling leaves, but they wouldn't be stilled. Seven-year-old Kevin Neal smashed the cover above—hard. Whatever was out there didn't shake back.

Going Home

Kevin heard the sounds of birds. Cold and alone, he had to get away. He could still feel Mrs. Sinnott holding tight as she ran. He threw off the branch, that he was hiding under and stood up.

"Mr. Murtagh needs me," he said. Staring at the mountain range, he told it, "Mr. Púca, I'm going to find Anty." He picked up his little stick and added, "and someone is going to stop the monster. I know it." Kevin crawled over the three-foot wall and headed back to the mountain road.

Maybe Da's at home, and Aiden and Seamus know how to stop it. Shivering, he smashed the ground with his stick and started swashing and jabbing the air as he had seen his brothers do.

The boy looked back at the vacant quiet and ran until the next turn in the road. After slowing to a walk, he returned to the vision of his mother on this road. Her eyes were dark, hair scattered, and her shawl wasn't tied properly. He wished she were here so he could feel her hand.

He didn't remember talking to Kathleen much. It was just her and Fiona, walking ahead. He folded his arms and stared at the ground as he kept on. Later, he dragged his stick behind and walked emptily for a very long time. Every once in a while he'd pick up a stone and throw it at something, like Seamus did.

From behind, he heard someone screaming. He stepped back and watched what was coming. His hand clutched his stick tight and checked for places in the fields to run to.

Three children came running. A boy, similar in age to Douglas, ran in front. A girl a little older than Anty and a boy, with a grey cap, a couple of years older than him, raced behind.

Kevin remained frozen as the oldest ran past him.

The boy turned, stopped and said, "What are you looking at, stupid?" He pushed a long wave of locks away from his right eye. There was a big rip in his jacket under the armpit as if something had tried to tear off the sleeve. When the other two caught up, the older boy told them, "You're all useless." He grinned and Kevin could see that he was missing a front tooth.

"You're bigger," the girl said.

"Where are we going?" the youngest asked.

"The look of you," taunted the oldest boy.

"What?" asked Kevin.

"Look at your hands and your pants," said the girl as she stepped closer to him

"yeh, look at his face," added the youngest.

Kevin looked at his bloody hands, and the marks on his pants and shirt where he'd wiped his hands. "Why don't you go away," he said.

The oldest rushed at Kevin and pushed him so hard that he fell back and smashed the back of his head on the ground.

"Hey, what are you doing?" shouted the girl. "You hurt him."

The boy quickly backed up and replied, "I don't like him. I'm leaving."

"Does that mean we're going home?" asked the younger boy.

"Don't know about you, but I am," said the oldest as he started walking ahead. He looked back and waved for the young boy with the grey cap to catch up.

"Are you sure you know where our Mam is?" he asked.

"Shut up and let's get out of here," he ordered and, without turning around, waved in the air, beckoning the girl to follow them.

The girl stared at Kevin, blankly, and said, "I have to go." She quickly left him and yelled to the others, "Wait for me."

Kevin sat up and felt his aching head while watching the others approach the bend in the road. He picked up a rock, stood up and threw it ahead of him. "Black tooth, you're bad. I don't like you. I don't like any of you. Stay away," he yelled, and threw another stone.

When they disappeared beyond the road's line of trees, Kevin yelled, "Hey," and he ran after them. When he reached the bend, he didn't see them anywhere. He walked for a long time and still didn't see them.

As he scratched the sore on the back of his head, he thought more about the mean girl than the boy. Why didn't they like me?" he asked. He stared at his dirty hands and wiped them on his pants, but the dried blood wouldn't come off.

Kevin remembered when Thomas Brien, the storyteller, had told them stories in the evening on that Sunday when they had returned from Mass on the top of Cloroge More hill. Around the fire he told stories about Irish heroes like Cú Chulainn, Fionn McCool, and his ancestors, the Neals. The stories about brotherhood, righteousness, and adventure were the best part. He remembered Anty asking him about the good and the bad faeries.

"He was the most fearsome creature that ever lived," Thomas had told them. "He's good, does amazing and wondrous things, is a defender of good people and gives bad people what they deserve." The storyteller had told him where the Púca lived, and swore that he knew him well. Thomas Brien and his brother Denny were friends of his da, and Kevin's mam liked him and his stories.

Kevin also liked the stories about the Irish sorrows. He remembered when a friend of Thomas had asked him about it after an evening of storytelling in their backyard. The man told Kevin that his name was Harry Keane. He was tall like his da and he had been dressed in black leather, grey stockings and sturdy boots without tears. His shirt was light, his waistcoat dark, and he wore a common brimmed hat. *The Púca must be dressed like that*, Kevin thought.

Mr. Keane had asked him, "What did the King try to destroy in the second sorrow?"

"It was the fir trees," he answered. "He tried to chop them down, but each time they grew back together again."

"What were the birds given in the third sorrow?" he asked.

"The birds were given the gift of singing, and they got to keep their human language, reasoning and senses."

Kevin picked up another stone and tried to throw it at a tree, but missed. He picked up a handful more and kept stepping closer until he was able to hit it.

Kevin remembered that he had been feeding the chickens when Mr. Keane asked him to tell his father to give Captain Kelly a message on his behalf.

"If Mr. Kelly asked the Púca to fight, we'd all be safe. Isn't that right?"

"Well, that's a thought. I…"

Kevin tossed some feed to the chickens.

"Just tell him that Mr. Keane would like to have a word with him. At the place where we first met."

Kevin remembered that when he had turned back, the man was gone. He hadn't had a chance to ask him why he didn't ask his da himself.

He kicked rocks on the road with his Sunday shoes. After walking for another couple of hours, Kevin approached a string of bodies lying along the road. He moved to the far right side of the road in order to keep away from them as he walked past. He didn't see any movement but held his stick tightly in case he needed it to strike any bad men. There were seven people strewn along the ground. Two women had some clothes bunched around their lower legs. The rest were partially clothed. Kevin stopped looking and picked up his pace. He heard groaning by a stone wall on the other side of the road. He stopped, but wasn't sure what to do.

A bad thing happened here, he thought. It smelled, and he watched a fly crawl on a man's leg and he didn't move. He was afraid, so he turned with the intention of walking on but was startled by a cough. When he looked back, he saw a hand with a raised forefinger wave.

Kevin cautiously stepped a bit closer and saw that the hand belonged to an old man who was lying next to another body. He looked like a grandfather, but he just had on an undershirt and underwear. His raised arm fell back to his chest.

"Mister?" asked Kevin.

The man asked him, "Can you help me?"

Kevin cautiously stepped towards him until he could clearly see his face. "Are you a bad man?" he asked.

The old man grumbled something. He tried to stand up but was clearly having a problem. *He doesn't look right*, Kevin thought. *He's hurt.*

The man managed to sit up but appeared dazed. He looked at the dead bodies around him and coughed a couple of times. He attempted to stand again but wasn't successful. He reached his hand out.

Kevin noticed that the man had big bleeding gashes on his head and that blood dripped over his forehead. He had front teeth missing. There were bloody wounds on his left arm and there was blood on his side.

The man groaned something. Every once in a while he would say, "Can you help me?" It made Kevin more nervous.

"Are you good?"

The old man nodded.

"Mister, I think we better go," he said, and when the man reached with his hand, Kevin grabbed it and tried to lead him to the centre of the road.

The man could barely walk. Blood dripped from his nose to the ground.

Kevin looked back and saw a jacket in the ditch. "Mister, you need a jacket. Do you want a jacket?"

The man groaned, and Kevin interpreted that as an answer. He led the man to the jacket. Kevin dropped his stick and tried to pull the jacket loose, but a sleeve lay under a body. The man bent down and helped him pull on it. With two hands Kevin lifted the jacket up to the man. He managed to coax the man to put an arm in the good sleeve. After they got one side of the jacket, the man tried to put on the other sleeve, but the half torn shoulder tore worse.

Kevin took the man's hand, and he led him down the road. He had a difficult time getting the man to keep moving. *If I had my stick I'd hit him,* he thought, *but that probably wouldn't be nice.* Kevin looked at the man's bare feet. He could tell the man didn't like walking on the dried dirt.

"Mr. Man, there's Mr. Murtagh and we have to feed the chickens." He looked up at the old man, but the man didn't look back at him.

The old man groaned as they walked and motioned with his free right hand that Kevin should run ahead.

"Man, we have to feed the chickens," said Kevin and started crying.

The old man stopped, let go of the boy's hand and placed a hand on his back, and then grabbed his hand again. He seemed to straighten up slightly. With his other hand he pointed a finger to Kevin, himself and then to the road, and he restarted their slow moving shuffle.

The solitude of their journey was short-lived. Threads of families passed them by. A young girl and later a middle-aged woman offered Kevin and the man some help, but they refused their help. The young girl was impatient and in too much of a hurry. The woman didn't look or sound right. She scared Kevin, so he huddled close to the man to avoid her.

Much later another girl, who was about Kathleen's age, grabbed Kevin's stick hand.

"You've got to come with me," she ordered.

Kevin pulled back, let go of the man and flapped his stick at her. "Go, go away," he replied.

The girl tried to take the stick from him, but the old man moved back towards Kevin, grabbed his hand, and flashed his own stick at her.

The girl muttered something inaudible and ran ahead to join a woman and another young boy that had rushed by them earlier.

The old man grumbled something and raised his stick in the air. He looked down at Kevin and put his hand on his shoulder. Kevin looked up at him and raised his stick in defiance and grinned. The old man grabbed his hand, and they continued their slow march to the Neal cottage.

"Do you like funny stories?" asked Kevin. He didn't hear the man say anything. Kevin was quiet for a couple of minutes.

"I don't think I know any funny stories. Seamus does, but he's not here." Kevin looked up, and the man gave a barely noticeable wave with his free hand.

"Mr. man, I know a story. Thomas Brien told it to me. Do you like stories, Mister?"

The man gave him another little wave.

"It's about the first of the Irish sorrows. It's the children of Tuirenn. Have you heard it?"

The man didn't say anything.

"There were three brothers. And way up there, somewhere," Kevin said, as he pointed up the road.

"They were attacked by the father of the King. The boys defended themselves against him." Kevin waved his stick around in a pretend sword fight. "They got him. It was too bad because he died."

Kevin the old man a quick look and then stared at the road ahead. "The King came and got them," he said. "And they fought a war and won." Kevin raised his stick sword high. "Touché," he yelled.

"The King didn't like them because he found out they killed his da, but he made a deal. He said he would forgive them for what they did if they got treasures for him. There were lots and lots of things they had to get. He didn't tell them that it was impossible to get them.

"The King, however, didn't know these were the smartest and best warriors in Ireland, and they fooled everybody." Kevin flexed his biceps. "When they fought to get the last treasure, the boys got hurt real bad. They had a prize with them that could fix their wounds, but they returned it to the King as they promised.

"The oldest boy told the others that when the King gets this he will forgive us, and then he'll heal us. Well, the King got all the things, but he was a bad man. He didn't heal them, and the boys died. Their da was so sad he died too."

The old man stopped and put his hand on Kevin's right shoulder as tears came to them both. Together, they felt a warm breeze on their skin, a still silence, and breath pumping in their lungs. Kevin patted the man's arm, and they walked on.

After a few minutes, the boy told the man, "When I grow up as old as my brother Aiden, I'm going to fight the bad men." He looked up and said, "I'm Kevin."

The old man looked back at him, coughed, pointed to himself, and said, "Alistair."

Kevin wasn't sure if it was the man, or something whispered in the wind, but it sounded like a laugh.

Kevin recognized that they were getting near home. He remembered when his father came home the last time. While his father and the Captain rode into their yard, his brothers remained with the horsemen on the road. He remembered his da pulling him up to sit on his horse. Captain Kelly rode up beside them. The Captain looked into his eyes and asked, "You've spoken to someone I've been looking for, and you have a message for me, isn't that right?"

"After the campfire, I was feeding the chickens…"

"Kevin, I'm sure that was really exciting but what was it you wanted to tell me," interrupted Mr. Kelly.

"You have to go the Duffry forest and get the Púca. He'll fight with you. You have to."

Kevin remembered the Captain nodding, and then asking him what Mr. Keane looked like.

"He wore well-made dark clothes. There were no patches on him. At times, he looked kind of blurry. Maybe I was tired, but he must have moved really quick. It was almost like he disappeared, because I didn't see where he went and he didn't say goodbye. He told me that he first saw you when you were as old as me."

"Yes, but what was the message that he wanted to relay?" asked the

Captain.

"Mr. Keane told me that he wants to talk with you. You're supposed to go to see him at the place where you first met."

Kevin remembered the Captain thanking him and leaving. After his father lifted him down to his mother, Kevin remembered telling his father, "And promise me you'll make sure Captain Kelly will get the Púca."

Kevin remembered his father hugging him tight, giving his head a kiss and him saying, "Right you are, I'll make sure, he doesn't forget."

Kevin wanted to ask the old man why the Púca didn't show up, but as he glanced up, he noticed that the old man was tired and sick looking.

When they finally reached Kevin's home, he led the man to his parent's empty bed of straw. He removed his mother's kerchief from it, and let the old man fall into it. Kevin returned and offered some bread that he found, but the man didn't respond. He looked like he was asleep. Kevin just put the piece beside him. Kevin didn't know what else to do. He left the room and went to bed. He grabbed his blanket and curled up on the straw of his brother Aiden's side of the bedding. When sleep started to overtake him, he thought he heard voices, but he was much too tired to pay attention to monsters.

The light from a hearth fire woke Kevin from his sleep. He loosened his grip on Seamus's pipes that were left laid across the straw mattress. *Mam must be making me something,* he thought. As he wiped his eyes, he saw a dark outline and heard a deep voice. *If it's not Mam, who is it?* he wondered.

It was a tall, sturdy-built man who didn't have a hat.

Kevin heard him say, "Alistair, it's almost done." As he watched him stir the pot, he saw a leather sleeve. *It's Mr. Keane,* thought Kevin.

The man's face turned and, even in the dark, he sensed a hawk like stare, similar to his mother's. "Mr. Neal, I see you're almost awake. You can join us if you like."

The man's jaw was square and solid, but the man always seemed to wear a grin, like he was always laughing at something even when you didn't say anything. His hair tended to curl in front, and although it flowed over the top of ears, didn't reach his collar. Everything the man wore was leather. Kevin had never seen a man dress like that. *He must be like the landlords*, Kevin thought. *He must be rich*. His odd ways reminded him of old Mr. Kavanagh.

"You didn't bring your pipes. I thought you were going to play us a piece," said Harry Keane.

Kevin just stood and tried to wipe sleep from his eyes. When he neared the hearth fire, he saw that the old man was sitting up. He had bandages on his head and around his chest. His arm was braced in a sling. There was soup in the pot, and it was bubbling. Mr. Keane filled a bowl and passed it to Alistair.

As Kevin approached the table, Mr. Keane said, "You've been through harrowing times, haven't you? Change and wash-up please. There's water in the bucket for you to wash-up. After you get changed leave the clothes there and I'll take care of them."

Kevin kept staring.

"Kevin, hurry. Alistaire here has a good start on you. He'll be finished before you look at your first bowl." Mr. Keane flicked the back of his hand, suggesting he needed to scoot off and get changed.

Kevin came back in a nightgown and washed his hands. Mr. Keane wiped Kevin's face with a rag before directing him to take a seat next to the old man.

"He needed some patching," he said. "He took a bad blow to the head, but it looks like he's going to live… Well as long as those wounds don't go bad. He needs rest. I can tell you've been a brave lad. Quite an ordeal, I'd expect."

Kevin, after taking a sip from his bowl, looked at Mr. Keane cautiously. "Have you seen the Púca?"

"Were you expecting him? How about me?" he replied. "I'm the one making you some soup. Is it good?"

Kevin nodded and sipped from the bowl again.

"You still look tired," Mr. Keane said.

"Did the Púca find Da, or Mam or Seamus or Aiden or—," Kevin asked, and he started to cry.

"No, but I believe your father and brothers were with Captain Kelly at New Ross when the fight took a bad turn."

"Mam, me and…" and he wiped a sleeve across his eyes. "We were there."

"I see."

"And where's Anty?"

Mr. Keane had a perplexed look on his face.

"Who?" he asked.

"Anty Kelly. She lives over there. Maybe the Púca can find her?"

"Maybe, but no promises," he said.

"Kathleen's gone. Everybody is gone. Mrs. Sinnott is gone."

"Come here, lad," Kevin heard him say. Mr. Keane hugged him until his tears stopped.

"There are some things that can't be changed and just don't seem right," Mr. Keane said in a soft voice.

"If the Púca was there, he would have shown them. He would have gone in there fighting and shown them how to stop." He threw a fist at an invisible opponent. "He would have been with my da and he would have brought him back. My mam wouldn't have had to look for him because the Púca was there. He would have shown them."

Mr. Keane put his hand on his shoulder and telling him, "From what Alistair told me, the two of you have not been properly introduced. Kevin Neal, may I introduce you to Alistair Alcock. He is related to the Alcocks of the Wilton estates. Young Kevin here is the son of John and Bridget Neal of Wheelgarrow townland. Their neighbours are relations of the renowned Captain John Kelly. For your gallantry and service, young man, please take a bow."

Wiping the sleep out of his eyes, Kevin attempted an elegant bow.

Alistair managed a light laugh.

"While you're waiting for your soup, I'll pour you some tea made from some wild flowers I collected."

After finishing his tea, Kevin got up and started punching the air.

"I'm impressed," Mr. Keane told him. "You have a very good stroke," he said. He put a hand on his shoulder and told him that he was a powerhouse.

When Kevin asked what happened to Captain John Kelly, Mr. Keane told him that he was warned to wait for reinforcements, but that events prevented him from following that advice. "He was prepared to wait for more men and weapons, but others got impatient," he said.

Mr. Keane crouched down and looked him in the eye and told him, "They'll not bother you now. You're the man of the house. It will be your job to take care of the animals and Mr. Alcock. They need you and, unfortunately, I can't stay."

He told him that he would let Mr. Alcock's people know where he was and that he'd get help. He lifted the old man and settled him back into his bed. He poured Kevin another bowl of soup and, without another word or offering a hug, he left.

While eating from his bowl of soup, Kevin walked to where the old man was resting.

"How did he know we were here?" Alistaire asked him.

"Mr. Keane?"

The old man nodded. "We didn't have a fire, and it was dark," he said. "I'm glad he found us."

"The Púca," Kevin said.

The old gentleman closed his eyes.

Kevin, after putting his empty bowl on the table, stared at the empty beds on the other side of the cottage and said in a quiet voice, "It was that stupid, stupid Púcaman that told him."

He went outside and sat against the cottage, staring at the chickens. *The Púca could have helped. but he didn't,* he thought.

"He's bad. He's very bad," he told himself and tightened the grip of his arms around his knees. The sun was shining and there wasn't much of a wind, but Kevin was shivering.

That day and the next passed quickly. Mr. Alcock's coachman took him away in the afternoon. Kevin was left huddled with a blanket in front of the open cottage door, staring at disappearing shadows. The only thing he remembered him say was, 'Thank you,' which was followed with a quick pat on the back. 'Maybe the next time we meet,' he said, 'I'll bring my violin,' and then he left.

They left me alone, Kevin thought. *There's only me, Mr. Murtagh and the chickens. I think Mr. Murtagh is mad because I left him.*

Kevin remembered his mam glaring at his brother Seamus when she said to him, "You don't have any intention of going to the hurling match, do you?" He told her that he was going to visit the neighbour, but he went with Aiden to learn to fight instead. He remembered Seamus cautiously looking up to her, and then she yelled, "How dare you."

Kevin watched her raise her hand and Seamus start weeping. Without saying a word, Seamus just got up and went outside into the dark.

There was a look of shock on her face. He had forgotten it until now. She never hit anyone or tried, but she almost did—then.

Seamus ran away the next day with Da, Kevin remembered.

Maybe they all ran away and they don't want me anymore, he thought.

He remembered the feeling of Mrs. Sinnott's shoulder as they ran.

"The bad men," he said.

"Mam and Kathleen aren't coming home," he told himself. He grabbed some stones by his foot and threw one of them away.

"Aiden, where did you go? Did you fight the bad men?"

He stared at the blackness for a couple of minutes.

"Maybe you're with Da and Seamus and Captain Kelly. Something happened to Captain Kelly. Mr. Keane said he was sorry. What does that mean?"

He wrapped the blanket tightly around his shoulders and grabbed his knees.

"'You're the man of the house now,' Mr. Keane said. What does that mean?" Kevin asked as he started to rock back and forth.

Kevin dragged his blanket and sat down against the cottage across from the chickens.

"Mr. Murtagh you're still awake," Kevin said. "I found a letter to-day. Anty must have left it. It has my name on it. I saw her write it for Father once. Where do you think she is?

"Mr. Murtagh, how come Alistaire had to go? I'm going to miss him.

"Where's the Púca? Do you think we'll ever see Mr. Keane come back?"

"I don't know either."

"I fed the chickens already, Mr. Murtagh," Kevin said. "They'll get too fat."

Kevin lay down, wrapped the blankets around, put his head on his forearm as he looked into the pig's cage, and held Anty's letter close. In the morning, the rooster woke both of them up.

In the afternoon of the next day, a man who said he was Nick Walsh told Kevin that he had come to bring him home. He was older and fatter than his father, and he was there with his two sons.

"Did Mr. Keane talk to you?"

"Who?" he asked. "Don't know the name. It was the priest that came to see me. He told me that you needed help until your parents returned."

"But Mr. Keane said…"

"I don't know. Anyway, this is my oldest—Padraig," he said. "He's a hard worker, but he's always got his head in the clouds. Liam here is a tad impulsive. They could both use a good hit on the head, but generally they're good lads."

Padraig had curly, reddish-brown hair whereas the other two had plain tussled dark brown. Kevin thought that Liam looked like he was a little older than Anty.

"If your da comes back, we'll see him at Sunday Mass," said Mr.

Walsh.

"What do you mean if he comes back?" asked Kevin.

"Well, they might have shot him or stabbed him," said Liam.

Kevin threw his handful of stones at him.

"Hey," screamed Liam. "You little…"

"Boys—enough," Mr. Walsh ordered as he quickly moved between them and he put his arms up to separate the two of them. "I can tell we're all going to get along just fine. Kevin, it will be at the Sunday Mass where your parents will find us, and that's where we'll all give thanks."

Mr. Walsh, with his finger, directed his boys to help collect some things from the cottage.

Kevin looked down at Seamus's sling. *I wish I knew how to use it,* he thought.

Mr. Walsh helped him wrap up a bundle of his clothes. The only personal things Kevin brought other than clothes and bedding were his letter, a pillow, and of course, Seamus's slingshot. He was going to bring Seamus's pipes, but Liam broke it.

As they prepared to leave, Mr. Walsh raised a couple of bags of food that he had collected from the Neal garden and told them, "Potatoes and beets for tonight."

"What about Mr. Murtagh and the chickens?" asked Kevin.

"Oh, yes, right you are. Don't worry your little head about that. My Missus is expecting us and we can't be late."

For the next couple of months, Kevin ate well at the Walshes', but meals were bland after that. When helping in the garden one day, Kevin asked Mr. Walsh, "Where are the chickens and Mr. Murtagh?"

"They had to go away," he replied. "The landlord was looking for them and he would have done awful things to them."

Emptiness and Loss

The years after the rebellion were hard for everyone in the parish. Eight-year-old Kevin accompanied the Walshes on a walk down the Kiltealy mountain road to another Sunday open-air Mass. Mrs. Walsh grabbed her husband's right hand again, while Kevin walked on her other side. The Walsh boys, Padraig and Liam, ran ahead to be with their friends.

Nick Walsh loved to tease. He was one to pat a man on the back or touch a sleeve when he was having a conversation, while his wife Judith was more reserved and focused. Her friends trusted her with their confidence. Although she was shorter than some, she was strong-minded, beefy, and had a sensible, practical disposition, which made the women she knew pay attention.

More than a year had passed since the Battle of New Ross. The crown had thoroughly squashed the rebellion in the county. The hungry months of summer had been difficult. Food stocks were bare, and it was too soon to harvest.

It wasn't as worrisome as the six months before, when the majority had suffered sickness and starvation. The bloodshed had kept most from finishing last year's plantings.

That Sunday the open-air Mass was being held in front of the Jordan cottage. The farm was next door to old Mr. Joseph Kavanagh's property. It stretched along a gentle hill that overlooked fields of thatch browns, and shamrock greens, and was trimmed by thick dark green trees. The sea blue sky was filled with clouds thick and puffy like the treelines. An Irish autumn had begun, but it felt much colder than it should have been.

Kevin stared up at Mr. Walsh and asked, "Why did you give Mr. Murtagh away? He needed me."

"Ughm, well…" Mr. Walsh said and looked to his wife. "That was a long time ago. Why…?"

"Look, we're here," interrupted Mrs. Walsh. "Now both of you be on your best, please. The priest is coming." She pointed to the boy's feet and told him, "Don't kick stones, Kevin. Those are your only shoes." She gave her husband a look and told him, "Mind him, please. I'll be with Mrs. Jordan."

A noisy gaggle of men and women clustered in front of the stone cottage.

When Mr. Walsh saw Kevin staring up at him again, he said, "Well look there, if it isn't Danny Scallan." He hurried ahead as he gave him a wave. He checked back and told Kevin, "If you're waiting for the King of England, you'll be there a long time." He beckoned him with a finger and said, "Come on, you don't want to get run over when the priest comes in." Mr. Walsh drew closer to Danny Scallan, who stood near the Jordan cottage.

An elderly lady with a shawl over her head, who was approaching Kevin from the road, tried to shoo him towards Mr. Walsh. "You don't want the priest to give you more penance and fasting, do you?" she told him.

Kevin moved a couple of steps away from her. In front of him, men and women huddled in clusters in the Jordan's front yard. Like the other properties, the cottage was set less than a hundred feet from the main road. There wasn't much room for people to avoid each other, and everyone seemed to have something to say.

The thatch roof of the cottage was grey, gnarled, had some rot showing. The grass was wild-looking.

Kevin noticed that thirteen-year-old Catherine Jordan carried her late sister's colicky baby in her arms. He knew it was her sister's because Mrs. Walsh had said it was. Catherine's eyes were tired and shadowed. Mrs. Walsh had told him that the only one left at the cottage with them was her grandmother. He saw her standing near Catherine, steering gossip in an orderly but not necessarily righteous tone. Kevin had been here before the rebellion with his mam. The small cottage used to be a household of twelve.

He walked towards the cottage door.

"What do you think you're doing?" asked twelve-year-old Phillip Scallan.

"I don't know."

"There's no-one in there and there's not supposed to be."

Kevin just stared at him.

"We're waiting for the priest. He has to get prepared for the sacrament of the Mass in there. That's why."

"But you said he's not there."

"Go away. Do you hear me? Shoo," Phillip said as he waved him away.

At that point, Phillip's father, Danny Scallan, came over. When he got near, he said, "Phillip, leave him alone, and I don't want to have to go looking for you when the Mass starts."

"Did you see my da?"

"You're John Neal's boy, aren't you?"

Kevin nodded.

"You should really be talking to Nick Walsh about that," he said.

"But he sent Mr. Murtagh away."

"Mr. Murtagh?"

"He's our pig. They took him away."

"Well, I don't know anything about that, but… Anyway, Nick is a good man. I'm sure your Mr. Murtagh is in a better place."

"He said that if my da came back the priest would know."

Mr. Scallan looked at Nick Walsh's back. "Well, I was there. John Kelly died, and a lot of our boys went with him. If you haven't heard from him …. I mean, it has been more than a year. Anyway, Nick told me that you already had that talk, at least a couple of times, he said."

"But Aiden. …And what about Seamus?"

Mr. Scallan looked back at Mr. Walsh. "I think I've said too much. We should get back to Nick over there," he said, and he gave Kevin's hair a brush. He turned to go back to the group but noticed that the boy didn't budge. "Well, lad, is there something you're waiting for?"

"The priest. He's supposed to be here." Kevin felt Anty's letter in his pocket.

"Well, he's late. No use waiting if he's not there, don't you think?"

Kevin nodded and ran over to Mr. Walsh. Mr. Scallan hurried to catch up.

"If the French fleet hadn't floundered, it would have been a different kind of war," Mr. Kavanagh told a half circle of men.

"If we had them at New Ross, we wouldn't be in these straits now, would we?" added Mr. Scallan.

"It was always too little and too late. If they were serious about fighting with us, they would have been here when we needed them," said Mr. Walsh.

When Kevin reached Mr. Walsh, he heard his wife call him. "Nick, I brought Padraig and Liam with me. Mind them…and do you know why the priest is late?" she asked.

"We've been told that his horse is lame. Tom Neville, with his cart, is bringing back the priest, the small Mass stone, the Mass kit, and the Murphy couple." Nick Walsh looked back at Kevin and told him, "When you see the cart you'll know the priest's coming," and then he gave him a wink. "Keep an eye out for us."

"Do you think we'll ever see a church built?" Mrs. Walsh asked.

"Maybe, but I don't think Father will live to see the day," answered Mr. Walsh. "He's not in good health."

Kevin pulled on Nick Walsh's pants.

"What is it, Kevin?" he asked.

Kevin pointed to Joseph Kavanagh.

"Joseph, the young lad wants to ask you a question. Better you than me," Mr. Walsh said. "Lad, go ahead."

"Mister Kavanagh, do you know where the Kellys are?" asked Kevin. "Do you know where my parents are? Did you see my brothers?"

"Nick, he was asking me the same, and I suggested that the two of you should have a talk," said Danny Scallan.

"Well, I thought I covered that a couple of times already, but I guess not," Mr. Walsh replied.

"Young Kevin, I can see that you've learned to walk on your own," said old Joseph Kavanagh. "Good on yeh. I'd say you deserve an honest answer to your questions. Kevin, I don't know anything about what happened to your family, but I do know something about the Kellys."

"What happened?" asked Padraig.

"Yes, and what did you see?" asked Padraig's father.

"There were a few young fellas sent from Enniscorthy and we were supposed to back them up," said Joseph. "We didn't get there soon enough. Speaking of that, Nick, what fighting did you see?"

"I fought with my oldest son, Terry, in Carlow, after the battle at Newtownbarry. I saw Terry go down when they surrounded him. I'd rather not talk about it, if you don't mind." He hesitated, wiped his nose on his sleeve, and asked, "Did you see him?"

"No, sorry, I didn't," answered Joseph. "It tears my soul, Nick. The best of us, lost in such brutality. I share your loss." He put a hand on his shoulder and nodded.

"The people I marched with were young, inexperienced, and too self-confident. They were in a hurry to get to the battle before it ended. They kept a fast pace, and I fell behind. A pair of them saw a Loyalist helping one of their own and so they ran ahead. I don't know if they knew what they were going to do when they reached him. Fool-hardy farm boys, they were."

"What happened next?" asked Padraig.

"It was a trap. The enemy heard their bluster and hid. They encircled the whole platoon and hacked them to pieces. If you're going to fight in a war, you can't act stupid."

"Then what happened?" asked Padraig.

"Lad, you certainly are impatient, aren't you? When the Loyalists left, I ran to see if I could do anything for those boys. I said prayers with two of them before they died. Their faces were badly cut and smashed in. I marched with these boys and I couldn't tell one from the other."

"Did the soldiers come back?" asked Nick.

"No, they didn't, but they left their wounded man behind. He wasn't quite dead. His skull was smashed in and I could see what was inside. I sat with him until his life passed on. I don't know if he could hear me, but I did my best to say some Protestant prayers. God probably thinks I was as foolish as those dead boys.

"Joseph, you did a good thing."

He shrugged his shoulders and said, "The man had a musket and some shot, so I took it. There were too many to bury, so I kept following the Slaney River until I met young Seán Kelly."

"Did you see Anty?" asked Kevin.

"I don't know anything specifically about Anty. Sorry, Kevin, but he told me some things and I'll get to it in a minute. I was getting some water from the river when I saw him come out of the forest cover. He waved and motioned for me to join him in the forest. I collected my gear and ran up the hill. Seán wasn't carrying weapons. He was a miserable sight. His hand was covered in blood holding a wound on his thigh.

"He told me that I was a fool for being out in the open. He was right about that, and then he babbled something about his brother killing someone mercilessly and then described the terrible battle scene that he had just escaped from.

"As you know Newtownbarry was lost. Our boys chased out the Loyalists, but they came back and routed them. Poor Seán saw his father and older brother hacked to death. He got hit by shrapnel from return cannon fire. Seán told me that he pulled out a big piece of metal from his thigh, but he still had a small piece in his leg and another in his shoulder. I gave him some water and food. 'Everyone was surrounded and killed,' he told me. I did my best to cut out the metal bits and patch him up. I used pieces of my shirt for bandages."

"You must have been cold without a shirt," said Kevin.

"I had a waistcoat and a jacket but went back to the dead and took one of their shirts."

"Oh," said Kevin.

"Lord Almighty," said Liam.

"Not as awful as looking inside someone's head," added Padraig.

"Boys, let Mr. Kavanagh tell the story, please," pleaded Padraig's father.

"Seán told me that he had to get to Enniscorthy to warn them that Loyalists still controlled Newtownbarry," said Mr. Kavanagh. "I told him that families from all over were crowding around Vinegar Hill, which towers over Enniscorthy. 'It was idiocy,' I said. 'Farmers with pikes on a bare hill will not be able to protect their families from an English regiment with cannons'.

"I asked him what he was going to do.

" 'I guess I'm a fool, but somebody has to fight for them and how many of us have muskets?' he told me as he slung it onto his back. Seán asked me if I had seen his mother or his sisters, and I told him I hadn't, but on the hill I did see their neighbours—the Murphys and the Nevilles. I wished him luck and told him that from what I saw I knew the war was lost, and that I was going home to take care of my garden. I am old and if I am going to die, that's where I am going to be."

"Does that mean the Kellys aren't coming back?" asked Kevin. "Is that what you are saying?"

"I saw them," said a voice.

It's one of the young Scallan boys, thought Kevin. *It's that stupid Phillip Scallan.*

"I saw Seán talking to his mother and his two sisters on the hill," Phillip said. "I know because I was there. I heard his mother ask 'Did they suffer?' But he didn't say anything. It must have been terrible I thought."

"What else?" asked Kevin.

"Father Mogue Kearns, who led the failed rebel assault at Newtownbarry, was there at the top of the hill with them."

"What about Seán and Anty?" asked Kevin.

"Seán's mother didn't want him to leave, and his sister called him a fool. Seán told his sister Mary that she had to do whatever she could for her mother and Anty. Seán wouldn't let his mother hug him, and he put his musket back on and hobbled down the hill, and I remember Mary saying, 'God Almighty, my broken brother Seán is our soldier. God in heaven above, it's up to Seán to save us. My Lord, my Lord.'

"I remember seeing Anty tugging at her hand and telling her not to cry, and her sister pulled her hand away. Mrs. Kelly sternly told Mary to stop crying and ordered her to tell him how proud she was of him."

"Did they get away?" asked Kevin. "Did they leave? Where did they go?"

"My mother grabbed my hand and led me off the hill. When the soldiers started firing at the hill, we hid behind some trees a long way away. I saw cannon blasts hit some people where I had seen them standing. The soldiers followed with swords and bayonets and killed everyone in their way on their march to the top of the hill."

"But they must have gotten away," said Kevin as he stared up at Mr. Kavanagh.

"Sometimes bad things happen," Mr. Walsh replied.

"Kevin, I don't know. I wasn't there," answered Mr. Kavanagh.

"And they caught up to our Moses—that young Father Mogue Kearns—and hung him again, but he wouldn't die so they cut his head off just like they did to our John Kelly," said Padraig.

"Cutting off heads of the likes of Lords Blacker and Annesley would do us right," said Mr. Danny Scallan.

Mr. Kavanagh put a hand on Danny Scallan's wrist, and without looking at him told him, "Not here. You can't say that. These are changing times."

Mr. Scallan looked at him as he pulled his arm away and told him "I respect what you say but no-one stops me from speaking my mind, do you hear?"

"Well, if it isn't the devil," said Mr. Walsh. "That's Tom Neville's cart coming in. Everyone back there, clear a path for him, please."

Kevin touched Anty's letter. This was the first chance he had to get the priest to read it to him. He ran towards the cottage door.

The two-wheeled cart steered around the outside of the crowd and rode to the side of the house. A couple of men followed the cart and offered to help the priest and the old couple.

When Kevin got to the door, he realized there was something else he wanted to ask the priest. He wanted to ask him if it would be wrong to ask God to bring her back to life. He wondered if it would it be a sin.

The old priest was led to the door, but young Kevin blocked the way.

"Father, Father," he asked. "Is it wrong to ask God for something….?"

"Out of my way, boy," the priest said, "I'm late."

"Excuse me," interrupted Tom Neville as he pushed Kevin out of the way and led the priest inside.

Judith Walsh hurried over and grabbed Kevin's hand, and after reflecting on the priest's lack of concern, said, "Some people have no sense." She led him away to her place on the women's side of the assembly. She told Kevin, "I know you have something to ask him but it's just not the right time. The Mass is about to start."

Before Kevin could complain, he heard the door of the Jordan's cottage open. He saw Mr. Kavanagh holding the door while a robin flew in. There was a roaring scream inside which was followed by the priest racing out the door with his vestments in hand. Once outside he was muttering something in Latin and he looked disoriented. After capturing his breath, he ran around to the back, and Tom Neville followed.

Kevin looked up at Mrs. Walsh and saw her jaw drop.

"That means someone is going to die," moaned old Mrs. Jordan.

"What kind of priest is that?" asked Mrs. Walsh. "Running away from evil. Some people have no sense and no faith. He needs to go back in there and bless it with holy water."

"Maybe some charm-water," said Mrs. Evelyn Scallan.

Mrs. Walsh gave her a quizzical look and then looked down at Kevin.

Kevin had his head down and his hand in his pocket. He was still touching Anty's letter.

"Don't you dare go and bother that poor priest," Mrs. Walsh ordered. She led Kevin over to where her husband was standing. "Nick, please have Father give the Jordan's cottage a special blessing before Mass." She looked at old Mrs. Jordan and said, "I hope he has enough to console her?"

Nick nodded, told Liam and Padraig to stay where they were, and hurried to the other side of the house. A few minutes later the priest walked out from the side of the cottage, dressed in his vestments with Nick Walsh and Tom Neville hurrying to follow. The priest refused to stop at the entrance. He grabbed the Mass kit basket that was offered to him and continued marching towards the altar near the trees. Tom Neville placed the small altar stone on a makeshift table. The priest organized his chalices, containers and pieces of bread across the table. His plain treed backdrop provided shadows in sharp contrast to the vibrant, colour-laden landscapes of rolling hills, towering mountains, and the brilliant blue open skies behind the parishioners.

Kevin stared up at Mrs. Walsh but didn't know what to say. He needed to talk to her about the loss of all those people on Vinegar Hill. He pulled on her skirt so she'd listen to him.

The crowd was still rearranging itself. As per tradition, the men shuffled to the right side and the women to the left.

The priest, with his bible in hand, walked towards the altar.

"Kevin, I know you want to talk," Mrs. Walsh said as she moved out of the way of people shuffling around. She avoided his eyes, pointed, patted him on the back and said, "Maybe after Mass, but for now I think it's best if you go over there with my husband. Pray and we'll talk later—it's best." She grabbed his hand and led him towards Mr. Walsh.

Kevin pulled his hand out of her grip and said, "No. You're not my mother."

Mrs. Walsh stared longingly at her husband.

Mr. Walsh came towards them and told him, "Kevin, it'll be all right. For now, I want you to follow me over there." He gently pushed the young boy on the back to direct him to walk in front. Once he got back to his place, Mr. Walsh separated him from the other boys.

Kevin stared up, but Mr. Walsh ignored him. Kevin turned and looked back at sad, old Jeffrey Connors. His face was dirty, and the eyes were dark and sunken. His shirt wasn't buttoned properly. The pants seemed to be falling off. He saw poor, thirteen-year-old Nancy Hennessy, alone. And he didn't see Joseph Kavanagh anywhere. *He told us the story*, he thought. *It would be a sin to leave.*

Kevin heard some noise. Mr. Walsh elbowed Liam and scolded him about something. *His sons are fighting again,* Kevin thought.

Mrs. Walsh kept looking back at them. *She's not supposed to be doing that,* Kevin thought. *She's supposed to be praying. The priest is going to give her a lot of prayers to say at confession,* he thought. Kevin felt as miserable as the dour looking people around him.

The priest stepped forward to give his homily. His face was gaunt and eye sockets dark, and he seemed to have difficulty walking.

"We, in Wexford, at one time, had the greatest respect for the French," the priest said. "I would even have used the word admiration. We depended on them for support, and they did provide it, but the attempt to send ships to our west coast was, according to some—insufficient, and lagging.

"I have told you, on more than one occasion in my homily, that just a couple of months before the battles began here, the French kidnapped our Pope. A commander, by the name of Napoleon Bonaparte, was responsible for capturing and imprisoning him. Summer has come to a close, and the most recent news I have to tell you is grim. The French have committed the worst type of sacrilege. The rock of our church has died while being held captive. Pope Pius VI, who has been on the throne longer than any Pope since St. Peter, is no longer with us."

"Dear God," said Mrs. Walsh. "Mercy, dear Lord."

"For him to have left this world at the hand of such scoundrels is an abomination," said the priest. "May God have mercy on their souls. We pray that God will bring an enlightened replacement to the current French regime. May God show mercy to us, for we are truly lost. Over the last year, Wexford has lost many of its priests. I do not know what future I have in this place."

"We need a priest with more stamina," whispered Padraig to his father. "Maybe someone that talks like a man." His father gently nudged his elbow in his side. "Keep it down," he said.

Did the Púca get Anty in time? Kevin wondered. *He could have picked her up and run away, and no-one would know. But if he did that, he could have done the same thing for my sister and Mrs. Sinnott. Why didn't he? Why aren't they here now? How come da, Mam, Seamus and Aiden aren't here? Maybe the Púca doesn't exist. If he does, he can't be good to let this happen.*

"Now that they've won, they will have their way," said the priest. "Let us return to our offering and our prayers."

"It's a lot of hot air," grumbled Mr. Walsh and slipped one of the last dried bilberries into his mouth, breaking his communion fast as he joined the others by falling to his knees.

Kevin stared at Mrs. Walsh when she glanced back. She ignored him and returned her attention to the priest. She tightened her shawl around her neck and folded her arms tightly as if she were warding off a terrible chill.

Eight-year-old Kevin stared at the cracks in the stumps that supported the altar-stone and whispered, "Not true, ...not true." He gulped and a little louder said, "What they say is not true." He looked at the mountain on his left and then felt the paper in his pocket. "I know it. I know it," he softly told the mountain.

He felt like he needed to stand up and hit the man in front of him, but this thought was interrupted by a lady arguing. "His nerve," she said.

"Maimeó, no. Hush," said another voice.

Who would say such a thing—during Mass? Kevin wondered. He, like others, twisted round in shock.

He saw old Mrs. Jordan staring at her cottage door. She replied with,

"Don't hush me. Why did he let more bad luck fly into my home?" She turned back to the front and muttered, "Something needs to be done."

Kevin saw old Mr. Kavanagh shuffling at the back, trying to avoid people's prying eyes.

The baby in Catherine's arms started crying. Gently bouncing the baby in her embrace wasn't helping. The old priest stopped saying his prayers. Some in the crowd started shuffling and whispering.

Kevin noticed that although people were supposed to be looking at the front many refused to turn around.

The voice of an old lady somewhere ahead of Catherine repeated, "Hush."

"Yes, yes," Catherine said, and the baby's cries got louder.

"Dear Jesus, please protect us," groaned old Mrs. Jordan.

Catherine, who was trying to soothe the baby, looked at the old priest for consolation. The old man looked frail and disoriented. He met the girl's eyes and waved her away.

"This is foolish," Catherine said. She caressed the baby's head, patted her back, and then stamped off to the back of the congregation. Kevin watched her and the baby disappear behind the cottage.

"It's a sin," said Mrs. Jordan. A lady joined her, put an arm around, and tried to quietly console her.

Kevin looked up at Mr. Walsh, who just scratched the back of his neck and directed him to pay attention to the priest.

"…but something's wrong," Kevin said.

Mr. Walsh pointed to the altar again.

Kevin looked over to the mountain. "She's alive," he said.

He stared back at Mr. Kavanagh and muttered, "And I'm going to FIND her. I know it."

PART 2: Swept Up (1803)

Learn from what your eyes tell you. (Ned Scallan)

A Torn Button

Joseph Kavanagh bent down and grabbed a piece of earth from the garden behind his cottage. "Young Kevin… finally, after five years, we have some good news," the old man said. "Your pestering paid off." As he stood up, he added, "…and your coming with Nick Walsh tomorrow. Something to lift your spirits-won't that be something?" He rolled the hard, dry bit of dirt through his fingers until it crumbled and fell to the ground.

He looked back and watched the young Jordan girl cross through his spring planting of beets.

"Catherine's not so young anymore," he said, "…and goodness gracious, thank the gods for small miracles, she's brought a basket of eggs."

"Mr. Kavanagh, now, what are you doing?" she asked.

As he turned around, he wiped his hand on his pant leg and replied, "It will be a bad year for bread, Catherine. You make sure you tell your grandmother that. It will be a long, hot, dry summer,

I promise you."She adjusted her sunhat so she could look at him. "Now, how is it, that you know that? Do the faeries come down the mountain and tell you? Mr. Kavanagh, you haven't put your shovel in the ground and you're telling us the way it's going to be."

"I've been here a while and I just know. Would you put them on my table inside before you leave? Thank you very much, Catherine."

She ignored him and stopped within a few feet of him. She put the basket down on the grass.

"Why did your grandmother change her mind?" asked the old man.

"You mean about bringing you the eggs? She thought you were getting thin, that's all."

"It's been years, and just because someone gets to church late after the homily… Besides, from what I heard, some of what the priest said was questionable.

Catherine bent down and took the napkin off the basket of eggs and put it into her dress pocket.

"…and when nature calls, an old man has to go," Mr. Kavanagh told her.

"You peed at the Mass?"

"Catherine Jordan, how old are you, girl? You're just being silly."

"Well, you did let that robin in before that—and the poor priest…"

"The poor bird, if you asked me. And where on earth did you ever get the idea that I tell animals where they should or should not go? Such a workup over nothing."

"Mr. Kavanagh, I'm going home."

"Shush!" he said.

"What?"

"Sorry, but… will you look at that?" he said as he stared upward.

A bird slipped out of the sky as it struggled to keep its wings flapping.

"It's a raven… unusual to see them out here. It's not going to make it. It's a sign of something bad."

There was a wind blowing upwards toward the mountain, but the wounded bird wasn't strong enough. It crashed and rolled across the grass.

Catherine wiped the sweat off her forehead. "Oh, yes. Oh, yes of course. Mr. Kavanagh, you're being foolish."

"No more than your dear grandmother and speaking about her, tell her not to bother with wheat this year. Grow more corn. It'll be a very good year for corn."

As she walked off, Mr. Kavanagh picked up his shovel, and told her, "Don't forget."

As Catherine watched him repeatedly smash the raven with his shovel, she said, "I'll do no such thing. Mr. Kavanagh. You're just a foolish old man."

⁓⊚⁓

"What an eejit," yelled twelve-year-old Kevin as he impatiently swiped a hurley stick down the mountain not far from Mr. Kavanagh's. "Ned Scallan, you've got a face like your arse and you're worse than a cow's fart. What a useless place to meet."

The rough, scrubby hedges on both sides of the road were almost as tall as he was. There was a roll of a hill beyond one side, and a line of tall trees separating him from a view of the mountainside on the other. Kevin kicked the ground again.

"Is he bringing enough for a match? Stupid or what? …waiting here for nothing?"

"Not even a rock to sit on." He used his hurling stick to smash a stone and then dropped it to the ground.

Looking into the trees, he muttered, "Bet I could see him from the top of the mountain."

He stared farther down where trees grew on both sides. Branches interlaced over the road, giving the appearance of a tunnel.

"Maybe not," he said. "He's a brainless weasel and the trees would hide him."

"Take this, take that," he yelled as he launched his fists against an invisible opponent.

From his pocket, he took out something from his past life. He put a stone into his brother Seamus's sling and gave it a powerful swing. It missed the tree trunk but was close.

"Touché," he yelled.

He had a blurry memory of Seamus yelling that at his brother, Aiden.

He missed and felt guilty for wrongly making the call. He whipped another at the trunk. He hit it and yelled, "Touché." He hit it again and felt justified this time. He picked up a pile of stones and put them in his pocket. It took him seven throws with his sling, but he hit it again.

He yelled, "touché," only the once, and the sound of it was so sweet he punctuated it with a "yeh!"

The other thing he had from the past life was a crumpled letter. It had been handled so much it was now broken into six pieces. Touching, folding and putting it into his pocket was destroying Anty's writing.

He took out one of the pieces.

The priest was a mean one, Kevin thought.

'Want to find out what it says? Then read the bible stories first,' he remembered him say.

I wonder why he was trying to punish me? He thought as he looked at one of the pieces in his hand. *It wasn't until Ned Scallan's mam—Mam's friend Evelyn read it to me, that I finally heard what it said. And soon it's all going to be gone*, Kevin thought.

From memory, he recited the message. 'Looking for my brother.

Be good. i won't see you at Mass.

Say your prayers. Bring more flowers.'

She never signed it, but Kevin knew it was her. After reciting, he always added, "Come home, Anty." He used to say please before 'Come home Anty', but when the paper started to break up, he stopped saying it. The older he got, the more he realized how childish the letter was.

If I stop saying it, I'll forget them all, he thought. He patted the pocket that had the remaining bits.

When Mr. Kavanagh talked to him about his and Anty's families, he instinctively knew he'd never see them again. He had returned to the ruins of his father's cottage many times, and it made him feel cold and empty.

They left me alone, he thought. He put the piece of paper back in his pocket with the rest.

"They're all fools," he told himself.

Although it got late and no-one showed up, he kept slinging stones.

—⊙—

The next morning Kevin walked along with Mr. Walsh to Mr. Kavanagh's. Kevin was focused on a button that was coming undone on his tweed vest.

Mr. Walsh said, "You know, if you were going any slower, you'd be stopped." He took a deep breath of the sweet, cool spring air. The view on both sides of the road was unimpeded. The wild grass in front of the untrimmed three-foot hedges bordering the road was spotted with buds of yellow and white wildflowers. Fields of green rolled out beyond.

"Why did you want me to help?" Kevin asked. "I like Mr. Kavanagh and all—I'm just asking, why not Liam?"

"We're in a rush for the plantings and Liam and Padraig know what needs to be done."

"You're saying Liam's faster than me?" he asked, as he stared up at the man.

"But Kevin, have some sense. He's got four years on you. You're really getting ahead of yourself. Well, don't you think?"

"I can hold my own."

"You've nothing to prove. At least not on my account.

"You're here because I think it's time you learned to work with thatch. Since the landlord took your land, it wouldn't hurt to learn other ways to make yourself useful. We're going to fix a leak. Actually, it's more than that. A whole section of it needs to be replaced. Anyways, the old man shouldn't be up there. 'Stay off it and I'll fix it,' I told him."

Mr. Walsh lightly slapped the back of Kevin's shoulder as he asked, "Are you up for it?"

"Of course I am," Kevin said, as he stood straighter. He picked up his pace and looked away from him.

"You look like you're insulted I asked."

"No. It's just…"

"I heard you and Liam had a lively discussion about last night's hurling match. What was that about?"

"It wasn't a discussion. Liam was acting like an eejit," answered Kevin.

"He can be a bonehead like his father on occasion," said Mr. Walsh.

Kevin gave a light chuckle.

"Is that a stomach infection or a laugh I hear?" asked Mr. Walsh.

"There was supposed to be a game, but no-one showed up. Liam was just picking away. That's all."

"Well, that's a kick in the arse, isn't it? Who was it that set it up?"

"Ned Scallan."

"Those damn Scallans. His father, Danny Scallan, owes me. Damn them to hell. Sorry for my language. It's just—well, never you mind. Kevin, you need to take your revenge. So, when there's a next time, you have him wait while you go take the lads somewhere else. That's what I'd do. Now buck up. We've work to do for the old man. I can see Joseph right there—playing in the dirt."

Kevin drew slightly closer to Mr. Walsh as they followed the trail into Mr. Kavanagh's yard.

Mr. Kavanagh had a short walking stick in his right hand. When they got close, he told them, "Took you long enough."

"What's that Joseph?" asked Nick Walsh.

"It's almost the middle of the day. Did you sleep in?"

"We're not even there and you're going on about work," said Nick, as he walked along the side of the cottage.

When Kevin got close, he looked up at the roof and then at Mr. Walsh.

"And did you bring the money?" asked Mr. Kavanagh.

"Not yet," said Mr. Walsh, as he dragged his hand across his nose and looked away.

"You know it's a sure thing and you're going to lose out?"

"I never doubted you, Joseph," said Mr. Walsh.

"A horse race?" asked Kevin. "I know you love to talk about horses, Mr. Kavanagh."

"Never you mind, Kevin," interrupted Mr. Walsh as he stared at him.

"It's an adult thing. Mrs. Walsh…" he said as he looked away.

"Mrs. Walsh, the horses, …I hear you," said Kevin.

"This morning I found something important," interrupted Mr. Kavanagh.

"Is it worth something?" asked Mr. Walsh.

"It's not like that. Were you aware Thomas Brien was missing?"

"No."

"Well, I've just learned, that no-one has seen him since last autumn and I'm pretty sure I've found him."

"What do you mean? Either you have or you haven't. Did he forget who he is?"

"It's not like that," Mr. Kavanagh said. He felt his bristly cheek and then he pointed beyond the road and added, "Yesterday, I was collecting wood along the river over there beyond the Duffry forest…"

"You mean the stream? …the Urrin river I mean."

Mr. Kavanagh nodded. "Late last night, I found a shoe and a cap," he said. "I'm sure the shoe belongs to Thomas because it's got a tear on the right side. He was never very good at stitching."

"Kevin here could use a needle and thread," interrupted Mr. Walsh. "He…"

"Anyways, I recognized the tear," continued Mr. Kavanagh, and he looked towards his cottage. "It's his cap. I used to tease him about it."

"So he's missing a hat and a shoe," said Mr. Walsh.

"No. There's more to it." Mr. Kavanagh's lowered gaze was tailed with the phrase, "I'm afraid."

"Joseph, get on with it. What is it?"

"There's a foot in his shoe. It was cut off at the bone. Whatever killed him didn't leave much."

"He was such a nice fella," Kevin said. "Why would someone kill him?"

"It was the work of a devil. A man wouldn't do that. What about the Púca?" asked Mr. Walsh.

"Don't get ahead of yourself," said Mr. Kavanagh.

"Well, what kind of creature cuts off a man's leg at the bone? What else could it be?" Mr. Walsh looked at his friend curiously and added, "You've met him, haven't you?"

Mr. Kavanagh brushed his hands together as if to brush off dirt and said, "There's only one Púca around here.

"Why?" asked Kevin.

"Don't know exactly, but that's just the way it is. Thomas had a lot to say about him, and never anything bad. Don't go round starting rumours until we know what we're dealing with," said Mr. Kavanagh.

Kevin noticed that Mr. Kavanagh wouldn't say if he'd met the Púca.

"Thomas Brien was the best story teller," said Kevin. "My da, …we all, liked him a lot. I met him and his brother, Denny. He was nice and told good stories. The neighbours would come and we'd sit around a fire in the backyard." Kevin looked up at him and said, "So you did meet the Púca."

"Let's just say I've seen things I can't explain," Mr. Kavanagh said.

"Thomas will be missed by everyone. It's a very sad thing," said Mr. Walsh.

Kevin stared at him, scratched his thigh, and wondered why Mr. Walsh didn't want to know more.

"Why don't I make a small coffin to bury him in?" asked Mr. Walsh.

"Not much left to put in one, I'm afraid," said Mr. Kavanagh. "I want you to come with me to have another look in the forest. Maybe we'll find the rest of him. What do you think, Kevin? Are you up to it?"

"Ugh, Pieces of him," he replied. He looked at the other two. "It's a terrible, thing but I'd like to help."

"You can go in the cottage and have a look at what he's already found if you like," Mr. Walsh said.

"No, not really," answered the boy.

"Nick, give us a minute," said Mr. Kavanagh, and he waved for Kevin to follow him.

"But Joseph, I was only teasing," said Mr. Walsh.

"Kevin and I are going to get that needle and thread. We won't be but a minute,"

As they left for the cottage, they could hear Mr. Walsh mutter, "Joseph, you're getting to be like old Mrs. Jordan. And maybe you should have some tea while you're at it, why don't you?"

Once inside, Mr. Kavanagh had Kevin sit on a stump near the hearth fire while he searched through his belongings. Kevin looked around for a sack of body parts and then put on Mr. Kavanagh's hat that was next to him.

A couple of minutes, later, the old man brought out a bowl. He took out a wooden needle and a roll of thick thread and gave it to Kevin.

"I'd show you how to make a needle for yourself, but we don't have enough time," Mr. Kavanagh said as he looked down at him. "Don't get Mrs. Walsh to do it for you, have her teach you. Do you hear me?" he said as he slightly bent down and stared into his eyes.

"I hear you, Mr. Kavanagh," Kevin said as he put the needle and thread into his pocket. "What can you tell me about the Púca?"

Mr. Kavanagh ripped off the loose button on Kevin's jacket and told him, "You better put this in there as well. You don't want to lose it in the woods. Trust me."

As the boy turned to leave, Mr. Kavanagh told him, "Hold on, Kevin, I'm not finished.".

"But Mr. Walsh…"

"I made a mistake…"

"About Mr. Brien?" Kevin asked as he tilted the hat back.

"No. I need to tell you something."

Kevin wondered if it had something to do with the Púca or the hat.

"Remember when I told you about what happened at Vinegar Hill?"

Kevin pulled the brim of the hat down, as he said, "They killed the Kellys."

"Well, Anastasia Kelly is alive," Mr. Kavanagh told him.

"I knew it," Kevin said as he pounded the air with his fist. "Anty is alive. But you said that Phillip Scallan saw them die."

"I don't know how you knew, but it's nice to have some good news for a change. As it turns out, someone picked her up and took her off the hill before the soldiers made their final run at it. She's living with an aunt near Tintern Abbey."

"Where's that?" asked Kevin.

"Tintern Abbey is an old monastery in Tintern parish. It's south of the town of Wexford. It's near the sea."

"She's going to be a nun?"

"Don't get carried away. I doubt she's going to be a nun. There aren't any religious in the monastery. The landlord has been using it as a private home."

"What's the name of her aunt?" asked Kevin.

"Sorry, I don't know, and neither does the person that told me. The family that took her emigrated to England.

"So how am I going to find her?" asked Kevin.

"Ask around," said Mr. Kavanagh. "…and don't forget the local priest. By the way, the owners of the Abbey are cousins of your landlord—Caesar Colclough. Your landlord is referred to as Adam's Caesar. Adam was his father. The boys at the abbey—Caesar and John, are known as Vessey's Colcloughs. Vessey was their father. When you're older, you should pay her a visit."

"I think, I'd like that," Kevin said as he stared at his feet.

Mr. Kavanagh took his hat back, grabbed a basket and an oak staff, opened the door and told him, "Don't just stand there, we've got to go… and bring the other two baskets."

"But…" said Kevin. He wanted to ask him more about the Púca.

"Come on, we don't have all day," he replied.

Once they got outside, Mr. Walsh said, "You had time for tea and you didn't bring us some. If you put things off any longer, we'll be doing this in the dark."

"Quit your complaining," Mr. Kavanagh said, as he marched past him with his staff. Mr. Walsh followed, and Kevin ran to keep up.

"Do you think the forest will be haunted?" asked Kevin, as he gave a wicker basket to Mr. Walsh.

"I hope not," said Mr. Walsh. "But whatever did this, I hope it only comes out at night. To be safe, we'll say a decade of the beads before going in."

While walking on the road, Mr. Walsh, without waiting for him, started with an "Our Father". Mr. Walsh used his knuckles to keep count for the rest.

When they finished, Mr. Walsh asked, "Are you really keeping the bits of Thomas in your cottage? I mean, the body has been dead for who knows how long."

"Took you long enough, Nick," said Mr. Kavanagh. "Kevin figured it out when he asked me for the wooden needle and thread for his button. Of course, I'm not keeping him in my cottage."

"The bag is hanging from a tree," said Kevin. "I saw it as I walked out of his cottage."

"Animals will probably get it," said Mr. Walsh.

Mr. Kavanagh led the other two across the road to the green cover of hardwoods that followed the stream. Each of them carried a straw basket.

Kevin straggled behind as the other two disappeared into the trees. Kevin saw a robin fly into the forest cover on his right.

"Mrs. Jordan's cottage," he told himself. *That was supposed to be bad luck and someone's going to die, and Mrs. Jordan and her grand daughter are still there. What does it mean?* He stopped in his tracks. "They're in danger," he said and ran in after them. On the other side of the trees, he saw the other two staring at him.

"I was going to go back for you. Were you having second thoughts?" asked Mr. Walsh. "Joseph, is it really a good idea to bring the boy with us?"

"But Mr. Kavanagh, I saw a robin."

"That's nice."

"Was there anything chasing it," asked Mr. Walsh.

"No, but it was like Mrs. Jordan's cottage… They say, if a robin flies into your house, someone in the parish is going to die," said Kevin.

"It's Mrs. Jordan and the silly bird again, is it?" asked Mr. Kavanagh. "It's just nonsense from people who don't like birds."

"Well then, I guess that's for poor Thomas," said Mr. Walsh, "and that's why we're here."

"But this bird just flew in like… I mean…" said Kevin as he looked around the stream. Mr. Walsh checked to see if there was anyone else.

The place was quiet, except for gentle, rustling of leaves above them.

"Maybe I should have come alone. I would have gotten more done," said Mr. Kavanagh.

"But what do you want us to do?" asked Kevin.

"Let's spread out," the old man replied. "You two, scout the other side of the stream, and I'll check this way. We're twenty minutes from where I found him, but animals might have brought parts of him down here."

"Mr. Kavanagh, how come no-one found Thomas before this?" asked Kevin.

"Well, I suppose no-one knew he was missing. First time I heard about it was from his brother, Denny. It was three weeks ago at Mass, when he asked me. Thomas did love to travel and was rather unpredictable. I just stumbled on him, so to speak. I wasn't really looking for him. I don't usually have a reason to go that far up stream. I was just looking to get me a good piece of wood.

"So if it's around, it could tear our arms off, couldn't it?" asked Mr. Walsh. "I mean, look what happened to Thomas."

"Nick, I didn't see any sign of it, the last time I was there. If it was here, it would already have heard us by now, don't you think?"

Mr. Walsh stepped through the stream. It was only about a foot deep. He waved for Kevin to follow.

After walking around for about five minutes, Kevin checked behind and scratched the back of his neck.

Mr. Walsh noticed his nervous ticks and asked, "Is it flies on yeh, or what?"

"No, just I thought… no, it's nothing I guess," said Kevin.

Mr. Walsh, for the next few minutes, also kept looking back.

Kevin stopped to look at something near the water. He called and waved for the others to join him. Mr. Kavanagh tramped across the shallow stream. When he reached the other two, he said, "Looks like the bones of a rabbit. They're too small."

A couple of minutes later, Mr. Walsh found another piece of a bone.

"Don't think it's him," said Mr. Kavanagh, "but put it in your bag, anyway."

"What if the beast is here?" asked Mr. Walsh.

"Then, we'll find out what did this to him, won't we?" said Mr. Kavanagh.

"Yes, but…" said Mr. Walsh.

"Shh," said Mr. Kavanagh, and he put his finger to his lips and waved for them to keep moving forward.

Kevin froze. He sensed something staring at him. He didn't see anything but sensed that it was there. Mr. Kavanagh looked at him and gave a raised hand for Mr. Walsh to stop. As he went down on one knee, he gave a sign for the others to do the same.

They kept quiet and waited for five minutes. There wasn't any sound, but Kevin knew there was something ahead of him.

Mr. Kavanagh looked at Mr. Walsh, who pointed to a quick way out of the valley.

Both men were stunned when they watched Kevin get up and start running ahead. Mr. Kavanagh moaned, "No, Lord. No."

"Damn," groaned Mr. Walsh, and he ran after him.

As Kevin ran, he moved his basket from his right hand to his left. He saw Mr. Walsh waving wildly at him. Kevin ignored him and raised his right hand.

Kevin slowed down, and Mr. Walsh stopped.

"Mr. Keane," yelled Kevin as he gave him a wave. "Harry Keane." He saw that the man was standing next to the stream and looking at something on the ground.

"Kevin Neal, is it?" he asked, without looking at him.

"Yes."

"You should wait up for Joseph," said Mr. Keane. "He's not as young as he once was, you know." He bent down and touched the ground.

When Mr. Kavanagh caught up, Kevin said, "It's Harry Keane."

"I know, we've met," Mr. Kavanagh said. "Harry, I take it, you're looking for poor Thomas."

"What do you think happened?" Mr. Keane asked.

"It was the Púca," said Mr. Walsh.

"What do you think happened, Joseph?" Mr. Keane repeated.

"A huge animal got him, but it's not something from around here. And what do you think it was?"

"I don't know what to tell you," said Mr. Keane. "It certainly was something fearsome. I've collected some remains. They're in a pile behind me. Not much, I am afraid."

"We didn't find much of anything either," said Mr. Walsh. "I found some bones, but I'm not sure they're him," he said as he raised his basket. "Joseph has more at home."

"You can keep looking if you'd like, but I've searched upstream and around the forest. I don't believe you'll find much more than what we've already got."

"I found Thomas' cap and boot ten minutes upstream from here," said Mr. Kavanagh.

"I'd hate to run into the monster that did this," said Mr. Walsh.

Kevin ran past Mr. Keane to look at the small pile of body parts that Mr. Keane had collected. "Isn't that frightful?" he said. He noticed that they were mostly just a collection of bones, but there was some tattered flesh with something moving in it.

"Kevin, would you mind putting those remains in your basket, please?" asked Mr. Kavanagh.

The boy crouched down and used a piece of a branch to scoop them into the basket. He watched the others walk back towards the roadway.

"They're going home. What are they doing?" said Kevin. He looked around to see if there was anything else here with him. "If you think I'm staying here alone, you're crazy," he told himself. He quickly pushed the heap into the basket and stood up.

He went over to where Harry Keane had been staring at the ground. All he saw was wild grass. He backed away a step and, after looking more carefully, he made out what he thought were old impressions of large dog-like footprints. *Lord, they're at least a foot across. Why didn't he say something? They must belong to the Púca.* Kevin cautiously looked around but didn't see anything else. *Mr. Walsh was right. It was the Púca that did this. He's a monster.*

"Time to get out of here," Kevin told himself, and he rushed after the others.

Mr. Walsh stood waiting for him, but the others were gone.

Kevin asked him, "Where did they go?"

"Back to Joseph Kavanagh's cottage. Harry Keane's going to make the coffin."

"I thought you were going to do it?"

"He wouldn't take no for an answer. He knows the brother and he's taking the remains to Denny Brien himself."

Kevin persuaded Mr. Walsh to go back and look at the footprints.

After Mr. Walsh had a chance to look at the prints from different angles, he said, "I don't know, the rain might have made marks in mud, and grass grew over it. There's nothing in this world that has feet like that. We'd have to find fresh footprints to really be sure it's what we think it is."

"Well, whatever it was, it had no problem ripping apart poor Thomas. I hate to think about what's going to happen next. The beast is still loose and there's no reason to believe it won't kill again."

When they climbed out from a cover of trees, Mr. Kavanagh was there waiting for them.

He pointed to Kevin's basket and said, "I'll take that."

"Where's Mr. Keane?" asked Kevin.

"He's waiting for me at the cottage." The old man hurriedly grabbed the basket from him.

"But…" said Kevin.

"Not now," said Mr. Kavanagh. "I have to go. I'll see you Saturday, won't I?"

"Saturday morning," said Mr. Walsh. "But…"

Mr. Kavanagh hurried off without replying.

"Why is he in such a hurry?" asked Kevin. "And why didn't he just stay at home, and let us bring it to him?"

"Well, he's got pieces of a dead body stinking up his property and someone has offered to take it away and make a box for it. Pretty good reason to get back to Mr. Keane before he changes his mind don't you think?"

"Maybe," said Kevin. "But I think he looked nervous about something."

"Having poor dead Thomas hanging in a tree outside the cottage is enough," said Mr. Walsh. "I'm sure of it. Imagine if the sheriff came calling."

On the walk home it was quiet between them. Kevin was caught up in his thoughts. He remembered looking at Thomas's shoe tapping on the dirt floor of their cottage, near the hearth fire as he smoked his pipe, listening to his father talk about farming and the people he had seen. He wondered why anyone would have a reason for hurting him.

He remembered Thomas telling him that to get help from the Púca he had to be nice and offer him something.

What would a Púca want? A good cup of tea, or to tear a man apart and devour him like an animal? What is this Púca creature?

Thomas also told him that in order to send him on his way and persuade him to 'see a little of the world', you needed to thank him, and give him a nice coat. "He prefers a red one," he said. "Those that had seen him leave referred to him as the 'red man' (an Fear Dearg), for the bright colour of the coat."

Thomas seemed to know much, but how did he get himself killed?

"What's that?" Mr. Walsh said as he was woken from his own musings.

"Why couldn't it have been a man that cut Thomas up?"

"You mean a big fella, with a huge axe? But why all the parts? They mustn't have liked him. I mean this goes beyond killing someone. It was really excessive. And where's the rest of him? Really, to me it looks like something ate him and what we saw were leftovers."

"Well, if this was done a year ago, is it possible someone else got killed?"

"Not that I know. I mean. you'd think we would have heard about it. Worth asking the congregation, though. ...I don't know if I should have brought you. It's not something a lad at your age should be thinking about. You should be putting your mind to other things."

"Like?"

"You're too young for girls, but there's hurling, learning to farm, and next week I'll show you how to fix a thatch roof. That will do for a start." He spat on the ground.

Kevin looked up at him, stared at the ground, smiled and gave the ground a similar gob.

Kevin woke up the next night, sweating and shivering with fear. He was repelled from sleep by a vision of flames, a bird's wing and screams. *It's something terrible.* He was upright and shaking.

On the shared pile of straw, he noticed that both Padraig and Liam had rolled facing away from him. He imagined himself rolling and grabbing towards Liam when he was struggling against the nightmare. It made him shiver. "Dear God," he groaned. The memory of it was as revolting as the bad dreams.

He went outside into the dark and overcast night with the intention of going for a pee. He recognized Mr. Walsh, who was standing on the road talking to a stranger on horseback. The other man was dressed in black.

"You're a good man, Nick," he heard the man say. "Good luck, with your fortune and take care of your boy Padraig." Without looking back, he rode away.

Kevin heard somebody moving inside the house, so he ran around to the backyard so he could have privacy while he took a pee.

He heard Mrs. Walsh call for her husband. Mr. Walsh told Judith to leave him alone. By the time Kevin had finished urinating, he saw the two of them arguing at the road. She attempted to put her arm around him. He pushed it away.

Drunken fool, thought Kevin. Somebody else came out of the cottage. Kevin slowed his walking pace along the side of the house. He saw Liam run towards his parents.

"Leave her alone," Liam shouted.

Mr. Walsh staggered. "It's not right," he said. "No, it's not right and where can we go?"

"Nick, calm down and come to bed," Mrs. Walsh said, but she was interrupted by Mr. Walsh's swiping. "We've got to keep them away."

"What are you talking about?" she asked.

"I don't want to talk about it," and he slapped at her but missed.

Liam ran up to him and pushed him. His father came back at him and punched him in the face. Mr. Walsh looked stunned and told him he was sorry, and he started weeping. Mrs. Walsh started screaming. Liam got up and started yelling. Mr. Walsh started swearing at no-one in particular.

"Lord Almighty, I'm going back to bed," Kevin told himself. He walked towards the front door, but it almost hit him in the face. "Padraig," he grumbled. Kevin moved back as Padraig came out. "Your da's drunk," Kevin said as he went inside. Padraig followed.

Once in bed, Kevin started to ask, "Do …?"

"Kevin, I don't want to talk about it. I'd like to get some sleep. Good night."

Kevin was still awake when the other three tried to settle in.

The next evening, after a late, argumentative supper, Kevin went outside to the dark. He found Padraig lying on crossed arms on the ground in the front yard, away from the house, and staring at the moon and the stars.

"I don't want to talk about it," Padraig said.

"Your father hits your brother and your brother defends him against your mother. What's that about? And what was that about last night with him and the stranger?"

"I don't want to talk about it," Padraig repeated.

Kevin stretched out on the ground near him. He lay there for what seemed to be a long time. He saw that Padraig had closed his eyes and asked him, "What do you see?"

"There's a lot of places to see and imagine as long as it's any place but here. I wonder what's on the other side of the mountain. I wonder what it's like to live along the Newtownbarry Pass or on top of the White Mountains. There's lots in this world to wonder about. What do you dream of?" asked Padraig.

"I try not to. I'd rather forget my dreams," said Kevin.

"Me too, sometimes. My father looks at Liam like he is a younger version of himself. When he makes a mess, he takes it out on my brother."

"Sounds stupid."

"You got that right."

"I see why you don't want to talk about it."

"You got that right."

Kevin heard footsteps behind him. He turned back and saw Judith Walsh. She was stopped near the cottage where she tried to take in the full expanse of the clear, star-lit sky. Kevin could feel a warm wind pass over him that he figured must come from the direction of the Irish Sea. He stared up at an undisturbed, open sky.

Padraig's mother took her time coming over to them. She paced around in a circle. She reminded Kevin of a wild dog circling before settling down. Once she found her patch of ground, she lay down on it like the others, but her legs stretched in the opposite direction.

Each of them set their eyes to their own portion of the sky. There was a long period of quiet, and eventually they all forgot what took them there in the first place.

Roughed Over

On Saturday morning, Kevin and Mr. Walsh approached the turn in the road that led them to Mr. Kavanagh's. "Are you sure he has enough thatch for the repairs?" asked Kevin.

"From what I can see, it's only for a bad section at the peak," replied Mr. Walsh. "I'm sure it'll be fine and if not we'll have to go back again. That's all."

When they came to the straight section of the road, Mr. Walsh said, "And will you look at that, he's standing there waiting for us."

When they got within earshot, Joseph yelled, "So, you've come to do some work, have you?"

"Come back Saturday, you said, so here we are," replied Mr. Walsh.

"Where are we on the other thing?" asked Joseph.

Mr. Walsh approached him and dropped a pile of coins into his hands and said, "Could you take care of this?" "Where did you get this?"

"A good turn, that's all."

"You're not going to tell me. I guess you have your reasons. You know, this is going to make you rich."

"Men like us never get rich, Joseph. We just do what we can."

"I'll put it away. In the meantime, you can go and start the work," said Joseph. When they reached the property, he headed towards the cottage door. The other two headed towards a ladder that was leaning against the roof to the right of it.

Once Mr. Kavanagh disappeared into the cottage, Kevin asked, "Was it from that man?"

"What man?"

"The rider?"

"Don't know what you're talking about."

"What did you do to get it?" asked Kevin.

"No good will come of this if you tell anyone, so never you mind," said Mr. Walsh. He stared at him and started to say, "Swear to…"

"But where's the thatch?" asked Kevin.

Mr. Walsh had a blank look on his face.

Kevin repeated his question, "The thatch for patching the roof—where is it?"

"It's right there at the side of the house. I can see it from here," said Mr. Walsh. He shook the ladder to make sure it was sturdy and then brought a couple of bundles back. Kevin returned with another.

Mr. Kavanagh came out and said, "By the way, I heard from Denny Brien."

Kevin came out from around the side of the house with another bundle. "What did he say?" he asked.

"Obviously, he's overwhelmed with depression. He asked the Púca for answers, but he didn't get any."

"That's because it was the Púca that did this," said Mr. Walsh.

Mr. Kavanagh started to say, "That's…"

"What did Mr. Keane say?" asked Kevin. "He seems to know things."

"He didn't say much."

"Do you know Mr. Keane well?" asked Kevin.

"Like you said, he knows things. He travels and is worth listening to. He has amazed me many times with what he's seen and heard, but I can't say I really know the man.

"Are you thinking of doing something about the monster?" asked Mr. Walsh.

"What do you mean?" asked Mr. Kavanagh.

"The neighbours will want to know that something tore the man apart. They'll want to organize a search party and hunt it down."

"But there hasn't been any activity for almost a year."

"But how do you know that?" asked Kevin. "Nobody but us knows about what happened to Thomas Brien."

"I've asked around if somebody was roughed up or killed under suspicious circumstances and nobody has reported anything," said Mr. Kavanagh. "Well, at least not around here."

It's important that we don't reveal our troubles to the wrong people," said Mr. Kavanagh. "There are bad sorts that can make use of others' misfortune."

"Like the landlords," said Mr. Walsh.

"They're not men to be treated lightly," said Mr. Kavanagh. "The sheriff works for them."

"My landlord—Adam's Caesar, wants to move to Dublin and wants to get rid of us," said Mr. Walsh. "How do you think he's going to make money without his tenants?"

"I've heard that he wants to use the land for raising horses."

"He doesn't like people but likes horses?" said Mr. Walsh.

"It's not that he likes horses. It's just that they don't usually talk back," said Mr. Kavanagh.

"Usually?" asked Kevin.

"Racehorses. If someone damages a racehorse, there's no end of problems with the courts."

"So typically Adam's Caesar will always have a preference for less than the best," said Mr. Walsh.

"He's getting married soon," said Mr. Kavanagh. "I've heard there's an engagement party coming up, and he's in a rush to fix the Big House."

"The harvest is the busiest time of year and he's going to want us to help," said Mr. Walsh. "The man is an insensitive cad."

"I know, but you're well behind on the rent, Nick, and you didn't plant corn like I told you to," said Mr. Kavanagh.

"I know. You were right. I've had a couple of bad years, and this year hasn't helped. Maybe our luck will turn."

"You mean the races?" asked Mr. Kavanagh.

"We can only dream, right?" said Mr. Walsh.

"Maybe, but right now we should get the roof fixed, don't you think?" Mr. Kavanagh put his hands on hips, stared at the ladder and told the others, "There's a big hole in the roof. Are you waiting for me to do it, or are you stalling until it rains?"

"Fine. I'll go ahead and tear apart the bad patch," said Mr. Walsh. He motioned for Kevin to carry up a load of thatch ahead of him.

Three days after repairing Joseph Kavanagh's cottage, Nick Walsh was ordered to do the same for the landlord's residence at Duffry Hall. Kevin watched Mr. Walsh put down his bowl and sneeze again as he put on his coat.

"You're not in any shape to be going out in a night like this," Mrs. Walsh told him.

"They've no sense. It's the busiest time of the year. We could have done this months ago, but no, no…Anyway, we have no choice in the matter," Mr. Walsh said, and sneezed again. "We'll be back when we can."

Kevin watched him hurry across his neighbour's fields to avoid an approaching downpour.

"That Colclough. A witches' curse on him, is what I'd say."

"Mam," complained Liam.

"I didn't mean that. Lord knows," she said as she blessed herself.

Late after dark, there was a loud knock at the door. Kevin opened it and recognized Michael Fortune standing there. "It's Nick. He's been badly hurt. I ran ahead to warn you that Matthew Keogh and Danny Scallan are carrying him. "He slipped off Colclough's roof in the storm. The people over there have no sense."

Kevin, with Judith Walsh and her sons, hurried out and intercepted the men. Judith hugged her husband and, in a light rain, shared her tears and caressed his face.

The procession carried the man to his bed at the cottage.

Mrs. Walsh took off his soaked clothes to mend his wounds. She washed and wiped him down before tucking him in. Liam brought in some more blankets. Kevin made the men some hot tea with herbs from the mountainside. The story of what had happened was repeated around the Walsh hearth fire.

"What a scoundrel that Martin Bennett is," said Danny Scallan. "It was him, that ordered him up to the roof. Nick told him he wasn't going to go and Bennett threatened to persuade Colclough to kick him off his land."

"And imagine Bennett forcing him to leave on a night like this," said Matthew Keogh.

"They should have cared for him until he was better. There's no Christian charity there. They're beneath contempt," said Michael Fortune.

"We've a harvest to take in and we're going to have to do it without Da," said Padraig. "This is a great way to force us out, isn't it? What a monster."

"That he is," said Matthew. "He's a monster." He and the others drank the last of their tea and left without saying much else.

"He doesn't look well," Kevin said as he stood in front of the bedroom door. Mrs. Walsh was dabbing a cloth across her husband's forehead.

Padraig moved behind Kevin to hear the answer.

"He's still breathing, but he's hot. We'll be in God's grace if he doesn't take him from us tonight. We're in desperate need of fasting and prayers. I will watch him through the night, Padraig, but I'll wake you early."

Padraig pulled on Kevin's shoulders and directed him to go back to sit next to Liam by the hearth fire. "Do you two want some more tea?" he asked, and beckoned them to pass him their bowls.

"Is he going to die?" asked Kevin.

"Don't be a fool," said Liam.

"How bad is he hurt?"

"Don't know," answered Padraig. "I know he doesn't look well and we don't know what's broke. Even if he gets better, we don't know what he's going to be able to do. They said he fell off Colclough's house."

"But it wasn't off the roof," said Liam.

"We'll just have to wait, see and as mam said, we have to pray," said Padraig. "Maybe it's not his time yet."

"But if he dies?" asked Kevin.

"You really like to hit it on the head, don't you?" said Padraig.

"We'll be orphans like him," said Liam.

"You got your Mam," corrected Kevin.

"Well, the farm goes to me and whether da gets better or not, the three of us are going to have to work long days and it's been a really bad growing year," said Padraig. "The landlord wants us out because he says he hasn't been paid what he's owed. Not having Da's help makes something bad a lot worse."

"Do you know what the landlord is owed for the harvest?" asked Liam.

"No, but Mr. Kavanagh might be able to tell us."

Liam stared at Kevin and said, "And if he dies it's no skin off you, is it? He's not your da."

"Liam, throw your head over the hedge to the Kellys, why don't you?" said Padraig.

"Might not be my da, but I'd miss him," replied Kevin. "Wouldn't miss you, but I would him. He taught me things and sometimes he talked to me when he didn't have to. He's good at showing how to do things. Your mam is right—whether he gets better or worse we got to pray."

"Let's pray we don't lose the farm," Padraig said. "Sláinte," he added and raised his bowl of tea to them.

Kevin quietly raised his bowl in turn.

⚬

Joseph Kavanagh joined Nick Walsh, who was working in the gardens behind the cottage. Mr. Walsh ordered his sons to stay put and keep working.

"Are you up for the work?" Mr. Kavanagh asked.

"It's been about a month," he said. "I can't stay in bed forever, can I? Padraig made the crutch and the boys helped me with the brace for my foot."

Kevin raced around from the front of the cottage, and said, "You mean I did."

"Hello Kevin," said Mr. Kavanagh, and he put a hand on his shoulder. "I see you've been working hard. Keep it up, they need you."

"Well, Liam worked in the garden. Everyone helped out," Mr. Walsh said. "If it wasn't for your herbal soup, I don't know if I'd be here to-day."

"Just glad to help."

"All this happened in the hunger months of summer," said Mr. Walsh. "Caesar Colclough is a miserable human being."

"He thinks he's above that sort of thing," said Mr. Kavanagh. "Being human, I mean."

"Colclough's man came here last week. The agent warned me that I have to get off the land. He complained about how I owe back rent. He went on about how the troops on the continent need food for the war effort."

"Do you owe?"

"yeh, but everyone's suffering. It's not just us."

"How long did they say you have?" asked Mr. Kavanagh.

"Until spring. They clearly don't have confidence in this year's crop."

"Judging by what I see, neither do I," said Mr. Kavanagh.

"You mean we don't have somewhere to live in the spring?" asked Kevin. "What about my parent's property?"

"The landlord shouldn't have had the right to take it, but they do," said Mr. Kavanagh. "Don't worry about it, Nick will figure it out."

"Kevin, you should be helping Liam in the garden," said Mr. Walsh. "Joseph and I need to talk."

Kevin reluctantly headed back to the garden. He stopped at a plot that was closest to them so he'd still be able to overhear what they were saying.

"Why so soon?" asked Mr. Kavanagh. "You're supposed to get at least a year's notice."

"The agent said the papers were filed in the spring. Didn't come to see me, of course, but he said he did—the lying serpent."

"My landlord has been doing the same thing. The Jordans, next to me are also in a miserable state.

"The landlords have no decency," said Mr. Walsh. "I've seen the likes of some miserable types that they employ. And that just reminds me of that damned Martin Bennett, I'd dearly like to make him pay, and he has a lot of sins to account for."

"Things might look dire, but cheer up. The big race is in a couple of days. Your winnings would turn things around, wouldn't they?"

"With likes of Colclough and the others, I wouldn't be too sure," said Nick Walsh.

The next day, Kevin walked with Liam and Big John Reilly on the Kiltealy road that was leading them to a hurling match near Mr. Kavanagh's property.

"I heard about your da's bad fall," said John. "My da saw him on the ground."

"When they brought him home, he looked really bad," said Liam.

"We thought he was going to die," said Kevin.

"Too stubborn for that."

"I heard him cursing Martin Bennett," said Kevin.

"Who?" asked Liam.

"One of the landlord's fellas, I think."

"Makes you wonder what would happen if he died," said John.

"Reilly, shut up," said Liam as he glared at him and clenched a fist.

"He's a man that can get rough, and he's not great managing the rent, but we'd be lost without him," said Kevin. "And Lord…"

"What?" asked John.

"I see Ned Scallan ahead of us on the road. He stood me up the last time and didn't bother to tell me that they changed the place.

"Don't look at me. I didn't go," said Liam.

Liam and John veered off to sift into a cluster of other boys, while Kevin headed on towards Ned Scallan.

"Hey you clod, how come you gave me the wrong address for the last game?"

"What do you mean, I told Liam."

"He didn't go."

"So what, I told him."

"I'll tell him you called him a liar."

"That's not what… Go ask him and learn from what your eyes tell you, you fool."

"I've got a game to play," Kevin said, as he scooped up a rock on his hurling stick and repeatedly, but lightly tapped it into the air as he walked.

Liam approached him and asked, "Who's a liar?"

"Ask Scallan. He knows," Kevin said as he kept tapping the small rock.

Kevin slipped amongst the rest of his team who were arguing positions. He looked back and saw Ned and Liam arguing. Liam glared at him.

"Should have figured. Liam was just being an ass," Kevin muttered.

He considered the five of them that made up their side. He, being twelve-years-old, was the youngest player on the field. He was hefty and was a capable passer. Liam had four years on him and was usually pretty good with a hurley. Ned Scallan, who was a year older than Kevin, was a capable runner but not a great passer. Big John Reilly had presence. Ed Williams, like Big John Reilly, was a year younger than Liam. Ed wasn't up to the task but could be good at distracting if he was motivated.

"Boys, let's go. This is it!" Liam yelled, and he waved them ahead. The boys on the other side were running down the road towards them. When Liam's line met the other gang, they all stopped.

Tall Johnny Byrne from the other side shouted, "So you've come back for more punishment. Have you? We tore into you last time and we're going to tear into you this time."

"Johnny Byrne, you're going to kiss my arse," yelled Liam. "Who's that with you today?"

"Behind me is Big Kenny Summers, Black Tommy Hogan, and Fast Michael Bulger, and Solid Danny Turpin."

"Johnny, you lads stink and we are going to clean up. We've set up like before, so let's get on with it, here and now."

"Right you are, Liam," said Johnny, and he gave him a nod. "Have you got it?"

Liam nodded, showed him the sliotar and took a forward step.

"No, let the runt do it," said Johnny Byrne.

Liam tossed the leather sliotar to Kevin.

Kevin threw the stuffed leather ball up into the air. A melee ensued, and out of it came Liam running. Kevin ran on after him. He knew Liam lived for the game. The goal line was within sight.

Johnny Byrne smashed into Liam. Kenny picked up the ball with his makeshift stick, spun in a turn and lost the sliotar. Kevin scooped it up with his stick and twisted to manage a pass to Liam but was blindsided by Black Tommy. The ball bounced twice but was picked up by Michael Bulger who ran three paces and tossed it. The throw went wide. Young Ned Scallan jumped onto the short stone wall at the side of the road, raised his hurley above his head and redirected the ball back to the road.

"Danny, what were you doing?" yelled Johnny Byrne. "You had the ball! Why did you stop? Why did you throw it over there?"

"That's a puck—that's a foul and it's ours. We start from there," yelled Ed Williams. The rest of his muttering wasn't audible.

"Ned, they're right, it was a foul and you can't do that. Good pop, though," said Liam.

"Big Kenny Summers scraped his knee and is walking with a limp," yelled Ed Williams.

"Tommy, off the road," yelled someone.

Ned Scallan smashed the ball. Kevin spun but was surprised by horses that raced towards him and Tommy. Kevin rolled and narrowly avoided being stomped on. "Scoundrels. They could have killed me," Kevin yelled. He looked back towards Tommy. He was all right, but the riders rode on without looking back.

Kevin had scraped his arm and ripped a hole in the thigh of his pants. When he got up, the others joined him.

"That didn't count!" yelled Ed Williams.

"Yes, it did," Danny Turpin yelled.

The arguing was short-lived. The teams started re-positioning on the road around a centre line.

"Kevin, what are you doing? The sliotar is up here," yelled Ed Williams.

Kevin ignored him and walked to the side of the road. He noticed that the riders had turned into Mr. Kavanagh's farm.

"Kevin, are you playing?" yelled Liam.

Kevin saw that Mr. Kavanagh kept digging something up in his garden in the back while one of the men rode up to him and dismounted. He was in his late twenties or early thirties. He was powerfully built and looked like a bully. The other man dismounted his horse in front of the cottage. He removed a club from his saddle. The one in front of Mr. Kavanagh yelled at him and then pushed him.

"Stop the game!" yelled Kevin. "Stop the game! Hey! Johnny. Liam. They're beating up old Mr. Kavanagh. He needs help!" He pointed to what he was looking at. Once he got the attention of Johnny Byrne and Liam, the others stopped.

"Well, come on," Kevin said as he skipped over a short hedge.

"Hold on, Kevin," yelled Liam. "Do any of you recognize them?"

"No," said Big Kenny.

"Me neither," said Johnny Byrne.

Kevin stopped and looked back at them.

"They must work for the landlord," said Johnny Byrne. "When I see people I don't recognize, they are usually there to get people off their land. I don't think the other one is a Bailiff."

"Kevin, you know if we interfere, the landlord will do the same to us," said Liam.

"And when they do it at another cottage, no-one else is going to stop them either. Liam you're acting stupid," said Kevin. "Stop wasting time. Mr. Kavanagh needs our help. Anyone that isn't coming is a coward."

"What if they are carrying pistols?" asked Liam.

"When they kick people off their land they don't need pistols," said Black Tommy. "They're good at beating people up and if anyone tries to stop them, the landlord puts up rope." All the boys stopped.

"We're not cowards," yelled Kevin, and he raised his hurley and waved for the others to follow as he ran.

A few cautiously jogged after him.

Kevin saw that Mr. Kavanagh was sprawled on the ground.

One of the men rode out from the back, and the other came out of the cottage and left the door open. He carried a bulky bag and attached it to his saddle.

"He's stealing stuff," Kevin told himself. He noticed that the man's left hand had bad burn scars and that he wore a black scarf. When he climbed onto his horse, Kevin didn't see any evidence of a weapon. The riders headed out and rode past where the boys were playing.

Kevin rushed over to Mr. Kavanagh. He found him still breathing but saw a lot of blood dripping from his head and shoulder, and there was a bad cut on his chest.

Ned Scallan rushed up alongside Kevin and asked, "Is he dead?"

"Don't stand there. Go get Mrs. Jordan," ordered Kevin.

"I don't take orders from you," complained Ned Scallan.

"Go get Mrs. Jordan or I'll punch you in the nose," replied Kevin. "Mr. Kavanagh can you hear me?" he asked.

Mr. Kavanagh didn't reply.

"Somebody, get some more clothes," ordered Ned Scallan.

"Tommy, get Mrs. Jordan," said Kevin. "And hurry it up. Ned is totally useless."

The boys circled around the body. Liam pushed his way through the crowd. He saw the bleeding, so he ran into the cottage to find some cloth. He returned and started ripping a nightgown into strips.

"His chest is bleeding," said Kevin. He had pressed Mr. Kavanagh's shirt on the cut.

Liam knelt down and elbowed Kevin out of the way. He put some cloth on the wound and said, "Kevin, hold it until Mrs. Jordan comes."

"What if it's her granddaughter?" asked Black Tommy Hogan.

"She's useless. Get Johnny to send her away," said Ned Scallan.

"How come all of you are standing around doing nothing?" asked Liam. "They broke his fence. Go fix it, why don't you?"

Liam attempted to make a bandage for Mr. Kavanagh's head.

"You should have cleaned it first," said Danny.

"Mind your own business," said Kevin.

"Mouthy runt, isn't he?" said Danny, as he looked at others.

Amongst the commotion, Kevin said, "Mr. Kavanagh don't leave us. I need you. Please. And Ned, if you don't get your foot away I'll break it."

He stepped back from Kevin and replied, "You and who else?"

Old Mrs. Jordan came running into the yard with her granddaughter. "Oh dear Lord. Oh my, how could this happen?" she asked.

"They hit him and cut him," said Liam.

"Catherine, go round up all the other boys. Tell them that fixing the fence can wait."

After Mrs. Jordan heard her daughter yelling at them, she started waving for the boys to hurry up. When they arrived, she directed them to pick up Mr. Kavanagh and follow her into the cottage.

They didn't do a good job of carrying the old man. The bigger boys held the arms, Danny held his head, and a boy grabbed each leg, but his rear bounced on the ground. The stress on his arms and chest caused him to moan in pain. Mrs. Jordan ordered them to put him on a makeshift table she had assembled. They got his torso on, but his bum got stuck and the ones in the front had to let go so they could lift him up the rest of the way.

Kevin tried to keep the bandage pressed on his chest, but it wasn't easy and blood seemed to be leaking in spite of his attempt to keep it there.

"Catherine, bring me a container of clean water, please," ordered Mrs. Jordan. "Liam and Johnny, get me some more clean cloth please."

The boys brought back shirts and put them on the table. "You know if we rip up all of his clothes he's not going to have anything to wear," said Danny.

"Let's worry about saving his life. One thing at a time," she told them.

Old Mrs. Jordan persuaded most of the boys to move towards the doorway, but Kevin refused to leave Mr. Kavanagh's side.

Mrs. Jordan tore off the old man's shirt and cleaned the wounds, and bandaged them properly.

When she finished, Kevin asked, "How is he? Mr. and Mrs. Walsh are going to want to know?"

"He has a bad cut on his chest. I think he'll be all right, but it's hard to say. He's not young anymore, and I'm worried about that bump on the head." To the others at the doorway she yelled, "Now I want all of you out," and waved them off. Looking at Kevin, she added, "You too."

Kevin went outside and tried to fix a fence, but Ned Scallan kept bothering him.

Catherine came out and told Kevin, "Granny wants you inside."

"Your fault and she's going to set you right," yelled Ned. "It's on you."

"Ned Scallan, you couldn't find your arse if it was stuck on your face," yelled Kevin.

"Kevin, she's waiting," Catherine reminded him.

When Kevin entered the cottage, Mrs. Jordan beckoned him to where Mr. Kavanagh was lying. Before you go, he wants to tell you something. I told him he was too weak, but he'd have none of it. Keep it short."

The old man said something, but Kevin couldn't make it out, so he got right in close.

"Yes, Mr. Kavanagh," Kevin said. "Could you say that again?"

He softly said, "Tell Nick—we won."

"Now, now, Kevin. You've got to go," Mrs. Jordan told him. "Joseph needs his rest."

As Kevin moved back, Mr. Kavanagh reached for his hand and told him, "Don't give up." He dropped his arm and closed his eyes, and Mrs. Jordan quickly led Kevin out of the cabin.

"Best you keep him in your prayers," she said as she shut the door behind him.

Mr. Walsh limped along with Kevin to Mr. Kavanagh's house the next morning. He used a cane for support.

"What did they look like?" asked Mr. Walsh.

"The one that gave the orders wore dark clothes and a worn belt. His shoes and broad-brimmed hat were in really good shape. Maybe he stole them," said Kevin. "The other one wore rags. The one with the good shoes, had a square jaw, a solid build, and looked like he was a few years older than Padraig. He didn't have a big belly, and his right hand was badly scarred. Padraig told me that he didn't think it would be difficult to find him because only landlords are allowed to have fine-looking horses."

"I can't believe we won," Mr. Walsh told him. "I never really thought any good would have come of this."

"So it wasn't a small bet?"

"It was a long shot, but I put down a good sum. Thanks to Joseph's good judgment and my good fortune, I don't believe we'll have to worry about the landlord."

"What are you going to do?"

"With the money, you mean? No idea. Judith will probably want to give it to the priest."

Kevin looked up at him.

"Well, maybe the church. Maybe set some aside for a burial." Mr. Walsh stared back at him and added, "Let's just see what Joseph has to tell us."

As they drew near to Mr. Kavanagh's cottage, Kevin found the air still, dry and quiet. He felt like hitting something to make a noise—just to let himself know something was alive. Mr. Walsh was there, though, and it didn't seem right to disturb his good luck.

As they crossed into Mr. Kavanagh's yard, Kevin straggled behind. He watched Mr. Walsh step unevenly. He stepped faster and reached out quickly with his cane. He started running and dropped the cane. Kevin looked at the open door.

Mr. Walsh was hobbling as fast as he could. Kevin watched him get far ahead of him, and he hesitated.

Out of the door staggered Catherine Jordan. She wasn't wearing her shawl. He watched her bend over as if to throw up, but she didn't. Kevin recognized the emptiness. He didn't remember much of what had happened at New Ross, but he remembered the feeling. He recognized fear and the effect of bad things coming. He wanted to yell stop at the top of his lungs but was frozen. He wanted Mr. Walsh to stop but the closer and faster he ran, the more Kevin felt the evil of bad things coming. He couldn't yell stop, so he ran. He raced as fast as he could after Mr. Walsh, and he squeezed his fists.

Mr. Walsh stopped near the girl. Over the sound of crying, Mr. Walsh said, "Catherine". Kevin instead heard the words, "Kathleen"—his sister's name.

As Kevin rushed toward the doorway he heard her say, "They're…",
Mr. Walsh yelled, "Don't…"
Beyond the doorway Kevin noticed that the pot wasn't hanging over the hearth. A body was sprawled on the floor in front of him. From the plain grey colour of her stockings and dress, he knew it was old Mrs. Jordan. She was motionlessness, face down, and he saw a pool of blood above her hand.

In the shadows to his right, he recognized Mr. Kavanagh. He was on the floor next to his bed, face up. His vacant eyes were still open.

Mr. Walsh blundered in and pushed Kevin aside so he could take in the view.

"Joseph!" he yelled. "Dear God. What have they done?"

Kevin rushed to him. As he drew closer, he saw that blood was pooled around Mr. Kavanagh's head.

Mr. Walsh felt his face and then his hand and listened for breath. "I'm afraid he's gone," he said.

He hurried over to Mrs. Jordan and rolled her over. There were bad gashes on the side of her head and her cheek. He pushed back her hair and closed her eyes.

"They're cold and the blood is dried. It happened last night?

"What kind of evil…?"

He moved back a bit, still sitting on his heels and asked, "So what happened here?"

"It was the pot," answered Kevin.

"You're right. So they grabbed it as they came in, hit poor Mrs. Jordan until she was down, hauled Joseph out of bed and kept smashing him. It's over there in the corner, dented and marked with blood. It must have been the men that you saw yesterday. Oh dear Lord, I should have been here last night. I don't know if I can bear this."

"You told Liam you weren't going to see him because he needed his rest. That was right. I mean, no-body could have known," said Kevin.

"I'd love to kill those monsters," said Mr. Walsh as he changed to a kneeling stance. "How about saying some prayers?"

Through the brightness beyond the doorway Kevin looked at Catherine Jordan, who was staring back. He recognized fear and despair in her face. Her arms were crossed as she looked around and shuffled about. She looked like a small bird in an open field, looking for a way out but not sure which way to go.

"Catherine needs our help," Kevin said. He picked her shawl off the floor and walked out into the light.

⟿⟾

In the weeks after Mr. Kavanagh's murder, Kevin had many restless nights.

In a dream, he found himself running scared. A thing behind him was so close he was sure he was going to be taken. He slipped, and fell, and rolled through a bitter darkness. Confused, he started screaming. He couldn't tell if he was going up or down.

A softness of, "there, there," and something on his head stilled him.

Through blurry eyes, he saw the shadow of her. She combed his hair with her fingers.

He propped up and felt her caressing his hair. She patted his chest to calm him.

"Another bad dream. It was a terrible thing. Mr. Kavanagh…"

Her bosom was loose and rolling. She adjusted her gown to make herself look respectable.

Kevin turned and wrapped his hands around her waist. It was Mrs. Walsh who was with him. She caressed his back.

Kevin remembered Mrs. Sinnott holding him tightly against her chest… And there was screaming. It was Mr. Kavanagh, and he didn't want to look.

Mrs. Walsh held him tightly until he was ready to let go. When he settled back, she pulled the blanket over his shoulder and tucked him in. Before leaving she said, "Mr. Kavanagh might be gone, but the good are always with us. Kevin Neal, remember that. You boys have lots of work. Try to sleep now." She gave his forehead a kiss before leaving.

After spending a long day working in the fields, Kevin sat around the hearth fire with Liam and Padraig for a late supper. The sun had already set.

Kevin stared tiredly at the bowl in his hands.

Padraig, who sat across from him, wiped his lips and said, "You haven't said a word."

"What?"

"Kevin, you've been sitting there all this time, and you've barely touched the soup. Hurry up or you won't have a second bowl because I'll get it first."

"Not hungry."

"You should talk about it."

"Go away and leave me alone."

"You're in a fine mood, aren't you?"

They both heard the sound of shouting.

"Suit yourself," said Padraig, and he got up and went outside.

After finishing his soup, Kevin followed. He passed Mrs. Walsh, who was standing next to the door. Padraig stood at the other side of the door. He was watching his father, who was sprawled next to a hedge by the road.

"Can't stay here. It's not safe," whined Nick Walsh. "Have to go somewhere else."

They watched him take another drink.

"...have to run," he shouted.

"Well, go bring him in," ordered Mrs. Walsh.

"Da's where he wants to be," Padraig said, "so, let him stay."

He walked away from the house in the dark, and Kevin followed him.

"What's going on?" Kevin asked Padraig, when he caught up to him.

"Da feels responsible for not being there for Mr. Kavanagh."

"But he'd be dead," said Kevin.

"It doesn't need to make sense. That's just the way he is. He's avoiding Mam because the rent isn't going to be paid. He won the most he'll ever see in a lifetime, but because Joseph died, there's no way for him to prove the winnings are his. It's all gone with Joseph."

"Was that why they killed him?"

"Maybe. I think da is afraid that they'll come for us too. He's more upset about that than not having the money. And since the race, he's been going on a paranoid rant about the Púca. He talks about it as if it were an evil ghost or something. It might be the drink that's making him see things that aren't there. And then he goes on with repeating, 'And I can't trust him, I can't trust him'."

Mr. Walsh knows something he's not telling us, Kevin thought. *The man on the horse that he was talking to that night must have something to do with it. Whoever he is, he must be trouble.*

"We're in a really bad place," Padraig told him. "Soon we won't have a place of our own and we won't have anywhere else to go. I really hope da's wrong about someone else knowing about the money."

Padraig turned around and headed back towards his mother.

"Where are you goin?" asked Kevin.

"To bed," he answered.

After Padraig went inside, his mother followed.

A week and a half later, Kevin learned that something else had happened. It was Big John Reilly that told him. He heard that the landlord had sent someone to look for Martin Bennett because he hadn't shown up for work. He was in his cottage. Parts of him and his son were distributed throughout different rooms.

Since no-one would have been willing to live in such a desecrated place, the landlord had the cottage burnt and torn down.

"Da says that the stone is going to be used for patching Mr. Colclough's road," Big John said.

Reaching Out

Padraig, Liam and Kevin walked ahead of Mr. and Mrs. Walsh. Padraig walked between Kevin and his brother. The family was going to Joseph Kavanagh's wake.

"Carrying Da on a cot would have made a lot more sense. It's going to take forever to get there," said Liam.

"If you don't work, you die, is what the old people say," replied Kevin.

"Liam, he's not as slow as that. At least he's alive," said his mother from behind. She walked ahead of her husband while she recited the rosary.

Padraig told Liam and Kevin, "I'm thinking of joining the French army to fight against the English."

"That's crazy," said Kevin.

"How's that going to help us?" Liam asked as he wiped his brow.

"I'll send money back."

"We'll all be old and dead when that happens," said Liam, "or maybe you'll end up dead yourself. Besides, who's going to help run the farm?"

"What about Joseph Kavanagh's crop?" asked Kevin.

"The Jordans are going to get it," said Padraig.

"Whiny Catherine, you mean?" said Liam.

"And the Scallans," added Padraig.

"Why's Kevin running off?"

"Must be you," Padraig said.

They watched him race towards Joseph's property.

Kevin saw Denny Brien playing the pipes next to a fiddler. Next to them at the cottage doorway he thought he saw Harry Keane. Kevin ran across the yard and into the cottage. The coffin was there with Joseph in it. Matthew Keogh, a friend of Mr. Walsh, was next to it.

"You can tell Nick that he did a marvellous job on the coffin," Mr. Keogh said. "Joseph would have been impressed."

"Yeh, he put a lot of work into it. They were good friends," said Kevin. He stepped back with surprise. He saw Harry emerging from a dark corner. "Uh, oh hello Mr. Keane," Kevin said and stepped closer to him.

"I heard that you were here, when Joseph was beaten up."

"Two riders beat him and they stole some stuff from him. Somebody came back at night and killed him."

"Why?"

"Well, the landlord has been trying to get people to leave. Mr. Walsh thinks they might have thought he had money."

"They killed him for money?" asked Harry.

"Or maybe they killed him because he didn't have any," said Denny.

"Maybe," said Mr. Keane as he stepped past Kevin to the casket. He looked down at him, touched the wood coffin and said, "Joseph was a good man. We knew each other for a long time."

"Our landlord is going to take the Walsh farm that has belonged to the family for generations. He wants us and our neighbours off the land because he's moving to Dublin and wants to use the land to raise horses.

"They can be quite mean-hearted when it suits them," Harry Keane said, as he backed away from the coffin to give the boy more of his attention.

"Mr. Walsh almost died because the landlord forced him to do something he didn't want to do. They were supposed to give him at least a year's warning before forcing him to leave but didn't. They lied."

"You'd need a barrister to defend you, but you won't be able to afford it. What is Nick Walsh going to do?"

"Don't know. Maybe there's a way we can change Mr. Colclough's mind. Do you have any ideas?" asked Kevin.

"If Caesar Colclough wants something, it's pretty difficult to stop him. You'd need similar resources to even get his attention."

"So you're saying that he is going to get what he wants no matter what we do?"

"No. I'm saying you should understand who your allies are. You might just have some. For one, Mr. Alistair Alcock is in your debt."

"I don't know about him. I just remember him disappearing after I took him home."

"Maybe so, but I know he hasn't forgotten. I know because I have talked to him over the years. More important to your cause is that there is another Caesar Colclough."

"What do you mean?"

"He's one of the two brothers who live in Tintern parish."

Kevin's jaw dropped. *Lord Almighty, that's where Anty is,* he thought. He drew back.

"Kevin, I take it—I'm boring you," said Mr. Keane.

"No. No. Go talk to the cousin is what you're saying. Mr. Kavanagh told me about them. You're talking about Vessey's Caesar and John. Our landlord, who's a barrister, is Adam's Caesar."

"Right you are. He got that right. Anyways during the rebellion, John sided with the rebels, and your landlord sided with the crown. John believes that your landlord has stolen from him and from his brother and has had cause to exchange pistol fire."

"Sounds like a lovely bunch," said Kevin.

"Vessey's John is in the county, but Vessey's Caesar is in Europe. John's attempting to acquire a political seat, and he's very popular. They live near the sea."

"So you're saying we should talk to John Colclough?" asked Kevin.

"I'm not saying they'll be able to stop your landlord from stealing the farm, but it wouldn't hurt to talk to someone that has influence and shares some of your concerns. Mr. Walsh has been unfairly treated and I'm sure that Vessey's boys would be interested in hearing about it."

"So how do I meet him? Do I go to his house and knock on the door?"

"Kevin, give me a few minutes so I can consider the options. I'll get back to you when I'm ready," said Mr. Keane. Without listening to what else Kevin was going to say, he left.

When the door closed after him, the twelve-year-old realized his mouth was hanging open. *Lord Almighty, isn't that something,* he thought. Kevin turned and walked over to the dead man behind him.

"Mr. Kavanagh, you were a fine old man. Mrs. Jordan thought you were an old coot, but you told everyone the way it was even if they didn't want to hear it. I liked you a lot and I'll miss you."

He stared at the corpse in front of him with curiosity. "I don't like talking to dead people much. Mr. Kavanagh, you were a strange man. Well, you were a good man—don't get me wrong. To me—it's just like you're still alive. It wasn't right, Mr. Kavanagh. I'll try to find out who did this. I'd like to help you out by saying some prayers, if you don't mind." Kevin knelt down and recited a decade of the rosary. It made him think of Anty and berry picking, which made him hungry.

After paying his respects, he went outside. Denny Brien and the fiddler were leaning against the house, near the door. Kevin complemented, Denny and his friend on the music. He told Denny that he used to have similar pipes, but he lost them. "I also remember the last time you came to our house with your brother," he told him.

"And when was that?" Denny asked.

"In '98. It was the week before my da and brothers went to fight. I remember your brother Thomas telling us the story of the three Irish sorrows. I still remember most of it," Kevin said.

"To the sorrows," Denny said, and he tipped the broad brim top hat.

"And to the end of monsters and killers of good men," replied Kevin.

Denny and the fiddler played another tune.

"I can help you, if you like," Harry Keane said. Kevin jumped. He was standing behind him. Kevin looked at him with shocked surprise. He hadn't heard any footsteps.

"That would be good," Kevin replied.

"Adam's Caesar is throwing an engagement party in a couple of weeks," Mr. Keane said. "Vessey's John is going to be there with a lady friend. If you're up to it, we'd catch them on their way to the party. Is that something you want to do?"

"Yes, of course," replied Kevin.

"I've already discussed this with Mr. and Mrs. Walsh, and they've agreed to it. Make sure you're dressed up, bathed and ready to go."

Kevin said, "Yes," and looked over at the musicians. When he looked back, he saw that Mr. Keane was gone. He looked in the house, but there wasn't anyone there except poor dead Mr. Kavanagh.

How did he do that when I'm standing by the door? he wondered. *He must have snuck out through the thatch. What a strange one,* he thought.

Kevin didn't see Mr. Keane again for the rest of the wake or at the funeral. Afterwards, he helped Mr. Walsh bury Mr. Kavanagh. They made sure his feet were pointed towards his cottage. After they covered the coffin with dirt, he and Mr. Walsh told him that they missed him.

The day of the landlord's engagement party arrived. It was the middle of October and although the skies were clear, there was a chill in the air. Breakfast for the Walshes was finishing up. Despite the conversation Harry Keane had with the Walshes a couple of weeks ago, the couple had changed their mind and developed a plan of their own. They didn't think Kevin should talk with John Colclough.

"Kevin, let it go," said Mr. Walsh. "It'll work itself out."

"But he wants me to go with him," argued Kevin.

After collecting all the bowls, Mrs. Walsh started into her husband.

"Nick, that's enough of it. Don't go on—and put that drink away. You've got us into a mess, and how are we going to get out of it? If we lose everything, what are we going to do?"

"I'm going," Mr. Walsh said.

"Don't go on about it, because you're not. You can't get up and it's not because you're injured and you know it," she said.

Kevin left them and ran outside. He went looking for Padraig. He heard Liam in the cottage yelling, "Mam, leave him alone."

"Both of you squabbling with no words to git and go," replied Mr. Walsh. "Pour yourself some tea and you'll be fine. Just let us be. Here's a toast."

I'm supposed to be ready and they're just acting stupid, Kevin thought as he walked to the garden plots in the backyard. He found Padraig with his head down, apparently looking at the dirt.

"What did you say?" Padraig asked.

"You know your father."

"Mam wants me to go," said Padraig.

Kevin kicked away a planting of beets. "It's worthless. A crows' curse on all of you," he said. "And what are you doing, anyway?"

"Better fix that," ordered Padraig. "And since you asked, it's rabbit trouble I see here."

"So, make a trap and we'll have rabbit stew."

"Like I haven't thought of that. Go way."

"Lord, there he is," said Kevin. "He's coming out from the trees." Kevin caught Padraig's eyes, and he flicked his nose in the direction of the neighbours. "He's there. It's himself. Lord, look at him. Mr. Keane is dressed up as fine as Mr. Alcock."

Today, Mr. Keane was dressed in a full trench coat, vest, proper breeches, top hat, and sensible long black leather boots. The boys watched him cross the property, pick up a basket of potatoes, pass them by and walked on to the cottage.

Mrs. Walsh appeared at the side of the cottage. Mr. Keane approached her with a gentile manner and tipped his hat to her.

"I saved your boys the trouble," they heard him say as he raised the basket of potatoes to Mrs. Walsh.

After the exchange of greetings, she invited him in.

"You'd think he was another John Kelly or Father Mogue Kearns himself. The way he is I'd say even the Pope would tip his hat. What do you think?" Kevin asked Padraig.

"You're dreaming, Kevin," he replied and gave him a laugh. "And fix your mess."

—❦—

Mrs. Walsh bombarded Mr. Keane with lots of questions as her husband quietly smoked his pipe next to the hearth fire across from their guest.

"Are you a tinker and storyteller like Denny Brien?" she asked.

"I get around like he does," he said.

She got him talking about people and places he had seen. It became clear he had travelled widely and seen much. It had come up that he had spoken to strangers speaking in other languages. The man was an enigma, but he made a good impression on her. Once the tea was ready, she asked him who he knew in these parts. He skirted the question by just saying that he travelled long distances and that he was passing through to his next stop in County Waterford. His lack of candour made her feel a bit uneasy.

"Mr. Walsh, have you heard anything more from the landlord?" asked Mr. Keane.

"He's planning to move to Dublin and would like to change how he manages his properties," he said.

"Marriage always changes things, doesn't it?" said Mr. Keane. "If we're going to meet the landlord's cousin, we will have to leave very soon."

"What are you going to ask him?" asked Mrs. Walsh.

"We are just going to make his acquaintance," said Mr. Keane. "We'll know what to ask once we get to know who we are dealing with."

"Mr. Keane, I would like to go with you, but I overdid my last trip to visit poor old Mr. Kavanagh, and my leg won't manage it."

"The passing of Joseph is Wexford's loss. He was a good man. He'll be sorely missed," said Mr. Keane.

"I would be more comfortable if my oldest went in Kevin's place," Mrs. Walsh said.

"I understand your concern, but Kevin is peculiarly suited. He's young, unassuming, and his connection with Alistair Alcock is unique. Did you know that John Colclough's young Miss is his cousin? I am sure Kevin will make a good impression. Don't worry, he will be in good hands."

Kevin came into the cottage.

"Would you like some tea?" Mrs. Walsh asked Mr. Keane.

"Young man, I asked you to have a bath, and your clothes and shoes cleaned," said Harry Keane. "Hurry on, or we'll be late."

"I tried, but…"

Harry gave him a small swat with the back of his hand and ignored his excuses.

"I didn't think it was necessary," said Mrs. Walsh. "I didn't want him to go."

"I *suggest* you help him," insisted Harry Keane. "I'll be outside waiting."

When Kevin came out to join Mr. Keane, he saw that he was already walking away across the neighbours' property. He had to run hard to catch him.

By the middle of the afternoon, the two reached a bend in the road that wound around the main part of the Colclough's property and led south to the main road.

"You're going to keep on this trail until you reach the Mocurry Crossroads," Harry Keane told him. "That's where you're going to speak to Mr. John Colclough."

"What?"

"You'll have to keep up a good pace to get there in time. You wasted a lot of time dawdling."

"I thought you were coming with me?"

"Sorry, but I have to go. Have a nice walk. Oh, and here are some berries and piece of bread," he said, as he took them out of his pocket and put them into Kevin's hand. Mr. Keane left without saying another word. Kevin watched him run away through a line of trees behind him.

"Well, of all the most ludicrous, stupid, gob-infested things," Kevin ranted. "What am I supposed to do? There's no sense to the man." He reached for the sling in his pocket in hope of destroying something, but instead started running. To *hell with Harry Keane. I'll just have to think of something.*

After a few minutes, he had to stop to catch his breath.

"How am I going to be able to stop a fancy coach? Stand in the road, waving my arms madly until he runs over me?

And if the coachman stops, what am I going to say to the man to get his attention? he wondered.

Well, hello there, your lordship. Do you mind stopping for me, out of the goodness of your heart?

No.

And why would you want to stop? You ask.

Because I'll spit on you if you don't and I'll be in a sour mood all day. You wouldn't want that now, would you?"

"*What do I want from you? You ask.*"

"*Well, I want to tell you that your relative is way worse than you are.*"

"*How bad is he?*"

"*Well, he's a liar, a thief, and a traitor to the Irish people.*"

"*And aren't we all? You say.*"

"*Well, he's especially awful.*"

You know that already and you're leaving, you say.

Well, you know your ladyship there, should be proud to be beside such a great noble gentleman like yourself.

You know that already and you're going to run me over if I don't move?

Do you like berries? How about a piece of bread?

Harry! Damn you, Harry. This is not going to work at all.

Kevin took the sling out and used it to throw a stone at a tree. He missed the trunk but hit a branch. He put it back in his pocket, and aloud said, "Lord Almighty," and started running again.

When Kevin finally approached Mocurry Crossroads, he wondered if he had got there in time. Three main roads crossed at the junction. There was a farmhouse to his right, and another across the road. When he walked across the crossroads, he was caught off guard by the appearance of Harry Keane. He was smoking a pipe and having a chat with a farmer in front of the cottage that was on his right just off the main road.

Kevin watched Harry say goodbye to the farmer and calmly take his time crossing the yard to meet him.

"Why…? How did you get here?" asked Kevin once he got close enough.

"You know, when nature calls… The coach is going to stop at this crossing before going to Duffry Hall down there," Harry said, as he pointed down the road away from Kevin. "Are you ready? You look all sweaty."

"You told me I was going to be late."

"Maybe I exaggerated a little, but really, are you ready?"

"To talk to Mr. Colclough? Yes. Well, maybe. Well, actually…"

"I suppose you're as ready as you'll ever be. So how old are you now?" asked Harry.

"Twelve."

"You're tall for twelve."

"And short for thirty," replied Kevin.

"Right you are. For you that must feel like an eternity away." Harry gripped the leather waistcoat, putting on airs like an influential gentleman, and asked, "How's things?"

"They are not good. They want me to leave, and I think Mr. Walsh is beating up Liam. Padraig is talking about going to France. Liam is smashing me and I hit him with a stick."

"Did he deserve it?"

"What?"

"For you to hit him with the stick?"

"I don't know. Maybe not, but he's almost twice my size. It's not fair."

"You will find that little in life is fair. You'll need to learn to fight. If you learn to use your fists and acquire some confidence, maybe you won't have to use a stick." Harry hit him in the shoulder.

"Ow. What are you doing? Why did you do that?"

"Put up your fists and protect your nose," Harry said as he jabbed the air in front of him. "Come on, Kevin, protect yourself." He jabbed his forearms hard enough that they hit his head.

"That's no fair, you're an adult."

"And you're whining like there's a tomorrow. Now keep them up or a big bloke will give you a black eye," after which he jabbed his arm again.

"Watch your footwork. Be steady. In tight spots, make your stand until you can find a direction to run."

Harry had them jab around in semicircles. "Now there's three of us. Me in the middle and two on each side. Keep it up, Kevin. You're doing great. Better than the last time."

Harry sat in a crouch and hopped like a rabbit.

"What's that you're doing?" asked Kevin, as he gave Harry a smash in the left forearm.

Harry in turn gave him a soft jab in the stomach.

"That, Kevin, is a rabbit punch." He bounced back, away from him and then stood up.

"Kevin, find someone that fights better than you do and get them to teach you."

"Why don't you teach me?" asked Kevin.

"I'd like that, but I can't. Sorry. Besides that, I don't think I'm the best boxing teacher to be honest. Learn to become a blacksmith. I believe you'd like it."

"Why do you say that? Why not a farmer?"

"There's a bitterness there and you've been hit down on. You could use a bit of smashing, and that's what blacksmiths do. They smash and reshape things in fire. Kevin, it's just an observation. You'll do what you want."

"Something killed Mr. Thomas Brien. Some say it was the Púca."

Harry looked away from him and focused on the road. "Padraig wants to go to France, you say. It's probably for the same reason Liam is hitting you."

"Yes, but…"

"The bad things your landlord does causes desperate people to do strange and foolish things."

"I saw Liam with a bruised face after Mr. Walsh got drunk."

"Nick Walsh probably sees himself in young Liam. There is no good excuse for why it happens. They should be kept apart. Padraig needs to smarten up and stand with his brother, and that's whether Liam likes it or not."

Kevin was quiet for a while. He thought of his brothers, Seamus and Aiden, sword fighting in their backyard a long time ago.

"Anything else bothering you, Kevin?"

"Mrs. Walsh lost a son in the war, but she never acknowledges that she lost their only daughter before. I find it strange."

"Well, Nick lost his baby girl and then his oldest son. Some people hide the worst of things. Just because people don't talk of them doesn't mean they are any less important. Sometimes things are just too hard to come to terms with. Mrs. Walsh might believe that talking about an old wound that can't be fixed might cause him to go on a bender. I don't know, Kevin. This is something you're going to have to find out from them."

"Harry, you've got a sense of things," Kevin added

"Me? Well, I get around. I talk to people and I'm older than your pair of shoes.

"Don't look glum," said Harry. "I'm sure we'll see them here. He's bringing his sweetheart. Even if he didn't want to go, she would do her best to persuade him."

"Why would he bring his lady friend to a party with people they don't like?"

Harry opened his mouth to say something, but he stopped. "Well, Kevin, you have a good point. They live in a strange world. That's all I'll say."

"I've heard that the Púca hasn't been seen by anyone in a while. Has he been busy?"

"From what I hear, he's likely waiting for a call to go to America," said Harry.

"Why would he be thinking like that?"

"Everyone has things they have to do. They have their work cut out for them. I'm told there are things he's got to do there. He has to fill in for someone, or there'll be hell to pay."

Harry looked at Kevin. "You don't know what I'm saying."

Kevin shook his head.

"That's fine. There are times when I don't understand it either."

"Well, there's been hell here."

"Right you are, young Kevin. Right you are."

"Will he miss this place?"

"More than you can imagine, Kevin."

"Has he travelled to America before?"

"No, but he has travelled the world. He does get around. It's what púcas do. They get around."

"So, there are others?"

"You're curious today, aren't you? There are, but they have their own names and their own stories."

"Harry, do you like travelling?"

"Kevin, are you working your studies? Is the priest keeping you up with your reading?"

"The new one isn't like the last. He's pretty busy," said Kevin.

"How's the music coming?" prodded Harry.

"The spirit is there." He shuffled around.

"Not a bit. Not even a tiny bit. Eh?" said Harry and gave him a good stare.

Kevin gave a laugh as if he was being tickled.

"If you want the girls chasing after you, you will need to learn to keep them hopping. Cup your hands. I have something for you. It will keep you occupied," said Harry. From his coat pocket he pulled out a cloth. Within it were more berries, and bread. He put them in Kevin's cupped hands. "I picked the berries and the bread is from Mrs. Walsh's kitchen."

When Kevin took a bite of the bread, Harry gave him a friendly swat between the shoulder blades. "Don't spill them now, do you hear?"

About ten minutes later Harry told him, "I can see the carriage approaching."

"You must have good eyes. I can't see a thing."

Harry smiled and said, "They've made good time. Kevin, this is who we've been waiting for." As he hurried across the roadway and waved an arm, he added, "Come with me, Kevin."

When the coach got near the crossroads, Harry started flagging his arms above his head. He rushed to the other side of the corner to address the stopped coach. "Hello Mr. Colclough," he said. "It is good to see you again. I see you brought along your charming lady."

"Oh no, we're not…" John Colclough said and coughed a couple of times. His face was red with embarrassment. "It is a coincidence to see you again, Mr. Keane."

Harry Keane pointed to Kevin, who was running across the street, and told him, "This is young Kevin. Nick Walsh is his father. Mr. Walsh is the one that does stonework."

"Hello sir," said Kevin as he struggled to catch his breath.

"How do you know Mr. Keane?" asked Kevin.

"While I was on my way to meet my dear Elizabeth at Wilton Castle, I came across this young man's misfortune. He told me that robbers accosted his his carriage. We gave him passage to the road that leads to Adamstown. That was early this morning. How on earth were you able to make it here?"

"I had access to a remarkable steed. I expect you and your party are in a hurry to reach your engagement. As I mentioned earlier, Mr. Walsh will soon be without a property, and I believe he and his sons could assist you on those new designs and renovations that you told me about."

Kevin was going to repeat the question to Harry as to how he got there, but the woman beside Mr. Colclough asked, "What is this about, John?"

"Well, Elizabeth, it's not exactly a secret, but I was hoping to surprise you later. I have some plans for a wonderful new set of gardens. The place could use some colour, and the abbey hasn't had a good garden party in a very long time. The mill needs work, and the abbey definitely needs attention."

"John, when would you like to have a word with this boy's father?"

"That must be young Kevin, who you talked to me about before. Well, Mr. Keane, Elizabeth and I will discuss it some more, and then I expect I will have my man look into it very soon."

Kevin remained quiet.

John Colclough asked, "Kevin, what do you think about moving to Tintern Abbey?"

"Yes, we would like that very much, sir. All of us would."

"Mr. Keane tells me that your landlord is forcing you to leave your farm."

"Mr. Walsh got hurt because Caesar Colclough made him work in a place that wasn't safe, and he decided to take his land because he got hurt."

"How is he now?"

"He's walking around and feeling much better, thank you."

"Yes, I have heard my cousin brag about raising horses. It is not something out of character, I am afraid. He has done this before. He is not a likeable man and we detest each other. If I asked Caesar to do something, he would do the exact opposite."

Kevin said, "Well, how about asking him to take our land and maybe he'll do the exact opposite."

John Colclough gave him a grin. "Maybe you're right," said John. "The boy might have a future in politics." He winked at Mr. Keane.

Mr. Keane suggested, "Maybe you should work on a way to get your brother back into the county. Together you would have a strong presence should you need to stand against Duffry Hall."

John said, "I won't make promises, but I will give it serious consideration." He looked down at the ground and waved the coach on. As the coach left the intersection, Mr. Keane added, "Mr. Colclough, keep in mind that Kevin here maintains connections with the Alcock family." John in the carriage was startled. Before he could say a word, the coach moved beyond conversation distance.

Kevin gave Mr. Keane a disappointed glare.

Harry responded with, "I didn't say anything specific. Did you know that the lady beside him is Alistair's cousin?"

"No," Kevin said. "You just told me that he was bringing a lady friend."

"We have exchanged a few words with an influential man and polished some connections. Mr. John Colclough can be a reasonable man, when it suits him. You may not have a solution here, Kevin, but at least now you have some open ears in influential places. It's better than a kick in the head."

"Why did you tell him Mr. Walsh was my father? He's not," said Kevin.

"It is time I headed back," Harry told him. "Sorry to leave you Kevin, but I have to go," and he quickly marched down the road away from Duffry Hall.

The long walk home was lonely and boring, and Kevin felt let down. After he kicked the dirt, he reached for an empty pocket. It had been several months since he had had Anty's papers. He rolled his fingers together as if he were feeling it. It made him remember something about a mean boy who was running from him.

I didn't like him, he thought. *Was Douglas his name?'* He remembered something sticky on his fingers.

Didn't want to go with her, he thought *And who was that:* Something about not wanting dirty hands."

"So stupid," he said to himself. "This is stupid. Liam is stupid. This whole idea is stupid."

"His lordship wants to build a garden for his lady friend and have a

few things fixed. How secure is that?" He gave the ground some spit. *What does 'I'll have a man look into it' mean? When Harry asked him when he was going to meet Mr. Walsh, there wasn't an answer. And he doesn't really know where we live. If he hates our landlord, he's not going to talk to him, now is he? Lord in heavens, didn't we mess up?*

The more I think about this, it might just be so much of nothing, he thought. *And who is Harry Keane? And how did he get around so fast without a horse?*

His shoulders sagged. The pace slowed. He shuffled his feet through the dirt and angrily kicked some stones. He found the stillness of his surroundings menacing. It bated him.

I used to think that Harry Keane was there for me, but I believe he arranged the meeting for himself. He has decided to leave, and he needs to develop connections.

More than a month had gone by since Kevin had reported on their meeting with the landlord's cousin. Judith Walsh stood beside the cottage door, looking at the path out to the road. "Well, will you look at that," she muttered. "The landlord sent another one to tell us we're out. Heavens, I'll be at the mercy of the priest for things I'd like to say to that one. Where's his bailiff?" She looked around and didn't see anyone other than the man on horseback who was riding onto the property.

"Lord Almighty. More to the point, where is…? Oh, poor Nick." She rushed around to the back of the house and she waved to get her husband's attention.

Padraig, who had been digging the ground near her yelled, "da, someone on horseback is here."

The lone rider wore a black top hat, a colourful red waistcoat and a fine gentleman's coat. *He's one that must be worth more than the last,* thought Mrs. Walsh. *I'd say he was a tad overdressed for his line of work, but that's not my concern.* She walked back to the front and asked the stranger, "Sir, how can we help you today?"

"Would you be Mrs. Walsh?"

"Yes, I am."

"My name is James Kennedy. I am here to have a word with your husband, Nick Walsh."

"He hasn't been well since the accident. Can you give me an idea, of what you would like to discuss with him?"

"Well, Mr. Colclough of Tintern Abbey was expecting a man that was capable and reliable and knows how to work with stone. Maybe a mistake was made."

"That's my husband in the garden. He'll just be a minute."

"Nick was close enough to hear the man's name and who he represented. When he got within hearing range, he waved his cane."

"Mr. Kennedy, Nick Walsh at your service. Judith, make us some tea, please. Mr. Kennedy, please forgive my wife. She is a little overprotective these days. You know, with the rebellion and all, you can't be too cautious."

They went inside and Mr. Walsh offered him a stool by the hearth fire. "Your employer sounds like a fine, upstanding gentleman from what I've heard," said Nick.

"I have been in the employ of John Colclough for quite a few years now. I provide him assistance in many things, including the maintenance of his estate. He has been quite occupied of late, and his properties are in need of serious repair. Getting a capable and reliable resource with knowledge of how to deal with stone would be a great asset. You see, Mr. Colclough lives in an abbey."

"Is he a religious?" asked Mrs. Walsh as she poured some herbal tea into a small bowl for her guest.

"No. No, he's not. The abbey hasn't been used for prayer for a long time. The religious left it before the Colclough family acquired possession, and they've had it for centuries. He and some servants are the only ones who live there. He is considering having part of it rehabilitated so his mother can move in with him."

"That's nice," said Mrs. Walsh. "Is he old?"

"Judith," groaned Nick.

Mrs. Walsh passed the bowl of tea to Mr. Kennedy.

"No. He is currently courting a young lady friend. He is very captivated by her."

Padraig and Liam came in. "Do you need some help, Da?" Liam asked.

"No. No. We're having a sociable conversation with a dear visitor. Boys, this is Mr. Kennedy. He is in the employ of Mr. John Colclough. They are in need of a good stonemason."

"Mr. Kennedy, this is Padraig, my oldest. Boys, they have a huge house like Duffry Hall. The funny thing, though, is that it looks like a church. Well, it's an abbey to be exact. Mr. Kennedy, I have done similar stone cutting for Mr. Caesar Colclough. I've had the boys help me. Although we've had our differences, I am sure the men at Duffry Hall would provide references for my craftsmanship."

"Very good. I notice that you have a bad limp.

"Caesar had me repair a roof without proper supports in a rain storm. I was hit hard, but I'm a tough man to put down. As you can see, I am getting about just fine."

Mrs. Walsh passed cut pieces of bread in front of her guest and her husband.

"You have another lad here, don't you?"

"You mean, young Kevin. He is probably still working out back. Liam, go fetch him please," ordered Nick.

"Mister Colclough was taken by him for some reason," said Mr. Kennedy. "The reason is not clear to me, which makes me curious."

"I am very interested in this opportunity, but I'd like to discuss this with my family first. When would you need me?"

"Well, you've got quite a limp there, haven't you?"

"On my way back I am going to make a stop at Duffry Hall and look at work that you have done. Don't worry, I'll mind my tongue with the upper crust. They don't need to know everything. It's the men and women that run the place who are in-the-know. If that goes favourably, I expect that I might return in a couple of weeks. I'd give you a week to get settled in, and at that point we would assess if you can keep up."

Mrs. Walsh was speechless. She couldn't decide if this was a good thing or another disaster in the making.

"Nevertheless, Mr. Kennedy, I thank you for considering me," said Mr. Walsh.

Kevin came into the cottage with Liam following.

"So you must be Kevin," said Mr. Kennedy. "You must be a fine lad. You're doing all the work while the rest of us are all wasting time in the kitchen. You made a good impression on his lordship."

"Mr. Kennedy tells me that his estate requires a proper stone mason," said Mr. Walsh. I let him know that I've done the same type of work for the landlord here."

"That sounds like a good thing," said Kevin.

"How did you come to meet Miss Alcock's cousin? Mr. Colclough overheard that you have some sort of connection."

Kevin looked down. "I helped him out when he was hurt, that's all."

"Look up, lad," said Mr. Kennedy.

Kevin looked at him cautiously. He didn't trust him.

"I understand that he has business ties with both branches of the Colclough family. I can confirm that Tintern Abbey has the greatest respect for dear Alistair. Well it was nice meeting you, Kevin." He gave his small bowl back to Mrs. Walsh. "I am sorry to cut the niceties short, but I have a long way back and I have some stops to make."

They followed their visitor out. He quickly mounted and steered the horse back to the road. He didn't look at them as they waved and said their goodbyes.

"But he's just one of Colclough's men," said Liam. "Da, why did you tell him that you're a stonemason? You're a farmer. They're expecting a stone mason for Lord's sake."

"Well, a stone mason's work is what they had me do at Duffry Hall. He just wasn't paying me for it."

"He's well-dressed for hired help, if you ask me," said Mrs. Walsh. "He has well-made shoes. There are no patches on that one. Nick, are you in any shape to do this? And we'd have to leave the farm before spring. Is that what we want?"

"All of you have been saying for months that we needed a way out. Now there is one," said Kevin.

"There's nothing in this that says it's going to happen or whether it's even a good thing," said Mrs. Walsh.

Late that night, after Mr. Kennedy's visit, Kevin woke from a bad dream. He was wet with sweat and shaking with fear. He had seen a vision of a monster stamping by the sea and surrounded by people running around. After seeing it eat its human prey, the dragon-like thing showed its dirty fang-like teeth and there was a bellow of a ferocious bellowing scream. He wasn't sure if it was the scream of the monster or the sounds of its victims. The monster had stepped with many feet and its' breath smelt like rotted dead things. A young version of himself had confronted the beast on the beach.

Kevin screamed at it, as loud as he could, but no sound came out. He dared not move because he was defending someone behind him. He didn't know who it was, but knew it was important. Everything froze, and that's what woke him up. He was shivering, and he looked at the others sleeping and didn't know what to do. He didn't want to walk out into the night. He just grabbed his legs, put his head on his knees and asked Mr. Kavanagh what he was supposed to do.

In the shadows, he remembered him say, "Follow the river to the Irish Sea. It has huge fish in it and they're bigger than both of us. They can eat you up." Kevin imagined him sigh and repeat, "Choose wisely, young Kevin." He fell back onto the mattress and stared up into the darkness until sleep took him again.

A month and a half later, the Walshes still hadn't heard anything from Tintern. Mr. Walsh told the boys to fill up baskets with produce from the garden.

"Liam, you've got a dazed look on your face," said Padraig. I haven't seen you look that way since the Watkins girl said she could see your balls hanging out from the rip in your pants."

"That was a lie, and it wasn't true. Her brother made that up. It was his pants that were ripped." Kevin tried to poke him. "Get him away from me," complained Liam.

"Kevin, move away," ordered Padraig. "What did you hear them say inside?"

"da was telling her he wants to go now," said Liam. "And she's not saying no."

"What are you talking about?" asked Kevin.

"I mean, he really wants us to get ready to go."

"To Tintern?" asked Padraig.

"yeh, to the place by the sea," said Liam.

"But they haven't told us they want us. That's stupid."

"We know they need someone, so he's just going to go there before they say no," said Liam.

"da has a bad leg. Why don't I go in his place?" said Padraig.

"It's Da, they want."

"So, I'll go with him."

"Mam says she wants all of us to go."

"That's the stupidest thing…

"She'll not break up the family, she says," said Liam. "And Da says he's not going to stay here. For some reason, he wants to leave now. I asked him why, but he wouldn't tell me anything."

"I think something scares him—and it's not just the eviction," said Padraig.

"Shite," said Liam as he got off his knees and picked up his basket.

"What's your point?" asked Padraig.

"We've got a fresh harvest and we're leaving it to go to who knows where and possibly starve and lose everything. Padraig, what do you think?"

"I don't know," he said.

Kevin pawed at an empty pocket. Since he could no longer read the few remaining pieces of the letter, he added them to the hearth fire.

"I'm packed," he told them.

"You've decided, have you?" asked Padraig.

In spite of the warnings in his dreams, Kevin replied, "I suppose I have." He brushed the top of his nose and looked away.

"I thought you wanted to know who killed old Mr. Kavanagh?" said Liam.

"Who says I'm not coming back?" Kevin replied, and returned to weeding.

Stepping Off

Liam stepped outside the cottage doorway with a sack on his shoulder to where Kevin stood waiting for him.

"You've a confused look on your face," snapped Liam. "What are you doing?"

Kevin hefted his own bag over his shoulder, while he stared at Padraig and his mother who were waiting on the road for them. He replied, "I don't know what we're waiting for. They're leaving and your da is still plodding around the garden. There's not much there, so why is he wasting time?"

"That's his business," said Liam. He saw his mother stare at him impatiently. "You can go ahead with the rest of them. I'll get him." Kevin didn't argue. He hurried to join the others on the road.

Liam walked around to the back where he found his father in the middle of the field. Without acknowledging his presence, his father pinched a bit of soil while staring at the neighbours' fields. He flicked the dirt back onto the ground.

"Da, who are you looking for?" Liam asked.

Mr. Walsh stammered, saying, "Never you mind. Nothing. Nothing at all." He stared at his wife and the others on the road. It's time to go. Sorry, boy. I really wish things were better for us. This is not the way I wanted it to be."

"Da, don't. We'll get through it."

Liam watched his father nervously looking around again. "Go tell your mother it's time to go," his father said as he put a backpack over his shoulders. "No time to waste. It's time to go."

Liam looked back at his mother. She moved the back of her hand away from her face and had a disgruntled look. Liam turned back to look at his father and said, "Good Lord." He went off in a different direction. He scrambled over a stone boundary wall and continued rushing across a neighbour's field as if wild dogs were after him. The others ranted with a stream of complaints as they came back to follow him. It was winter in Wexford and no-one was eager to think about the coming cold night.

After hiking for a little more than an hour, Kevin left the road to look at a stream that followed the road. "It's the Urrin River," he yelled. Liam ran after him. When they came back Padraig snapped, "Why are we standing here waiting for the likes of you? We'd leave, but you don't know where the hell we're going. For the Lord's sake—I don't even know where we're going." Padraig took a look at Kevin and started laughing. "Lord. Well, … the look of you. If you're going for a swim, take your clothes off first. Don't complain about having cold feet."

"He was gawking at a stream, and he slipped and fell in. What a fool," laughed Liam. "Urrin River? You don't know that. What a fool."

Padraig looked at Kevin's right stocking, which was wet up to the calf, and ordered, "Kevin, don't just stand there. Put on another one."

As Kevin changed his stocking at the side of the road, Liam asked, "Why are you acting like an idiot?"

"You're one to talk," replied Kevin. As he squeezed out his stocking, he added, "Well, the stream got me thinking."

"Cold like this? You got soaked. How do you figure you're thinking? Come on, it's time to go."

"I still don't know much about who killed Mr. Kavanagh."

"Well, the Jordans and the Whelans said they saw the man in gloves."

"Yeh, but we don't know who he is or why he did it. And we don't know anything about who killed Thomas Brien."

"Of course we do. It was the Púca," said Liam.

"You're being stupid."

"Ned Scallan thinks so," said Liam.

"You told him. That was stupid"

"He said he knows something."

"What?" asked Kevin.

"Don't know," Liam said. He looked back at the others. "He wasn't at Mass yesterday."

Kevin started pulling on his shoes.

"So you're staying here? Then good riddance," Liam said and he ran after the others.

"Kevin, come on," Padraig yelled, as he and his brother rushed to catch up to their parents.

When Kevin caught up, he settled in line next to Padraig, who was to the right of his mother. Liam walked to the left of his father.

"Nick, where are we going from here?" asked Mrs. Walsh as she touched her husband's arm."

"The road goes to Enniscorthy, which is on the river Slaney."

"And we follow it to the sea?" asked Kevin.

"No," answered Mr. Walsh. "According to the map that Julia persuaded our priest to draw for us, we have to go south across the county. The place is by the sea, but we won't see it until we get there. I hope we don't get lost. I've never been in these parts."

"You think you're up to walking there, dear?" asked Mrs. Walsh.

"I'll be fine. I just won't get there as soon as I'd like."

As the day progressed, Mrs. Walsh became more depressed and withdrawn, but she was determined to keep going. To keep occupied, she repeated decades of the rosary.

Knowing the others were straggling, she quickened her walking pace. She didn't notice that Kevin wasn't far behind.

"This is a hard thing we're doing and mercy if I'm going to let it get us —Nick Walsh, you're such a bag of shit. You are lying to yourself, as much as to the rest of us. That farm was worked by your family since before your grandfather's grandfather. You will whine about this for the rest of your life. You're such a shit. You'll ignore this all day long and then come to me before it's time to sleep. If only the rest of them would stay out of it."

Without turning, she shouted, "Kevin! Liam! Pick up your pace. Get on with it."

When they walked through the shelter of tree cover, the walk was calm and peaceful, but in an exposed spot, winds brought the winter cold. Thick storm clouds moved in from the road ahead.

"Good Lord, us here, and that line of trees—so far off."

Her desire to go back to the trees they passed was overridden by the need to get away from where they'd been, and fear of the landlord's men and of strangers coming to the cottage. She tramped harder.

"Come on, boys. Get to work," she yelled. "The rain is coming and we are not going to have any cover. Boys, help your da."

"Judith, don't," Nick Wash replied. "Go on with you. A little rain won't bother me."

She kept going.

'He'll be good to you.' "That's what my mother said." 'The matchmaker made some good points.'

"But he's got bad shoes, and he's old."

'He's not that old,' she said.

"He's missing a tooth."

'Don't you think he'll be nice to you?' Mother had asked.

"When he wants me," I told her.

'It won't hurt to talk to him,' she said while caressing beads on the rosary. "I saw him smile, and he gave me that wink. I was surprised to find that he listened to me. It was all over when I realized I wanted him. How foolish young girls can be."

All around were unfamiliar hills and landscapes.

"A lifetime together and we have nothing but the clothes on our backs, what we can carry and two days of potatoes and beets. All those difficult years in that cottage and we have nothing left. We have nothing."

"Mother, you told me, 'It won't hurt to talk to him.'"

"Oh no, no, no. Of course not. Look at me now. Well, look at us now. What's the best we can expect? Labourers don't make much. The boys will leave because there's no farm. When we're old, we'll still have nothing."

She didn't stop, but she slowed her pace a little because the day was succumbing to a threatening darkness.

"Liam tries to be like his brother, Terry. Poor Terry, God bless his soul. Padraig is determined to leave us—and I don't know if there's anything Nick and I can do to show we love him and keep him close. Dear Lord, I don't know what to do."

She kept walking.

"And Kevin's a poor lost soul."

Cracks of thunder made her stop.

"If I go running to Nick, I will be lost. I can't depend on him. I don't know what to do."

"Mam." It was Liam calling.

"What?" Judith Walsh replied without looking back.

"Mam, Da can't keep up. You're going too fast for him."

She turned and was startled to see Kevin so close, and she was surprised at how far behind the others were.

She didn't go back. She waved for them to hurry on, and she pointed to the clouds overhead.

She kept moving ahead.

When the rain began, she turned, and saw that the others had almost reached her. Her husband wore Padraig's coat, and her son had his arms around him, and Nick was shivering.

Facing into the storm, she directed the family to race for protection behind a hedge which was braced by a short boundary stone wall. The drenching rain quickly turned into hail. The sounds of running in wet shoes were interrupted by a painful barrage of pebble-like hailstones against bare heads and poorly protected skin.

As soon as her boys lifted their father over the roadside wall, she followed and ran ahead to a spot that looked sheltered. Mr. Walsh was lowered to the cold ground where he sat against a wall of stone. Judith squeezed next to him and hugged him tight. Padraig and Liam knelt next to their parents and wrapped their arms around them to protect them. Liam felt Padraig shivering.

Kevin curled up in the corner of the stone wall. He was in the process of taking off his coat in order to make a tent.

"Kevin, over here," Mrs. Walsh called as she beckoned him with both arms.

"I'll be fine," his lips said.

"His feet must be freezing," said Mrs. Walsh. "Kevin, come over here this minute." She gave her husband a squeeze. "It's a new day. Get over here," and she pointed to the ground beside her. "And you are one of us." She didn't wait for him to answer. "Liam, go get him. Carry him if you have to. Such foolishness."

Kevin gave Liam a warning glare, and Kevin quickly rushed and put his coat over Padraig, who was starting to turn blue. From his pack Kevin pulled out two pullovers. He put one on and wrapped the other around his head to form an improvised hat. Mrs. Walsh moved Liam aside and let Kevin sit beside her, and she put her arm behind Kevin and Liam as they huddled closer.

Padraig unwrapped a couple of blankets and had everyone huddle under them.

The freezing rain was overtaken by a blowing snowstorm, which continued unabated.

It's getting so bad I can't see anything in front of me. I just want to fall asleep. In spite of being huddled together with the others, Judith Walsh was freezing. *We are all shivering like Padraig. It's so very, very cold. I wonder if we're all going to die. We've a day of walking ahead of us. Mercy. How are we going to manage?*

Kevin hid his face in his arms. He felt Mr. Walsh move his arm around her.

After about forty-five minutes of silence and shivering, Nick whispered to Judith, "Trust me, we have to move. There's a break in the storm. Now is the time to go." He released his arms from her, got up and waved for everyone to follow. When they got back on the road, he told them that he was leading them to Monart House.

"It's only about half an hour away," he said. "I've worked with men from there at Duffry Hall. I'm sure on a day like this, I can persuade them to let us stay in the barn for the night."

As Nick Walsh had hoped, the proprietors of Monart House allowed the family to remain in their barn until the bad weather had passed. The family made their way back to the road after a stay of two days.

Judith Walsh and Liam followed Padraig to the road.

"We were fortunate, Liam," said Mrs. Walsh. "If it weren't for Christian charity of the good people at Monart House, I don't think any of us would be here today. If your father didn't convince us to move, it would have been dire indeed."

"Look at the snow, will you? It's disappearing fast. Maybe it will be gone by the time we get to the abbey," said Liam.

"It was nice of those Monart people to let us stay, and that wonderful Mrs. Sutton—she gave us those blankets and milk and porridge. It was truly a time of grace."

"Yes, it was. It was very nice of her," Liam said.

"We are in their debt. We should say some prayers for them. We'll say all the decades of the beads with all the joyful mysteries and we'll include all the saints…" Liam picked up his pace to catch up to his brother.

Kevin stood near the road, waiting at the end of the drive to the Big House for Mr. Walsh. Nick had stopped because someone called him.

"Aren't you Nick Walsh?" Kevin heard someone ask.

Mr. Walsh gave him a perplexed look.

"I'm Tony Mullins. You're the one that had the bad fall, aren't you? I was there. I see you're walking again. When I came in last night, I thought I recognized you, but you disappeared. You were a very lucky man."

"Why do you ask?"

"They're looking for you."

"Who?"

"Relatives of the Scallans."

"What are you talking about?"

"Young Esther Redmond, a neighbour, found them."

"Who?"

"She opened their cottage door and do you know what she saw?"

"What?" asked Mr. Walsh.

"It was the Scallans. The parents, children and even a pig were on the floor. Not only were they dead, they were all ripped apart. Even young Ned Scallan. It was monstrous, what happened.

"Poor Esther. It's not something she will ever forget. It was like they were attacked by a pack of animals"

"So what does this have to do with me?"

"You know them, don't you?"

"Lots of people know Danny Scallan's family. Apparently you do," said Mr. Walsh.

"Darren Redmond said that he saw you there that day."

"Maybe he's mistaken. It was a terrible thing, but there's nothing I can do about it. Sorry, but I have to go. My family is waiting for me."

"Nick, I just thought you'd like to know. By the way, where are you going in such a hurry at this time year?"

"I've got to go," Mr. Walsh said as he waved his hand to the others.

Kevin was shocked at what he heard. Although he had been listening to Tony Mullins, he hadn't looked back. Mr. Walsh ignored him as he rushed past. He hobbled quickly to reach his wife, who waited for him farther up the road.

Kevin watched the stranger who had relayed the story return to the Big House. *Mr. Walsh knows something about this*, he thought, *and that explains why he wasn't willing to wait for his leg to heal.*

Kevin turned and watched Mr. Walsh reach his wife. He didn't speak to her, and after taking a moment to catch his breath, he quickened his step again and waved for her to follow.

The idea of Mr. Walsh having a secret like this and not telling them scared him. He needed to confront Mr. Walsh but right then, not having a place to stay and potential starvation scared him more.

Mrs. Walsh stared back at him and waved for him to hurry up. Kevin returned a wave and started moving. *I'll ask him. Yes, I will,* Kevin thought. *And then maybe we'll find out what killed Thomas Brien and Mr. Kavanagh.* The words were reassuring, but he wasn't convinced he'd act on on them.

Hearing Mr. Walsh admit to something terrible could rip us apart, he thought.

Kevin took a spit at the dead remains of a weed as he passed, but missed.

PART 3: Extreme Unction (1804-1809)

Our local stories about heroism tell us about brotherhood, righteousness and the struggle against adversity at whatever the cost. (Thomas Brien)

Tintern Abbey de Voto

hree boys meandered across the bridge to Tintern. It was the second day of a new year. They were going to the beach.

Fourteen-year-old Samuel Boyse followed his older friends Richard Caulfield and Walter Glascott. Samuel was lanky, and his hair blew upwards towards the clouds in a scrawly, twisting mess. He had his cap in hand. It was torn, yet well-patched. Less could be said for the pants, which had holes at the knees. He stopped and stared curiously across the river and above the treeline to the abbey.

His friends stopped when they reached the path to the beach. Walter was seventeen and Richard was a year younger. Richard yelled, "Samuel, what are you doing back there?"

"A buzzard… I thought I saw a buzzard," he replied and ran after them.

"You can't eat a buzzard, and what would it be doing here in January? Go on," said Richard, when Samuel got close. Richard pushed his long, straight hair away from his eyes. He was wearing his brother's pants, which were too tight at the waist and too long over the shoes.

Samuel put his cap back on and followed the others on the trail to the beach.

Walter Glascott led the way. He carried a fishing pole over his shoulder with a basket in hand. He was appreciated for his wide, strong shoulders, but not always for his opinionated, bull-headed disposition. The other two carried fishing poles at their sides.

When they got to the beach at Bannow Bay, the tide was out. The bay stretched for six miles to their left, three-quarters of it bared a long expanse of mud and sand flats.

The three of them took off their shoes and hid them under rocks on the beach. Samuel followed the others barefoot onto the cold mud. The place made him feel lonely, calm, and free. He pulled the brim of his cap down so the wind wouldn't blow it off as he stepped into the wind.

The long peninsula that made up the flat far shore ended at the strait that opened into the Celtic Sea. The water and the sky were a similar bluish white, and there was a chill in the air, but everyone was comfortable in their thick wool clothes.

The cold mud on Samuel's feet and the sweet smell in the air made him feel raw and vital. "Yeh, I hear you," he said. Richard, who was facing him, asked, "Are you talking to me?"

"Nope," Samuel replied, as he pushed up the brim of his wool cap.

"I'll take that into consideration, Anty," Samuel replied.

Richard looked behind him and saw fifteen-year-old Anastasia Kelly.

"Sea urchins? You like sea urchins? I get it," said Samuel.

"Maybe," she said as she walked past both of them.

"'They're the best,' you said. A bit squirmy, if you ask me. 'Eat it raw,' you said. You know they have needle-like things poking out?"

Samuel interpreted the waiting in her stare as meaning "Come on, read my mind and tell me what I want and get on with it." She was strange. He was sure he'd never figure her out. After all, she was a girl. *Oh yes, she definitely is a girl*, he thought.

Her woollen shawl looked too long because when she talked to him she fidgeted with it. Her short ponytail looked like it was trying to get loose, and the frizzy hair on the left side had a life of its own.

"You'd be fine. My aunt Sarah Finn told me that they won't make you sick as long as you know how to eat them," she told him. "Jacob, her husband, loves it. Eileen Jeffers and I got our catch already. How about getting us a scrumptious flounder?"

"Why are you listening to her, Samuel?" complained Richard. "It's a powerful day, and we've got to get the basket back to the Duggans."

"Anty, I have to go," said Samuel. "I'll see, but I'm not promising."

"You see here. You tell the boys your mind," she said.

"And if I get it, what's in it for me?"

"Well…" She was quiet for a moment. "I won't be mean to you."

"So you're saying… you're going to be nice to me?"

"Hmm. I have to go. I'll see, but I'm not promising anything," she said. She left him and headed for the bridge that crossed the river."

"Hey, what's taking you so long?" yelled Walter.

"It was that Kelly girl," said Richard. "He's got a terrible soft spot for that Anty girl, doesn't he?"

"He needs a good kick in the head if you ask me," replied Walter.

She's got him around her finger and he's not old enough to know which way is up yet," chided Richard.

"She's sprouting, and she has a way. Are you going to marry her?" teased Walter.

"Go away," replied Samuel.

"She really likes to tell you your business, that one," said Richard. "She'll take you away and you won't even know it."

Samuel didn't have a clue what they were talking about, but he wouldn't let on.

None of them could have known that Walter Glascott would greet another friend of the Kelly girl in two days' time. It would happen on the other side of the estate.

Padraig with Kevin walked ahead of his parents.

He heard a laugh from his father—who had his arm around his mother, and Liam stepped away from them and said, "He made that up. That's not what happened."

"It's that girl again," said Padraig.

"What?" asked Kevin.

"Liam likes that Watkins girl, and he doesn't even know it."

"How's that possible? Besides, I've never ever heard him say a good thing about her."

"People are strange. You got that right. But look at that smile on my mam. She sees it, too."

Everyone had muddy feet, but they weren't wet or cold. The woollens helped keep out the dampness. The longer they walked, the smaller the patches of melting snow got. The light of a clear blue sky made them comfortable and hopeful.

"Are you still thinking of leaving?" asked Kevin.

"Without a farm, I'll never have a family, but I can get one if I become a soldier."

"Why not go to America?"

"…costs too much."

Kevin was looking at the ground.

"What are you thinking about?" Padraig asked.

"The Scallans." Kevin checked back and stared at the others laughing.

"What about them?"

"Nothing. Maybe things will get better," said Kevin.

"You might be right, Kevin," Padraig said and gave him a swat between the shoulders. Kevin stepped back and balled his fists. Padraig followed his lead, and as he bobbed back and forth threw playful jabs. Kevin launched two more, and he almost got him in the stomach.

About twenty minutes later Padraig told his parents that a young boy he had spoken to confirmed that the Tintern estate was only a few minutes up the road.

"I sure hope Vessey Colclough's boys are more goodhearted than

Adam's Colclough's," said his mother.

Mr. Walsh grabbed her hand.

"They're all the same," said Liam.

"Doesn't matter," said his father. "We'll do what we have to. Just don't cause problems when we get there and we'll be fine."

Liam didn't listen, and he ran ahead. He followed the narrow tree-lined road around a bend to a crossroads where he met a group of three boys playing hurling. They had crude hurley sticks in their hands.

"I'm Liam. You boys look like you're a bit short for a game, aren't yeh?"

"Depends on how you want to play," said the boy, who was about Liam's age and wasn't wearing a jacket.

"Walter here plays the net, and we just hit him," said the youngest of the three.

Walter Glascott, who was as big as Padraig, looked like he was a couple of years younger.

"You're blowing smoke rings out of your backside," said Walter. "Go find your head, stick it on, and tell us something we don't already know."

"Where is John Colclough's place?"

"He doesn't have one," said the boy without a jacket.

"What are you going on about? It's right there," said the youngest. He pointed to the entrance to the Tintern Abbey estate. It had short walls on each side of the gate.

Liam kept a close eye on the bigger boy. Walter didn't seem to like him much.

"It's not his," said the boy without the jacket. "His brother owns it. He just minds it until he gets back, and he does a terrible job. He's not interested in the place. He lets it go to rot and couldn't care less about the rest of us here."

Kevin caught up to Liam and moved alongside.

"Hey, mind what you say," said Walter. "…and who are you? Why do you want to know? And where do you come from?"

"Up north of the county, by Stua Laighean," said Kevin as he stepped towards Walter. who was over a head taller than he was.

"They're papists," said the boy without a jacket.

"That's our business," interrupted Liam. He turned around and saw Padraig approaching him on his right. His parents were following behind.

"Who says we're letting you through?" said Walter.

"You don't think your stick would stop us? Do you?" asked Kevin.

"It would certainly teach you to mind what you say," answered Walter.

Padraig patted Kevin on the shoulder and directed him to the Tintern Abbey entrance. "That's it. We're here," he told his parents.

As Mr. Walsh walked past Padraig, he said, "Now go lightly on them. We wouldn't want his dear parents to worry. It would be such a shame."

"Now that's enough, all of you. You boys go on," ordered Mrs. Walsh as she walked by. "You'll just find yourselves in a bad turn." She grabbed her husband's hand again and walked through the gateway to the Tintern estate.

"Well, that's rich," said the one without the jacket. He stared at Padraig and said, "Walter here is going to knock your head in."

"Hey," said Walter. "How about you show us how it's done, why don't you?"

Out of the corner of his eye, Padraig watched Kevin and his parents disappear around a bend blocked by a line of tall trees. Liam stood waiting in the entranceway.

"Liam, you hold on there," said Padraig. "Come over here and kick this kid's legs. It will shorten him up."

The boy without the jacket rolled his shirtsleeves up and looked back to Walter. The boy backed away.

Padraig returned a gaze with firm resolve. "What are we waiting for, lads?"

"That's enough," said Walter. "The others are waiting for us. We have a game to play. Are you staying here?"

The boy, with his sleeves rolled up, without saying anything, turned and walked away, and Walter followed.

Padraig walked around the boy with his shirtsleeves rolled up.

"So what is it to be?" taunted Padraig.

"But you're bigger than me."

"How about you have a talk with Liam?"

Liam started walking towards the boy, but without saying another word the lad chased after his friends.

Liam managed to throw a couple of soggy clods of earth at him.

"Lord, you've got a terrible throw," said Padraig. "Maybe if he was as big as his mother you'd hit him."

"So Kevin disappeared in a hurry. Still, we could have taken them on, no problem," said Liam.

"Maybe, but we don't know these people and we don't know what we're getting ourselves into," replied Padraig. He followed Liam through the landlord's gate. The road was bound by tall, dark, thin-branched trees on the left and open pastureland on the right.

"The man who Da believes is going to offer us a place here doesn't own anything," said Liam. "Did you hear that? It gets better and better, doesn't it?"

In response, Padraig threw a dirt ball at him.

Once he got around the bend, Padraig could see the huge form of the abbey. There were a couple of elaborate towers on the left side and a long, low extension to the right. He could see the outline of the castellations and precision stonework at the top of the adjoining wall. There were cottages scattered about in the large open fields in front. A long hill on the far right was covered with a mix of grey, green and brown tree cover. There was very little snow left in the valley. *The trees must protect the fields*, he thought. Although the road that led to the ruins took a sharp turn towards the centre of the field shortly after the entrance, for the most part it followed the woods on the left.

"Where do you think he lives?" asked Liam as he skipped over a puddle on the trail that twisted through the flat, open field.

"James Kennedy?"

"No. The landlord. Maybe he lives behind the church or maybe in the woods."

"A landlord living in the woods? I don't think so," said Padraig.

"Da's talking to someone. We'd better move. Come on. I'll race you."

Padraig followed the carriage road, but Liam ran a straight line across mud-pooled, grassy fields.

Nick Walsh watched his sons race towards them through the muck. He reached for his wife's arm and escorted her off the messy carriage road to the tall wild grass in front of the abbey. The boy they had been talking to disappeared around the building before them.

"Padraig, I am glad you could make it," said Mr. Walsh. "If you're going to race, run fair. You've got longer legs and running ahead doesn't make it much of a win, does it?" He looked at Liam, who was choking for breath. "If you had any more mud on you I'd send for a priest to give you last rites."

"Aside from that, you boys look like you fared well. They didn't keep you back, I see."

"So, where are we going?" asked Padraig.

"Well, Mister Colclough lives there in the abbey."

"Isn't that a sacrilege?" asked his wife.

"I don't know. If they kicked someone out, maybe, but if it was empty already, who can say? Part of it looks like a castle. Those people like their castles."

"The part on the right looks like it could use a lot of work," said Padraig. "Maybe, that's why we're here."

"The cottages around here need fixing too," said Kevin. "That one back there only has half a roof."

"Someone's been taking the thatch from it," said Padraig.

Mr. Walsh left the circle and headed towards the side of the abbey.

"Nick, shouldn't we wait?" asked his wife. "The boy Jimmy Doyle said…"

"Keep them here, I'm going to the servant's entrance," he replied.

Padraig ran after him.

Nick Walsh gave a few soft knocks on the door at the rear of the abbey. When he didn't get an answer, he banged harder. Padraig turned away from him and gave a disgruntled look.

A servant came to the door.

"Could you tell Mr. Kennedy that Nick Walsh would like to have a word with him. He told me that he had some urgent stonework that needed to be done."

The servant told him, that he would pass on the message and closed the door. Fifteen minutes passed without an answer.

Mrs. Walsh and the other two boys appeared from the side. She asked, "What's going on? Have you talked to him?"

"Maybe you should knock again," said Padraig. "Maybe he's not here."

"If he's not, where are we going to go?" asked Liam.

Nick raised his hand to knock but stopped. The others were staring at him so he knocked again, first softly and then louder.

"May, I help you?" a voice behind them asked. "I was told you were looking for me".

"Ah yes. Ah, Mr. Kennedy, you told me that his lordship might be in need of a crew to work with stone."

"I did, did I?" Mr. James Kennedy looked at the buildings behind him. "Well, Mr. Colclough has been very preoccupied with other matters. Leave it with me and we'll review his wishes." Mr. Kennedy opened the servant's door and proceeded to enter.

"Ah, Mr. Kennedy, do you mind if we wait?" asked Nick Walsh.

Mr. Kennedy looked at the family behind him and said, "Suit yourself," and closed the door.

All was quiet for a minute, and then Liam said, "I mean, can you beat that? All this way and it's like we don't exist. I mean…"

Mr. Walsh put a finger to his mouth and pointed to Liam and then pointed it towards the side of the abbey.

"Be patient, Liam. That's all we can do," said his mother.

Padraig walked away from the back of the abbey and followed a path which followed a river to a bridge at the back. Kevin chased after Liam around the side of the abbey towards the front. "Lord Almighty, I can't believe this," Mr. Walsh muttered, still standing in front of the servants' entrance.

After waiting for about fifteen minutes, Nick and Judith Walsh and Padraig joined Liam and Kevin at the front. The two boys were talking to a beefy man, who had a bit of a pot belly behind a blacksmith's apron. His cap was tilted back and he didn't seem to mind the cool air on his arms below rolled-up shirtsleeves. His hands, stubble around his mouth and chin, and front of his hair were blackened. The stain of coal dust also marked his sleeves. The hair hanging down either side of his face was greasy. His hands moved as he talked—normal for a man whose daily rhythm involves smashing things.

"Da, Mr. Sevens, is the landlord's blacksmith," said Liam.

"Mr. Walsh, your son tells me that you're here to rebuild the abbey. You can see they really need the help. No shortage of work if you know what you're doing. For tools and metal pieces, I'm your man. For your cart and where to get the stone, you'll have to talk to Mr. Stewart. Mr. Kennedy is probably avoiding you because he can't get his lordship to commit. It's not that Mr. John Colclough isn't a good manager, it's just that he's focused on running his businesses. He tends to let things go at home."

"A lady's touch is what he needs," said Mrs. Walsh.

"Right you are, Mam. And I see Mr. Stewart has decided to join us." Mr. Sevens raised his hand to a man wearing a waistcoat with bright buttons. "He might only be a coachman, but he's the one that gets things done."

Mr. Stewart was a thin man of average height. He walked towards them at a leisurely pace. Along with his black frieze pants, waistcoat and jacket, he wore a worn, wrinkled brimmed hat. He didn't acknowledge Mr. Sevens, he just gave the ground a good spit.

"Hiding in the straw and it's not half past morning yet," yelled Mr. Sevens. "I was telling these people about how you've been letting things go."

"A fine kick in the arse, aren't yeh?" Mr. Stewart replied.

"Nick Walsh, the new stone mason, is here with his family to make things right. James is hiding."

Mr. Stewart tipped his hat to reveal a bald spot with greying hair on the sides. "We'll get you settled, and we'll get a fire under his lordship's feet," he said. "That will get James going. I'll go inside and sort things out. I'll send young Jimmy Doyle to lead you to an available cottage."

He turned and saw James Kennedy approaching.

"Well, speaking of the devil. There he is, himself," said Mr. Sevens.

The round-faced gentleman was dressed in a white shirt, a red vest, and tails. He might at first glance appear to be a tad chubby, but on closer inspection he was burly and muscular. He walked with intent, fists closed, and had a stern, unrelenting stare that exuded self-confidence and self-importance.

"Mr. Kennedy, sir, I was just telling them, that I was going to have young Jimmy escort our new stone mason's crew to their cottage."

Mr. Kennedy stopped and raised a finger, but hesitated. "Ah, yes." He looked back beyond the stables. "The mill needs work," he said. "Yes, bring them to their cottage. Very good. Thank you, Mr. Stewart. Nick Walsh, is it?"

"Yes, sir," he replied.

"Get settled, and we'll talk. Mr. Stewart, his lordship is leaving for New Ross in the morning. Make the necessary preparations."

Before Mr. Stewart could tip his hat, Mr. Kennedy headed back to the servant's entrance behind the abbey.

A couple of minutes later, a young boy who was about a year younger than Kevin's thirteen years, came running from the side of the abbey. He had wild, unkempt hair, a trim frame, and he had the appearance of someone looking for something besides the people he was approaching.

"This is Jimmy Doyle. He and his mother live in the cottage just outside the estate entrance," said Mr. Stewart. "Jimmy, this is the Walsh family."

"Mr. Kennedy asked me to take you to Anderson's cottage. Are you going to be with us long?"

"Uh. Well, if we make an arrangement, it's possible. Have you…" Before Mr. Walsh finished his sentence, Jimmy Doyle ran off. He picked up a stick and pretended to fend off invisible attackers as he ran.

"Boys, you better keep up with him," Mr. Walsh told them. "Your mother and I will be along. Off with you."

Kevin was the first to start running after Jimmy. He stopped to pick up a branch and continued the chase.

When Mr. and Mrs. Walsh reached Jimmy Doyle they found him and Kevin mock sword-fighting.

"Boys, is this the cottage you're supposed to be taking us to?" asked Mr. Walsh.

Jimmy stopped and told him, "That's yours." Kevin also stopped and turned, but Jimmy hit him on the head with his stick. Kevin twisted and tried to smash back, but Jimmy fended off his attempts.

"The roof is worse than the one you pointed to Da," said Liam. "I'd say we'll have to make a new one."

"Well, the plot is workable. Not as big as home, but we can get something from it." He bent down and grabbed a bit of wet earth. "It's good soil. You know, it might be better than what we had at home."

Padraig stepped out from behind his father and said, "Hey, put the stick down or I'm going to clobber you. How come no-one's living here?"

"You're good, but you're not as good as me," Jimmy yelled to Kevin. He put up his hand and angled his stick. Halt," he ordered. Jimmy relaxed and proceeded to turn to address Padraig, but Kevin smashed his hand.

"Says who?" shouted Kevin.

"Touché" laughed Jimmy.

"I will smash both of you if you don't…" said Padraig.

"I have to go. I can hear my mother calling me," Jimmy said.

"I don't hear anything," said Liam, who stepped out from behind his father.

As Jimmy walked away, he yelled, "Oh, you can do anything you want to it. Mr. Kennedy says it's yours."

"And how come no-one's here?" shouted Liam.

Jimmy spun around and yelled, "Because they're dead. Don't worry. No-one's coming back." He turned and continued running.

"With our luck there's a body in there," said Liam.

"Now Liam, you've quite an imagination," said his mother. "Let's all see what we can do to make this place a little more respectable." With the back of her hand she directed Padraig into the stone cottage, and her husband followed. She stopped at the door and waited for them to say something.

"The place is pretty well empty. I am glad we brought our pot," said Padraig. "If there was one, someone took it."

A quarter of the roof was without thatch, and a support beam was cracked. The remaining thatch looked old and stale.

"If we had the material, I'd just as soon rebuild the roof from scratch," said Mr. Walsh.

Kevin peaked into the cottage and asked, "What killed the person that lived here? Was it the neighbours? A disease? A beast?"

"Kevin, stop it. You're making Mother nervous. A beast? What's with the beast? We've enough going on," complained Padraig. "Maybe your new friend hit you on the head too hard."

"Boys, go get us some water, something for sweeping, and something for a fire," ordered Mrs. Walsh. "It's cold and damp, and this place is a mess."

About an hour later Jeremy Molloy arrived and informed Mr. Walsh that some of his neighbours were going to help him rebuild the roof. He also told him where to get food, thatch and farming supplies. Mr. Walsh drew close to his wife and patted her forearm, "Well, isn't that a wonder?"

The next morning Mr. Kennedy pointed out to Mr. Walsh and the boys what work, needed to be done. The landlord's residence and the property in general was in a terrible state of disrepair.

"Mr. Colclough almost died during a rainstorm when the roof caved in," Mr. Kennedy told them. "The entrance in the main square tower needs to be rebuilt, and a second storey in the Lady Chapel has to be added to accommodate his lordship's mother. The flour mill needs more work and the landlord is working on a design for elaborate walled gardens on the other side of the river.

"Mr. Walsh, I'm not expecting you to be familiar with all the intricacies of good precision stonework. Old Anthony Thornton, who has served us for many years, will show how things are done and what's expected," Mr. Kennedy told him. He took off his hat and pushed the curls back and away from his eyebrows. "The centre aisle of the nave will be converted into a Georgian-Gothic style residence and the arched gateway of the cloister will be used for the coach-house." He pointed to it as they walked through.

"You told me what you want us to do, but is the land mine?" asked Mr. Walsh. "How much of my harvest is expected to go back to Mr. Colclough? How much cash money are we being paid?"

"Mr. Walsh, you need to show your worth. Perhaps in time, by showing value, Mr. Colclough will give you the security you are asking. By county standards, the gentleman has an exemplary reputation for fairness, for loyal and capable tenants. If you need help settling in—Jeremy Molloy is your man. Take three days to get settled and then we'll start you off with building a wall next to the mill. I'll notify Mr. Thornton."

"But that's Sunday," said Mr. Walsh.

"Saturday morning then. You'll start Saturday," Mr. Kennedy said, and he returned to the abbey.

"That was a mixed blessing, wasn't it?" Padraig said on the walk back to the cottage. "We are indebted to them for food and accommodation, but they haven't committed to anything. For all we know, we could be prisoners here."

"We'll have food and a roof over our heads, and you'll pick up a skill," said his father. "Working with stone is good work."

"Maybe," replied Padraig. "As long as we don't break our necks. Mr. Kennedy told us that the landlord lives under an old leaky roof. Look at the place. Da you're not up to it."

"Well, we're not going back to the mountain. We're near the sea and you might actually like it here. Besides, Mr. Kennedy says he wants us to start on the other side of the river."

"Da, if you don't ask, you won't get. Don't let him take advantage of you."

"Oh, leave us alone, Padraig. It's up to me and I'll take care of it."

Padraig shifted away, exasperated.

The boys helped Mr. Walsh and Anthony Thornton extend a stone wall from the flour mill. The boys used a horse and cart to haul stone from a ruins across the river. Nick did the cutting and Padraig trowelled the mortar. Mr. Thornton did whatever he thought needed to be done and acted as a general overseer.

Kevin was unloading the cart when Jimmy joined them. He was eating a bit of cake that he picked from his coat pocket.

"How come you're always at the abbey?" asked Kevin.

"My mam gets me to bring baked things to the cook and sometimes Mr. Kennedy lets me have some."

"I'd like that job," said Kevin. "Does she get paid to do that?"

"I suppose so." He scratched his head. "Actually, I don't know."

"It's just that if she were a cook, it'd be easier. I mean, the abbey has a big kitchen, doesn't it?" Kevin said.

"Mam takes care of the farm outside the abbey gates, and there's just us. Tomorrow's Sunday. Want to go to a castle after Mass?" asked Jimmy.

"You mean the abbey?"

"No, a castle."

"Anybody in it?"

"No. It's been empty for a long time."

"Yeh, that sounds good. Is it haunted?"

"Probably. What do you say?"

"Absolutely. After Mass, then. I'll bring my sling," said Kevin. He looked at Liam, who had just dropped a load of stone near his brother. Kevin pretended to ignore him. *He left me out of those matches so he's not going,* he thought. *Revenge is sweet.* Kevin tried not to smile, but failed.

Jimmy and Kevin left on their trip after Mass. Jimmy used a staff as a walking stick.

"Where are we going?" asked Kevin.

"It's on the bay and it's going to take a couple of hours to get there."

Kevin took out some leather from his pocket.

"What's that?" asked Jimmy.

Kevin put a rock in the sling and wound it. As the rock hit a tree, he said, "It's a sling. I have another. Do you want to use it?"

Jimmy threw a rock up and bashed it with his staff. "No, I like using this," he said.

In the afternoon they came to open fields that had a half dozen old stone ruins. Jimmy took him for a quick tour through a church and a house and then escorted him to the door of the castle.

"A real castle is it?" said Kevin.

"Yeh, and it's called the Black Tower."

"Does anyone live in it?"

"No, but a landlord owns it. There's only us and his sheep here."

From a dark first floor, they walked up a stone staircase to a big room on the next floor.

"Your Da doesn't have a problem with you coming here?" asked Jimmy.

"They're not my parents. My family died in '98, at least that's what old man Kavanagh told me."

"Who?"

"He was a neighbour, but he died. Actually, he didn't really know for sure. He just told me he didn't think I'd ever hear from them again."

"What do you think?"

"Makes sense, I suppose. I was with my mother and sister at New Ross. When I left there, I just remember screaming, fire and lots of running. I try not to think about it too much."

Jimmy started poking at piles of dirt on the floor with his staff. Most of the room was dark except for the light that came in through one small window. "I guess you miss them," he said.

"Who?" asked Kevin.

"Your family."

"I guess I do. You know, Liam is such a stupid fool sometimes, but Padraig reminds me a bit of my brother, Aiden. I don't remember much about him because it was a long time ago. You remind me of Seamus."

"Who?" asked Jimmy.

"My other brother. I sort of remember him sword fighting and my Da talking to him."

"About what?"

"Don't remember. It was a long time ago. I just remember people doing things, mostly. You said, it was just you and your mam, so you don't have any brothers?"

"No, I'm an orphan," answered Jimmy. "There's just the two of us. She never tells me anything about my father. I don't know why. All she ever said was that he's a good man."

"So maybe he's dead. Maybe in '98."

"I don't know. She did say that 'he is a good man'. She said *is* and not *was*. What do you think?"

Kevin threw a rock at the wall, and it almost ricocheted near Jimmy.

"We've got a puzzle. I'd say you're right. He's probably still alive. Maybe you have brothers. Maybe even some sisters."

"Never thought of that."

"There might be a dozen sisters. What would you think of that?"

"Don't know what to think. Never had one, so don't know what a dozen would be like."

"You might meet him and then find you have to take care of a lot of babies. What do you think about taking care of babies?"

"Kevin, you're talking crazy. I don't think he's alive, and I don't want to talk about it."

Kevin looked out the small window at the sheep in the field. He thought about his sister, Kathleen. He knew he missed her, but for some reason he didn't want to remember.

Jimmy headed down the staircase and out, and Kevin followed him.

When Kevin caught up to Jimmy outside, he told him, "I have someone here."

"What do you mean?" as he walked along the river looking at some birds.

"There's a girl here. Her name is Anty. People here might know her as Anastasia Kelly."

"Well, that's a fancy name, isn't it? So why haven't you gone and seen her?"

"I haven't had the time. Besides, I don't exactly know where she is."

"You said she was here."

"Mr. Kavanagh…"

"He seems to know a lot of things."

"Well he did, but he's dead."

"Gone on to better pastures."

"Yeh, right," said Kevin. "Anyways, he told me that she moved here to be with a relative, but he didn't know who it was."

"Why didn't you ask a priest at Mass?"

"Don't know. How come we didn't see any ghosts?" asked Kevin.

"Maybe we'll have to go there at nighttime."

"At a full moon, maybe."

"Maybe we need to bring ghost bait."

"Like what?"

"Goat brains and kidneys maybe," said Jimmy.

"You carry them. Maybe with berries, bark and dried corn."

"What kind of ghost bait is that?" asked Jimmy.

"Less messy than animal guts."

"Bet more show up with mine than yours."

It took them a couple of hours to return home. After returning from the hike, they followed a trail uphill from the bay to the abbey. When they approached the rear of the abbey, they saw that there were a couple of coaches parked close to the Abbey's servants entrance. Men were unloading boxes from inside and the top of the coaches.

As they passed one of the coaches Mr. Kennedy told them, "Keep it down, boys, I'm trying to count." Mr. Kennedy was rechecking the inventory and directing his men where to take the boxes.

"Mr. Kennedy gets them from France," said Jimmy.

Kevin told Jimmy, "I don't think they're supposed to be doing that. It's against the law because there's a war going on." To the chief steward, he asked in a louder voice, "Mr. Kennedy, are you a smuggler?"

"You're Kevin Neal. Aren't you supposed to be helping Mr. Walsh?"

"No, today's Sunday. I was just saying."

"I know what you're saying, and if you want to find yourself here tomorrow, you'll forget what you think you know. I am sure we can find lots of others willing to lay stone for us."

"Kevin, we have to go," said Jimmy.

Once they made their way to the front of the abbey, Kevin said, "So he's a pirate."

"Kevin, pirates don't want the sheriff to know that they are pirates."

"Do you think he'll get rid of me?" asked Kevin.

"Maybe. How about we scrounge up a game of hurling? What do you think?"

"Maybe I should go back and talk to him?"

"He can get nasty when he's in a mood. I'd just stay away from him if I were you."

"Lord Almighty," said Kevin.

"A good smash will set it all right," as Jimmy used his stick to smash at an invisible sliotar.

"Right," muttered Kevin. "Jimmy, I can't, sorry, but there's something that I've got to do. I'll see you later."

Kevin left Jimmy and asked some neighbours about Anty Kelly, but they didn't know who she was. He would have liked to talk to the priest, but he travelled to churches all around the district and it would have been difficult to find him. A woman suggested that he talk to Mr. Stewart, the coachman, because he belonged to the Church of Ireland. 'If her aunt lived on the other side of the river, he'd give you directions to someone who would know,' she told him.

Mr. Stewart suggested that he ask a woman from his church who knew everybody. He gave him directions. She lived about a half mile from the village on the other side of the river.

Kevin had thought that talking to someone from another church would have been a waste of time but was surprised to discover that the lady had heard of her.

Anty's aunt, she says, is married to a Finn and he's not Catholic. She's married to a pagan. Of all the things. Anty's turned Protestant, has she? That can't be the way of it. Slow down lad. Just because that's her aunt, it doesn't necessarily mean anything, does it? But then again, maybe people in the parish don't really know her. So where am I going with this? Lord, if I know?

The woman's directions led Kevin to the Finn cottage. The cottage was on a gentle slope. The fertile fields stretched openly to the south for a very long ways. Lines of trees acting as windbreaks bound the edge of the farm, like they did in the rest of the county. The cottage had two windows in the front and a door in the middle. He saw a boy talking to someone. He was a tall, thin lad who was close to his age.

"Samuel, that's very thoughtful," he heard a girl say.

That sounds like her voice, he thought. When he got closer, he said, "I'm looking for Anty Kelly."

"And who'd be asking?" she said, and she stepped forward. She stopped for a moment. "Oh my Lord, it's not Kevin Neal, is it?" She grabbed the front of her shawl firmly.

"Yes, it's Kevin," he said and looked at the ground.

She ran over to him and gave him a big hug. "Kevin, Kevin, Kevin," she said. "I was told you were all gone."

"Somehow, I'm here. Anty, Anty it's really you?" and he squeezed her as tight as she was holding him.

When he let go, he said, "I'm the only one left. They're all gone. Walshes took me in. They all told me that you died at Vinegar Hill in Enniscorthy."

"I almost did," she said, as she stroked her hair, and looked at Samuel. "I was carried away. Now I'm here with my aunt."

"Old Mr. Kavanagh, just a year ago, told me about that."

"You mean Joseph Kavanagh?"

"Yes, it's himself. He's dead, though."

"What happened?"

"Beaten up," Kevin said and brushed his locks from his brow. "The landlords up there are a bad bunch. Some of our people who suffered in the bad times were chased away."

"They can't do that."

"Maybe not before '98, but things got bad since. The Walshes couldn't keep up so they came here."

"Kevin, this is Samuel Boyse," said Anty and she patted his elbow. "He's a friend of mine."

Samuel touched his cap and then put his hand on her left shoulder.

"Yes, Kevin, we're friends." He took his hand off her shoulder and reached to shake his hand.

"Ouch," Kevin said as Samuel crushed it. "Think you're king of the hill, do you?" he added as he made a step back.

"Our farm was next to theirs when I lived up north," said Anty.

"That's very nice," said Samuel as he gave Kevin an icy stare.

"Anty, I got your letter, but over time it just came apart. Sorry."

"It was so long ago I forget, what I wrote. Actually, I don't remember much of anything at that time. The war was so horrible and…" She hesitated. "Well it was terrible."

"I know what you mean," said Kevin.

"So what are you doing at Tintern?"

"We have a cottage, and his lordship has us rebuilding the abbey."

"You're working as a stonemason?"

"They're teaching me." He stood tall and tried to look hefty, "and I'm going to be a blacksmith soon." He looked at Samuel and asked, "And what do you do?"

"I help my Da on the farm." He gave another icy stare to Kevin, "I'm an heir and my cousin is a very prosperous gentleman, I'll have you know."

Kevin stared at tears on the knees of Samuel's trousers. They had been sewn up before they got too noticeable.

A woman from the cottage doorway yelled, "Anty."

"That's my Aunt. Sorry, Kevin, but I have to go. We should talk some more."

She walked to the house, and Samuel followed.

Once the door shut, *And who is he? steeped* Kevin's thoughts. *Don't like him at all and what kind of name is Boyse, for Lord's sake?*

The door opened again and Anty's aunt looked him over with a hawk like stare.

He turned away, spat on the ground, and rolled his eyes. *And Lord Almighty, does she have a witch for an aunt? What's wrong with this world?* He hopped over a two-foot hedge and ran across a tenant farm. *But she did say we should talk some more, didn't she? We've got to look out for each other, don't we?* He gave a very wide grin.

other, don't we? He gave a very wide grin.

Smashing

A week after his first visit to the Finn's cottage, Kevin showed up a second time. He knocked lightly on the cottage door.

"Hello Mrs. Finn, would Anty be home? It's Kevin Neal."

"So, you're Kevin. The way she spoke of you, I thought you'd be taller."

She's a weird one, isn't she, he thought. He decided that she really didn't look like a witch. It was the shade of reddish-brown in her hair that had unnerved him a bit, and she seemed to have stern, prying eyes as if she were going to catch him in the act of doing something he shouldn't. She seemed like the kind of woman that if she didn't like you, would smash you with a hurley without a moment's notice.

"You're a young sprout, aren't you? Well, there's more meat on you than the other one, isn't there? Relax, boy. I'm just teasing you. You'll find her out back with my husband."

Once he reached the garden, Kevin saw her talking to someone who was digging. He waved, and she came back to meet him.

"Is this a good time?" asked Kevin when she got close.

"It's good enough by me," she replied. "Let's go sit over there by the trees."

"You don't want to go for a walk on the road?" Kevin asked.

"My aunt doesn't think it would be appropriate for me to go anywhere without a chaperone," Anty replied as they approached some cut logs next to a treeline. "If we went on the road, she'd come running after us. If we stay in the backyard, it'll just be us and my uncle."

"Do they always do that?"

"You mean having one of them watching?"

Kevin nodded.

"If there's an adult with me that they know, there mightn't be a problem," said Anty as she sat down on a log. "If I'm going to get shellfish though, sometimes I just go. It takes too long to get a chaperone and the tides don't wait for anyone."

Kevin sat on another log on her right side towards the road and crossed his legs towards her. "That's your uncle?" he asked.

"How did you know?"

"It was your aunt?"

She smiled. "We don't get along. Me and my aunt, I mean. I get along better with my uncle. Two of their sons left for America just after the rebellion, and the other one here is only three."

"And you're Catholic? You haven't been going to Mass. I've never seen you there and people I've asked told me that they didn't know who you were."

"There's a church closer. It's the other way. And sometimes I just don't feel like it. It's not the same for me anymore. I feel locked up inside. It's just —where was God?"

"Lord Anty, that's a sin and you know it."

"The priests were there with us, and we were mostly families with nowhere to go. We were defenceless, and they shot at us and came with bayonets. I mean…"

"Well I sort of know what you mean."

"Do you think about it?"

"I try not to."

"It's a difficult place for a Catholic to live."

"What do you mean?"

"Your aunt's family is Church of Ireland, isn't it?"

"So?"

"I just know some people around here don't like us."

"There's people that get along and there's people that don't," said Anty. "Living near the mountain, there were good people like Joseph Kavanagh who could be kind to anyone and there were other's willing to hurt anyone that was different. Most folk here have been very charitable—to me, anyway."

"You said you don't like your aunt."

"I don't think she likes anyone."

"She yells at her husband?"

"Whenever I'm working in the garden with him, she always telling him what to do."

"Do you think the boys left because of her?"

"I don't know. They were wild ones and I don't think they liked farming much. It wasn't a surprise to see them go. Maybe it's just me she doesn't like."

"Maybe."

Kevin saw Samuel Boyse on the road. Samuel turned and walked away. Kevin saw Mr. Finn watching both of them. Kevin crossed his feet towards the road.

There wasn't a window at the back of the house, but Kevin felt like her aunt the witch was somehow was staring at him.

⁓◦◎)

The next day, Samuel was behind his family's cottage turning up the garden with the help of his friend Richard. "Look who's coming," he said, when he saw Walter Glascott approaching.

Walter had a square jaw and struck a pose as he looked at them from the corner of his eye. He wore an Irish cap with the brim up as if to dare the wind to blow it off. He was a big man, and Richard and Samuel liked to load him up with things to carry, to let him know how useful he was.

When Walter got close, he asked, "The boys still working at this hour? Heathen ways is it?"

"And if you were here with us, wouldn't that be torture enough?" replied Richard Caulfield. He pushed away his hair from the right side of his face, but it stubbornly flopped back.

"I do enough digging as it is, and it's going to be dark soon," Walter replied.

"Richard's helping me dig this plot out," said Samuel Boyse. "We were supposed to patch the roof, but the thatch hasn't shown up.

"So you're done?"

"You can take my shovel," said Richard. "No. Didn't think so. What's on your mind, Walter?"

"There's a new family in Tintern. Smells like trouble."

"How so?" asked Richard.

"They're papists, and they tried to start a fight. I mean, the nerve of them."

"And?"

"Not much of anything. It's just that they were pushing for one. We can't let something like that get out of hand. Scullabogue is enough to remind us what they're capable of."

"I know more about it than you do Walter. It was the rebels that killed my uncle there," said Richard.

"Anyways the boys are bothering me to let them know, who sets the rules here."

"Is it Kevin Neal you're talking about?" asked Samuel.

"Him and the Walshes," said Walter.

"We hear yeh," said Samuel.

"Samuel, and me already had some words about them. Do either of you know if they're staying? They're just doing some fixing, aren't they?"

asked Richard. "Maybe they're just passing through."

"I saw them working on the abbey and I'm told that the landlord gave them a cottage," replied Walter. "They're nothing but trouble." He pulled the peak of his cap down and stared at Samuel.

"Walter, why are you looking at me?" asked Samuel.

"Because friends of mine need information about the rebels hiding near the mountains," added Walter.

"How would I know what's going on up there?"

"Anastasia Kelly."

"How in God's name would she know?" replied Samuel. "She's been here for years. Go bugger off. Use your head to hammer nails or something, why won't you?"

"She knows more than she lets on. I am sure of it," Walter replied.

"So point them to the new people," said Samuel.

"And they'll tell him what?"

"Does it really matter," answered Samuel. "That's their problem, and what exactly are they looking for?"

"Is it FitzGibbon again?" asked Richard.

Walter held the peak of his cap as if he were going to hide under it.

"What does he want, Walter? Go on," said Richard.

Walter looked behind him and then said, "The sheriff is hiring men to clean out the last of the rebels. FitzGibbon is one of them, and he's not the kind of person that's willing to be treated lightly."

"The sheriff and his men are tied to the landlords," said Richard. "The likes of them are never going to do you any favours."

"Don't know about that," said Walter. "He gets paid more than most and if they're getting rid of rebels, they need our help."

"Well and good, but we do have to get this done," said Richard as he started digging again. "Samuel's da will have our necks. Go have him bother someone else."

"We'd like to hit back tomorrow night. Are you boys in?" asked Walter.

"If it's not far from here, sure we'll skip out and give him a good kick in the head," replied Richard. "What you say, Samuel?

"We know what side we're on," Samuel said, and he raised his shovel in acknowledgement.

"Sure you won't help us dig here?" asked Richard.

"No, I've got to get home, but I'll see both of you tomorrow," Walter said as he gave them a nod and left.

Once Walter was out of sight Richard pushed his hair back, wiped his brow with the sleeve of his grey sweater and asked, "I know you're not going tomorrow, so what was all that about?"

"I told him what he wanted, but I didn't promise I'd show up."

"That's not the way it sounded to me," said Richard.

"Maybe you're as daft as he is. Big Walter stirs things up, but he's big, noisy, and everyone sees him coming a mile away."

"And the likes of Samuel Boyse is not going to be there to save him from himself. What kind of friend are you?" Richard grinned and dug deeper with his shovel.

"Show me how to trim the ragged ends of thatch at the eves, and I'll go," said Samuel.

"Your father has me doing it so you won't break your neck."

"Well?" asked Samuel.

"Promise me you're not going to break your neck until the brawl."

Samuel noticed that the sun was about to set. He dug deeper and added, "Let's get this done. We're running out of time."

Harold Wheeler nudged his horse to follow the trail up the slope to Three Rocks. The area was at the eastern end of Forth Mountain. "Come on, girl, don't be stubborn," he said and made a clicking sound. When he reached the top of the slope, the land looked relatively flat. He saw Douglas FitzGibbon in the distance plodding around an overgrown, wild-looking field. His horse was behind him and tied at a line of trees that marked the edge of the property, which obscured the forested rocky rise beyond. The mountain separated them from the flatlands on the other side that stretched to the sea. A trail, to Harold's left, wound towards the town of Wexford, which was about two miles away.

Harold twisted in his saddle and took a careful look around. The land behind stretched out from the base of the hill and gently rolled to a horizon a long way off, bound by mountains whose outlines were softened in hazy sunshine. He didn't see anything to suggest he was being followed. He kept riding, and when he got close, he didn't dismount. Douglas didn't acknowledge him.

"Why Three Rocks?" Harold asked. "Why'd you want me to ride all this way? There's nothing here but bad memories. No building, animals, crops. Nothing, I mean, look at this place. You've let it grow wild."

"I'm selling it."

"Is this your da's farm? The only things you ever talk about are work and your da's farm." Harold watched Douglas turn away from him. "So, it is. You used to say that rebuilding your father's farm was all you ever wanted, and now you have it—and it looks like this," Harold told him. "The weeds are almost taller than I am."

"Don't exaggerate," Douglas said as he walked towards his horse.

Harold rode closer. He caressed his thick scruffy beard as he asked, "Why don't you rent it out?"

"Couldn't find my way back here," Douglas said as he brushed his greasy hair back and untied his horse. "It reminds me of things I'd rather forget. I'm getting rid of it."

Douglas looked at the land ahead of him and said, "If I decided to do something else, where do you think I could go?"

"Colclough would probably have you killed."

Douglas looked at him.

"They'd kill you because they wouldn't want you working for anyone else. …too much chance that someone else would hire you to tear out their throats. You're too good at what you do and your reputation will always precede you. We don't get to make those kinds of choices."

"I'm not saying I'd do it. Just wondering that's all," interrupted Douglas.

"If you killed Colclough, you'd have to deal with the Sheriff. Then you'd have to deal with landlords like Loftus and Annesley. Then the likes of Blacker in Dublin. Behind them there's the crown. Ireland didn't stop them and neither did the likes of Napoleon. And there's nowhere else for you to go. The crown has significant influence in America and Australia. You won't be going to the continent because you don't speak their languages, and I don't see you taking orders in someone else's war."

"They tried to kill me when I was a boy. Did you know that?"

"Who?"

"The cavalry," said Douglas.

"Leave it alone. That was a long time ago. Douglas, the way I see it, there's nowhere for you to go and there's nothing to be done about it. You either keep your head down like the farmers or you give them a little something special like we do. That's just the way it is. You've sold your soul and now Duffry Hall owns it and there's no way out."

Douglas looked at his horse and patted it. "Anyway, we've got work to do. Colclough at Duffry Hall has been trying to round up others to do our business. He's a buffoon. He knows they're useless, and he's just doing it to try to influence my price."

"yeh, that and the Púca business," added Harold.

Douglas filled in some hoof prints with his boot. "I provide the landlords with consistency, dependability and persistence." He mounted his horse, grabbed the reins, and looked at the trail beyond the property. "I hate dealing with fools. Do you remember Mark Jarvis?"

Harold looked around nervously. "You strangled him with your bare hands in front of us for lying," he answered. "How could any of us forget? Why? Do you have a problem with my work?"

"Just keeping you focused. We've done fine work together, Harold. There's more that's gotta to be done and it's not time to get sloppy. There's a Tony Rankin who lives on this side of Tintern Abbey. When I locate him, I'm going to have you break his arm."

"Why just his arm?"

"The Sheriff wants it that way. He probably asked him for information, and the man didn't listen. As long as he pays us, I'll go along with what he asks."

"So where is he?"

"A boy by the name of Walter Glascott promised that he'd find him. We're going to pay him a visit tonight. Walter thinks that this has something to do with putting down rebels, so watch what you say. After you take care of Rankin, you're going to display some muscle. You're going to play peacekeeper for the boys if you know what I mean."

"I thought that the sheriff wanted us to round up the rebels around Killoughram Forest"

"You heard right. That's by the Blacker estate. Taking out the rebels will be more profitable. The sheriff wants us to go out and maintain order."

"You mean, he doesn't want to see them?" asked Harold.

"Him? Not a chance," answered Douglas.

Jimmy tapped the sliotar to Kevin, who twirled and smashed it to young George Sutcliffe. He lost it and someone from the other side got it. It was early February, and the field was still pretty oozy from a rainstorm they had earlier. It was messy, but the players were having a lot of fun trying to keep upright on wet grass and pools of liquid muck.

Kevin saw Liam tramp slowly out from a line of trees. He wasn't walking right. *Something is wrong,* he thought.

Kevin told Jimmy, "I'm sitting this one out." and he ran off to see Liam. Jimmy, without saying anything to others ran after him.

Liam had his hand to his neck.

"It was that Samuel Boyse and Walter Glascott. They came out from nowhere. They started hitting me, saying they didn't want any more Catholics here. They kept hitting me and blaming me for things and people

I've never heard of. I think they're crazy. They had sticks, and they got me on the neck and head."

"Eejits," replied Kevin. "There's a red mark on your head."

"Is it bleeding?" whined Liam.

"No. It's just a scratch. Knowing you, it will likely set you right," said Kevin.

"Feck off."

"Jimmy, are they mad or what?" asked Kevin.

"I just know what I am told," replied Jimmy. "Dozens of Protestants from this parish were killed at Scullabogue. It's a small place near New Ross. After losing at New Ross, some rebels set a barn on fire. More than a hundred people died. Women and children were burnt alive.

"Obviously you don't have anything to do with that. They are just being stupid. They don't know anything. Some of those people burnt were Catholics. Those fools are from here so you'd think they'd already know it."

"Now I sort of know why the cottage was empty." said Kevin.

"Let's go get 'em," said Jimmy. "Liam, are you ready to get them now?"

"My head really hurts. I don't know," said Liam.

"We only have about an hour of light," said Jimmy. "They live on the other side of the river. We need to clobber 'em now. They won't be expecting us."

"Give it a rest, Jimmy," said Kevin. "You want them following you home? Well?"

Jimmy scratched his head and said, "Next time."

Kevin wiped the sweat off his brow again and added, "Liam, your mam is going to want to look at that."

Padraig peeked into their cottage and called for his father, but didn't get a response. He closed the door and looked around. Something smashed him on the back of the head, causing him to fall forward. Padraig lay sprawled with his face to the ground.

Harold Wheeler dropped his wooden club, bent down, grabbed, and pulled up Padraig's wrist and stamped near his elbow. He heard a break, and said, "Lord, wasn't that easy. Less fight in this one than old Rankin."

Harold reset his cap, looked around, grabbed his club and casually walked back to the forest where he had left his horse.

When Kevin showed up at the forge, he found Mr. Sevens, the blacksmith, fixing a brace for Padraig's arm.

"I didn't see him, if that's what you're asking," said Padraig.

"Not someone from here, if you ask me," said Mr. Sevens. "He was too brazen. The lads who'd pick a fight with you lot wouldn't do it near the abbey. Too much to lose. The one that did this didn't care. The broken arm was a message, but the hit on the head was so you wouldn't recognize him."

"But who could afford the likes of him?" asked Kevin.

"That's the question, isn't it?" said Mr. Sevens.

"It's not hard to figure who wants it done," said Kevin.

"The worrying part of this is that they were able to persuade this oaf to help them," said Mr. Sevens. "Padraig, I am not belittling what happened to your arm, but this fella is more trouble than the scalawags, if you know what I mean. It's a bad sign."

"Did you hear him say anything, Padraig?" asked Kevin.

"No, he was fast and I guess he knew what he was doing," said Padraig.

"You'd expect he'd say something or write something," said Kevin.

"He didn't have to. You and I know who's done it," said Padraig.

"What happened to my boy?" asked Mr. Walsh as he quickly hobbled next to Kevin.

"He got beaten up by a thug. Nick, I'll leave you with your son. I have to inform John Colclough," said Mr. Sevens.

"Both my boys beaten down, one after the other. Kevin, you'll have to keep your head down. I can't afford to do without you. Not getting the work done isn't something we want happening.

"Kevin?" Mr. Walsh looked around, didn't see him anywhere and asked, "Where did that fool go?"

Kevin had run home to pick up a hurling stick. He left the Tintern estate to go to the Doyle's farm. When he got there, he found Jimmy working in the field at the back.

"They got him," Kevin yelled.

"Got who?" asked Jimmy as he brushed the dirt off his knees.

"They broke Padraig's arm," said Kevin when he stopped in front of him.

"Walter Glascott had something to do with it, I'll bet," said Jimmy as he brushed dirt off his hands.

"Mr. Sevens said he didn't think he was from around here," Kevin said.

"Maybe, but I'm sure Walter was behind it—and what are you going to do with that?" Jimmy asked as he pointed to the hurling stick in Kevin's hand.

"I'm going to give him a good smashing. Are you coming?"

"But he's as big as Padraig. Are you thinking right?"

"Are you coming?" Kevin repeated.

"Oh. The two of us," said Jimmy with hesitation. "I should tell my mam."

"You think so?"

"Well, maybe not."

"So, where are the Glascotts? I need to know. You don't have to do this."

Jimmy looked around. "Don't see my mam. We better hurry."

They crossed tenant's fields, a river valley forest and more farm plots on the other side. About a half hour beyond the valley forest, Jimmy pointed out the Glascott's cottage.

When Kevin got close he wasn't sure what he was going to do.

"Thanks Jimmy, if I find him, I'll tell you how it went," Kevin told him. When he checked back, he saw him run towards someone's backyard.

"Jimmy, what are you doing?" Kevin whispered.

As he neared the Glascott's cottage, he didn't see anyone. *And if he's not outside?* he thought. *Hide in the bushes and wait? Lord, what if he has older brothers or cousins? Or his father?*

And if it's his mother? he wondered. He looked around. The land was flat, but there were hedges along the edges of the farm.

"Lord, that's him," Kevin whispered.

Walter was digging in the backyard. He seemed to be alone, so Kevin tapped his hurley on his hand and marched towards him. Walter kept digging.

"And you think you're going to hit me with that?"

When Kevin got close, he saw that his opponent stood more than two heads taller.

He ran at him yelling, "For Padraig," and smashed his chest with his hurley. Walter hit back with his arms and punched Kevin in the side of the head with a left jab. He powerfully and deliberately smashed him full in the face with the other hand, causing Kevin to fly backwards towards the ground. Before he could protect himself, Walter kicked him hard in the side and the thigh.

"Neal, before I'm finished, you'll wish you were never born."

Kevin tried to roll away. Before Walter could kick him in the back, something screamed, "Aaaagh," from behind. Before Walter could turn around, it raced past him.

It was Jimmy with rolled-up pair of pants in a raised hand. "Come, get it," he yelled. As he rushed around the corner, he again screamed, "Aaaagh."

"My pants?" asked a surprised Walter. Without looking at Kevin, he left in quick pursuit.

"In for it now, aren't you? Can't have your mother after you," Kevin mumbled as he tried to get up from a crawl position. He held his side and moaned when he tried to put weight on his right leg.

He managed to stagger across the yard, wiping a bloody nose and spitting blood. He kept hobbling until he couldn't walk any farther.

Eventually he found a cottage wall to hide behind.

Within a few minutes, Jimmy joined him. He leaned over trying to catch his breath.

"And what were you thinking of?" Jimmy asked.

"Me?"

"You. Of course you. Your face is a mess and look at your shirt."

"A little bit of colour," Kevin said as he looked at the bloodstains on his shirt. He wiped his nose. It was still bleeding a bit.

"Surprise him. Smash his shins and run. I mean standing there and bleeding all over him, it's just…"

"I know what you mean."

"You let him beat you up, didn't you? Like you wanted him to. What were you thinking?"

"It's nothing. Go on."

Jimmy moved back and looked around the corner.

"Still chasing you, is he?" asked Kevin.

Jimmy nodded.

"What a wonder?" Kevin said sarcastically and caressed a sore. He didn't see any blood on his fingers when he drew them back from his nose.

"Why don't you stay here with him?" Jimmy asked and started running across the front yard.

Kevin looked at the pants in Jimmy's hand and said, "No. His dear mother will have him," and hobbled quickly after Jimmy.

When Kevin couldn't run any longer, he looked back and saw Walter staring at him from the road near his home.

"Not much in him. He gives up easy, doesn't he?" said Jimmy.

Kevin, who was bent forward trying to catch his breath, just nodded. He stared at the pants in Jimmy's hands and said, "Those aren't Walter's."

"Caulfield's," said Jimmy.

Kevin started in a fit of laughing and coughing.

Jimmy ran again and raised a hand, letting the pants flutter in the wind, and yelled, "Pirates."

Kevin tried to keep up and echoed his chant.

The next day Kevin limped quietly alongside Liam, who was driving the cart with a full load of stone. He saw Mr. Stewart wave at them from the front of the abbey.

"Hello boys," he said when they got close.

"Hello, Mr. Stewart," Kevin replied.

"My, your face is quite a state, isn't it?"

"An accident," Kevin said as he looked towards the cart.

"Hello, Mr. Stewart," Liam said.

Mr. Stewart nodded back.

"Kevin, I'll have you know that we've got Richard Caulfield's mother shouting at us."

"But why would she bother Mr. Colclough?"

"It's not Mr. Colclough she's talking with. It's me. I know the Caulfields. I see them at church. Did you know that Richard Caulfield is missing his pants? They were hanging out to dry in the back, and someone took them. ...and wipe those smiles off both of you.

"But Mr. Stewart..."

"I know. Why would I ask saintly fellows like yourselves about others' misfortunes? Well when you see young Jimmy, tell him that he has to give them back."

He stared at Kevin.

"But..."

"And don't rip them up." He stared at Kevin again, then looked up and added, "And don't put anything in them or make them unwearable, or he'll have the trousers of one of you lot. And if either of you think I'm teasing, then we'll have another talk—and trust me—you won't like it." Mr. Stewart stepped out of the way and waved for Liam to move the wagon close to the stone pile that the others were drawing from.

Hours later, when the boys had almost finished unloading the cart,

Kevin noticed that Mr. Sevens and Mr. Walsh were approaching them from the bridge. "Uh oh," he said. "They don't look happy."

"What are you going on about?" asked Liam.

"It's a bad sign, that's all," Kevin said.

"It's nothing on me—so keep up," said Liam.

"So you've been busy, haven't you?" said Mr. Sevens.

"Well, yes. We…" replied Kevin.

"We weren't asking what you were doing," said Mr. Walsh. "We know."

Mr. Sevens stared at the ground.

He looks like he's trying to figure something out, thought Kevin.

"What were you thinking?" asked Mr. Walsh.

"Me? Well…" said Kevin.

"How old are you? How old is Jimmy?"

"Thirteen. Twelve," replied Kevin.

"Walter is almost as old as Padraig, for Lord's sake," said Mr. Walsh.

"Stealing Caulfield's pants, then this," said Mr. Sevens. "If stupidity was worth anything, you'd both be rich."

"You beat Walter Glascott with a stick," said Mr. Walsh. "How did you know he had anything to do with it?" asked Mr. Walsh. "And why did you go to his home? It gives them an excuse to hit back here."

"Well…"

"Don't say anything else. I don't want to get into it," said Mr. Walsh. "If you're going to have anything to eat from me, it's not going to be to-day."

"Kevin, sometimes tussles can't be avoided, but things can get out of hand. When adults get involved, sometimes people die," said Mr. Sevens. "Houses get burnt and people can get sent away. Sometimes the sheriff or bailiff gets involved, and you know what that means."

Both Kevin and Nick froze with shocked looks on their faces.

"Do you understand the difference?" said Mr. Sevens.

"Yes sir. I understand what you're saying," said Kevin. "I'm sure it won't happen again, and as you see, we've a lot of work to keep us busy. I'm sure the worst is behind.”

“I strongly suggest you work really hard to prove yourself because at the moment it looks like you’re more trouble than you’re worth.”

Four days after being confronted by the blacksmith and Mr. Walsh, Liam, Kevin and Jimmy went on a run to collect more stone for the walls around the flour mill. Liam and Kevin sat at the back of the rickety cart, while Jimmy guided with the reins from up front.

“Jimmy, you know we could get there faster if we walked,” said Kevin.

“She’s old. Allow her some grace, please. It’s not her fault,” replied Jimmy.

“Where’s the stone?” asked Liam.

“It’s a demolished cottage. Your father wants the stone for the wall. No-one’s there, so it won’t be missed,” replied Jimmy.

After the boys completed loading up the cart with stone chunks, Jimmy gave a pull on the reins and called for the old horse to move on.

“Liam, don’t think of sitting back there,” yelled Jimmy. “This is more than enough for her. We don’t want to pull this cart back ourselves, trust me.”

As the cart turned to leave the property, they were stopped by a rain of stones.

“Ouch,” yelled Liam when he got hit on the shoulder.

From their left side Walter Glascott shouted, “Damned papists, put the Presley’s stones back. They’re not for shits like you.”

Kevin made out three assailants on both sides of the road. Besides having stones in their right hands, they had heavy clubs in their left.

“Boys, this is it. We make our stand. Jimmy, you’re on the right. Liam hit the easy targets and I’ll cover the left.”

Kevin took a sling out, filled a pocket with small stones from the back of the cart and then ran to the left side.

Kevin heard Jimmy give a yell. Liam followed in kind.

"Here, boys," yelled Kevin. He steadily let out a string of shots. Out of six swings, he reached one of his targets. A touch to a wound on the side of his head confirmed that it was bleeding.

"Got one," yelled Jimmy.

Liam didn't hit anything, but managed to send them dodging a lot of stones.

"Let's get them, lads," screamed Jimmy as he ran towards their assailants. Kevin and Liam followed behind him, and they copied Jimmy's mad screaming.

The other boys ran off.

"We've got them on the run," said Kevin.

"We should get out of here," said Jimmy.

"Liam, two more good ones and let's go."

Jimmy got back up front of the wagon and grabbed the reins. Kevin walked on the left side of the wagon and Liam on the right.

"Do you think they're going to try to stop us?" asked Jimmy.

"It's been a long time and we're dealing with old Walter. He doesn't have the patience to wait around," said Liam. "We would have seen him by now."

"If Samuel was there, he'd wait until we got to where the road gets narrow. There's lots of tree cover there," said Kevin. "Walter likes telling people what to do. Samuel can put him right, but those others are useless."

"I'm filling my pocket with stones. I don't know about you, but I'm not going looking for some when I see them."

"Then, lets go. I want to get out of here," Jimmy said.

"You know if they attack us, the slings won't help up close," said Kevin.

"Are you coming or staying?" said Liam. "Jimmy, get her to move."

"Let's go," said Kevin.

When they got near the narrow section of the road, Kevin told them, "I'll run ahead to make sure we don't get surprised."

Kevin walked through the narrow stretch but didn't see or hear anything out of the ordinary. He looked back and listened to the sound of the wood wheels slowly turning. *Sounds like there's a wobble,* he thought. *Lord, if we lose the wheel with a heavy load, this will be one huge waste of a day.*

He looked up at the branches that covered the road and for some reason wondered if he should go back to see Anty. *And what's she doing with the likes of Boyse?* he thought. *She's crazy.*

His daydreaming was interrupted by the sounds of screams. Jimmy and Liam were getting battered with rocks. "It's Samuel!" Kevin said. He saw someone picking rocks from their pocket. "…and Richard is with him." He recognized his grey woollen sweater. Both kept throwing rocks from the right side of the road. The horse got spooked. It reared and then tried to race ahead to avoid the screams and rock throwing.

Liam tried to return the throws, but he got hit hard on the wrist. Besides Walter and Samuel, Kevin counted another four. He used his sling and almost hit one of them.

"Run, Liam," Kevin shouted. "Just run."

Samuel threw rocks at Kevin, but he wasn't close enough.

As the wagon got closer, Kevin saw that Jimmy was bent over and covered in blood. He also saw splotches of blood on the old horse's back and flanks. He slung stones as fast as he could to give the others cover.

Liam jumped on the rear of the wagon and climbed up beside Jimmy. He managed to get the horse to slow down. Kevin followed the wagon as it passed. When Liam managed to get the horse to stop, Kevin ran up beside it and did his best to calm it by petting it and talking softly.

"Poor, poor girl. Terrible, terrible people," Kevin said.

"Kevin, Jimmy is in a bad way," Liam told him.

Liam, help me kick the stones off. Get him to sit in the back.

The two boys moved to the back and did their best to kick and throw off the load.

"Kevin, they're coming."

"Faster," yelled Kevin.

"We got to go," said Liam.

They turned and carried Jimmy around to the back of the cart.

Jimmy's head was bleeding. There was a big welt on his forearm and a bad gash on his lower leg. "Ow," groaned Jimmy as he was dropped into the back of the cart.

"Don't let them hurt the horse or we'll really be in for it," Jimmy muttered.

Kevin got a sling from Liam, loaded some of his pockets with pieces of stone from the cart, and then jumped down.

"Take Jimmy home and I'll try to slow them down," he said.

As the others moved on, he slung stones at the six boys that drew closer. He looked at the dirt ground and didn't see any more rocks around. *They're not throwing rocks,* he thought. *They're waiting until I'm in range.*

"Isn't that a bother," he said to himself.

He focused his throw on Walter, who was in the centre, but they spread out with the ones on the ends getting more adventurous. When he hit a boy next to Walter in the chest, they all froze. Kevin tried to hit the boy on his far right, but he wasn't close.

"Damn," Kevin muttered. "Why hit the landlord's horse? That was pretty ignorant."

"You're ignorant," said Walter.

"It's the landlord's property," said Kevin.

"No, it isn't. It belongs to the Presleys, and he stole it," said Samuel.

Kevin didn't know what to say. He only had about seven stones left, and he didn't see any other stones on the road.

"Well, tell it to the landlord," said Kevin.

"Kevin, you're a blowhard."

I wonder how fast I can run, thought Kevin. He ran through a line of trees. Screams and shouting followed him. He managed to run across the first field but had to stop in the middle of the next one to catch his breath. The others were almost on top of him. His second attempt landed a rock on the leg of the boy wearing a brown jacket. His scream caused the others to stop. Samuel was still moving, but he was travelling wide. Kevin slung two more stones and didn't hit anyone, so he started running again. A thick forest was only half a field away. As he was running, he loaded another sling. He stopped, waited and managed to hit Walter in the chest again. He was the easiest target because he was the biggest. Kevin turned and made a mad dash for the last half of the field. *Samuel is the problem*, Kevin thought. He added a rock to his sling again and turned left and looked for his target. As he expected, Samuel was really close. He wound his sling, but Samuel hit Kevin's chest with a rock. Kevin's last throw was incomplete. He turned and ran into the forest. The trees protected the river valley that led towards the abbey.

Kevin kept moving left but didn't descend into the river valley. When the others poured down the hill towards the winding small river, he slipped back out into the field.

He ran across the clearing, where they wouldn't hear him. He crossed the river valley farther up and raced towards the abbey across fields on the other side.

When Kevin reached the abbey, he told the blacksmith that Jimmy had been hurt. Mr. Sevens rushed over to repeat the story to Mr. Stewart, the coachman. Kevin was surprised that he was ordered to sit up beside the coachman as they went out looking for him.

If it was me, they would have let me rot, he thought. *Is the coachman his father?* He stared at him but didn't see any resemblance.

When they met the other cart, Mr. Stewart gave Liam and Kevin grief for not fixing Jimmy's wounds. He didn't give them a chance to say anything. They also didn't want to say anything about the injuries the poor animal had suffered. He ordered them to help carry Jimmy into the coach and then told them to go back and get the stone they left behind. When Liam attempted to say something, Mr. Stewart told him that he didn't want to hear any excuses and that he was in a hurry to bring Jimmy home to his mother.

"I get hit just like him, but he sees his lordship there and he gets the royal treatment," said Kevin. "Hello, how are you? Are you dead? That's nice, so get back to work."

"Do you think Mr. Kennedy is his father?" Kevin added.

"Jimmy, you mean. Mr. Kennedy's wife, Mary, would have a few words to say about that, wouldn't she?" said Liam.

"Well, that would explain why no-one is talking about it," said Kevin.

Mr. Stewart, the coachman, led a horse into the stable.

"Your horse got some bad sores, didn't she?" said Mr. Sevens from the barn door.

"It's been a month," Mr. Stewart said while he undid a buckle. "She's much better now."

"I saw young Jimmy. He's still got a bit of a limp."

Mr. Stewart said, "The boy was lucky. If that bash on his leg had got infected, he could have lost it. His lordship was absolutely furious. He had James Kennedy threaten the wrath of God on everyone for fighting. Not much came of it. The abbey got some extra work from the Walsh boys. He almost lost one of them, though. Liam almost fell off the abbey roof, I'm told."

Mr. Sevens came over to the horse and grabbed the reins as he said, "And what about Walter, Samuel and the other boys? If they were residents of this estate, I'm sure there'd be many ways to show his displeasure."

Mr. Stewart started grooming the horse. They are from Ballyvaroge, which is across the river in another parish. I don't see that as being an issue. John Colclough and their landlord recently have had some fruitful discussions. His lordship has managed to get them to deliver six wagon loads of stone to his flour mill. That's one wagon load for each of them. And I'm told that their landlord has them hauling more stone for his own purposes."

"Did they clear out the Presley house?"

"No, John arranged to clear one that was closer."

"These skirmishes aren't going to go away," said Mr. Sevens.

"His lordship is bringing back Tintern's hurling matches. Like in his grandfather's day, he's going to mix the Protestants with the Catholics. Given a choice between the games and extra work, none of them refused to give it a go."

"Well, that's a turn up for the books. And Mr. Kennedy's not going to want to have anything to do with it"

"He was supposed to organize it, but he put it on me. As if I have the time—and what do I know about the game?" said Mr. Stewart.

"The only reason his lordship is doing this is because Jimmy Doyle's in the midst of all the trouble," said the blacksmith. "The boys were beating each other with sticks by themselves and now the adults are going to cheer them on. Well, isn't that an improvement? As long as there's some smashed skulls and the like, you can count me in. I'll be there."

"Maybe you should play. You could use a good kick in the head," said Mr. Stewart.

Sevens raised a fist and said with a laugh, "And wouldn't they love to see that."

Mr. Stewart gave the horse a look and said, "I'll let you pick at his shoes, I'm going back in. I'm having a word with the cook."

"Life's small privileges," Mr. Sevens said as he made a smack of his lips and gave a bitter frown. He bent, picked up the horse's hoof and began picking the dirt from its' shoe.

A fortnight and half later, a mixed hurling match came to pass. Samuel and Richard were walking home with Walter.

"Another one for Tintern's Yellowbellies," said Richard.

"If we were playing someone else maybe, but Richard, you played us and lost," said Samuel.

"It was Kevin Neal's fault," said Walter as he gave Richard a soft jab in the shoulder.

"Come on. You were ahead by just one goal. You'd think it was a dozen," said Richard. He turned, jabbed Walter in the stomach and hopped back and forth, moved his fists around and told him, "It was the goal keeper and those two saves."

"Don't let it go to his head, lad. It's too big already," and Samuel gave Walter a grin.

"I had a good laugh. I was yelling at Kevin Neal," said Richard. "I asked Kevin why he didn't smash Jimmy. He told me that it was because he had the sliotar, and it was yours for the taking."

"What did Jimmy say?" asked Samuel.

"He said that he was right. Next time he was rougher, and shoved him. Jimmy smashed him with his hurley and took the sliotar. They both have spirit, don't they?"

"Jimmy's a good runner but…" said Samuel.

"Yeh, but he's only twelve," said Richard.

"Both of them aren't old enough," added Walter.

"Kevin, sure can throw. Spends too much time thinking, though," observed Samuel.

"And you don't spend enough…" laughed Richard.

"Go away," replied Samuel. "And Richard, get that shoe fixed. Look at it. Three toes showing on the left foot. You'd be better to go barefoot for the next match."

"My Mam has been busy."

"Then tell her it's an emergency," said Samuel. "Tell her that his lordship won't let you play until it's fixed."

"Didn't see Anty Kelly there?" said Richard.

Samuel didn't answer.

"Did you ask her?"

"I guess her aunt didn't want to go. I don't know."

"Walter, what about Elaine Byrne?" asked Richard.

"Didn't ask her," he said as he pulled the brim of his cap down. "Too far for her to come."

"Maybe we should challenge Lord Carew," said Richard.

"Where did that come from?" asked Walter. "One lousy game, which you've lost, and you're going to take on the world?"

"Lord Colclough and the Yellowbellies used to do that sort of thing," answered Richard.

"Don't think so. Honestly, as a group, I think we're pretty terrible. We would need an awful lot of practice before his lordship would even remotely consider it," said Samuel.

"So this means you're now good friends with the papists?" asked Walter.

"Not necessarily," said Samuel. "His lordship has a soft spot for Jimmy Doyle, and we all know what the landlords are capable of. They can force us off our land, or even have us hanged if it suits them."

"So you're not against taking a strong hand?" asked Walter.

"If it doesn't involve Jimmy Doyle and happens at night, you'll be all right. But keep out of the landlord's way."

Walter lightly smashed Samuel's hurley, raised his, and said, "Right you are."

Two days after the hurling match, Kevin popped his head in the forge and said, "Hello—Mr. Sevens."

"It's you again. Kevin, isn't it?" asked Mr. Sevens, the blacksmith. He rolled a piece of metal in a measured grip as he used a powerful arm to smash it into shape. "I heard that you're playing hurling," he said. "Aren't you a bit young to be on that team?"

"Jimmy's playing and he's younger than me."

"So, Richard Caulfield is on your side. How's that going for you?"

"I try not to think about it. Anyway, I'm here because I want to learn how to become a blacksmith. What can I do?"

"And what can you do?" he said, as he lowered his tongs into a vat of water.

"What? Well, I help lay stone and do repairs for Mr. Colclough."

"I don't work with stone," the blacksmith said as he put the tongs down and wiped the pouring sweat from his forehead. "If you were here, what could you do for me?" He wiped his hands on a filthy apron.

Kevin stared at the forge. "If you teach me how to start the forge and cleanup, you could sleep in."

"God in heaven above, that's a twist, isn't it?" He swiped long strands of greasy hair away from his face and pulled back at the leather cord of the apron that was scratching the back of his neck. "But until you learn to do things, I can't pay you anything."

"What about that leather jacket?"

"It has been hanging there for a very long time. The jacket was there before I started here. It doesn't fit me. My arms are too long and maybe it is not quite right around the belly." He laughed. "The jacket also has a big, ugly red stain across the back. If you have the patience and the determination, I suppose you could get the women to tell you how to dye it." He reached up, grabbed it and handed it to Kevin. "Try it on," he said. Mr. Sevens took a careful look at him. "Long on the sleeves, isn't it? You'll grow into it soon enough."

"That's fine by me," Kevin replied.

Mr. Sevens scratched the side of his head and asked, "Now why should I think you're worth my time. I mean, I don't know if you're dependable. How do I know you're not going to run off on me to try to kick sense into some useless twit, when you're supposed to be here?"

"I won't," Kevin said. He looked around and started shuffling his feet. "Well, I guess you'd get the coat back."

"I'm not making any promises, but Mr. Kennedy and I will talk this over. Now off with you."

⁓❦⁓

While Kevin was talking to the blacksmith, Samuel left his family's cottage after having supper. He met Anty walking on the road near the Jeffers' house. He gave her a wave and ran over to meet her.

"Hello Samuel," she said.

A sweet, gentle wind blew in from the sea, shaking the shrubs on both sides of the road. The sun was large in the clear sky, but shadows from the trees stretched long towards the sea.

"Shouldn't you be with your aunt or something?" he asked.

"Absent minded, I guess. Haven't seen you. Thought you were dead. Where have you been?"

He looked down at her shoes and asked, "That Kevin Neal, hasn't he been keeping you busy? I've been helping my da."

"He's nice but you know, he's just a boy," she said.

Samuel shuffled and then stood up straight, opened his stance, and thrust his hair back. "Right you are. Never gave him a moment's thought," he said. "Your uncle—has he heard from the boys in America? I mean it's a big place, and it's interesting to hear about, you know."

"Nothing more than the last time I told you. I don't think they are ever coming back and I'm sure my aunt and uncle don't have any interest in leaving."

"Just wondering, that's all," he said. He stared at the shadows of the line of trees. "Didn't see you at the match," he said.

"Hurling? No, sorry. I've been too busy and my aunt didn't want to go. That Kevin is a talker, isn't he?" asked Anty.

"No, haven't noticed. Well, sometimes he goes on and on. That's true."

"Oh," she said.

"Do you see something in him?" he asked. He looked at her fidgeting with the front of her shawl. He noticed that she did that when she was thinking about something.

"Him? He's just a boy, but I told you that already," she said. "Are you going to stay?"

He saw the silhouette of someone at the Jeffer's cottage, but it looked so very far away. "Stay where?" he asked.

"Your older brother is going to get the farm, isn't he?"

"Well, I might split the farm with my brother, unless one of us goes to

America."

"Do you want to?" Anty asked.

"What?"

"Go to America."

"Well, Ireland is my home," Samuel said, and he stepped back and forth. "What's to make me to go to America? Do you think you'd leave?"

"What?" asked Anty.

"Ireland."

"If there's not anything to keep me here."

"Oh," said Samuel.

"I'd like to see some places," said Anty.

"I was in Tipperary once," said Samuel. "I was with my da. My cousin is there."

"I was just wondering," said Anty. "I was just wondering what my options are," she repeated. "I can't stay with my aunt. She's making life unbearable. Just wondering."

"About what?" asked Samuel as he marked a small awkward line in the road with the front of his shoe.

"It's getting late and I've got to get back before she misses me."

The next evening, after their chores, Walter, Richard and Samuel started demolishing one of John Colclough's cottages. When part of the wall was pushed over, they separated the stones from the mortar and then loaded them onto the horse drawn wagon.

"Maybe we should have blamed this on Harold Wheeler," said Walter.

"You'd be dead and buried, and we'd be running for our lives. Are you insane?" said Samuel Boyse.

"You don't like to work?" asked Richard.

Walter ignored him and dropped another stone onto the wagon.

"I would rather be like the landlord and order you louts around,"

Samuel replied.

"You'd better marry one of his relatives. Where are you going to get the dowry?" asked Richard.

"Right," said Samuel.

"What happened to the Kelly girl?" asked Richard.

"Nothing. Why?" said Samuel.

"Because he's interested in her, that's why," said Walter. "I mean, both of you are idiots. You can't find a half decent girl so you go rapping on the papists. You're going to get infected."

"With what?" asked Richard.

"You'll start drooling like lunatics. Look at Samuel. He's already looking like one."

"Walter, go away," said Samuel. "Better still, let Richard and me break up another part of the wall and you can load this lot all by yourself." Samuel dropped another block onto the cart.

"Both of you wouldn't be able to keep up," said Walter. "I mean, with Samuel drooling and Richard scratching himself, I'd be waiting here all day."

Richard lightly, but quickly, punched Walter in the side and said, "I'll show you who's scratching himself."

Walter plowed him in the shoulder with a punch, and Richard cried, "Ouch."

Samuel dropped another rock on the wagon.

"I was just teasing you, big fella. Maybe we should take a go at it," Richard said as he threw jabs with his left hand as he bounced by Walter.

Walter said, "Something is passing and the Catholics are not going to like it. They deserve what's coming."

"Change the topic, why don't you?" said Richard. "So, what is it?"

"You have to promise to keep your mouths shut," demanded Walter.

Samuel moved in front of him and said, "Fine. So spit it out."

"I was told that there's going to be another retaliation killing," said Walter. "I was told that it's rightfully deserved."

"Around here?" asked Samuel.

"We've got to put the papists in their place or they'll push us into the sea."

"Are you going on about this because Kevin Neal smashed you? I know you had Wheeler beat up Padraig," said Richard.

"Sometimes you can be so stupid. No, it's not me. It's them that's doing it."

"Douglas FitzGibbon, you mean?" asked Richard.

"Don't say that. You know better. The man's ruthless."

"So, how are they going to kill this fellow?" asked Richard. "And is it anyone we know? I hope not."

"They're not going to tell me and even if they did I wouldn't be stupid enough to tell fools like you anything, now would I?" said Walter.

"Walter, that lot is vicious. Get too close and they're going to tear out your better parts," said Samuel. "Why get near them at all?"

"Sometimes, we exchange favours," Walter answered. "Don't you two just stand there. Let's fill this wagon up so we can get out of here."

Connections

In January of the next year, Jimmy Doyle and Kevin Neal were escorted to the lawn behind the abbey by Mr. Stewart.

"If someone thinks we did something. It wasn't us. I swear," said Kevin.

"It was just you," said Jimmy.

Kevin tried to kick him in the shin, but Jimmy side-stepped away.

"Boys, if you know what is good for you, I'd suggest you keep quiet," Mr. Stewart said. He directed them to stand in line facing the servant's entrance.

Mr. Kennedy opened the door and ordered Jimmy inside. "Don't keep him waiting. Jimmy, inside now," he said.

Mr. Stewart followed Jimmy into the kitchen.

Kevin was left standing alone outside. He checked around but didn't see anyone else. "And if you didn't want to see me, why did you bring me here?" he asked. This is bloody not alright, you know! You know this is not alright," he repeated. Still no-one opened the door. After waiting for about ten minutes, he walked to the bridge to the mill and waited another few minutes. Still no-one came to the door.

"Gahd," he said, as he walked back to see if Mr. Walsh had work for him to do.

Jimmy joined him just as he started carrying rocks from one pile to another.

"What was that all about?" Kevin asked.

"His lordship doesn't want me to associate with you?"

"What does that mean?"

"I said it wasn't our fault. It was theirs and that I didn't want to play the fiddle and that I wanted to be a swordsman like his brother."

"His brother is a swordsman?" asked Kevin.

"Well, he was in the army, so he must know how to fight. Right?"

"yeh, I guess so," said Kevin. "So, what happened."

"Mr. Colclough said some stuff, but I lost track. I mean, I got some tea and biscuits. …with jam; pastries, even. You don't know what you were missing."

"Neither do you, by the sounds of it," Kevin added.

"Anyways, you got to play the fiddle," said Jimmy.

"What? Me? What do I know about a fiddle?"

"Not just you, but all of us. I heard that Mr. Kennedy is going to tell you," said Jimmy.

Two days later, Mr. Stewart again escorted Kevin to the lawn at the rear of the abbey. Samuel Boyse, Richard Caulfield & Jimmy already stood in line facing the servant's entrance. Kevin was instructed to stand in formation beside Samuel.

Mr. Stewart placed a small table beside two chairs. Mr. Kennedy placed a tray with a teapot and teacups on it and returned inside. When Mr. John Colclough came out, Mr. Stewart called the boys to attention.

The landlord walked around the boys and eyed Mr. Stewart.

"Samuel, why aren't those buttons done up?" Mr. Stewart bellowed.

"Yes sir," Samuel replied, as he did up a button on his shirt and another on his jacket.

"I've heard complaints about you boys," said the landlord as he continued to pace around them. "Problems related to the rebellion will always be here, but I'll not have any of it coming to me. Understood?"

James Kennedy had a sardonic grin on his face.

"Mr. Kennedy, you're not helping. Anyway, boys, you're here so we can keep a close eye on you. There are some that believe stronger measures should be taken, but your parents believe you can contribute."

The boys turned their heads and looked at each other.

"A good friend of mine, a Miss Elizabeth Alcock, is an aficionado of good music. Some young ladies are going to have a recital and we require some musicians."

Mr. Kennedy came out of the servant's entrance with a violin case and placed it on the small table in front of a tea setting.

"But Mr. Colclough, I don't know how to play and I am pretty sure Richard has never even seen one," said Samuel.

"Of course I have," said Richard.

"Enough, young man. I suppose there are lots of places you could go from here," said Mr. Kennedy. "Like maybe—Australia?" He paced up and down along the line in front of them.

"I have arranged for a tutor to assist in this endeavour. Who here is not prepared to do a masterful job for the recital?" He glared into each of their eyes.

"We keep our hands down if we're going to do it? Right?" asked Richard.

John Colclough ignored him and said, "I am glad we understand each other. The violins will stay here, but you may use them to practice in the courtyard. We don't want them damaged, and we want you to prove you are serious and capable. I am providing a rare opportunity. It is counter to what some would say is good governance. Should there be a re-occurrence we could consider transfers elsewhere. Lord Blackwell, I'm sure would be pleased to have some new tenants. And Richard and Samuel, don't doubt that we don't have your landlord's blessing. Do you hear me?"

The four nodded.

"His lordship, asked you a question and I didn't hear an answer," said Mr. Kennedy.

"Yes, sir," the four replied.

"Louder, boys," demanded Mr. Kennedy.

The four repeated their agreement loudly and in unison.

"Kevin, I was told that you have been bothering the blacksmith," said John Colclough.

"I did ask him a couple of months ago, sir. I didn't mean to be a problem."

"If you need to smash things up, I would prefer if it was for some utility. You can help him before you start your day with Mr. Walsh. Whether it leads to anything depends on Mr. Sevens' recommendations. Master Doyle, you know that is something you could do. Have you considered working with Sevens?"

"Thank you, sir, but I'd like to join the army like your brother."

"My brother, Caesar, sets a bad example. My brother's military training didn't last long. After learning to defend himself from Adam's Caesar my cousin took up a different interests."

Mr. Stewart escorted a gentleman from around the corner to a chair next to the tea set.

"Sir, Mr. Alistair Alcock has arrived," said James Kennedy.

"Bring him in, James. Boys, that will be enough for now," said Mr. Colclough.

"Hold it," ordered Alistair Alcock as he pointed upward. "John, you left off the best part," he said as his overcoat, a top hat, and a walking cane were passed to James Kennedy. "While at University, in Dublin, Adam's Caesar challenged him to a formal duel, but your brother bluffed his way out. They really do despise each other, don't they?"

"Alistair?" said Kevin. He looked like a different man from the one he had met six years ago. He looked taller, straighter, and cheerful as he walked with the air of someone that was in control. He was smartly dressed like Mr. Colclough. His trimmed grey hair was combed down and away from a balding top.

John Colclough sat down in the chair in the backyard beside Alistair.

"When John and I got into discussing amusements for Miss Alcock, I suggested that he seriously consider a recital. The abbey is known widely for its appreciation of hurling. I suggested that it might be worth investing in the arts as well. Jimmy's name came up, but I suggested that we expand the small group. Seems that John has got a commitment from you boys, I see. If the feet are kept to the fire, we might see progress of a sort. What do you think James?" He looked to Mr. Kennedy.

"Hours of hard labour are what they need, if you ask me. If they make music the way they run off in a match, the sound of it will be torture. Sir, would you care for some tea?"

Mr. Colclough, waved the boys away and said, "You may leave us now. You will be summoned when you're needed."

"How you've grown, Kevin," Alistair intervened, calling him back. "Kevin, I mentioned that the next time we met, that we would play a tune. Unfortunately, my fingers are not what they once were. They sort of froze up with age. Instead, I have arranged for something else. The fiddle in that case is mine. I am leaving it with John. Should you acquire a proficiency that passes muster in John's view, you can consider it yours. In the meantime, he will keep it away from your ruffian competitors."

"Thank you very much, sir," said Kevin. "I don't know what to say. Sir, how did you know I was here?" asked Kevin.

"Actually, I found out by accident. I heard that your old landlord—Adam's Caesar, was looking for you. Coincidentally, I had some business with Monart House and the lady of the house let it slip that around that time they sheltered a family from the north of the county during a snowstorm. John, in one of our many conversations, recently let it out that you had popped up here. You've had remarkable turns and twists in your journey, haven't you? You don't look any worse for wear other than John's recent chastising, of course."

"I'm sorry that you heard about that, but it's good to see that you are in good health, sir," Kevin replied. He didn't know what to do with his hands so he put them behind. He was uncomfortable with both gentlemen staring at him.

Mr. Colclough with two fingers directed him away. Kevin tried to decorously back up. As he walked towards the side of the abbey, he heard Alistair Alcock say, "For our favour, I'm sure he won't bring displeasure."

He overheard James Kennedy ask, "Why wasn't the ringleader Walter Glascott here?"

"Nothing between the ears on that one," said John Colclough. "He's just muscle. He's a seventeen-year-old, and he's been shown up by a fourteen-year-old."

"Young Jimmy, you mean?" added James Kennedy.

"Samuel's the one to watch out for. He's young, slim, and wiry, yet perceptive. When the boy's older, he'll have influence. I know it. Besides, I am very familiar with his cousin and he's a good sort."

After Kevin had left, Mr. Colclough and Alcock retired inside to the living room. James Kennedy poured a round of whisky, and then said, "Sir, I can check on the status of the kitchen, if you like."

Mr. Colclough gave a nod in acknowledgement and took a sip from his glass.

Alistair said, "It has been a bad season for storms, hasn't it?"

"We haven't done that badly," John Colclough said. "Even my cousin, Adam's Caesar at Duffry Hall, continues to stock up on our French and German wines, brandies and cheeses. He even bought some silk for his new bride. He might not know exactly where they come from, but so far he has paid what he owes. If he knows, for the time being he doesn't seem to care."

"One has to be careful in these times, John. It's only been a few years since your cousin John Henry Colclough, along with John Kelly, lost their heads at the discretion of the crown. And wasn't John Henry found hiding on an island just off your shores?"

"I don't know anything about that Alistair."

"I'd like to remind you that at one time they were also popular, but people still used their heads for a nasty game of football."

"Yes, the wrong sort can get caught up with the most revolting pastimes."

"You have always had my confidence and trust, but I strongly advise you not to be flippant with politicians like Arthur Annesley," said Alistair. "He and Adam's Caesar are close business associates. He's dangerous and I know he doesn't appreciate your sense of humour."

John Colclough adjusted his scarf to protect his neck. "Alistair, I understand your meaning. I believe I understand the costs of being a populist in this climate. James, please put another log on the fire."

"On a different matter, John, I would like to raise my glass in a toast to the opening of your new bank in New Ross. To prudent investments."

John leaned back in the old but comfortable easy chair. "Sláinte Mhaith," he replied.

"This enterprise will enable us to establish leverage," said Alistair.

"Your insight and candour in these matters was most appreciated," said John.

"Don't you think your attention to my cousin Elizabeth will force you to put the renovations to the top of your priority list?" said Alistair.

John put his glass, to the side of his nose, and to change the subject he said, "A Mr. Keane introduced me to the Walshes."

"I know the man. He provided assistance in my recovery of injuries suffered in the rebellion."

"A curious man," said John Colclough as he took another sip from his glass.

"I am using some of my returns from the bank to finish work on the mill and the abbey."

"We were discussing my cousin. Your brother is thirty-eight and you're a year less," added Alistair.

"A year and a half, actually. There is an Irish thing. We wait until the time is right."

"If you wait too long, you will be fifty, and the women won't want you."

"Alistair, I make no secret of it. I am very smitten with young Elizabeth. My intentions are purely honourable."

"I hope so. You have much to make up for, considering your father's philandering and wanton reputation."

"I, and my brother, are not like my father."

"Does Elizabeth know about the Doyle boy?"

"Jimmy? I'll…" He took another bite of a piece of jam covered soda bread and said, "Well, I'll address that with Elizabeth in time. The timing is delicate. I don't want to lose her. She means everything to me. I was in a bad place at that time. The Doyle girl was very compassionate. I am sorry if anyone thinks I led her on. I don't intend to shirk my responsibilities. The innocent need not suffer for our indiscretions."

"Does he know?"

John sipped his cup of tea and said, "I don't think so," and leaned back in his chair and crossed his legs away from Alistair.

"When I am in Elizabeth's presence, I feel like a young schoolboy. I feel completely irrational. My only hope is that she won't become bored with my relentless babble."

Mr. Kennedy entered the sitting room and asked, "Sir, the cook would like to know if you requested more of Mrs. Doyle's cornbread?"

"No. No, you misunderstood. Where's the cook? Uh, or where's Mr. Stewart?"

"John, relax," said Alistair. "I have known you for some time. You are naive in matters of the world. It is part of your charm, and it has enabled you to establish so many connections. You see how you want the world to be and you walk blindly on, and unfortunately a lot want to follow on. By the way, how is your brother?"

"Caesar is still in France," said John who attempted to lead the conversation away from the concerns of Lady Elizabeth. "He still writes the occasional article for Irish newspapers. He manages our trade connections from the continent. The French put him in prison for a short while before the Irish rebellion, but that was a long time ago."

"I don't understand why he likes being there so much," said Alistair.

"I manage our affairs. I am good at it and my brother is a bit irresponsible and has more cosmopolitan tastes. I do agree with you, however. I am concerned about this fellow, Napoleon. I don't believe his intentions bode well for a lasting peace."

James brought each of them a tray of Jimmy's mother's pastries.

John Colclough stared in amazement as James Kennedy placed it in front of him. "Uh, it's from the kitchen, sir," he said.

"Uh, yes, of course, James. Uh, as I was saying, it was your friend Mr. Keane that made me understand that together we make a good pair. I mean, my brother and I. Under the pretext of discussing our accounts, I convinced Caesar to return to the abbey. I am going to try to persuade my brother to take a run at politics. I believe he's suited for it. In the year after next, there should be a seat available. I would like to have him by my side. I am very good at managing assets and financial planning, and he has much more hands-on skills. He loves to tinker with woodworking and engineering. The abbey is in a terrible state of disrepair and my lack of attention to it is a frightful nuisance, which reminds me, I committed to Elizabeth a new walled garden on the other side of the river."

"John, I agree, keep your brother close and be very afraid of Adam's Caesar. He will take every advantage to find your weaknesses. He has gotten bored with being a barrister and is looking for a political position in Dublin."

Before John could reply, James returned from the kitchen and said, "Sir, young Jimmy wants to know if you need more soda bread? Sir, what should I tell him?"

John Colclough waved Mr. Kennedy away.

Padraig approached Kevin, who was sitting on a hill overlooking the bay. "Hey Kevin, aren't you cold?," he asked. "I mean it's the end of January."

"Go get some more clothes on if you're cold," said Kevin.

"I thought I'd find you here," said Padraig.

"It reminds me of what's on the other side of the mountain."

"*Stua* Laighean?"

"Sure. The other side of the world is over that line on the water. It's somewhere beyond that. Do you miss home?"

Kevin got up, pulled up the collar on his jacket, and walked down the slope to stroll along the beach. Padraig followed.

"There's nothing you can do about the past, so why dwell on it?" asked Padraig. "With blacksmithing, hurling, fiddling, putting people right, and a girl, you're a busy lad, aren't you?"

"Hasn't been any fighting for a while and I wouldn't say there's a girl."

"Where's that young Anty? Seems she's got you by the right and ready."

"Don't know about that. Someone older has her fancy, I guess."

"Samuel Boyse is it? Your time will come. Don't give up on it. I bet you'll have a beard on that face in no time at all. Well, isn't that something there," he said as he reached and threatened to pull out hairs from his chin.

"Don't," Kevin said, and he tried to slap his hand, but Padraig pulled it away too fast.

They sat on a rock next to the sand of the beach and were quiet for a few minutes as they looked at a setting sun. Padraig got up and said, "It's too cold to sit around. I'm going for a walk. He continued down the hill to the water. Kevin followed and caught up to him.

"Did I tell you I went fishing yesterday?" Padraig said.

"Did you catch anything?"

"Yeh, but I don't have the patience for it. Don't mind the eating though. Your friend Jimmy is over there," he said.

Jimmy ran down to them from the hill.

"You found me," Kevin told him.

"Mr. Walsh told me where you were," Jimmy said as he stopped to catch his breath.

"How is it your mother lets you stay up?" teased Padraig.

"Go away," he said. "I heard you say you didn't catch nothing."

"I didn't say that," said Padraig. "I just said it's boring."

"Probably wrong bait or you don't know how."

"You, go away," said Padraig. "I caught it and Da cut it up."

Jimmy laughed and said, "One fish and he gives it to his da. Oh, yeh, we have a real fisherman, don't we?"

To change the topic Padraig said, "Now, over there by the village they have boats, and they take them out to the sea. They've come back with some really big ones."

"Sea monsters," said Kevin. "I bet."

"We'll feed them little Jimmy—**he's** the best bait," teased Padraig.

After an exchange of another couple barbs, the conversation petered out. They walked in silence for another ten minutes.

"You think my da is still alive?" asked Jimmy.

"Well, you told me that your mam wouldn't tell you he wasn't. Is there anything else?" asked Kevin.

"No. Just wondering, that's all."

"Why didn't she get married again, if he ran off?" asked Padraig.

"I don't know. She likes her farm beyond the estate walls. She's independent, maybe. There's no figuring out, mam," Jimmy said.

"So you want to know," said Kevin.

"I don't know. I was just wondering."

"Well, I got a da, and sometimes I wonder if he's worth knowing," said Padraig.

"What are you talking about?" asked Kevin. "You just don't talk to him. That's no excuse."

"If Jimmy's da knows he's alive, he mustn't care about Jimmy or he would have said something. Maybe he should just be glad he has his mam and go on with his life."

"Padraig, you're not helping," said Kevin.

"What do you remember of your da?" asked Jimmy.

"Only a few things. I was really young. I try not to think about it." Kevin said.

"Why not?" asked Padraig.

"Because. Be quiet and just leave me alone," Kevin replied.

Padraig got up, ruffled Kevin's hair, patted his shoulder and walked down to the beach.

On the hill Jimmy asked, "Kevin, if you could go somewhere, where would you like to go?"

"The other side of the mountain," Kevin said as he watched Padraig walk away.

-ево-

Towards the end of March, Kevin waited with Richard, Samuel and Jimmy for their tutor, Michael, to arrive. They sat in chairs on the grass behind the abbey.

Kevin looked at Richard and Samuel and said, "No curse words. What's wrong with yehs?"

"Likes of him," Richard said, as he glanced towards a smartly dressed man that was shuffling in the distance on the path that followed the river.

"Who's that?" asked Kevin.

The man that Richard had identified was now walking unsteadily towards them from the bay. There was a woman with him.

"That's the landlord's brother," said Jimmy.

"Vessey's Caesar—the one from France?"

"That's him."

Caesar walked around the backyard with a woman in an elegant pink dress by his side. They both had drinks in their hands. Neither of them was walking very steadily. Kevin didn't know what they were saying, but he knew it wasn't English or Irish.

James Kennedy came out with a silver tray with an assortment of treats. There were slices of fresh fruit, cheeses, seafood, breads, chutneys, and baked treats. Each of them took a plate and picked from the selection. Caesar said something and rudely shooed Mr. Kennedy away.

"He doesn't have his brother's manners, does he?" said Richard.

"Keep it down," said Samuel.

"That's right. Mind your place or I'll kick your arse out of here, you stupid ingrate," said Caesar.

The servant's entrance door opened, and out rushed Michael, carrying the violin cases and the music.

"Sorry, boys, for being late," he said.

The boys, without waiting, grabbed an instrument and sheet music from him. Half of the sheets spilled onto the ground.

Caesar noticed the dazed look on the tutor's face. The lady beside him tapped her wine glass against his and took a drink.

"So, Julie, why is my brother wasting our money on amateurs?"

"June."

"Oh Julie, so sorry,. I mean, I'm truly sorry my dear. It's all that travel. It confuses the mind. Yes, June, it's good to be home, to the sweet charm of Wexford. What a delightful little backwater this is. It does have the most delightful charm." He reached for her and tried to kiss her lips but got her cheek as she pulled away from him.

"And to my cousin the barrister, Adam's Caesar. May the sea swallow him up and the sea creatures enjoy his many parts," he said and took another drink.

"And may they enjoy his many parts," she repeated, and took a good swallow from her glass.

"My brother says he's making a garden. Let's see if we can find it." He looked back at the tutor and said, "I'll have my brother deal with you later."

After the couple was out of sight Richard said, "Doesn't look like a politician to me."

"More like his cousin I'd say," said Samuel.

"I hope he goes back to France," said Kevin.

Jimmy said, "His lordship is trying to persuade him to stay, so he can run for an election."

"He spends most of his time in Switzerland," said Michael as he browsed through the music stack looking for something.

"Where's that?" asked Kevin.

"Next to France," said Michael. "Now raise your instruments. We don't have a lot of time and we have a recital to prepare for."

"Are you sure?" asked Richard.

"Turn around. Get to work," he snarled.

On the second Saturday in April, Kevin slipped away from doing repairs on the abbey. He strolled down the hill towards the water and saw Anty tramping through the mud carrying a basket. Her hair was wrapped in a bun. She wore long stockings, and her dress was pulled up to keep it out of the mud. The tide was out and much of Bannow Bay lay bare. There were a half dozen other girls staring at the odd creatures left behind by the withdrawn tide.

He recognized Mrs. Jeffers sitting on the slope near where he usually sat. *Best stay away from the chaperone. If she's against me, that will be the end of it,* he thought. When he got down to the beach, he wondered what Anty was doing. He saw her staring at something in the mud. When he got close, he watched her pick up a clam.

"And what do you do with that?" Kevin asked.

"Kevin, is it? You're wild looking, aren't you? Long hair and there's not much stopping you, is there?" Anty said. "Aren't you supposed to be building a church?"

"I never said that. It was a flour mill we were fixing. To-day it's the abbey."

"No, you're not."

"Of course I am," he said.

"You're here talking to me," she said.

"Well…"

"It's a clam," she said as she stared at the thing in her hand. "You open it like this," she demonstrated. She grabbed the contents, put back her head, dropped it into her mouth and swallowed. "And you do that."

"Well, isn't that something," he said. "Looks revolting."

She walked over to a pool and waved him to follow her. She grabbed a minnow from a pool.

"Your turn. I dare you to swallow this."

"No way."

"You're a coward."

"Me?"

She tilted her head and was going to drop it into her mouth, but her eyes rolled towards him.

"Fine. I can do it." *I hope I don't throw up*, thought Kevin.

He raised his head, closed his eyes and dropped it in.

"Swallow it, stupid," she yelled and laughed giddily.

Kevin started choking.

"Swallow it. Don't think about." She hit him on the back a couple of times.

"I don't think you're helping. No problem. It was delicious," he said.

"If you like it so much, there's a lot more here."

"Do you come here with Mrs. Jeffers often?"

"Sometimes. That's her daughter behind you, and there's my friend from Newbawn—Elaine Byrne. She's with us for a visit. It's really her, why we're here. I convinced her to try the seafood."

It's a lot she's collecting, just for them, Kevin thought. *There's more than what she's saying.*

"Anty, I'll help you. Just show me what you are looking for," he said.

She retrieved another empty basket and gave it to him. She went back to filling her other one up. She pointed to a slimy sea creature, and he replied with a "Lord, what an ugly looking thing."

They both started laughing.

As he was filling up his basket, he noticed that Liam was coming looking for him down the trail that led to the abbey. He nervously kept collecting. When they finished, he carried both of their baskets up the hill towards Mrs. Jeffers. *So this is what she needs me for,* he thought. *It feels like it weighs more than me.*

She's crazy, and she can have me laughing like no-one.

Mrs. Jeffers didn't talk to him, but she gave a pole to Anty who used it to bear the weight of the baskets across her shoulders. Kevin noticed that the other girls had gone ahead, and that Anty was in a hurry to catch up to them. She took the baskets without saying thank you or goodbye, but Kevin couldn't keep his eyes off her.

Kevin watched Liam returning towards the abbey.

I have no idea what I'm going to tell Mr. Walsh, he thought. *And why didn't I ask her why she avoided me at the last match? Just stupid, I guess. And why do I bother?*

The next evening the Finns and their neighbours sat around a blazing fire in their backyard. There was a big party for four families and some invited guests. Samuel Boyse sat between Anty Kelly and her friend Elaine Byrne from nearby Newbawn.

"So what do you think?" Anty asked, who was looking at Samuel and Elaine. "That's a prawn, that's a clam. That's a shrimp and…"

"I'm not new to this," said Samuel. "My uncle loves shellfish and I love these."

"Scallops," Anty said. "No, they're not bad at all."

"Takes some getting used to," Elaine said.

"Thanks for coming to the last match, Anty," said Samuel.

"Hard to get away. Was lucky I could. Any time I can watch the boys beat themselves up, like sure why not?" said Anty.

"So, Samuel, you work on your father's farm. How long has your family been there?"

"It's where my grandfather was born," he replied as he gave her a quick, cautious glance.

"You intend to share the farm with your brother?" Elaine asked while giving Anty a quick glance.

"Yes, that's probably the way it will be," he said as he foraged through his bowl for another scallop. "Anty, we've got a big concert coming up. Maybe you'd like to come."

"It's difficult to say because my aunt has me doing all sorts of things. Elaine, do you like listening to music?"

"I'd like to, but it's difficult for me to get away too. It's just me and my da."

"Elaine, how did you get the bruise on your arm?" asked Anty. She noticed that the bruises looked like fingerprints.

"Oh, it's nothing. I must have got clumsy."

"Come on, look at me," Anty said, and she glared unrelentingly. "If you need somewhere to stay, the Jeffers would be more than glad to put you up. Do you hear me?"

To Anty she said, "Thanks, I'll consider it."

To Samuel, she said, "As I said before, can't this time Samuel, but maybe another one."

"Anyway, it will be fancy. His lordship will be there with Miss Elizabeth Alcock and his brother Caesar from France," said Samuel.

"Do you sing?" asked Elaine.

"No, I play the fiddle."

"No, flies on you, are there?" Elaine added.

Samuel took a quick bite without looking at what he was eating. Whatever it was, it was crunchy, and he choked on it.

"Here's the last of the soda bread," said James Kennedy as he passed it to Mr. Stewart, the coachman, after their lunchtime meal. "Don't ask. Trust me. You won't see any more for a long while. A good cup of tea and sweet cake is what you need with the cool nip of autumn weather, isn't it?"

Mr. Stewart quickly took it from the plate and added it to his saucer. "So we're going to see less of Jimmy—and his mother's soda bread and more of Miss Elizabeth?" he said. He took a drink of tea while his eyes feasted on the last of a much-appreciated treat. "What a pity, I was hoping the abbey could use another assistant," he said and laughed.

"Go on," said James with a straight face. "She has a farm to manage, and that's the end of that."

Mr. Stewart finished his snack quickly because he knew that James needed to talk about something. "So, do you think his lordship will cancel Jimmy's music lessons and the hurling matches?" Mr. Stewart asked.

"I think that's a good idea."

"Less work for you?"

"Well, there's something else. His lordship has gone to Herculean extremes to make it possible for his brother Caesar to run in the next election. So, do you know what happened?

"Caesar without giving it a second thought—informed him yesterday that he's not interested and he's leaving."

"Doesn't want to give up his Swiss chocolate, I expect," said Mr. Stewart.

"It's just craziness," said James.

"That's typical of Caesar," said Mr. Stewart. "He's always been flighty and irresponsible. You know that John is not going to give up, though. He's stubborn. He'll continue to tell himself that Caesar will change his mind at the last moment—and of course he won't."

"It might be better for John if he just dropped the whole idea. I've heard that his lady friend's brother, William, is being forced to run against him. He and William have been friends since their early school days. I'm sure this could take a nasty turn.

"And John knows that Mr. Pierce Newton King, the High Sheriff, has been paying William's lady friend for secrets."

"I know John," said Mr. Stewart. "And he's not going to tell William, because he knows he's got a soft spot for her." He took a last taste from his teacup.

"More like he wouldn't believe him—and he can't reveal his confidential informant, I'd say," said James.

"Bad business. Very bad business," said Mr. Stewart.

One Sunday afternoon, at the end of summer, a small luncheon for forty of their closest acquaintances was arranged in honour of John Colclough's brother. Miss Elizabeth arrived with her brother and his lady friend— Jennifer Bates. Alistair Alcock, who was a recent widower, had given his condolences for not appearing.

A small stage was setup behind the abbey. Six girls stood on an added step against the wall. In front, the tutor's wife held a flute, a man played scales on a cello, and a woman manoeuvred a harp. Samuel, Richard, Jimmy and Kevin sat behind. Chairs were being set out on the lawn for the audience. The performers waited for the tutor to lead them in a practice before the concert.

"What happened to Michael?" asked Kevin, who was on Jimmy's right.

"Inside eating maybe," replied Jimmy.

"Is this the last time we play?" Richard asked Jimmy.

"Padraig's going with Caesar to France," Kevin interrupted. "His da just told me."

"So why aren't you gone?" asked Richard.

"Because at least one of us has to know how to play?"

"So what are you playing, Neal? Your nose?" added Samuel.

"Where's Padraig going?" asked Richard.

Kevin didn't reply.

"He's…"

Kevin tapped Jimmy with his bow and told him, "Don't."

"So, it's a secret, is it?" said Samuel.

"The French. He's joining the French," said Richard.

"Oh shut up. You don't know anything," said Kevin. He put his fiddle next to his neck and started playing an arpeggio.

"Bricon," said a voice in French.

As he was playing, Kevin recognized that it was Caesar. He must have been standing behind him. Kevin didn't know what he said, but he assumed that it was an insult. He kept playing and pretended to ignore him.

Kevin watched Caesar approach Miss Elizabeth Alcock, who was standing in front of her seat.

"Your brother has been conspicuously avoiding me. I think he's afraid. You can tell him…"

His brother John rushed out of the servant's entrance and made a beckoning gesture to someone inside. "There you are, Caesar," he said.

James Kennedy came rushing out of the abbey. To John, he asked, "How can I help?"

"Would you care for another drink, Caesar? And where is that young lady that was with you?"

"Excuse me, Elizabeth, but John's right I seem to have lost my lady friend. Will you excuse us? James, a glass of brandy, please. You'll find me inside. I'm going on a treasure hunt, if you get my meaning."

"When you have a chance, James, have someone bring us out a Bordeaux with cheeses and biscuits, please."

After Caesar went inside, Kevin stop playing and pointed out to Jimmy, "Caesar's decided to leave and not go into politics, but his brother doesn't want anyone to know.

"How do you know that?" asked Samuel.

Kevin pointed to Jimmy.

"John Colclough's lady friend's brother probably hates him for planning to steal his seat. Do you think we'll see a punch up?"

"You don't know anything, Neal. That's not how they get even," said Samuel.

"So if they're not going to hit each other, what's going to happen?"

"They always get other people to do it for them—or they hurt each other's business," said Samuel.

"So why doesn't William take a bottle of wine and hit Caesar over the head? That would speed things up, don't you think?" asked Richard.

"Go over there and suggest it to him, why don't you?" asked Kevin.

"Michael, you're here just in time. It's getting a bit out of hand," said the tutor's wife. "The guests are moving to their seats and we don't have much time left.

Michael passed a dish of sweetmeats to his wife and the other musicians he brought along. To the boys he told them to begin a set of scales.

Jimmy watched some members of the audience eating bits of cheese and fruit.

"Wishing doesn't make it happen," Richard told him.

"Kevin, Mr. Stewart asks why you're not using the fiddle Mr. Alcock provided you," said Michael.

Michael looked at the three lady singers at the back and told them, "Scales please." They were from Mr. Stewart's church.

As Michael led the group in practice, someone started tapping a metal triangle inside the abbey. The guests were warned that it was time to take their seats.

Although the music was planned for the upper crust, the immediate family of the musicians were permitted to sit at the back in the last row. Walter Glascott got in because he told Mr. Stewart that he was Richard's brother—even though Mr. Stewart knew him from church. The families waited in front of the abbey after most of the guests moved to their seats. Mr. Stewart made it clear that they were not allowed to associate with any of the guests and that they had to leave immediately after the concert. Mrs.

and Mrs. Walsh waved at Kevin as they passed by. Mrs. Walsh had made herself an elaborate new hat and decorated it with blue flowers.

John Colclough introduced his brother to the crowd. His brother provided a travelogue of his recent business in Switzerland and France. His brother cut him off short when he noticed that some of their guests were either yawning or had started talking to their neighbours. John introduced the orchestra and then took his seat.

Richard's shoes and pants were sewn up. Samuel wore a fancy reddish scarf, which was tucked into his shirt. Jimmy wore a makeshift white bow tie over something that was supposed to be a white shirt under his vest. Kevin had taken one of Mrs. Walsh's blue wildflowers and attached it to his lapel. He stared at Mrs. Walsh and made sure she saw him touching it with his bow.

Miss Elizabeth sat next to John Colclough and his brother up front in the middle, but her brother sat near the back on the side closest to the abbey's river.

After some coughs, Michael waved his baton, and the concert began.

Later that night, after supper, Kevin followed Padraig out of the cottage. Kevin moved beside him and asked, "But do you really know what you're doing?"

"I think so." Padraig started walking away.

"Where are you going?" Kevin asked.

"The bay. Want to look at it before I leave."

Kevin rushed along beside him.

"Is the landlord going to continue with your lessons?" Padraig asked.

"Caesar said he hated it, but he was drunk and talked all the way through the concert. Miss Alcock's brother told the landlord that he needed to get a proper orchestra the next time. He told the landlord that he was going to have one after he won the next election."

"It was all negative?"

"No, a couple complimented the landlord for his charitable work. I think it was insulting, but I'm not sure."

"Is that the end of it?"

"No, his lordship said that Miss Elizabeth thought that we put in a remarkable effort, so he invited Michael back and told him that he wants us to do it again for the next election."

"Did Mam tell you she liked it?"

"Yeh, she told me that she was proud to see me up there, in front of all the fine ladies and gentlemen. Her hat was nice. Your da made a big fuss about it too."

"It was a fine night. Don't give it up. Don't give any of it up," Padraig said.

Kevin bent down and picked up a stone, and threw it at a tree. "So, when did you decide to go?" he said.

"Just before the concert this afternoon, Caesar told me to pack and join him in the morning. He told me that if I was ready to go with him, he wouldn't charge me anything. All he's asking is that I help load some cargo onto some ships. This is my chance. I mean I'm never going to be able to afford to get out of here. If Da gets to keep his cottage, Liam will have it after he's gone, so there's nothing to keep me here."

"That's not true. There's…"

Padraig patted his shoulder and said, "Time will come and you'll have to decide what you're going to do. You know, working with Sevens is a good idea. Find out what he can teach you. I don't know what else to tell you. I just know this is my time to go."

"But you might die," said Kevin as he slowed his pace.

"If I stayed here, that could happen anyway."

Kevin stopped, and he didn't know what to say. He had so much to say but didn't know how. He understood it was right for Padraig—but it was wrong for him.

"I'll miss you," he whispered and turned and ran home. He didn't see him that night, and he didn't go to see him leave in the morning. He did, however, remember someone patting his shoulder when he was half-asleep in the early morning.

Liam saw him that night. He and his parents watched the carriage leave in the morning. After Padraig was gone, Liam and his mam continually repeated how much they missed him. Liam's father kept to himself at nights, drinking whisky.

A couple of evenings later, Jimmy and Kevin stood in front of the Walsh cottage. It was starting to get dark.

"That wasn't much of a concert we had," said Jimmy.

"Wish Anty was there to hear it. I asked her, but she didn't come."

"Possible her aunt didn't let her," Jimmy said.

"Maybe."

"Is that why you didn't use Mr. Alcock's fiddle? I've never seen you take it out of the case."

"He wasn't there."

"Who?" asked Jimmy.

"Mr. Alcock. He was supposed to be there."

"And Anty?" asked Jimmy.

"Her too," said Kevin as he wiped the top of his nose.

"That Caesar was a real fool, wasn't he?" asked Kevin as he stood straighter. "He talked through most of it, and when we were done, they gave us a cup of tea and sent us away. I mean, really, why do it all?"

"John Colclough was upset that his brother told him that he wasn't staying and he didn't want to let him talk to anyone about it."

"That was strange. Anyway, it's a better place without the landlord's brother if you ask me," said Kevin.

Liam came out of the cottage to join them.

"That Caesar is definitely a fool," said Liam.

"Vessey's Caesar does whatever and goes wherever he pleases," said

Jimmy. "I overheard him tell Mr. Stewart a funny story that happened a week before the concert. You remember William Alcock?"

"Yeh, John's lady friend's brother."

"He started screaming at John when he saw him talking to a woman that wasn't his sister. It was at a party, but not the one we were at yesterday. Anyways, he saw him again at an inn with another woman, and he slugged him."

"It must have hurt," said Liam.

"Well, John was drunk and seemed to have forgotten everything, but his brother teased him about it for days."

"Then what happened?" asked Kevin.

"Well, the next day John started bawling that Miss Alcock's friend was going to leave him," said Jimmy. "He sounded awful. The way his brother told it, he sounded like a girl."

"Maybe he was still drunk?"

"Well, he definitely sounded sick. He kept repeating, 'I'm doomed. I'm doomed.'"

"Sounds sick alright," said Kevin.

"Yeh, that's really funny. Ha, ha, ha," Liam said sarcastically.

"What's up?" asked Kevin.

"If it wasn't for him, Padraig wouldn't have gone," said Liam. "He's a stupid fool."

"Caesar?" asked Kevin.

"Padraig and Caesar—both of them."

So Padraig is going to join the French in order to fight the English?" asked Jimmy.

"yeh, but the damned French killed the Pope.

Why isn't he going to fight for the Spanish or something?" asked Jimmy. "Doesn't speak Spanish maybe?"

"He knows a few words of French," said Kevin. "I think he's chosen the French because Caesar knows people there."

"I saw Caesar showing Padraig how to sword fight," said Jimmy.

"Why doesn't Caesar go and die?" said Liam.

Neither Kevin nor Jimmy answered him.

After Jimmy left, the Walshes had supper. Liam and Kevin didn't speak much. Liam left early, and his mother followed him.

Kevin stared at his soup, while Mr. Walsh took a puff from his pipe.

"It was a stupid idea," said Kevin.

Mr. Walsh didn't say anything and seemed to ignore him.

"Why didn't you tell him he had to stay?"

"I did."

"When?"

"Before the concert. We almost came to blows," replied Mr. Walsh.

"Oh," said Kevin as he started sipping his soup.

"I told him he was going to get himself killed, but he wouldn't listen. The talk didn't go well."

"Why was that man at Monart House telling you that they're looking for you?"

"What? What are you talking about?"

"The Scallans got killed, and he seemed to think you were involved."

Mr. Walsh looked at the door nervously. "Don't ever say that. Not even in jest. You know what the sheriff would do? And boy, you've got it all wrong." He gave the door another look.

"He said that before they died they saw you, and—I know you didn't like Mr. Scallans," said Kevin.

"You've got it mixed up. Danny Scallan borrowed money from me, but I didn't hate him. He wasn't paying me back, but it was because the landlord was squeezing him like me. Punching him wouldn't have helped. I was desperate at the time and I did go see him. He told me that, like me, he was afraid of losing the farm. We ended up sharing a drink by the side of the road to drown our sorrows." He looked away.

"You didn't want Mrs. Walsh to know."

Mr. Walsh nodded.

"I don't know what he was talking about. It was a terrible thing that happened to them. Whatever killed Thomas Brien must have done the same thing to them. It kind of scared me, and I felt that it was best for all of us to get out of there. There's something terrible out there. Whatever it is I pray it stays far away." He blew out his pipe and put it away. As he got up, he said, "I'm going to get some air."

Kevin wasn't sure what to believe. The story didn't sound right. He could imagine a beast attacking someone in a forest, but doubted it would attack people in a small cottage. Besides, Mr. Walsh still looked nervous. He wondered if there was more to the story that he wasn't telling him.

He took some more soup from the pot.

⤺◉

"Nick, come to bed," complained Judith Walsh. "It's cold. I need you."

She didn't hear him say anything. She left the bedroom and heard her husband gnawing on his pipe. The hearth fire wasn't lit, so it was cold and dark. She embraced him and kissed his ear, and draped a blanket over him.

"What are you thinking about?" she asked.

"It happened so fast. There was a party, and then his Lordship and Padraig left the next morning. Padraig's so impulsive. I know he's been talking about leaving for a long time, but he doesn't listen. He wasn't thinking. If I had more, time, maybe I could have found a way to make him stay." Nick held onto his pipe even though it wasn't lit. "And Padraig and Kevin really didn't say goodbye to one another. It was a bad thing. I think it was a terrible thing."

"Yes, they did. I saw them give each other a hug when he left," Judith said.

"Not really. Neither of them really talked about it. It's hard for Liam but Kevin depended on him more and Padraig feels responsible. His lordship left in the same fashion. His brother threw a party and then his brother left."

"Boys are like that," Judith said. "When they get something in their head, they just go for it. When they see something, they take it." She was beginning to shiver.

Nick bit on his pipe again. "Kevin has never heard from his father and brothers in all this time. They are all gone and he'll never know what happened. Dear Lord. I know how he feels. We're never going to see or hear from Padraig again. He'll be an enemy of the crown and Ireland. Judith, I tell you it's a terrible, terrible thing."

"Nick Walsh, don't talk like that. Come to bed now. It's late, and it's cold."

Worried Looks

Kevin lay on his back with his head propped on his arms over the roll of his wool pullover. The hill had a gentle slope that allowed them to watch the full of the sky and the spread of Bannow Bay. The mid-April sun warmed as thin strands of white clouds seemed to hover in a sky full of blue.

"You know, over there—that's the land of St. Kevin," he heard Anty say.

He looked up and saw her looking down at him. She lay down beside him, with her head against her crossed arms.

"Where?" Kevin said.

"There, to the left," she said.

All he saw was a road leading to some trees and fields.

"What did he do?"

"He took care of the wild animals—deer, boar, wolves, and the birds. Sometimes they'd come to him to be safe."

"Are you an animal?" he asked.

She rolled over and made her fingers like claws and roared like a lion.

"I'll take care of you, I suppose," said Kevin. "Does that mean I feed you grass?"

"No. I'd like some fine things."

"Then I'll find you fine things."

She lay back down and, like Kevin, she grabbed a strand of hay and put into her mouth.

"Where's your chaperone?"

"It's Mrs. Jeffers. She's with her daughter, around the bend."

"So this is your moment of freedom," Kevin said and grinned.

"It's a sad thing that John Colclough lost his brother Caesar again," she said. "But then again, you'd think his brother in France would have more sense. I mean they put him in prison once. Why wait around Paris and let them do it again? Now really."

"Last year, when he was here, he told Jimmy that he was coming back."

"So you talked to him?"

"It was Padraig, actually. He asked him loads of questions about when he was in the army. He got him going, and at one point Padraig and Jimmy beat him back in a stick fight and managed to jab him, but he got both of them in a return attack. His brother came out and saw them fighting, but didn't interfere. After that, Caesar taught them how to use their weapons. If Napoleon tries to cut him up, I think he'll probably get a good fight."

"Oh. It's so sad."

"What?"

"Him being locked in jail. Maybe they'll hang him or chop off his head. Have you ever seen someone get hung?"

"No, but I know people that have."

"People here were burnt. Did you ever see someone that was burnt?"

"Well, maybe. I don't know. Some memories aren't clear. I do remember seeing dead people though."

"What did they look like?"

"They were just dead. They just looked dead, and it was like there was no-one there. I'd rather not think about it. It can give you nightmares. You see people plodding around but then there's no-one. It's like they are going to take you and you don't want to go."

"What do you think John Colclough will do?"

"What do you mean?"

"He wants to help his brother, surely?"

"He'll probably want to work us harder and have us fix more things. That's all, I bet."

She rolled and kissed him on the lips.

"Why'd you go and do that?"

She got up and started to walk down the hill. "I've got to go," she said.

Fifteen-year-old Kevin was dazed. It was like she slapped his stomach. He was totally unprepared. He didn't know what to think. He watched seventeen-year-old Anty disappear into the trees, and then he sat up and watched the tide roll in.

On the next evening, the tutor left Kevin and Samuel Boyse alone in the courtyard while he gave voice lessons to the girls inside. Of the original six girls, only three had continued with the training sessions. Jimmy and Richard had also stopped coming to the practices.

Kevin kept on with it because Mrs. Walsh wanted him to. He had an image of her smiling and wearing that new hat of hers and was determined to play at the next concert. He fingered through his sheet music to see if Michael had brought anything new.

"Leave Anty alone," ordered Samuel.

"What?" asked Kevin. He was caught off guard. He replied with, "I'll talk to whoever and whenever I please. Go feck off. What's she to you?"

Samuel ignored him and started practising scales.

Kevin moved away from him towards the opposite wall and played a different run of scales.

Samuel started playing a marching song for King William. Kevin started playing a traditional Brian Boru marching song. Each played louder and kept spinning into other songs.

John Colclough came out to the courtyard and said, "Lord, it sounds like cats fighting out here. Samuel, King William would be twisting in his grave, and Kevin, your rebels sound like gypsies drowning in mud. For the time being, learn ***The French Retreat.*** It might convince the French to leave us alone. You can have your differences but learn your art. Work harder."

He glared at each of them and warned, "So long as Elizabeth is amused with your music, I will keep her entertained but understand that I had better start seeing results."

Michael started nervously tapping at Kevin's music stand.

Kevin gave him a quizzical look.

"The other page," Michael ordered, and pointed at the sheet music.

John Colclough stepped away, but came back and said, "And Kevin, do what you can to get Jimmy back here."

Two evenings later, Kevin gave the Finn cottage door a light knock.

"Hello, Mrs. Finn. Would Anty be home?"

"Wait here, please," she said.

He backed away from the door. Anty came out, but her aunt called her back in. Her aunt poked out, to tell Kevin she would be out in a minute.

Anty came out again with a stool and some knitting.

"We have to go over there," she said, and pointed to a line of trees alongside the front yard. She sat on the stool and Kevin sat on the ground. Kevin noticed that Anty's aunt sat down on a chair next to the front door and was also knitting.

"Maybe I should get a log or something," Kevin said.

"Why are you going to do that?" she said.

"Whatever. So what am I supposed to do?"

"What do you mean? You do what you always do."

"So, I watch you knit?"

"Unless you want to do it."

"Me? What do I know about knitting?"

"That explains why your jacket is still ripped, and what about your shoe?" she said and pointed at it.

"Shoes are different."

"Is that what you're going to say when it comes apart? You'll have no stockings because it's not sewn and you'll have a bare foot because there's no shoe."

"I was going to get some help from Mr. Stewart."

"Does he do shoes?"

"He knows leather. There's always a thing to learn, I guess. What does your aunt think we're going to do?"

"Some boys have a way about them?"

"How's that?"

"Well… maybe you should just sit there and look like you're saying your prayers and I'll get this done."

"Maybe I could fix something."

"It's Sunday. You could always talk to my aunt."

"Talk to her and say what?"

"Then I'll sit here and pretend to say my prayers."

"Right."

"You finished the abbey yet?"

"We've just done the roof and worked around the top. It'll take forever to fix it all. We've still got more to do on the flour mill. The landlord wants us to get on with the wall for his flower garden. He wants to impress Miss Alcock."

"Would you build me a flower garden?"

"I'd have to have somewhere to put it, and even if I get a cottage, there's not going to be much space. Mr. Sevens tells me that people in America have lots of land. He says they have so much land that anyone can live like his lordship."

"Do you think that's true?"

"I don't know. Maybe not. I mean, he hasn't been there. I'm not sure who to ask for sure, but I'll find out." Kevin looked up at her and wrapped his arms around his knees as he tried to figure out what to say next.

"Do you remember running up Cloroge More?" Kevin asked.

"I remember you falling into the water."

"I did not."

"Yes, you did," she said, and laughed.

"Do you remember looking for your da?"

"No."

"Do you remember old Mr. Kavanagh?"

"Yes."

"He died."

"I know. You told me that someone killed him," she said as she looked away.

"Do you ever think of walking up to Stua Laighean?"

"No. I don't think about a lot of things."

"The Jordans are gone. The Murphys and Nevilles were chased off by the landlord. And if your sister…"

"Tarnation," Anty said as she made a mistake in her knitting. "Ahh," she groaned as she raised it up with the intent of throwing at the ground. She stopped, looked at her aunt and with reserve placed it on the ground beside her.

"It's pretty quiet back at my old house," said Kevin.

"Frightfully so I'd expect," she said, as she crossed her legs away from him. "You moved from there, though."

"The Walshes weren't far away, but they were in another parish."

She looked away.

Kevin wasn't sure if she was looking for birds or what.

"Don't remember it much anymore. It seems like so long ago," she said.

Kevin saw her aunt staring at them and didn't know what she was thinking. He felt uncomfortable.

Anty got out of her chair, so Kevin got up as well.

He stared at the preying eyes of her aunt, and said, "I guess I should be going. Some others have asked me to join them for a game of Hurling." He was lying, but he didn't know what else to say. He didn't know what she was thinking.

He stared at the outline of her breasts and the shape of her. Her hair wasn't bound up in a ponytail like it had been when she was a child. It was tucked in a bun at the back. The hair was long, wavy, wild and unkempt at the sides, but carefully trimmed at her forehead.

He thought she was going to hug him, but she crossed her arms. Kevin looked at the ground and kicked it. "I suppose I should go," he said. He felt nervous and confused. Something about her made him feel threatened, embarrassed, but curious. It wasn't like the way it used to be.

"A lot of bad things happened," he said as he looked at her chair.

She picked up her knitting and brushed off her dress, although nothing was on it.

"Goodbye, Mrs. Finn. Good to meet you again," he yelled as he waved.

To Anty, he said, "I'll see you again, but I better go." He intended to leave but without thinking about it stepped forward and gave her a long, tight bear hug. "I'm glad to see you," he said, quickly let her go and ran fast and far away from her. Something in him felt out of control. It was as if a beast was going to tackle him. To run fast and far away seemed to make so much sense, but he stopped to look back and smiled.

A couple of weeks later, in May, Kevin and Liam hauled stone to others who were repairing a wall next to Mr. Sevens forge. Mr. Sevens was talking to Nick Walsh and Mr. Thornton.

Mr. Sevens turned and said, "Kevin, I have some bad news. Mr.

Colclough has cancelled the concert.

"It's a shame because Judith and I were so looking forward to it," Mr. Walsh said.

"So like that lot, isn't it? Give something one minute and take it away the next," said Liam. "No skin off them."

"Mr. Sevens, is he in trouble?" asked Kevin"

"No, he seems to be doing quite well. He's making good investments, and he's even opening a bank. And from what I understand, he's all but won his brother a seat in the English Parliament.

"It's that cousin of his, I'll bet," said old Anthony Thornton.

"You mean that bastard Adam's Caesar?" said Liam.

"Right you are," said old Anthony Thornton. "Our landlord's father Vessey, was a really terrible businessman.

"Adam's Caesar was the one managing the paperwork for re-mortgaging the abbey. Most of it was borderline fraudulent, and the rest was downright illegal. It is well known that Vessey used most of the loans to support his womanizing ways and long list of bastard children. While the landlord's father was alive, John and his mother didn't benefit from any of it. He's spent years sorting out the mess, and I've heard his business associates brag that everything seemed to be organized and on the right trajectory."

"What's going on here? How come the wall isn't getting built?" asked Mr. Stewart.

"I was just telling Kevin, that you told me that the concert is cancelled. They want to know why?"

"I saw Mr. Kennedy sharing a drink with Mr. Colclough in the backyard in the middle of the day. Something isn't quite right. is it?" said Liam.

Mr. Stewart folded his arms and looked back at the abbey. "Well, I suppose it will all come out in good time. The fact is, Napoleon's troops locked John's brother up again. Someone informed the French that he's an English spy."

"Adam's Caesar?" asked Liam.

"That's what John believes," said Mr. Stewart.

"Adam's Caesar wants the abbey," said Anthony Thornton. "He's a low life criminal."

"His brother is Irish, for Lord's sake," said Mr. Stewart. "He speaks French fluently and has lived in France for more than a dozen years. It's incredible. No sooner did we find out that he was in jail again, Adam's Caesar put out the word that Tintern Abbey is insolvent and mismanaged, which—apart from his contribution, is untrue.

We know he is behind the incarceration because the ploy to smear the estate's management occurred before anyone else knew that the rightful owner of this property was locked up. John believes that the scoundrel may have kept some damaging and undisclosed financial information."

"So the concert is cancelled because his lordship believes that his cousin is going to steal the estate?"

"John's brother managed trading arrangements from Europe. John is sending Mr. Kennedy to calm our trading partners. An English war with Napoleon seems imminent, and our support for local businesses and egalitarian preferences are making the conservatives nervous. Mr. Colclough knows that knives are being drawn. It's time for some restraint."

"He believes that the property issue and the animosity might be distracting him from Adam's Caesar bigger purpose."

"Distraction from what?"

"Mr. Colclough is not sure," Mr. Stewart said. "I suggest you lads get that wall built. You wouldn't want his lordship to get someone else to do it."

A couple of months later, Mr. Sevens approached Mr. Stewart, who was feeding the horses, and said, "I've seen that the landlord has become nervous and argumentative. He's not been himself."

"He's preparing to run in the next election in November," Mr. Stewart replied.

"I don't want to appear simple, but he's already in government acting on his brother's behalf. Why would he drop this position and suffer the burden of another election?"

"His lordship found himself in an uncomfortable position. His brother Caesar never exactly gave him permission to have his name thrown into the political ring. John was sure he wouldn't have refused if he won."

"But?"

"Unfortunately Caesar didn't find out he was a member of the English Parliament until he was interrogated by French soldiers. He's in jail because they claimed he was an English spy. Obviously, he didn't take the news very well."

"His lordship feels partially responsible for him being there. Besides, his brother doesn't share many of his more liberal views."

"Is his brother aware of anything that transpired since the election?"

"He knows what John tells him in his letters."

"Very awkward indeed."

"What is more awkward is that Adam's Caesar and his associates have pressured Miss Alcock's brother, William, to run against him."

"Putting Miss Elizabeth between them puts her in an awful spot. No wonder he's distraught. Well, we'll keep him in our prayers for November, won't we?"

Liam, Kevin, the three Carley brothers and two of McCaffrey's carried stone for Nick Walsh and Anthony Thornton.

"When you have the lot of them piled there, I'll want the other loads brought farther up," said Mr. Walsh. "Anthony won't be doing your work for you."

After the youngest Carley boy threw a stone at the oldest McCaffery boy, he yelled, "Wasn't me, it was him," pointing at his brother. All the other boys, but one, dropped the stones they were carrying and started insulting each other. The one with the stone threatened to throw it.

Kevin started. Suddenly, there was a man in front of him. He was surrounded by a cacophony of screaming, swearing, animal-like boys. The man looked lost and confused.

"You don't look yourself," said Kevin as he backed away from the crazies running around them. "Don't mind them. They're just lunatics."

"Who's your friend?" yelled Liam, from behind Kevin.

When Kevin turned, he shooed Liam back. "Give us room, why don't yeh." As he walked past, he said, "You know Harry Keane. You saw him at the old cottage. He introduced me to his lordship." He turned back and said, "That's Liam. His da is the one building the wall over there."

Looking dizzy and not quite right, Mr. Keane said, "A word—Kevin, if I could."

"Certainly," replied Kevin. As they left the site of the walled garden, he thought, *Something else is coming. When he's around, there's always something bad.*

"You don't do well with crowds, do you?" said Kevin.

"I'd like to make this quick. The cousin of your landlord, Adam's Caesar of Duffry Hall, is setting a trap. John Colclough is going to meet some of William Alcock's voters, and a series of events have been arranged that will set him up as a traitor. The pretext will permit the court to have him and his brother hanged. This will have a disastrous effect on the local balance of power. Someone has to warn him to stay away. Kevin, and don't tell him that you heard this was from me."

Liam came out from the entrance of the walled garden and whined, "Kevin, we're waiting for you. What are you doing?"

"Liam, go away, I'm busy," said Kevin and waved Liam away. To Harry he replied, "Mr. Colclough isn't here, but Jimmy Doyle and I can tell him."

Harry backed away and turned to go.

"Uh, thanks, …but uh, Harry, how do you know this? And what will I tell him?"

Harry didn't answer.

"You still plan to leave for America?" Kevin asked.

"Leaving soon. …going to Canada. It's far," he said.

Kevin didn't know anything about Canada, but he did know that you had to cross the ocean to get there.

The last time we spoke, he told me it was the Púca that was leaving. He's not acting right.

Kevin caught up to him and told him, "Harry, I've got to give you something."

"I really have to go," said Harry.

"No. Not yet Harry—I really need to give you something. It's a gift. It's in the forge and it's just over there."

Kevin ran to the forge and came back with his old leather coat. "Thomas Brien told me about an old Púca custom. In order for the Púca to leave, and be free, he needs to be appreciated and given a gift. This coat is for him to wear on a trip to the big city. I did what I could to dye it. Can you give it to him?"

"Big city?"

"Where-ever he wants to go."

The dazed look disappeared and was replaced with a wide smile. Something in him seemed to really light up, but in a strange way. Something about his face looked not quite right. It seemed to change shape in a small, almost imperceptible ways. It made Kevin feel like he had just looked at him cross-eyed.

Harry put the jacket on and silently walked briskly into the nearest line of trees.

Lord Almighty, Harry Keane… The Púca. He really is the Púca. Lord Almighty, I've really met the Púca. God in heaven above, He's the Púca! Who'd believe it? Denny, I hope by giving him the coat, I've done a good thing.

And good Lord. …why didn't the Púca tell me Anty was alive all those years ago? I mean if Mr. Kavanagh knew, he must have.

"Damn!"

Kevin returned to the work site. "Mr. Walsh, I have to get a really important message to Mr. Colclough."

"The landlord isn't here," replied Mr. Walsh. "He can wait, but this work can't. Help Liam with that load. You can go running around after we're finished."

Kevin stopped. *Maybe he's right,* he thought. *No, he's not. I can't wait. Harry told me that somebody wants to kill him.*

"You don't understand, Harry told me that they're going to try to kill him."

"What did you say?" said Mr. Walsh.

"Never mind," Kevin said. "I have to go." He turned and ran out to the estate entrance.

When he reached the Doyle cottage, he found Mrs. Doyle in the backyard working in the fields. She directed him to find Jimmy at a neighbour's. "You see that plot?" she said. "It is not that one. It is the one after the next. You can see his scruffy hair from here."

"Thanks, Mrs. Doyle," Kevin said.

"You boys keep practising and give us another concert. You hear?"

"Yes, Mam."

Kevin followed a path around the gardens. When he got close he yelled, "Hey mud, wake up."

"Hey, if it isn't knuckle face?"

"It's something we have to do. It's really, really important. You up for it?"

"Well, I'm supposed to be working. Old man Reynolds is going to go in a pissing rage if I leave."

"You have to. Mr. Walsh is the same, but I'm telling you, this is really important. Like if we don't do this, something really bad is going to happen. I'm coming here not just because you're my friend, but you talk to the landlord all the time."

Jimmy leaned on his shovel and said, "Kevin, go on and spit it out."

"Someone wants to kill him. We've got to tell him."

"What?"

"Mr. Reynolds is staring at you," said Kevin.

"God." Jimmy turned and looked back at Mr. Reynolds, and said, "Life and death stuff. You sure?"

"Yes," Kevin replied. "Well—don't just stand there."

Jimmy dropped his wooden spade and started walking fast, and asked, "Where are we going?"

"I'll tell you on the way."

When they reached the abbey servant's door, Jimmy started bashing it loudly.

"I'm coming, I'm coming," said Mr. Stewart. "Jimmy Doyle. What's so important? What's with the commotion?"

"John Colclough is going to die if we don't save him. Can we come in?"

"No," yelled James Kennedy from behind him. He moved Mr. Stewart out of the way and asked, "Now what is it, that you want to tell me?"

"I was told by a reliable source that someone is going to do him harm if he goes to visit the voters," said Kevin.

"Whose voters?" asked the steward.

"I don't know, but it's important he doesn't talk to them," said Kevin.

"Who told you this?"

"I can't say. It's personal," said Kevin.

"Boys, I know you're excited, but it sounds like you're making this up. Mr. Colclough is not even in Ireland."

"Then he shouldn't come back. I think, they're going to hang him."

"Who?"

"Well, they… You know."

"No, I don't. Boys, when he comes back I'll be sure to ask him if he wishes to pursue this further."

"James, are you sure? It does sound serious," said Mr. Stewart.

"Boys, it is the middle of the day and you're supposed to be working. I am sure your people are looking for you." He closed the door.

"Let's go to the stables," said Kevin.

"Why?"

"To get a horse."

"You know what they do to horse thieves," said Jimmy.

"Oh, yeh. Anty hinted at that," Kevin said, as he felt the side of his neck.

"I think we'd better walk," he said and he turned around and headed back to the main road.

"Kevin, where are you going?"

"To see Miss Elizabeth Alcock, of course."

"Oh, of course."

When they left the gate, Jimmy walked towards his cottage.

Kevin waved at him.

"What do you think you're doing?" asked Jimmy.

"I'm going to Wilton Castle. It's a long way from here. It will take most of the day to get there. Thanks for the help. I'll see you when I get back," Kevin said, and he kept walking. About ten minutes later he heard some shouting. When he looked back, he saw Jimmy waving as he ran. Kevin waited for him and, when Jimmy caught up, he whipped a stick around and yelled, "Parry, thrust and we're in, let's go."

Kevin stared at him and said, "I see you and I see trouble."

"March on and raise your swords, boys," responded Jimmy.

"Whatever you say," Kevin muttered.

"What were you doing back there?"

"Had to tell Mam not to worry."

"And you told her what?"

"We're stopping the evil lords from destroying the abbey."

"Maybe you should have said that a little slower or used more words."

"And what would you tell her?"

"Good point. Maybe we should have just kept going," said Kevin.

"Oh, I forgot, I grabbed some bread. Want some?" Jimmy said as took out some bread and offered it to him.

"Sure, mudface."

"Do you know where we're going?"

"Sort of."

"What do you mean, sort of? We should have asked somebody. I could have asked my mam."

"Well, we know they live in Wilton Castle and that it's near Enniscorthy."

"I just hope we're not going the wrong way."

"Have faith."

"How's Anty Kelly?"

"I called on her a couple of times, but she wasn't home. Each time her aunt doesn't say anything except goodbye. I don't think she likes me."

"Anty?"

"No. Her aunt."

"I think she's with that Samuel Boyse again," said Kevin. "I'd like to pulverize him." He took a swing at the air and said, "Bam".

Jimmy stared far off up the trail, hoping to change the subject.

"Do you think they are going to chase us?"

"Who?" asked Jimmy.

"Mr. Stewart and Mr. Kennedy."

"They didn't listen to us, so why would they chase us?" said Kevin. "Thanks for coming on this trip, Jimmy. Well, mudface, did I ever tell you that you remind me of my brother Seamus?"

"yeh."

"Well, I'm telling you again. I don't remember too much about him, but I do know he was a real swordsman—like you—and he loved adventure."

"Thanks Kevin. I never had a brother."

Kevin put his hand on his shoulder and told him, "Well, I guess you've got one now. Here's to a life of adventure." They smashed the sides of their fists and, in unison, yelled, "Aahay".

They walked for a long time. Most of the direction advice they got from people they met, wasn't very helpful. The sun started to sink beyond a horizon of tree-lined rolling hills to their left. It was starting to get chilly.

"If we can't convince Miss Elizabeth, then we've got a big problem," said Jimmy. "There's not going to be any way of saving him."

"I don't know what else we can do," said Kevin.

"Well, at least we could say we tried. That's more than the rest of them."

"Adam's Caesar is behind this and at the abbey, I learned that he had John's brother Caesar imprisoned as a spy," said Kevin. "If he gets away with this, then no-one at the abbey will be safe from him. These brothers may not be saints, but speaking from experience, their cousin is a bad fella."

In spite of some misdirection, the boys managed to reach Wilton Castle about an hour after sundown. They walked to the servants' entrance.

"Well, here's to see if we live or die," said Jimmy.

"Want to toss a penny?" said Kevin.

"Do you have one?"

"Nope," said Kevin.

"It was your idea. You go first."

Kevin knocked lightly on the door. No-one came. He used the knocker. He smashed it hard.

The door opened.

"We're here to speak with Miss Elizabeth Alcock," said Kevin.

"Tell her that it is a matter of life and death," added Jimmy.

"Yes, tell her that it is a matter of life and death, please." said Kevin.

The man opened the door wider. "Could you tell me who you are and what message it is that you wish to convey?"

"I'm Kevin, and he's Jimmy. We are tenants of Mr. John Colclough and I have it on good authority that someone is going to try to kill him."

"Would you wait a minute? I will be right back." The servant closed the door.

Twenty minutes later the servant returned with a steward. "Mister William Alcock has requested your presence. Follow me," he said. They followed the steward through a series of hallways.

The boys were greeted by a middle-aged gentleman who stood in the entrance to a drawing room. "Thank you, that will be all," he said. "My name is William Congreve Alcock. May I help you?"

"Is this Wilton Castle?" asked Kevin.

"Yes, it is," said William. "This is my father's house."

"Does Elizabeth Alcock live here?" asked Kevin.

"What of it? Anything you ask her, you can ask me. I am her brother."

Kevin looked at him and didn't trust him. "We need to speak to her about a Mr. John Colclough," he said. "He lives at Tintern Abbey. He is a good friend of hers."

"William, I would like to hear what they have to say," Elizabeth said as she walked down a staircase.

"I don't know. I believe that it would be appropriate for me to vet what these boys' intentions are."

"These boys have a message for me. If you care to listen, then you may. Don't infringe on my business. You can be a frightful bore."

"I didn't mean to..." William said as he stepped back from the doorway.

Lord, if this rich lady doesn't believe us, this is really going to go bad, isn't it? Kevin thought.

"Fine boys, what is it that concerns us? I believe I saw you boys play a recital at the abbey."

"Yes, Mam, that was me and Jimmy. I'm Kevin."

Elizabeth smiled, but she stood waiting.

He looked down at her shoes and scratched the back of his neck.

"Well, Kevin," said Jimmy.

Kevin looked at her and said, "I was told by someone that Adam's Caesar, of Duffry Hall, plans to do Mr. Colclough harm. When Mr. Colclough is supposed to interview some voters, he is going to be framed for something that's going to get him thrown into jail, and then they're going to hang him and his brother. Mr. Kennedy told us to wait until he returns, but that might be too late. Perhaps you know where he is and can warn him."

"He's in London, trying to get support from members of Parliament for the upcoming election," she said, and hesitated for a moment.

"Where is he supposed to be interviewing these voters?" she asked.

"I don't know. That is all that I know."

"Stupid story. They are just silly boys, Elizabeth," said William. "Don't bother yourself in this.”

“I am not blind. I know you know those terrible people. Don’t be a cad by trying to tell me what isn’t true. It is not becoming.”

“Miss Elizabeth, I also know that Adam’s Caesar—the barrister—is responsible for having Mr. Colclough’s brother put in prison,” said Kevin.

“How do you know this?” asked William.

“I just know it,” answered Kevin.

“I don’t know exactly where he is at the moment, but I am concerned,” said Elizabeth. “This is definitely an important matter. You boys took a very great risk in coming here. This is what we are going to do. William, have the servants find a place for these boys to sleep. And that will be enough, William. Leave us,” Elizabeth said. After her brother left, she got her maid to pack her bags and organize two coaches for the morning.

“One coach will be for me,” she said. “The other will be for the boys. We will be going to Tintern Abbey in the morning. Have the kitchen take care of our guests. I hope with Mr. Kennedy’s assistance we will reach John before he makes the crossing.”

“Parry, thrust and onward,” added Jimmy.

Kevin gave him an ugly frown and rolled his eyes to the side towards Miss Alcock. *You can’t say that in front of a girl, you clod,* he thought.

On the coach ride back to the abbey, Jimmy asked, “Are you really sure something is going to happen to Mr. Colclough?”

“We took most of the day to walk there. We spent the night at the Alcock’s house. You didn’t have a problem then, so why are you doubting me now?”

“Are you really sure Harry knows what he’s talking about?”

“Harry knows things. He had to travel a long way to tell it to me. He wouldn’t have shown up for no reason.”

“It’s just that I’ve got to explain it to my mam. She’s not going to like it that I ran off without a good reason."

"Well, now that you mention it, Harry Keane didn't look quite right in the head. Lord, I hate thinking about this. You're going to tell your mam, that we're saving the landlord from being murdered. If it doesn't happen, then like everyone else you're going to blame me. And God forbid that will be a terror of a bad day, so maybe you could give me more of those dried apples."

"I threw the last one at a dumb bird."

"Jimmy, Jimmy. How do we ever put up with yeh?" Kevin asked and laughed.

John Colclough returned to the abbey three weeks later. He entered the sitting room with Elizabeth Alcock by his side. James Kennedy took her coat and hat. Jimmy Doyle and Mr. Stewart had placed some luggage further down the hall. "Mr. Stewart, please have someone bring in some refreshments," John Colclough ordered.

"John, you should have someone fetch the Neal boy," said Elizabeth.

"Oh, yes, of course. Mr. Stewart, take care of that as well, please," John said. "We'll have a word with him outside."

Kevin was hauling stone from a wagon to a wall next to the mill, when he saw Mr. Stewart coming his way.

"Hello Kevin," said Mr. Stewart.

"How can I help?" Kevin asked as he brushed the dust off his hands.

"As you know, the messenger reached his lordship in time. He has just returned and would like to have a word with you. Take a minute to wash up and I'll let you in at the back entrance."

"You know that Mr. Kennedy told me that he was never going to let me work for Mr. Sevens again, for approaching Miss Alcock without his permission."

"It is not for me to say. If you're looking for a formal apology from him, I don't think you'll ever get one. He has to maintain order, you know. Hurry, please. His lordship is waiting."

"Nothing like helping someone out to get you a kick in the head..." Kevin muttered.

Kevin and Jimmy were escorted to a pair of wooden chairs behind the abbey by Mr. Kennedy. Miss Alcock sat in a more comfortable chair next to Mr. Colclough.

"James, please offer the boys some biscuits. They've earned it," John Colclough said.

Facing Elizabeth, he said, "I owe my life to the three of you. And of course, a special thanks to Mr. Kennedy and Mr. Stewart. Your messenger reached us just in time. After leaving London, I reached Wales and purchased my return trip to Wexford. If there was any further delay, I would have been on that ship and I probably wouldn't be addressing you today."

"What did they intend to do?" asked Elizabeth.

"I had arranged to meet property owners on your father's estate to explain why they should vote for us. Adam's Caesar was convinced that your brother was going to lose the support of his own constituents. He arranged for witnesses with impeccable credentials to provide sworn testimony that I had done things that would brand me as a traitor. Kevin was right. There was a plan to lock me in prison, and I could have been tried for treason. For this plot to work, I had to make an appearance at the estate.

Fortunately for me, they printed and signed their false accusations, in spite of the fact that I wasn't even in the country. If the situation wasn't so dangerous, we could consider it almost humorous."

"That was weeks ago, so what happened?" asked Elizabeth.

"My good friend, political advisor and business partner John McCord was with me on that trip. While in London, we heard some rumours about something that Lord Earl Annesley was planning something. He and Wexford landowners, like my cousin, were intimidated by my call in Parliament for promoting fair and open elections. John McCord stayed on in London to get more information while I headed home. While I was boarding my ship home, Annesley arranged for his cronies to arrest me."

Elizabeth with her hands on her lap, looked at him warmly and looked down. "I'm glad you're here," she said. "But if those men took you back to England when you were supposed to be here, wasn't it a bit difficult to explain why you were picked up in the first place?" She looked up at him and asked, "…and why didn't they hold you for longer?"

"Elizabeth, I am glad you aren't in his employ. What you say makes too much sense, but that is not what Adam's Caesar did. Prison was a vile place. I hope I shall never see it again. I understand now why my brother doesn't return my letters. Fortunately, Mr. McCord found me and, with the right connections and great expense managed to get me released and brought home. The information I had acquired from the messenger in Wales, was of great assistance in explaining my case to the court."

"We're glad you're back," said Jimmy. Thanks for picking me up in the coach on our way past."

"You lazy lout," whispered Kevin.

"Enough, boys. Drink your tea," said James Kennedy.

"Mr. Colclough, why isn't your brother talking to you?" Kevin asked.

"He is still in a French jail. He is not amused by his current living conditions.

"John, have you considered not running in this election?" asked Miss Alcock.

"Someone with means has to represent local interests. Besides, if I told them I was not going to run, they would interpret it as a sign of weakness. Since my cousin Caesar, the barrister, is involved in this I will be in a much stronger position to defend our assets in the political arena than out of it."

"They've already attempted to have you hanged, what more can we expect?" asked Mr. Kennedy.

"They are under the spotlight. They'll be careful about doing anything rash. They are at a disadvantage because we are watching them. James, until the election, I'll have you arrange for extra security precautions. My friend John McCord is looking for some capable bodyguards. James, when it's time for Elizabeth to return, I would like you to escort her and her coachmen home. Bring a horse and a pistol with you, please."

James Kennedy gave him an acknowledging nod.

"Kevin, Mr. Kennedy tells me that you wouldn't tell him who gave you the warning."

"He doesn't want people to know and wouldn't like it if I squealed."

"I would like to know who it is. I am in his favour and please keep Mr. Kennedy aware if he has more information to share with us. I can be very appreciative."

"Elizabeth, this will all be behind us after the election, don't worry," said John. "Maybe my brother will get released and then there will be two of us in London with political seats. That would really get them going, wouldn't it?"

Elizabeth Alcock put her teacup down, crossed her feet, and folded her arms.

"Boys, I see that you are finished your tea," said John Colclough. "Mr. Stewart, please bring out that special something, would you?"

Mr. Stewart came back and gave Jimmy Doyle a box.

"Jimmy, for your determination and fortitude I am giving you a real sword. But you can't keep it yet. You need to be a little older. I don't want you to kill anyone—even if it is someone that deserves it."

Jimmy Doyle took it out of the box and started waving it and thrusting.

"Jimmy, over there with it please," said John. "Kevin, you have been working with Sevens without getting paid. Starting tomorrow, we are going to increase your time, and I will make sure he starts giving you the right sort of training immediately. When he says you're ready, you'll be paid a fitting wage."

It took considerable effort not to glance triumphantly at James Kennedy. He stared at Mr. Colclough's feet instead.

"Thank you, young man, for doing what it took to do the right thing. I am deeply in your debt. Boys, I still expect you to continue with your music lessons. I would like to have another concert to celebrate my election. Mr. Kennedy, would you please take Jimmy's sword from him before he cuts himself and escort the boys out? Mr. Stewart, please provide them with more tea and cakes in the courtyard. Elizabeth and I have much to discuss."

After the boys left the abbey, Jimmy shouted, "Parry, thrust and touché."

—ꙮ—

Later that evening, Kevin sat with Mrs. Walsh in front of their cottage. When she asked him about his reward, Kevin said, "Maybe. I should have asked the landlord for more."

"And what would that be?"

"Not sure actually, but after finishing, I did ask for two more slices. Jimmy thought it wasn't much of a reward, but honestly, it was really good pie." He grinned from ear to ear and took another sip of her herbal tea.

—ꙮ—

Three days later Nick Walsh yelled, "Where's that boy? I need him here to work the wall. I can't work this way. Liam go find Anthony."

"But Da…"

"Liam. I will be fine. I'll make do until you return."

As Liam was leaving, he saw his father trying to slide a large stone up a tall ladder, and he muttered, "Kevin, you useless shit, where are you?"

"Sevens," shouted Mr. Stewart, as he approached the small forge.

"What is it?" Mr. Sevens replied, as he rearranged some pieces of metal in front of him.

"Get the boy to make us a buckle and pieces for a new hip strap harness. The one we have is beyond repair. How is the wheel coming along?"

"Mr. Stewart, Mr. Walsh wants me to help with the stonework for the abbey. Now that Padraig is gone,he depends on me," said Kevin.

"You should have thought about that before persuading him to let you work with the blacksmith.

"The harness and wheel assemblies have been damaged ever since something worrisome happened before we met you at the Mocurry Crossroads. There were odd things that day, and from what I hear, there are stranger stories today."

"Mr. Stewart, what could have caused that kind of damage?" asked Kevin. "And what stranger things are you talking about?"

"The wheel needs fixing. That's your priority," ordered Mr. Stewart. "Finish that for me today and I need the set of brackets you promised me."

"But I also have some work for Mr. White and Mr. Sutcliffe," said Kevin. "They are expecting it today."

"I don't want to hear complaints from either of you. His lordship depends on all of us. Anything else will have to wait."

"But—," interrupted Kevin.

"Sevens, take care of it," said Mr. Stewart. "Tell your assistant that if he doesn't like it here, he can leave and move on."

"So, what am I supposed to do?" asked Kevin.

"The landlord wants the carriage repaired more than he wants the stones cut," said Mr. Sevens.

"What does he mean there are stranger things?"

"I don't know," answered Mr. Sevens. "Let's get to work. Now that you're going to be here all day, there's a lot for you to learn. As long as you listen to what I say and do what I tell you, you shouldn't have any more problems with Mr. Kennedy."

"What?" asked Kevin. "I'll be right back. Just like you said. I'm explaining it to Mr. Walsh. Right back, I promise." Kevin ran away in a hurry.

"That boy has no sense. Trying to set things right will probably get him into more trouble than it's worth," muttered Mr. Sevens. He placed the metal into the fire.

Michael, the music tutor, placed music sheets in front of his students. They were arranged in a half circle with their backs to the abbey kitchen door.

"Busy at work?"

"No end to Mr. Walsh and Liam's complaints," answered Kevin.

"I mean that," said Jimmy as he pointed to a burn on Kevin's hand.

"Oh," said Kevin. "That I can handle; the rest I don't know. You changed your mind about being here?"

"No, my mam, she wouldn't let me…"

"It's the end of November and it's freezing," said Kevin. "His lordship came out and thanked us and he didn't even offer us a cup of tea."

"You can play in the barn with the horses," said the tutor.

"Anything's possible, right?" said Samuel Boyse with a snicker. He bragged and told us that maybe he'll have us play for the King of England."

The other two laughed.

"Bragging to his lady friend is all," said Samuel.

Michael said, "We don't have time for this. The concert is in two weeks."

"His lordship cancels. She bats her eyes, and…"

"Get to work," ordered Michael. "Kevin, are you going to use the fiddle that was given to you?"

"I don't know, maybe at the concert."

Michael shrugged and then palmed some of Colclough's cakes into his pocket.

"His grandfather sent a hurling team to fight against the crown, and they won. It was the Yellow Bellies."

"Jimmy, they'd kill us if we did that again. It's not going to happen," said Kevin. "It's a different time."

"Feck off," said Samuel.

"Why do you think you know Anty Kelly?" Kevin asked Samuel.

After placing his papers on a stand and placing his fiddle under his chin, he gave an obscene hand gesture and said, "…and you think you know Anastasia?"

Kevin wanted to smash him for using her formal name, but he hesitated. He wasn't sure if he had the right. He just waved him off, turned away and played the music that was set in front of him.

⁓❦⁓

That evening, Walter knocked at the door of the Caulfield cottage. Mrs. Caulfield answered the door and called, "Richard, Walter's here."

Richard tore a bite of bread from his hand as he rushed out. "What is it?" he asked. "I take it you're not looking for work?"

"Maybe, another hurling match with the lads," answered Walter as he nudged the brim of his cap back. He looked around and motioned for Richard to follow him away from the front door. "I heard something and I think you should know."

"With you, if it's not about a girl, it's about beating heads. So, what is it, Walter?"

"I heard from a reliable source that something terrible has been going on in the north-west of Wexford."

"Kevin, again is it?"

Walter looked back at the road, then he paced nervously around in a circle. "I heard from a reliable source that something terrible has been going on."

"Walter, there's always a terrible thing going on. What is it?"

"Where Kevin Neal is from, there was this Darby Brown. They found him with his guts torn out. There wasn't a single one of his family in the cottage that wasn't ripped to pieces."

"This reputable person wouldn't be Harold Wheeler, would he?"

Walter looked at the road. "It's just that I'm not sure I should be telling you this. It was a man who worked at Duffry Hall that told it to him. I didn't recognize him and I don't know who he is, but he sounded convincing. Harold told him that he knew that the same thing was done to Matthew Whelan and his family. They lived close to the Walshes."

"I just know that the man said that everyone in the parish was very nervous because none of the neighbours had heard anything out of the ordinary while their neighbours were being attacked. They're saying that only the Púca could have done this."

"Sounds like someone is releasing a pack of man-eating wild dogs," said Richard.

"Harold said that he heard people say that it's coming this way."

"If it's a ghost or a Púca or what, how could any of them know?"

"Harold sounded convinced. He said something like, 'it's going to put him out of business.'"

"Walter, I wouldn't go around repeating any of this."

Richard gave him a measured look and said, "Honestly, I think Wheeler is playing with you. He or someone wants you to pass on the story and get people worked up. I'm sure Samuel will tell you the same thing. I suggest—keeping it to yourself. So how about organizing a match? Just our lads—not the papists, if you like."

"I know I shouldn't have told you. It'll happen, and when it does, remember I told you so." As Walter walked away without turning back, he said, "Richard, I'll let you know."

"A bit touchy this evening isn't he?" muttered Richard

Stolen Passages

Kevin and Mrs. Walsh with Sevens and a small crowd of other tenants stood on the grass looking at a waiting coach in front of the abbey. It was the end of May. The trees and flowers were full of colour.

"The poor man," Mrs. Walsh said.

"What?" asked Kevin.

"He wins and six months later the government tell him he's got to do it all again."

"Where did you hear that?" asked Kevin.

"I heard Miss Elizabeth tell Mr. Colclough when I was talking to Nick in the garden," Mrs. Walsh said.

"Why isn't he here?"

"His lordship wants him working on the garden. It's for Miss Elizabeth. He's convinced he's going to win, and he wants to plant flowers when he comes back."

"…and if he doesn't win?"

She shrugged her shoulders. "Flowers look nice whether you win or not." She gave him a stare and added, "Don't you think?"

Kevin laughed. He looked at Mr. Molloy and mimicked his posture by grabbing the lapels of his jacket.

"My, you've grown," she said. "And you've done well for yourself, haven't you? A blacksmith, and a musician for his lordship. I'm impressed. And there's that friend of yours—Miss Kelly. You like her, don't you?"

Kevin lowered his arms, stared down at the ground away from the subject matter, and only managed to say in his defence, "Well…"

Mr. Sevens edged over and said, "Don't feed into him. He's got a swelled head, as it is."

Before Kevin could field a response, Mr. Kennedy called to Sevens from across the road, "Move over and make room." He moved onto the far side of Sevens.

"Are they moving in or out?" Sevens asked.

"A lady has to look presentable," added Mrs. Walsh.

"Good afternoon, Mrs. Walsh. Right you are," said Mr. Kennedy.

"They don't want to do this," said Sevens.

"They don't want to leave?" asked Kennedy.

"For him to win, her brother has to lose," said Sevens.

"He's a fool," said Kevin.

"Maybe, but the ones with money are on his side. None of them are supporting John this time," said Sevens.

"You don't think he has a chance?" asked Kevin.

"The lords aren't going to support him, but he's going to win," said Mr. Kennedy."

"How's that?"

"Dozens of freeholders—men that don't pay rent to the landlords, are supporting him," said Mr. Kennedy. "He's even going to win the votes from the freeholders on William Alcock's estates."

"It's quite a thing—a publicly supported candidate—It's unprecedented," said Mr. Sevens."

"Oh, he'll win, but don't go jumping up and down. It will probably get him killed," said Mr. Kennedy. "Mr. Colclough doesn't have any sense. Maybe that's why people like him. He does the unexpected."

"That's going to generate a terrible row in Parliament, isn't it?" asked Mrs. Walsh.

"Can't get much worse," said Mr. Kennedy. "At the end of the last session, he stood up in the English Parliament and demanded that this election needed to have an open and free vote.

I take it, that didn't go well," said Sevens. "I mean, the English wouldn't want to put up with an Irish man demanding anything, would they? They'll want him out and very far away."

"Locally, John Loftus, Lord Arthur Annesley—and Adam's Caesar of course—are very offended," said Mr. Kennedy. "Loftus and Annesley have taken a personal interest in William. They made sure he couldn't run for the family seat in Waterford. They are threatening to destroy him economically and personally if he doesn't do what he's told. I've heard Miss Elizabeth say that he's repeatedly threatened to leave the country."

"So why doesn't he?" asked Kevin.

"John Loftus is a Commissioner of the Irish Treasury," answered Sevens.

"Well, that is not quite right," Mr. Kennedy said. "He was last year. Now he is just the county governor."

"When he wins, I'm sure none of them would consider harming him," said Mrs. Walsh, and she put a hand on Kevin's shoulder.

"I hope not," said Mr. Kennedy as he wiped his hand across his jaw.

After the servants loaded the last of the luggage into the coach, Mr. Colclough escorted Miss Elizabeth to the crowd side of the coach. Before she stepped up, she pinned a pink wildflower over his heart. The crowd cheered and clapped. Once they settled inside, John Colclough waved his top hat out the window, Mr. Stewart flashed his whip, and the coach moved ahead to escort Miss Elizabeth home. The men chanted "Go maire hÉireann," while waving their hats, and the women showed their palms

Two nights before the election, Kevin was woken from a nightmare. Mr. Colclough had already left for Wexford town.

In the dream he had watched Mr. Stewart steer the coach out towards the front gate. Jimmy, his mother and the rest of the tenants were waving their goodbyes. As the dust in their wake disappeared into the trees, the monster was chasing them. It was moving with fire, had many arms and was cutting things down without mercy. He couldn't get back to sleep so he went out and took a piss.

The coach returned late on the day after the election. It didn't stop at the front door but continued to the back. Mr. Stewart didn't speak to Mr. Kennedy until he was on the ground. James stumbled to a knee but recovered quickly when he saw a crowd closing in.

"They killed him," he said. "He won, and they killed him."

Sevens and Mr. Walsh moved to the front and persuaded people to keep back.

After the body was carried onto the dining room table, Mr. Stewart tried to explain to Mr. Kennedy what had happened in Wexford town a couple of hours earlier.

The new High Sheriff, accompanied by an Army Captain and another man wearing a suit and top hat, demanded that John Colclough give up the controlling shares of his votes to his opponent.

They threatened him at the door of his mother's house, which was two short blocks from the Wexford court house. William Alcock remained in his coach on the street, as did a couple of parliamentarians. William refused to leave the coach. The challenge for a duel was made on his behalf by the sheriff.

A procession of carriages followed Mr. Stewart's lead away from John Colclough's mother's stone house on George Street. From the intersection with the muddy main road along the quay there was a clear view of the bridge, where Captain Kelly and John Colclough's cousin had lost their heads nine summers ago. The bridge stretched from the dockyard to the other side.

The procession of carriages followed the quay away from the mouth of the Slaney River to a pasture just out of town, where the duel was to take place.

Mr. Colclough wasn't given a chance to get his bearings. He was brought into formation without preparation.

"Good God, John," someone said. "All of Wexford's judges are here."

William Alcock was presented with black gloves and precision black-rimmed glasses and gloves by his instructor. Wexford's finest marksman tapped his back with a baton to make him straighten his stance. "Watch your footing, and remember your training," he ordered.

Mr. Stewart hurried over to John Colclough and clasped his hands and then on his shoulder to stop him from shaking. When he told him that, "William isn't half the man you are," his lordship looked frail and flush.

John Colclough put his hand on his friend's shoulder and then walked out to the field as he put his top hat on. The duellists lined up and their seconds loaded their pistols. The former sheriff, who had attended vote counting and threatened William Alcock's constituents if they voted for Mr. Colclough, proclaimed a change to the duelling rules. The duellists were ordered to fire at ten paces instead of the usual twelve.

Less than a month and a half after John Colclough had told the English Parliament that there should be an open and free vote in the new election, the ruling class had arranged to murder him. The bullet went straight through the pink flower pinned to his jacket. Mr. Stewart stood frozen in shock. He couldn't believe that Elizabeth's brother could ever have done such a thing.

—❦—

From these sad times, Lady Elizabeth became sickly. She remained reclusive and was reported to no longer be quite right in the head. Her brother William, similarly, succumbed to a lunatic's depression. Although he died four years after being moved into a lunatic asylum, he didn't lose his seat in Parliament. A revelation caused Jimmy to leave his mother and become a soldier. He would never return. While the owner of the abbey, Vessey's Caesar remained in prison for years, Adam's Caesar's scavengers sniffed around for the takings. Another ruinous infection had spread over the land.

After the burial of his lordship, Jimmy was called into the abbey. When he came out the front door, Kevin left the forge and ran after him.

"What did they want?"

Jimmy folded his arms, and told him him, "Leave me alone." He hurried toward the gate.

Kevin caught up and marched beside him, waiting for him to say something.

"Why didn't they tell me? They could have said something."

"What?" asked Kevin.

"Mr. Kennedy said he was my father."

"His lordship?"

"They told me now because me and my mam are in his will."

"So, what are you going to do?"

"I'm going to leave. I don't want to stay here. I've got some money for a military education, so I'll do that."

"So that's why Mr. Colclough paid for a tutor."

"The abbey is not going to pay for any more lessons. We won't see Michael anymore. Mr. Kennedy told me that you've got to pick up the fiddle that Mr. Alcock gave you. I wouldn't put that off."

"Why?"

"I saw Mr. Kennedy, Mr. Stewart and Mr. Sevens drinking Mr. Colclough's whisky."

"It's not like he'll miss it."

"But it's his brother that owns everything. Mr. Kennedy says he's going to run the place until he gets out of jail. I heard him telling the others not to worry. He said he was going to discuss this with John McCord who was Mr. Colclough's good friend and business associate. He also said that he was going to carry on managing the property paperwork and follow up with letter writing to John's brother. He said that he planned to economize by cutting back on coaches, and horses and the like, but repairs are going to continue. Before his lordship died, he promised to build a place for his mother at the abbey, and the frame is still missing a roof."

"You're leaving?" Kevin asked.

"Yeh, I suppose so. I don't want to be here."

Kevin walked with him to the gate in silence.

"I'm going to talk it over with my Mam. See you," said Jimmy. He walked alone to his mother's cottage.

Eighteen-year-old Anty Kelly pulled on her shawl. She moved it up a bit at her neck even though it was the middle of summer. She walked the road that passed the Jeffers' cottage. Eileen Jeffers kept near to hear more of the story.

"It just came over us and it was a terrible, frightful thing and I don't know what to do," said Anty.

"And…"

With her finger she pulled her shawl at her neck again as if it were too tight there. She then moved it from her neck and put over her head. It gave her the feeling like she was whispering under the cover of a blanket. "Well, we got talking. You know, that Samuel has definitely grown."

"He's filled out, he has. I noticed he's put on a little weight."

"He's not so little anymore, but I've still got a year on him," said Anty.

"Boys flower at different times and some are really late," said Eileen.

"So you're telling me that's not a problem with Samuel."

"We were talking behind the trees, then I, …then I remember his wet lips. Oh that was the second time."

"You were behind the trees?" Eileen asked.

"Well, he was mad at me for not watching him at the hurling match. He had a point. I mean, I don't see my future here. It's just that I looked into those pouty eyes of his. I didn't mean to hurt him. I meant to give him a gentle hug, but I felt those hands of his move down to the middle of my back and—foolish me—I moved closer. I could feel young Samuel come to life. I could feel the excitement as his hands moved to my hips."

"And then…" prompted Eileen.

Anty slipped the shawl from her head to the back, of her neck and pulled on it at the front. "I kissed the side of his cheek and he tried to find my mouth, but as I tried to avoid it, our knees started to buckle. I remember kneeling close to him on the grass with our foreheads touching and me staring at the first button of his shirt unfastened—It was a terrible thing. I could have been thrown out of heaven and damned for eternity."

"Aren't you exaggerating a little?" asked Eileen.

"Well I managed to pull it together and get out of there. But the next time was worse. I tasted his lips and as we rolled around on the grass it was like…"

"You didn't let him undo your buttons?" asked Eileen.

"Well one. Well, almost. But he put his hand in places that he shouldn't and I must admit I was curious as I put mine in places where they didn't belong either.

"Are you going to tell your priest?" asked Eileen.

"Tell him I'm up close with a Protestant?" Anty asked, and she hesitated with a perplexed look. "I suppose I'll have to. I'm really not looking forward to it. At least he's not going to force me to marry him."

"If the buttons slip, you might not have a choice."

"Holy mother…

"Well, the third time…"

"There was a third time?"

"Boys can be persistent.

"When he was on top of me, I said **Kevin** by accident," Anty said.

"Usually you'd bring up a name before you're in a compromised position."

"He stopped and backed away. He didn't take it very well," Anty said. "He tried to be nice about it but didn't stay long."

"You could have asked him about his music."

"I'd be swimming in deep waters way over my head," said Anty. "I'd only be coming up for air then and I'm sure I'd be doomed. Anyway, that didn't go well and I haven't seen him since."

"Well, I don't know what to tell you. Have you ever considered entering a monastery?"

"You're joking," replied Anty. "I don't think you even know the meaning of the word. I'm a farm girl. Handling the planting and managing the harvest is what we do."

"Well, seriously, is Samuel worth considering?"

"If I stay here, they'd want me to convert," said Anty. "I'm not going to put on a new hat because some fools tell me I have to? I'll follow my own fashion, thank you very much."

"Have people bothered you?"

"Sometimes," said Anty. "A couple of weeks ago there was a woman from the village, who I didn't recognize, called me a stupid papist. My aunt was with me and she lit into her like I've never seen anyone. She had her asking forgiveness to everyone before she left. It was quite something to see."

"What about Samuel's friends?"

"Oh, they're nice enough. A lot of people here are really set in their ways, though. Even if I did convert, I'd always be considered an outsider."

"Is that such a terrible thing?"

"Oh, I don't know," said Anty. "What I do know is that I have to get away from my aunt and I don't know how much longer I'll be able to stand being with her."

"Are you going to see Samuel again?"

"I'm afraid to." She slipped her shawl back over her head.

—❧—

"Hey, if it isn't Kevin Neal."

"Samuel Boyse," replied Kevin. "I take it you want something."

"I'm here to pick up some shoes for Mr. Sutherland. He asked for a buckle to get fixed."

"Can't you see I'm in the middle of something? I'll be a minute." Kevin was shaping a red hot metal piece with a hammer.

"You wish that was one of our boys," said Samuel. "Now that Colclough isn't here to protect you, you're going to learn what people think of you. It's time you people looked for another place. I'm just saying. I've heard stories about people doing terrible things."

"You mean like the Black Mob killing farmers above Stua Laighean's Newtownbarry pass?" said Kevin.

"What about your Corcoran Gang terrorizing around the mountains by New Ross?" said Samuel. "And what about the rebels of Killoughram Forest near Killann?—Babes in the Woods they're called."

"There' are a lot of crazies who can be quite spiteful. What about you?" said Kevin.

"What about you? Fool," replied Samuel.

"Boyse, if you weren't so full of yourself, Anty might give you the time of day. For some reason it's me she wants."

"It's on your head."

"It's not my head she wants," said Kevin.

"To hell with you!" said Samuel.

"Steal the blessing off the holy water, why don't you?" replied Kevin. "What the craic? Why would she want you? You're just a fart in the chapel."

"It's like talking to shit beaten up in a bucket," said Samuel.

"Hey, what's going on here?" asked Mr. Sevens as he came in the forge doorway.

"I am giving Boyse some shoes."

"Why doesn't he have them?"

"The ceiling strop had to be done just right. It's done."

"Well?" asked Sevens. "Well, why are you standing there with your mouth up your arse?" repeated Sevens. "Get him on his way. We have work to do. Samuel Boyse, I appreciate your business but keep your troubles out of here."

"Mr. Sutherland says it's on his account," said Samuel, and he gave a nod.

Sevens gave a wave of his hand.

Samuel said, "Good day," and left.

"You and that Anty Kelly are going to cost all of us. I'm just telling you," said Mr. Sevens. "Persuading your friends to smash heads because she's with the other one is something none of us can afford. Do you understand me?"

"Yeh. yeh. I hear it. Just leave it alone," complained Kevin. He undid his apron and walked away from the forge.

"And where are you going?" asked Sevens.

"I'm taking care of it," Kevin said as he walked away.

"Well, I didn't mean now," Sevens muttered.

When Kevin passed the Walsh cottage, he heard, "Where are you going in such a hurry?"

"Anty Kelly," he replied.

"You're not going like that." Mrs. Walsh said.

"Like what?"

"The look of you. Those hands and your face. She'll run from you and you'll never see her again."

"Is that true?" with an earnest look on his face.

"Go away. Get cleaned up. You've no sense."

"That's what Sevens says."

"Well, then he's right."

When Kevin came back out, he asked, "How's this."

"A bit better." She patted his hair back and fixed a button.

"Why in such a hurry in the middle of the day?"

"It's that Samuel Boyse."

"Well remember, she's always right."

"What?"

"Work with it. Maybe you'll learn something; And let her know you're listening to her."

"I always do."

"You? Right. And let her have her say. Be honest. Let her know she's important and lastly—"

"What's that?"

"She's always right."

"But you said that already."

"Good luck," Mrs. Walsh said as she hugged him "And tomorrow's another day," she added as she stepped away and laughed.

Rolling Tides

In the spring of the next year, seventeen-year-old Kevin helped Anty fill her baskets with fresh shellfish and seaweed. The tide was out. Anty noticed that he was lethargic and moping.

"What is it?" Anty asked. "Are you not awake yet?"

He stepped through the mud, threw up his arm, gestured with open hands as he said, "Well it's like—when I get close to something it gets taken away from me. I lost my family. I was close to Padraig and he left. There is no good reason why John Colclough had to die. He tried to be a good man. Jimmy was a fool. I understand he needed to leave, but I'll miss him."

"You still have the Walshes and…"

"And I have you?"

"You wish."

He ran after her along the narrow beach and tried to tickle her, but she was too fast. He returned to the basket he left in the mud. He continued picking up shellfish. He dug another clam out of the mud. He looked at a barnacle with something wiggling in it.

"What is it?" she asked.

"Oh, just a little something." He gave a hint of a smile.

She came over to look.

He picked her up and twirled around.

"No, don't. I don't want my dress muddy, it's so…"

He turned her, so her eyes were even with his. His right hand held her buttocks so her feet didn't touch the ground. His left held her lower back. As he let her slip down, he let her hips press against the fullness of his erection, secured by the embrace of his large blacksmith hands. When her feet touched the mud, his right hand slipped up her side and approached her breast as he playfully kissed her cheek.

"You know for the rest of it, they will kill you."

"Lord, Anty, you really know how to cut a man off." He slipped and fell on his backside into the mud.

As she laughed, she said, "Kevin Neal, keep the pants on or the hogs will be chomping on your balls."

"That's what I like about you, Anty. Right to what matters. The best parts, chomp, chomp—chop, chop. Fine, it's back to work."

"Why don't you swim to other side of the bay? I'll take the baskets to the Jeffers and get to you with the boat. Prepare a fire and collect some of this for us."

He stared at her with a jaw-dropped-look.

"Don't just stand there, we've got to fill the baskets first. The tides not going to stop for the likes of us."

"No, the tide is not going to stop for the likes of us," repeated Kevin, and he got up out of the mud.

When they were done, she put the staff on her shoulders and Kevin fixed the baskets hanging from it.

"You sure you don't want me to carry that home for you?"

"A mud drenched body with that sausage sticking out past your buttons. You're kidding, right?"

"I'll wait for you then," he said.

Kevin watched her approach the bridge. They had been alone on the beach.

He took off his clothes, rolled everything into his muddy pants, and tied the legs around his neck. The young man glanced back and saw her watching him from a distance.

He kept walking in the mud. Kevin had to go a long way out before the water was deep enough for swimming. The water got cold in the deeper parts and a current tried to push him off course. He liked the challenge. Kevin thought of how he wanted Anty. Lord, she wasn't a girl. She was fully a woman, and he felt fully a man. She wasn't far from twenty and he was seventeen and the spring was full of colour, health, sweetness and wonder. When he thought of her, he felt so alive, so full of power, desire, and hope. When he reached the other side and started walking into the shallows, he thought, *Lord, I'm hungry.*

Once Kevin reached the shore, he unrolled his clothes. Kevin took his pants and shirt back to the saltwater and washed the mud stains out. He hung them on the seaside of the tree so the sun and the wind could dry them. With a bit of flint he lit a covered fire and cooked shellfish in clam shells he had collected. As he ate them, he leaned against a tree and daydreamed, as his skin felt a gentle, sweet ocean breeze caress it. He eventually moved to the grass where he sprawled out and fell asleep.

He woke with a startle. Kevin thought he heard something. He got up but didn't see anyone. The trousers were dry enough, so he put them on.

Was I asleep for hours? he wondered. He looked at the far shore, where the sun was in the sky. *Possible,* he thought.

His shoes were still damp, so he didn't put them on.

She should have brought the boat over. Where is she? he wondered. He walked through the tree covered peninsula to the beach on the other side, so he could see the shore across the bay. He stepped into the calm water of the protected inlet.

He saw Anty, but she was far away from the shore in front of a line of trees. *What's she doing?"* he asked himself and started waving both arms.

It looked like she was waving him away.

"What the…" Kevin said as he scratched his head. He went back and got the rest of his clothes and a log. He stripped, rolled his clothes in his shirt and secured them to a branch on the log he dropped into the bay. As he flutter kicked his way back to the mainland, he noticed that Anty occasionally disappeared into the treeline. When she reappeared, she continued to flag him away. A line of horsemen riding out from the direction of the abbey followed the sound of a pistol shot. Kevin snagged his roll of clothes and held it under water. The strangers rode along the beach. Some had oak clubs. Some had swords. Kevin noticed that two of the swords were marked with blood.

Kevin, slipped down in the water, and moved close to the log with only one eye staring beyond the end of the log. He let the log float him towards the sea.

The riders were clearly looking for someone on the beach. Since they didn't find what they were looking for the men rode back from where they came.

After the riders disappeared Kevin hurried to reach Anty. Once he reached the beach, he quickly put his trousers on and ran barefoot towards the forest cover. Anty came to him and gave him a bear hug. "Why didn't you stay there? How could you be so stupid?"

"What? What are you talking about?"

"They're looking for you?" she said.

"How do you know?"

"I heard one of them say it. I heard people screaming."

"I wonder why they're looking for me. Did you see James Kennedy?"

"I heard Mr. Stewart tell them he wasn't here."

"You need to go back to where you were," Anty said.

"I have to make sure the Walshes are safe. I'd feel more confident if you went home." He put his soaked shirt and shoes on while they were talking.

"Kevin Neal, I am not going home."

"Anty, shh, they'll hear."

"I'm going where you're going."

Kevin scratched his head. "Fine. We'll follow the tree cover along the river until we get near the cottage."

He reached a place where he could make out the Walsh cottage.

Anty, who was next to him, touched his shoulder and warned, "They'll see you."

Kevin pulled his arm away. He saw Mrs. Walsh standing in front of the cottage entrance. A man with long, scraggly, black hair dismounted his horse. He yelled something and then threatened her with a short sword. He seemed to be distracted by something. *Maybe it's the others*, Kevin thought.

A body was sprawled in front of the cottage across from her. Mrs. Sutcliffe stared terror stricken. *That must be young George Sutcliffe,* Kevin thought. Mrs. Walsh pointed to the body.

"Kevin," said Anty.

"Not now," Kevin replied.

The horseman said something and then stabbed Judith Walsh hard in the chest.

Kevin froze. "No, no, no," he moaned. Kevin raced to the cover of the Sutcliffe cottage. When he came round to the front, he saw that the rider was on his way out of the front gate of the estate.

When Kevin reached Mrs. Walsh, he found Mrs. Sutcliffe kneeling over her body.

"She didn't tell them. I didn't tell them," Mrs. Sutcliffe said. "Both of them are gone. He killed my George."

"No. No," Kevin repeated. "Oh, my God." Others talked, but he wasn't hearing anything else.

Anty ran up behind him and meant to put a hand on his shoulder, but she pulled it back.

"It doesn't make any sense. Why did this happen? I should have been there," he said.

"And you would have been dead," said Anty.

"They would still have been alive."

"You can't look at it that way," Anty said.

Kevin wanted to touch Mrs. Walsh, but the cold, empty stare and blood made him hesitate. He knelt down and held her limp hand.

Mrs. Sutcliffe closed Mrs. Walsh's eyes.

Mrs. Molloy joined them. "After they killed my son, everyone left to get to the other side of the hill," she said. "I couldn't leave my boy. I hid in our cottage. Judith told that beast that her husband was dead and her children had migrated to America. After telling him that young George was you, he killed her."

Kevin stared at the circle of blood around George Sutcliffe's head and asked, "Mr. Walsh?"

Mrs. Sutcliffe shrugged.

He noticed that Anty was staring at something approaching from the direction of the abbey.

Kevin turned and, as he got up, he saw Liam running madly. His father and Mr. Stewart followed behind. Kevin backed away from Mrs. Walsh's body.

"No, mam," Liam screamed as he got close.

"Liam, she's gone," Mrs. Molloy said.

He bent down, grabbed her, and hugged her, as he repeated, "Mam no," again and again.

"This can't be," Mr. Walsh said. "This is not the way it's supposed to be." He put his hand on his son's shoulder.

Liam stood up and went over to Kevin and said, "They wanted you dead, but they killed my mother. Why?"

"I don't know?" Kevin replied.

Nick Walsh got up and said, "Kevin, I'm glad they didn't find you. Those monsters. They were the worst. They must have been from hell itself."

Anty put her hand on Kevin's shoulder, but he moved it off.

"If you move my hand off your shoulder again, I'll kick your arse, I will," she said.

He turned and hugged her tight and didn't mean to let go. "If something happened to you, I don't know what I'd do," he told her.

Mr. Stewart moved towards him and told him, "Whoever came for you thinks you're dead. If I had to guess, I'd say the Adam's Caesar knows you were the one that warned John Colclough."

"Mr. Stewart, the man that killed Mrs. Walsh believes that's Kevin Neal over there," Anty said as she pointed to George Sutcliffe's corpse.

"I'd suggest you keep your head down. Why don't you and Mr. Sutcliffe prepare some coffins. We know that Mrs. Walsh and young George are not the only ones that died to-day. See Sevens about the nails and I'll see what I can do about getting some good wood." Without waiting for an answer, Mr. Stewart tipped his hat and turned to confront a growing crowd.

A mob of tenants returning from the hills were blocking his path back to the abbey. A farmer screamed, "What's the abbey going to do to help us?"

"Give us room, and please have some respect for the dead," Mr. Stewart replied. "Loved ones need to be mourned and bodies prepared."

"What if they come back?" yelled another tenant.

"What happened this afternoon was despicable. I, like the rest of you, know that we need to protect ourselves, and I'd like to see the men that attacked us brought to justice.

"The crown won't touch the likes of them," yelled Mr. Molloy. "That's just talk."

"The abbey will have more to say about this once Mr. Kennedy has been apprised. We'll address this in the next couple of days. Now, please, let me through. We all have to get back to work."

A line opened up for him to pass, but grumbling continued.

"Mr. Stewart is right about the work," Anty said.

"The coffins, you mean?" Kevin asked. He saw Mr. Molloy, nod at him. "I guess we're committed." He noticed that Mr. Walsh had his hands in his coat pockets. He looked frozen.

Liam must hate me, Kevin thought.

"How are you feeling?" Anty asked.

"It's that damned Harry Keane! …telling me to warn John Colclough, William Alcock tells Caesar that I saved him and then this."

"You did stop them from killing his lordship," Anty said.

"The first time. Not the second time. It didn't work out."

"Oh, go on. You did some good," Anty said. "Life can be cruel and unforgiving, but you still keep living it."

"I don't know. I've got to go. I'll see you later."

"When?" she asked.

"Don't know. I can't stay here." As he turned away, he added, "I'm going back to the forge."

"You're such a bonehead," he heard her say.

"What?" he asked when he looked back.

"Nothing. Never mind," she said with her arms crossed. "Go on," she added and shooed him away.

Confused, he continued to walk towards the forge.

"But," he said, and when he turned, he saw that she was running away.

A couple of days after Mrs. Walsh's death, Kevin Neal crossed the bridge with the intention of finding Anty. Walter Glascott approached him from the other side of the river.

"Well, if it isn't that damn Neal. Aren't you supposed to be dead? They thought the old bitch was you."

Kevin took a run at him. Big Walter Glascott blocked a swing with an arm. Kevin swung around and pulled his arm and managed to make him stumble. An exchange of punches led to a wrestling match on the ground. When Kevin had him down, he punched Walter in the face again and again and again.

"You're the one that caused this," Walter said. "You thought you could stand up to the likes of Duffry Hall. He showed you, didn't he? You're the one that brought the Púca here."

"What the hell are you talking about?"

"The Browns and the Whelans—they died brutally."

"You're crazy," Kevin said, and he hit him again and again. "Glascott, stay away or I'll kill you," he said, and he ran because he was afraid of what he'd do if he stayed. Kevin raced across the bridge. He didn't stop until he was surrounded by open country fields and had no breath to spare. After straightening from being bent over, he could see that he was alone, and that made him think of Anty.

In one of her recent lectures she had told him, '*They left, and you didn't say a thing. Terrible things happen, and you pretend they don't. You just lock it away, but you know very well it all comes back. Maybe then it's too late to work things out.*'

When she said it, he didn't say a thing.

Kevin started walking.

"So what do you expect?" he told the air. "Padraig and Jimmy are gone. Mr. Kavanagh, I mean how can… It's too much. And Mrs… I remember her dying." Kevin paused "And you, the way you talk about your aunt. What's so terrible about it? It's really not about her is it? You're just describing yourself and…"

Kevin found himself almost running, so he slowed his pace. "Lord, I'd better find something else to say or she'll leave me for good. Poor Mrs. Walsh would have something good to say, wouldn't she?" He walked in quiet for what seemed a long time.

Behind the Finn cottage, he found Jacob Finn shovelling in the garden.

Before Kevin could ask anything, Mr. Finn told him, "She's not here."

"What?"

"She's gone."

"But…"

"Check with the Jeffers'. She's with Eileen. There's been a dust up but I'm sure we'll get it sorted. Now, if you don't mind, I've got to get this done."

"Uh, yes. I'll leave you to it, then," Kevin said as he scratched his head.

When he passed Richard Caulfield's cottage, he caught sight of Anty on the road coming his way. *She went to see Boyse*, he thought.

When they got close, Kevin asked her, "Why didn't you tell me you were moving?"

"You're acting crazy. You're like a little boy."

"Well, I…"

"Go away."

"Well, I just wanted to know where you were. I was worried."

"Why do you treat me so?"

"What? What do you mean?"

"Go away. I need to get away." She kept on walking past.

"You're right."

She turned around and asked, "What was that?"

"You're right. It felt like if I stayed in the same place, I'd lose you. I didn't know what to do."

"Kevin, sometimes you surprise me.

"You went to see Boyse, didn't you?"

She eyed him over and looked like she wasn't sure how to respond. "And what's it to you?"

"I'd rather you stayed with me."

"Aren't you supposed to be working at the forge?"

"I told Sevens that I was looking for you."

So where are you taking me?

"To the top of world, I guess," he said.

"And then?"

"One step at a time," he said.

She grabbed his hand and pointed him to the tree covered river valley that ran along the abbey to the bay. "We could do with a private place where we can talk."

Kevin squeezed her hand and so very much wanted to get to the last field.

When Kevin returned to the forge, he met James Kennedy by the stables.

"Sorry, I didn't see you sooner. My condolences, Kevin," said Mr. Kennedy. "The death of Judith Walsh was a vile, gruesome thing. Why were they looking for you?"

"It was Adam's Caesar. William Alcock told him. He heard me tell his sister that I knew Adam's Caesar arranged to jail John's brother."

"You're probably right. He might try to do the same to rest of us. I'll get Mr. Stewart to draw up an audit of our ammunition and weapons. We'll upgrade our provisions and defences."

"I heard that the abbey intends to move everyone."

"News gets around, doesn't it," he said as he brushed a hand across his nose. "It wasn't my idea. Vessey's Caesar, who's still in jail in France, in his letters is demanding that tenants on abbey grounds have to move. He wants to relocate everyone to the other side of the river. He's going to rebuild the village in Salt Mills. I wouldn't be concerned. It will take a long time before anything happens and other than having to walk a bit farther to the abbey I don't see a problem with it."

"You don't really believe that, do you?" asked Kevin.

Mr. Kennedy looked away from him and looked towards the bay. "Mr. Sevens is starting to have trouble with his hands, and I'd like you to take more of his workload. I've made arrangements for you to move into a small cottage near the forge, and I've recommended that Liam and his father move to another cottage as well."

"Thanks, Mr. Kennedy. I appreciate that."

"Kevin, for your gallantry in saving John Colclough the first time, I will order a tombstone for you. You can add your name along with Mrs. Walsh if you like. He tipped his hat and headed towards the servant's entrance of the abbey.

"Mr. Kennedy wants me to learn your secrets," Kevin said as he put on his leather apron.

"Does he?"

"You've problems with your hands, he says."

"It'll pass."

"Probably."

"How's Mr. Walsh?"

"Anthony is with him full time and since there's not a landlord around I don't expect there will be much of a rush to get things done."

"That's not what I meant."

"He's been drinking heavily. He's in a bad way."

"Anyway, boy, you've been watching long enough. See what you can do with this horseshoe. It's not about bashin'. There's a way about it."

"We should start making lots of pikes. They're going to need them."

"Focus on shaping iron first, boy, and get us better quality coal."

❧

Nick Walsh had difficulty sleeping that night. It was cold without her next to him. She wasn't there to stop him rolling on his back. He was now more aware of sounds like the wind and birds and insects that hadn't bothered him before. He got up and went outside.

Lord, it's dark. Not a light in the sky. It must be really late because there's no-one around, he thought. He went for a piss outside the door. Nick took a deep breath and went back to his bed, hoping he could get back to sleep. Once back on his hay mattress, he pulled up the blanket to protect him from a chill around his neck. He rolled over on his left side, and both hands held a grip onto the blanket as he focused on the image of his dear Judith. Nick was interrupted by the roll of a body against his back. He turned and the body was cut open and leaking, and Mr. Walsh heard a gasping voice say, "Da, run."

❧

The first light washed over his face. Kevin forced himself to open his eyes. "Ahhhhrg, he groaned and stretched his arms out wide. The young man went to a cold pot of water and splashed his face and naked body. Kevin grabbed a wad of dried bread and proceeded to get dressed while he was chomping on it. He went out in front of his cottage and took a piss, and then hurried off to the forge. The young man was eager to get to the forge before Mr. Sevens, so he could heat himself some gruel while he stoked the coal fire. By the time he got the fire started, the sun had risen and the morning had begun.

"I see you're ready," said Mr. Sevens as he entered the forge. "Kevin give it some more air. Ease up on the coal. I don't want the abbey on us because we waste. Watch where you stand. And don't fart because you'll burn us into the next life."

"Good morning, Mr. Sevens."

"I see you've had your gruel without me."

"I was starving. I would have fallen over by the time you showed up."

"Fair enough. Just make sure the forge is set by the time I show up, that's all. Let's see if you can remember from yesterday. Let's see if you don't mess up the horseshoes."

When the bar was hot enough, Kevin pulled it from the coal fire. He turned and shaped it with respectful admiration of fire's almost magical transforming properties.

Michael Dwyer, a labourer, came to the door. "Kevin, have you seen Mr. Walsh or his son this morning?"

"No. I'm kind of busy right now," replied Kevin.

"There's a bunch of us and he hasn't told us what we are supposed to be doing this morning. Do you know where he is?"

Kevin gave a muffled groan when the bent steel was turning as he expected it to. "He lost his wife," he replied. "Maybe he's drowning in whisky. Then again, Liam should have shown up. Go see if he's sleeping in —and …Christ almighty," Kevin shouted when he lost a firm hold on his work.

"Stick with it, boy, you can save it," said Mr. Sevens. "Keep the thing moving. The fire can be your friend. Understand it. Firm legs, strong back —boy. It will be a long day and the abbey has high expectations of us." Sevens inspected his work and said, "You didn't do too bad. We'll keep it.

Into the water with that one."

When Kevin was done, he raised the horseshoe in the air with his tongs to show him and he quietly moved on to the next one.

—◦◦◦—

"Kevin," said David Sutcliffe from the counter. He lived near the Walsh cottage.

Kevin was finishing up straightening a metal bracket. "David, I am in the middle of something. Mr. Sevens?"

"Is there something I can help you with?" asked Mr. Sevens. "How about a pike?"

"Kevin, Nick and Liam have been murdered."

"What did you say?" asked Kevin.

Mr. Sevens yelled, "Boy, go!" and he elbowed him out of the way while he grabbed tongs from his hand and attempted to rescue the reshaping of the bracket.

Kevin reached David, as they passed the front of the abbey. "Are you sure?" asked Kevin.

"That they're dead? Yes. It's them. The site was horrendous. What came at them was monstrous. Something literally tore them apart. No man would do such a thing. Mad dogs perhaps. Some terrible beast, maybe."

"Why do you say that?" asked Kevin.

"They were torn open and their insides were scattered all over. I don't know if you should see this, Kevin. It is not the way you should remember your people."

"Poor Nick, poor Liam…" Kevin left him and ran as fast as he could to the Walshes' cottage.

There was a crowd of people around. Mrs. Sutcliffe met Kevin at the door of the Walsh cottage and said, "Kevin, I don't think you should see this. It's terrible."

"Sorry, Mrs. Sutcliffe, but I have to see for myself. I need to know what was done to them."

He saw Mrs. Sutcliffe's daughters cleaning the bodies next to the hearth. Her sister was blowing on some kindling in order to light a fire to boil a pot of water. When he entered the cottage, the smell was nauseating. The front of both bodies had been cut open, and the internal organs were being collected from the hard dirt floor and placed onto a pile. "Good God," sighed Kevin. *It's such a horrendous thing the girls have to do*, he thought. Kevin couldn't bear the sight. He went outside, bent over, and threw up. *Holy mother of God,* he thought.

Kevin tried to pull himself together, and he stood up. *I can do this. I need to know what did this.* He turned and prepared to walk back in but felt he was going to heave again. The young man turned and took a big, deep breath. He felt like running away. The young man took another deep breath and walked back in.

"What in the name of God happened here?" Kevin asked young Annie Sutcliffe.

"Kevin, come outside and I'll tell you," said her mother. She stared at him from outside the open door. "Kevin, please," she said.

"We dragged them near the fire so we could clean them." Once outside she said, "I'm so very sorry Kevin for your loss. They were hardworking, good spirited people. It's a terrible thing."

The smell in there is wretched. The men are going to carry them out and the rest of the preparation will be done outside on a table."

Mr. Walsh helped us prepare my son. I thought it was fitting that we set things right for him.

"In the name of the Holy Trinity, what happened here?" came from behind Kevin.

"Mr. Kennedy, I don't know," said Kevin.

James Kennedy slipped into the Walsh cottage.

"Mrs. Sutcliffe did you hear anything out of the ordinary last night?" asked Kevin.

"No. My husband asked around and no-one heard anything. What could have done this without waking any of us up? It's terrifying."

"Kevin," said James Kennedy after he came back out of the cottage.

"I have work to do, Kevin," said Mrs. Sutcliffe. "I have to leave you." She took his hand and gave him a hug, and then she said, "You've suffered a terrible a shock, but dear, please know that we will do everything that has to be done here."

Mr. Kennedy waited until she left to tell Kevin, "I took a walk around the cottage, including the bedroom. There was blood on the stone walls and the dirt floor. Sorry, I don't mean to be insensitive, but I've never seen anything like this. Kevin, I have no idea what could do something like this."

"David said that he thought it was a wild animal."

"It would have taken a pack of animals to do this," said James. "Animals kill to eat, and I don't see any evidence they ate anything," said James. "Mrs. Sutcliffe is right. They have things well in hand. Go dig the graves, and I'll get someone to make the coffins. I don't think you should remember them this way."

Another lady who was one of their neighbours approached him and said, "James is right, Kevin. Go do some digging. You need to work things out. The shroud and preparations for the Mass are being taken care of. Go."

When Kevin started to walk back towards the abbey, he was hit by the horror of what had happened. The young man headed into the forest covered river valley behind the forge. Kevin slipped, and only a hand on a tree held him in place. He let go and slid down the side of the slope.

Kevin had barely adapted to the loss of Mrs. Walsh, and now the rest of his second family were brutally torn away from him. He curled up, couldn't breathe and started shaking. A memory of his dying sister, Kathleen being attacked by a monster, seemed to come from nowhere.

Kevin eventually rolled to a kneeling position with his head on the ground.

"How can they forgive me," he moaned. "It keeps happening over and over. What in God's name am I going to do?"

James Kennedy found Kevin looking at the waves from a slope above Bannow Bay Beach.

"I didn't think you'd be ready to start digging so I brought you a little something," he said. He handed him a bottle of whisky. "It was John's," he said. "He won't be needing it anymore. I've sent someone to find Anty."

Kevin accepted it and didn't start drinking it until James was long gone. When Anty found him he was half asleep. She caressed his hair. She saw that a quarter of the bottle was gone.

"You still have eyes in your head," she said. "So I guess I can snuggle in there."

She lay down on the ground next to him.

Kevin put his forehead against her cheek and put a hand through her hair.

"Can you talk about it?" she asked.

"Can't. Not now. Be with me. Please."

She placed an arm around his neck and held his shoulder. She leaned back against the hill and together they watched thick clouds move in.

Kevin rolled on his side looking away from Anty. He curled up in a fetal position, shivered and moaned, "No. No."

She knew he was re-living something. She rolled towards him and gently touched his arm. When it didn't look like she was helping, she rolled onto her back again. The horrendous scene she'd seen at the cottage, and the gruesome attack on Mrs. Walsh made her relive the screams of her mother, sister and others at Vinegar Hill. She also felt numb, and too vulnerable. As she watched Kevin's drunken shivering, she rolled away from him and tried to forget that she was afraid.

As Stewart approached, he watched James Kennedy and Kevin argue with each other in front of the boy's cottage.

"Well, sometimes he acts like a real fool himself and…" Kevin added in his defence.

Mr. Kennedy curtly waved him off and marched back towards the abbey. "Maybe you can talk sense into him, as he passed by."

"Hello, Kevin," Mr. Stewart said. "I know things have been difficult for you, but Mr. Sevens, is very concerned."

"Yeh, I know. Yeh have lost your attention," Mr. Kennedy told me. "You're not getting the job done, you're too slow and you're wasting coal. It's not true. He just doesn't like working with people."

"Mr. Sevens tells me you're argumentative and in a foul mood most of the time."

"Me?"

"I see," said Mr. Stewart, "And Anty Kelly isn't around, is she? Even now you look half asleep, unkempt and out of sorts.

"Mr. Kennedy came to see you because he wants you to tear down the Walsh cottage. The stone will be used for the wall.

"Mr. Sevens suggests that when you're done, you' should organize the men to do some touch ups on some slate roofs. I believe it's a good idea. We'll leave it to Mr. Kennedy to decide how argumentative you are after that.

Kevin stared back at the Walsh cottage.

"I'm going to suggest that in his next letter to Caesar, that James should mention Padraig. Unfortunately, I doubt he's going to know how to contact him, but it's worth the effort."

"I miss playing the fiddle, but without Jimmy Doyle, I don't see the point," said Kevin.

"Lord, with you and Samuel Boyse it would be an accident ready to happen. That's the end of that. Off now. James will decide what to do with you, when you're done."

⁓⊙⁓

It was another five months before Kevin returned to the forge. He replaced most of the tenants' thatched roofs with slate and he built a new set of latrines. The roofs of the latrines were in better shape than the dilapidated abbey

The farmers were terrified. The men of the parish didn't uncover any leads as to who or what was responsible for the recent horrific killings. They talked brave, but everyone felt vulnerable and powerless to prevent a recurrence. Arguments and brawls between protestants and papists became more common and more obvious. Uncorroborated rumours about tenants being forced from their land were rampant.

⟶⊛⟵

"What's with you and your girl? It's Anastasia, isn't it?" asked Mr. Sevens.

"We keep leaving each other and Lord, then we can't let go," replied Kevin. "Sometimes we start talking about the old times, but it stops. Everybody is gone, and it's all too terrible. Anyway, she needs a husband and I know it and it's just, well, I'm not ready. I don't know if I'll ever be ready. I don't think her aunt likes me. It's Boyse she likes. When Anty isn't with me, she's with Boyse."

"The aunt should marry Boyse then."

Kevin laughed. "She's already married."

"Just teasing you, boy."

"Anyway, we had a big fight a week ago, and I told her I never wanted to see her again. I don't know what started it, but that's how it ended. Mr. Sevens, I really don't feel right in my mind. Padraig, then Jimmy, then the Walshes… When it all happens, I'm losing all my family over and over again. Mr. Sevens it's too much. And Lord if anything should happen to Anty… It's all my fault that these people died. Maybe I should just leave."

"And go where? Australia? Pretty expensive if you ask me."

"If they arrest me they'll send me there for free," said Kevin

"If Vessey's Caesar, sees your face, you'll only feel the noose. That would really straighten you out wouldn't it? Besides, you can't be so hard on yourself, because everyone else isn't in their right minds either. You're not the only one suffering. You know if you talked this out with her, you'd probably find a way around this."

"Maybe I could save money and take us to America. I'm not ready to be serious, but tomorrow, or the next …who knows? How was it, with you? Why aren't you married?" asked Kevin.

"I knew a girl I liked, but I didn't make enough. It was before I worked here, and I wasn't working as a blacksmith. I barely made enough for myself and I didn't like farming. Now I raise what I have to but working at the forge is what I like. I just got used to the way I live. I hear you built a big, new set of cottages with slate roofs. You know people are going to remember that for a long time. Maybe people can change."

"You mean like you?" asked Kevin.

"Go on. Get back to beating shoes. I can't have you falling asleep on me."

After finishing the horseshoes, Kevin left him and took a walk down to the bay to get away from the heat of the coals.

He saw Anty pacing barefoot along the reach of high tide in the host summer sun. She wiped sweat from her brow with her sleeve. The waves lapped to the sandy beach. Eileen Jeffers stood in the water, farther up the shoreline. Neither of the women had their shellfish baskets. It wasn't that time of year.

Kevin saw her glance at him as he approached him but she was ignoring him.

"You still staying with Eileen?" he asked when he got close.

"What's that to you?" she replied.

"Was just wondering if things were still bad with your aunt?"

"That's meaningless nonsense and you know it."

"No. I mean… It's just a question. I mean…"

"You made yourself quite clear, so why are…?"

"Sometimes I say things that…"

"that you know exactly what you mean," she corrected him. "It's too dangerous to be around you, is what you meant."

Kevin walked into the water and folded his arms as the waves washed over his shoes.

Anty had one bare foot on the sand, the other in the water and a hand on her skirt, holding her shoes by the laces to keep them from getting wet.

"I asked you to leave this place. Mr. Kennedy told you the same thing and you're still here. Heaven help us. There's not too much to discuss, now is there?"

Kevin moved towards her and reached to touch her as he said, "Anty."

"No. Don't…," she replied as she recoiled backwards.

"Sorry, I…" he said as he backed away. He stepped out of the water.

She stepped toward him and touched his arm, "You were right. It's just not the time."

A strong wind from the sea brought with it an unexpected chill. She waved at Eileen to join her.

When Kevin looked away, he saw Samuel Boyse and Walter Glascott walking down the hill from Salt Mills village towards the bridge. He stepped back in the water as Anty passed him and Eileen ran after her.

"Didn't I make a mess of it? I should have stayed at the forge," muttered Kevin. He turned away and walked along the shoreline in the other direction. Minutes later he turned back and sat on a rock. His jaw dropped. As he took off his soaked shoes and stockings he saw that Samuel and Walter walked slowly up the trail towards the abbey, and the women on the other side of the bridge raced towards the hill to Salt Mills.

Lord God in Heaven, what did I miss? He felt like he needed to run but he didn't know where to go. Another strong chilling wind blew in.

As he closed his hand around his stockings and the laces of his shoes, he ran his thumb over the callouses on his palm that were caused by the blacksmith's hammer. Another gust of wind blew in and he raced barefoot towards the fire at the forge.

Phillip Jeffers lit his pipe from the hearth fire. His wife, Bridget, passed him a bowl of tea. Their tenant farm was a couple of miles from Salt Mills. "Bridget, how do you think the boys are finding themselves in England?" he asked.

"I have no idea, dear," she said. She stirred the pot that hung over the hearth fire. She walked outside and called, "Eileen, it's time to come in. Do you hear me?"

When she returned, Phillip said, "You don't have to yell. I am sure she could have heard you."

"And why were you sitting there while I'm cooking? Phillip, you get off your stool and go get them. Don't argue. It is getting late."

To the door she said, "Young ladies, you're here just in time. Take a seat, please."

While they were waiting for the meal, the girls talked of boys they were interested in and personal squabbles, which caused Mr. Jeffers to tune out and drink lots and lots of tea.

After everyone was served, Mrs. Jeffers asked, "Eileen, would you be so kind to say a grace for us?"

"Thanks, Mam. I'd be glad to. In the name of the Father and of the Son and the Holy Ghost…"

There was a knock on the door.

"Excuse me," said Eileen. "I'll get that."

"Are we expecting anyone else?" asked Mr. Jeffers.

Everyone shook their heads.

Before she reached for the door handle, the door slammed open. Eileen took a solid defensive step back. "You!" she said. "It's you. What are you doing here?"

Whisky in the Afternoon

Samuel followed a young woman who wore a green floral apron. She was carrying a couple of buckets of water towards the Jeffers' cottage. The remains of the roof cover had already been cleared, but three men were still busy removing burnt things from the cottage so the women could properly prepare the bodies. Samuel recognized that Anty's uncle Jacob was one of the men working on the cleanup crew.

"Young man you shouldn't be in here," said Mrs. White. She was managing the cleanup in the Jeffers' cottage.

Samuel pointed and told her, "That looks like a singed piece of Anty's shawl." Most of the bone of the skull on the burnt corpse was visible. A pile of ashen remains and flesh were piled beside it. Samuel dashed outside and threw up.

The woman with the green apron placed the buckets next to Mrs. White and told her, "She gave it to Eileen Jeffers."

When Samuel returned, Mrs. White repeated, "We've serious work here, and you're in the way, unless of course you'd rather take it from here."

Samuel stared at Mrs. White's ash covered clothes and the filthy rags she was dealing with. He saw another woman recoil after touching the charred remains of the arm of a corpse. The charred crust crumpled, and she recoiled with revulsion.

To the young girl with green apron Mrs. White asked, "Could you ask my husband when he's going to set up the other table in here? We'll need to get the other bodies off of the floor." To Samuel, she said, "These women require the privacy they deserve so you'll have to leave."

Samuel was perplexed. "I didn't mean… I just…" he said and left.

"Kevin you're getting ahead of yourself," complained Mr. Sevens. "Everything the abbey needs is done. The coaches are fixed and I've even fixed our door. I am not saying you are doing anything wrong. You're just throwing things around too fast. If you're too quick, your quality will suffer. That's all I'm saying."

"You're thinking that in another year or two I won't need you."

"There's no chance of that. You're too cocky and we're in a slow spell. You haven't seen half of what we need to do."

"Is the Walsh boy in there?" said a voice.

"No, he's not. He's dead," replied Mr. Sevens.

"Well, dig him out. We need to speak with him."

"Well?" replied Mr. Sevens.

"Thanks, Mr. Sevens, but I know who it is. It's Richard Caulfield." Kevin grabbed an iron bar and walked through the door to meet him. "I see you brought Walter Glascott and four of your friends. What's needling you?"

"We're here to warn you. You've got a lot to answer for bringing the Púca around," said Richard.

"Richard, in God's Holy Name, what are you talking about? Have you lost your mind?"

"There's been another murder. It's the Jeffers. They're south of Salt Mills."

"Are you saying the Púca did it?"

"What happened to the Walshes happened again to the Jeffers. Folks say that it's an animal creature called the Púca and they're blaming you for bringing it here."

"And those folks are you, Samuel and Walter. Right? No-one's going to pay attention to you. My family was killed. How is getting rid of me going to keep people safe?"

"We still think you should leave."

"Well, isn't that a surprise? And who's going to make the pikes? Is it going to be you or is it going to be big bone-headed Walter there?"

"Let's show him who he's talking to," growled Walter.

"The wake will be the day after tomorrow. I suggest you tell her family you're leaving."

"Whose family? The Jeffers?"

"No, Anty Kelly."

"What?"

"You didn't know?"

"Anty. My Anty. You stupid…" He raised the iron bar and made ready to smash something.

"Hold on there, Kevin," ordered Mr. Sevens. "What was that you said about Anastasia? Was that young Anty Kelly?"

"Richard, quickly, you ass, tell me what happened or I'll kill you myself."

"Eileen Jeffers invited a friend for dinner. Everyone was torn apart. It was disgustingly brutal. The thatch caught fire and everything was burnt. It's not something anyone should see, not even the likes of you, I suppose. Samuel Boyse liked her. I doubt he's going to be acting right."

"Boys, it's time for you to leave. Breaking things here won't help us," Mr. Sevens said. "Go boy." He brushed the back of Kevin's hand to let him know he needed to move on.

Kevin threw his apron to the ground and pushed Richard out of the way with both hands. Before he was able to lunge into a run, he smashed into James Kennedy.

"Ow," said James as he stumbled back towards a wall. He managed to regain his footing. "You're in a hurry, aren't you? Mr. Stewart saw Richard and Walter and summoned me. The two of them together usually means trouble. So, what is it?"

"There's been another killing on the other side of the river. They say it's the Jeffers and my Anty!"

"Good God. There's no end to it!"

"Sevens needs more coal for making pikes," said Kevin, and he left him and ran as fast, he could to the Jeffers.

There was a crowd of people in front of the Jeffers' house. "Holy Mary, mother of God," moaned Kevin. Jacob Finn sat hunched over on a stump with a couple of men talking to him. His face was ashen and his eyes were glazed. His short blond hair looked dishevelled. He was a solid block of a man, but looked like he was incapable of standing. Kevin didn't see any of the Jeffers' relations.

"Kevin," said a voice.

Kevin turned and recognized that it was Anty's aunt—Sarah Finn. "None of us can believe this. How, in the name of God could anything be so vile. You may not have known this Kevin, but she loved you. She just didn't know what to say." She beckoned for him to come to her with her hands. She stepped towards him and she embraced him first. His arms felt frozen, but he grabbed her shoulder blades and pulled and let his head rest on her shoulder.

The image, of the witch that Anty couldn't stand, melted as he felt himself go soft. He felt her breath. He didn't want to let her go. To see the face of a woman that he thought was cruel and unfeeling and to see her weak with tears scared him. When she moved her hand to the middle of his back below his neck, he had to pull away. She was beckoning him to cry but he wouldn't.

"Can't..." said Kevin. "Can't be gone. ...Have to see her. What is this?

What happened?"

Sarah pointed to the burnt building. "They're preparing the bodies inside," she said. "There's nothing to see. The bodies are badly burnt. My husband, Jacob is in a terrible state. He helped the men tear apart the unstable roof before the women dealt with the bodies. It was an awful, awful sight."

"What happened?"

"That monster killed everyone, and the thatch caught fire. The fire didn't stop the beast from doing its worst."

"This never happened before," said Kevin.

"The fire you mean."

"It's gotten sloppy. She must have tried to fight back by starting a fire. That's something she'd do. But God, no! No. It can't be Anty. For God's sake. It can't be my Anty. Why? It's not right. No way. I want to see her. Where is she?"

"It's terrible," Mrs. Finn said.

Kevin glared at her.

"The Whites are preparing the bodies. This happened last night, Kevin. You can't imagine, and you shouldn't."

Kevin glared at her again. "Mrs. Finn, you know I can. Why do you go on? And why didn't anyone contact me?" asked Kevin.

"What happened was only pieced together this morning. Everyone's still in shock."

When Kevin tried to walk into the remains of the Jeffers cottage, Mrs. White, who was a matronly, immovable presence, stopped him. "Where do you think you are going young, man? You're not going in. It would be indecent. We need to do our job."

"She's my Anty. Clear the way, please."

"Have you no shame? Sarah, who does he think he is?" she asked.

"Clear the way, or I will force my way in," he demanded.

"Marilyn, he just found out. He and Anty were close," said Sarah. "He just found out."

"Still, she's not ready. I'm telling you it would be indecent."

Kevin quickly squeezed his way around her. Once inside, he saw four bodies on makeshift tables of planks. A shroud was being sewn up around a woman's burnt body. Instead of a face he saw parts of a skull covered with strands of burnt shreds of flesh and muscle strands. He made out an outline of a blackened female breast. He couldn't tell if that or the other two bodies was her. The room stank terribly.

How can I possibly tell? If I had given her a ring or a necklace. He started to cry.

"Boy, you can't stay here. We have to get them ready," she said as she glared at him.

Kevin put his hand on the table next to the shroud and did a sign of the cross. He nodded in acknowledgement. From the door he watched her finish sewing the shroud around a girl's head.

She was right, he thought. *That was no place for little boys. She is right. I don't feel like a man.* He wiped at his tears. *I didn't do what I should have done. I've failed her. I failed them all. I didn't stop it.*

Kevin stepped out to where Sarah stood waiting for him.

"How does anyone know Anty is in there?" he asked. "I couldn't tell."

"My niece has had a difficult time finding her place here. We had some difficult arguments. She spent a lot of time with her friend Eileen Jeffers. She moved in with the Jeffers five weeks ago. I told Samuel Boyse on more than one occasion that we were very concerned. Earlier to-day he told us that he had found one of Anastasia's shawl's next to one of the bodies.

"So why didn't you tell me?"

"I was wondering if you'd sense something and besides it's a terrible way to remember her."

Kevin didn't know what to do or say. He just wanted to kick or yell at something. Sarah was being too helpful and too nice.

"I was told that putting the body parts back together was terribly gruesome work. The Whites have provided us with an incredible act of charity. You see Jacob, my husband there? Part of him died last night. I don't know if he will ever recover from this. My son doesn't know about it and I don't know what I'm going to say."

"Mrs. Finn, so long as I am alive I will do everything in my power to stop whoever or whatever did this," said Kevin.

It is nice to hear myself give them a promise but really what am I going to do: he thought. *Without Anty, I feel so cold and hopeless. Now that I know everyone is blaming me, it is going to get a lot colder.*

"I know it is a bad time for you now, Kevin, but I have to tell you that people are blaming this on the Púca."

"Richard and his friends made that up to associate it with me. I've heard this before. I thought people would have more sense."

"People are terrified and they are desperate for answers."

"So, the Protestants are blaming a Catholic for something they don't understand. What else is new?"

"Kevin, you're not being fair," said Sarah Finn. "It is not just the people here who believe this."

"Kevin, until tempers settle, you should keep a low profile." She stepped forward and gave him another warm hug. When Kevin stepped away, he wiped tears from his eyes.

"James, what are we going to do about this?" asked Mary Kennedy. Her voice trembling as she spoke. She was talking to him in their cottage, in Salt Mills.

"We are taking all kinds of precautions."

"Everyone is horrified. Families are being defiled in their homes. The landlord wants farmers removed from the parish. People on this side of the river are afraid of being terrorized by new neighbours. All sorts of vultures and bullies are trying to steal the Tintern lands. James, this is not a peaceful place. Have you considered joining your relatives near New Ross?"

"Working for the Colcloughs has served us well Mary."

"Being served well, is only worth considering if we have our health. Consider our daughter, James. This is no place for her. I am truly afraid of what is happening here."

"I need more time. I am trying to get permission for both of you join me at the abbey, at least until we sort this mess out."

"I am just as afraid of the people that killed Lord Colclough as I am of the monster who is committing these god-forsaken horrors," said Mary.

"For a start, I have instructed Mr. Stewart to accumulate armaments and organize a community militia. Have faith in me Mary. I am going to rid us of all these distractions."

Kevin sat on the hill where he remembered Anty putting her hand through his hair. He looked at the tide as it moved out. He took another swig from the whisky bottle and then took a look at it. *A long way to go,* he thought.

"God. Oh my God. How on earth could he? Well, we know how the Púca could, but why would he do such things? Thomas Brien told us sometimes the Púca could be a problem, but this? Is this what they do? Damn, then why didn't people kill them off a long time ago?" Kevin muttered.

Kevin took another drink.

"Maybe they were too smart.

"That Harry is smart."

Kevin raised the bottle to look at the contents.

"Oh, Harry, how could you?"

He took another drink.

"Harry, I've got to take a pee."

He stood up and took a pee.

"Piddle on you, Harry."

He stumbled.

"God, I'm not going to sit there," he said.

"A piddle on all of yeh. All of you go home and go away. Me and Anty are going to stay here. Hey enough!" he yelled.

He stumbled around and fell back on his behind.

"It's not right. There are too many bees. This world has too many bees and not enough honey. Do you hear me?"

He stretched back on the ground and looked at the slow rolling clouds.

"That's where I should be. Up there. Just like a bird," he moaned.

He remained there drinking for a long while. He heard someone approaching him from the waterfront path. He came and stood over him and looked down.

"Kevin Neal, you're a dog fucking snipe. I ought'a kill you where you lie."

It was the voice of Samuel Boyse.

"No, no, he's dead. The dogs ate him," replied Kevin.

Samuel kicked him hard in the side.

"You lying, evil pissing bastard," he yelled and kicked him again.

"That's right, there's no-body," replied Kevin, and he threw up.

"Lord, that's gross. That's vile that," said Samuel. He came downhill and picked up the fallen whisky bottle. He looked to see if there was anything putrid in it and then took a swig of it.

Samuel sat down on the hill when he got far enough away that he knew Kevin wouldn't throw up on him, he took another swig.

"And they wouldn't even let me put my tombstone next to her," whined Kevin. "Lord Almighty, that was so sad. Awful it was. She was such a darling."

"Stuff your ball in it."

"What does that mean?" Kevin groaned. "Don't you wonder where the Almighty is? You go to church and it's like there's no-one there."

"They didn't stop you. You just didn't go," replied Samuel.

"Oh, there's that. Odd how that is. Gimme another."

Samuel gave him the bottle, and Kevin took another swig.

Samuel took it from him and took a drink from it

"I have to go. Where am I goin' to go?" asked Kevin.

"To Hell I assume," said Samuel.

"Sure. Give me another, why don't you?"

Samuel passed the bottle.

Kevin took another swig and offered it to Samuel. "Here and off to hell," Kevin said.

Samuel lay back and stared at the clouds.

"So you're here to tell me she loved you. You god-damned son of an octopus fucker."

"Hard to keep on point with an octopus," Samuel said. "Well, she did like me."

"Go to hell." said Kevin.

"I'll miss her," said Samuel.

"Go to hell!" Kevin took another drink. "God damn it. I'll miss her more."

"When she was with me she mentioned your name."

"'God damned asshole,' she must have said."

"yeh, god damned asshole." Samuel took another drink.

"No she just said your name."

"What?"

"Shite. You're the shite," said Samuel.

"Probably. That's me." Kevin took another drink. "She would have gone with you if you were willing to go somewhere else."

"Where?" asked Samuel.

"How would I know?" asked Kevin. "We couldn't talk about the old days. It was like putting hands in a fire."

"yeh, needed a hit in the head."

"It's been said a hundred times." Kevin looked at the contents of the bottle again.

"Fuck off," said Samuel, and took the bottle and took another drink.

They started humming a short bar of the *French Retreat* until Kevin threw up.

"On the mark," said Samuel. He lay still and got dizzy watching cumulus clouds move.

Kevin stopped moaning and fell asleep.

When Kevin awoke, he couldn't find his bottle. "Lord, man. Go get your own," and he rolled back to sleep.

Richard, saw a horse tied up in front of the family cottage. He opened the door and saw that the hearth fire was lit.

"Hello Richard," said a voice.

"But…"

"No, there's no-one else at home. There's just you and me. Have a seat Richard. I made us a spot of tea. I didn't think anyone would mind."

Richard closed the door behind him. The man sitting by the fire had black hair and a coat. He didn't see any sign of a hat. The hair was short but wiry.

"Who are you?"

"I'm Douglas FitzGibbon." He was dressed in black, including a neck scarf and gloves.

"I've talked with your friend Walter Glascott a number of times. He's spoken quite highly of you."

"Why are you here? And why did you let yourself into our cottage?"

"It's been a busy day and I had long hard ride. Like I said, Walter told me how neighbourly you usually are. I thought I would pop over for a quick chat." Douglas grabbed a bowl and poured out some tea from the pot and passed it to Richard. He raised his cup of tea over the hearth fire and said "sláinte," before sipping it. Richard gave him the same greeting and took a sip.

"I tell you lad, the Púca is doing good work and miserable fools are getting what they deserve. Richard, what do you think?"

"Mr. FitzGibbon, what was done in the north wasn't necessarily a bad thing, but I am surprised by what happened at the Jeffers' place."

"For a good cause there are always unfortunate circumstances and casualties. The Púca is definitely a wily and controversial fellow, so let's move on. Caesar Colclough of Duffry Hall has plans for Tintern Abbey and Salt Mills. With the death of one of the landlords and the other in prison a change of management is evolving. For those willing to provide service for his lordship he's been known to be very gracious."

"Mr. FitzGibbon, clearly you want something from me. What is it?"

"Walter has helped us out in the past but lately he's been procrastinating and has required encouragement. Men like yourself, and your friend Samuel Boyse, are capable of seeing a bigger picture."

"You want Samuel and me to tell you how the abbey is being run?"

"That would be helpful, but we'll discuss this in more detail the next time I drop by. Richard, just remember that the next time you or yours are in a pinch, you'll appreciate knowing someone with the right connections. I appreciated this little chat." As he got up he added, "Give my best to the family when they get back from church." He dumped the remaining tea on the hearth fire, tossed his bowl to Richard and walked out.

"Mr. Stewart is going to bring you the coal and iron you requested," said James Kennedy. "We have good support for establishing a local militia. Do you have confidence you can make the pikes for me?"

"I made my share of them in '98," said Mr. Sevens. "The boy and I can make what you're asking. Arming farmers with pikes will make them feel better, but honestly, pikes aren't going to stop this thing."

"And I think you worry too much," said James.

Kevin carried another stone from the front of the Presley cottage to the cart. He walked around and gave the horse a carrot and petted it. "You've worked hard. You deserve it," he said.

When Kevin turned the cart into the farm, he spotted Walter and someone else slip through a line of wild six-foot-high shrubs that shadowed the road. Each carried wood clubs. The remains of the smashed cottage were about a hundred feet away. Taller trees followed the property line about twenty-five feet to his left. The other two sides were clear and open for a long way. Kevin kept loading the cart.

In another few minutes he heard clumsy shuffling from behind the line of trees nearest to him. "Well, I see you've brought some friends." He looked back and saw Samuel, Walter and three others come in from the road.

Kevin stepped in front of the horse which faced towards the road, and he put up his fists. "Fight like men, not boys," he told them.

Most dropped their sticks, but Walter didn't.

"You just need to move on. You know we don't want you here." said Samuel.

"The abbey sent me so I'm not leaving, so let's get on with it," Kevin replied.

"You're just being an ass," said Samuel. "There are other places to get stone."

Kevin rushed towards a curly-haired boy whose jacket was ripped at the shoulder. His punch hit the boy in the cheek and as he turned he pushed him towards Samuel.

The one with a cap and dark brown jacket, on the other side of Samuel, came rushing at Kevin with his club in full swing. Kevin kicked his shin, but the swing managed to create a long tear in the side of Kevin's tweed coat. The boy lost his cap and was screaming that his leg was broken.

"Nonsense," Kevin said, "He's just crying because he wants to go home."

"Walter, what are you waiting for? Your mam?" said Kevin.

Walter told the others to let him through. "You're all mouth," he said as he showed him his raised club.

Kevin ran around him and pushed the boy with the boy with the sore leg against Walter. He threw a punch to the back of the curly-haired boy and then kicked him in the side of his leg. He rushed forward and reached for Walter's club. He lost grip of it but managed to kick Walter in the side.

He re-grabbed the club from him, but the boy with the dirty sweater smashed him on the back of the head and then his back.

Kevin managed to toss Walter's stick away and kicked Walter's thigh hard, making him fall to the ground. The boy with the curly hair slugged Kevin in the ear, but his second punch was blocked by Kevin's left arm. Kevin lunged forward and took a swing at Samuel but missed. Samuel threw a punch, and hit Kevin in the face causing him to fall flat on his back. The boy with the dirty sweater smashed a stick across Kevin's stomach. Walter and the curly hair boy started kicking Kevin in the shoulder and the head. Walter after recovering his stick started smashing his arms. Kevin rolled over into a crawl position.

Walter picked up his club and smashed him hard across the back.

"Walter, get rid of that," yelled Samuel.

Kevin said, "Your turn, Samuel, where are you?"

"I'm right in front of you, fool."

"What are you waiting for? Put 'em up," mumbled Kevin, as he tried to stand.

"Stupid ass," Samuel replied and something smashed Kevin's face causing him to fall over.

Kevin tried to get up again, but something hit him in the face.

"Neal, stay down or we'll crack your head." said Walter.

Kevin moved and then he lost consciousness. When Kevin awoke, he found himself alone. The horse and wagon were gone. He was a few feet from the hedge that lined the road. "God, I'm not dead. Small wonders." He lay there because it felt like everything was broken.

He stared at the fluffy white clouds above. "Damn. Anty." In spite of the pain, he sat up and started crying.

Mr. Sevens came into the forge to find Kevin stoking the fire.

"Look at you. You were in bed for a week and a half. You're lucky there were people willing to take care of you. They almost killed you. Have you learned anything or are you going to keep doing it until they finish you? Kevin, none of what happened was your fault. Beating yourself up is not going to fix what's happened. Find a way of doing some good in the world. Your parents would be ashamed of you. As far as I'm concerned, before you do it again, just go somewhere else and jump off a cliff."

"Hard to find a good one around here," answered Kevin.

"Giving stupid people ideas, is not my intention," said Sevens. "Maybe it would be better if you just lay stone for a while."

"I need to get back to work, Sevens. Mr. Kennedy got us more iron and some half-decent coal."

"More pikes is what he wants," said Mr. Sevens.

"What about the poles?"

"Mr. Stewart is looking into that. Well, if you're up to it you can get started, but the abbey has a list of things that have to be done today. Kennedy's complaining that the place is falling apart. Right now, I need you to make a load of nails. If you're here with me, quit talking and get to it."

For the months that followed, Kevin spent most of his waking hours in the forge. James Kennedy complained that he spent too much of his time making pikes. "You are wasting too much iron and coal," he said. "We don't have it to spare. Leave it and make the things we need. We've got enough weapons for now. If Sevens thinks you're up to it, make us some nice door handles. You'll find that to be enough of a challenge."

By continuing to work long hours and producing a lot of work, Kevin was able to experiment with making new weapons. He made himself a small shield, a couple of long daggers, and even a couple of swords.

"If Mr. Kennedy finds you using the iron for your toys, it'll be on me," complained Mr. Sevens.

"Mr. Kennedy wastes a lot of money and it's not his money. Besides, we aren't getting paid enough for what we do, so stop complaining."

"What's that you're working on?"

"It's the Gáe Bulgha."

"You mean 'the Gáe Bulgha' used by the great Cú Chulainn."

"Yeh. Well, at least my interpretation of his Gáe Bulgha. It's a long spear with special blade-like barbs."

"Well, that is definitely a challenging piece of work. Have you ever seen one?"

"Mr. Sevens, you know I haven't, but I've heard the stories. It goes in easy but makes a mess coming out," Kevin said.

"Sounds bloody gory, if you ask me."

"I didn't ask you."

"Just don't go waving it at anybody around here."

"You can use the shield," said Kevin, and he laughed.

"Against that thing? No way."

"This is an early attempt. It will probably take me a long time to figure how to make it right."

"I'll see you later. Mr. Stewart is complaining about something in the coach house. It's probably one of the coach wheels."

"You know they have four of them."

"That doesn't matter. We do what they say."

"Where is Kevin?" asked James Kennedy.

"He probably swam across the bay," answered Mr. Sevens as he dropped a hot piece of work into the water bucket. "Kevin works a lot and then he disappears with his whisky and seafood and watches the tides. He hasn't been right since he lost Anty."

"Well, he hasn't hurt anyone so let him be," said James Kennedy. "I am returning to Wexford to stop John McCord from talking about removing the tenants from their land. These are bad times. Everyone is anxious. If I don't get this stopped, the farmers will have our heads. Mr. Sevens, I am sure you remember '98 well. You better say some prayers."

Mr. Sevens nodded and returned to the objects in the fire.

Sharpened Edges

Kevin knelt before Anty's wooden cross. Almost a year had passed since the gruesome assault on the Jeffers' cottage. The end of Wexford's autumn was in full form.

"Anty, really I tried to persuade your family to let me put your name on my stone, but they wouldn't have it," he said. *And of course neither would Samuel Boyse,* he thought and laughed.

He stared off vacantly into a field. Anty, *if you could talk I'm sure you would forbid me to do what I need to do,* he thought. "Find another way, you'd say," said Kevin. "Damn it Anty. I'm sorry. That's all I can say. There's not another way." He got off his knees and crossed himself. "Anty, I'm leaving in the morning. I just thought you should know," he said.

—◦◉◦—

Kevin sat by the hearth fire in his cottage. He dropped his empty cup to the ground. *Don't have much time if I want to get out of here before dawn,* he thought.

Kevin threw some dried food into his pack. Over his coat he put on a harness that held a sword, a small shield, and the Gáe Bulgha, which was about ten feet long. He had them wrapped with some thatch. His coat concealed the knife attached to his belt at the back. In a small pack he kept a rock sling similar to what he thought David might have used against Goliath.

The eighteen-year-old wore a grey waistcoat covered by a black frieze coat, over a white cotton shirt. His black knee breeches were tucked into his grey stockings. The knife sheath on his right leg was covered by a stocking.

"This is it," he said, as he swept a hand through his long, wavy, dark brown hair.

He stamped out the fire and threw some water on it. Without the fire, it was pitch dark. *I don't want Jimmy Doyle's mother, see me leave*, he thought. *I'd rather not have to explain what I'm doing or where I'm going.* Although Kevin didn't think he would ever return, he didn't want to say goodbye to anyone. He felt alone. Considering what he was up against, he preferred to embrace the feeling.

Kevin made the journey on foot. Wherever he saw birds or small animals, he slung the sling at them. He came close to hitting his targets a couple of times.

Thomas Brien used to say that the Púca can be friendly, but it can be terrible to people that are bad, he thought. *There was nothing bad about Anty.* He remembered when they lay together on the hill overlooking the bay. "Well, except maybe that she loved me," he said aloud. He gave a painful sardonic laugh. *The Jeffers were a harmless old couple. Eileen was just a young girl. Liam and Nick Walsh... how dare he. There was no reason. The Bennetts didn't deserve to die.*

Walter said something happened to the Browns and Whelans. I wonder what that was about. I could go back and ask him, but that would be a coward's way out. If I went back, I wouldn't have the courage or the insanity to do this again. He picked up a handful of rocks and continued slinging them against targets along a hedge.

"How can someone be as nice as Harry and then become such a monster?" he said. *As a Púca, he would always have been that monster. I only met him a few times and most of those times I was just a kid. I can't really say I know him or how he thinks. Why didn't the Púca help us fight at New Ross? He could have easily rescued my father and my brothers. Anty's father might not have died. He could have been there at Vinegar Hill. I'm sure he could have found a way to lead them away before the cannons fired. The Púca didn't do anything then and now it does this. It's an outrage for God-fearing people. The sheriff is corrupt and the politicians are villains. My people are left to themselves so there's just me. If I had money, I could join Jimmy in Dublin and truly learn to fight, but they'd send me somewhere and I'd probably never come back.*"

Kevin checked the dagger sheathed to his belt at the back. He slid the knife out and then slid it back in. "Yes, there is just me. I'm here and there's no-one else," he repeated.

He met many people on the long trek to the Duffry forest along the mountain. They didn't know what to make of him so they remained aloof and kept their distance.

When he passed the road to Wilton Castle, he felt pitifully sad.

Poor Lady Elizabeth, he thought. *No longer quite right in the head.*

'Her brother William similarly succumbed to a lunatic's depression,' he had heard Mr. Kennedy say.

"But only if Adam's Caesar lets him go," Kevin added. He took a bite of some bread and tossed a piece to the grounds to ward off the spirits.

⤙⥄⤚

Kevin slept in a forest on Lord Blacker's estate in Woodbrook. He considered himself lucky for not being accosted by the landlord's men on his long walk. Lord Blacker, like Lord Annesley, maintained considerable influence.

If they discovered a free roaming labourer with weapons, they'd string up a noose on the nearest tree. Best not let that happen, he thought. *The best place to hide is on the man's property. Landlords spend more attention looking at other people rather than minding what they have.* It had taken him a little less than ten hours to walk from the abbey to the Woodbrook estate.

He snuggled up for the night behind a fallen tree in the forest on the grounds and nibbled on pieces of bread and dried fruits. Blacker was a neighbour of Caesar, the barrister. Kevin was sprawled out a little more than a mile from Kiltealy Village, which lay below the hill of Cloroge More.

Kevin awoke with the sun. He ate as he walked. He was aware that men working for Blacker or Duffry Hall might try to stop him, so he picked up his pace. When he walked through Kiltealy Village, he didn't see much activity. *It's like a village of the dead,* he thought. He listened more carefully. "Well, a village of the dead, with the exception of some fowl and a couple of cows," he muttered and then added some soft laughter.

Uprighting a Wrong

Kevin followed a path to the Urrin stream. When he got there, he removed his coat, a load of weapons and the harness. He made an impression in the sand and, with his cupped hands scooped some water and filled the small pool. The water was cold, and there was a thin crust of ice along the slow-moving edges of the stream. It was the end of Autumn and the chill was to be expected. From his pocket he removed some plants, crushed them together and mixed them with a bit of water and spit. The noxious paste included poison hemlock, evergreen yew leaves and wolf's bane and he smeared it onto the spear blade and barbs of the Gáe Bulgha. Kevin washed his hands in another pool. He destroyed both pools so an animal wouldn't drink from them. The want to be warrior put his weapon harness on again without his coat but left on his waistcoat. He ran across the stones and into the trees. Kevin slowed and carefully followed the trail upwards towards the Duffry forest.

If Captain Colclough was here, what would he tell me? he wondered. With an English accent he growled, "Go home and don't come back until you're fully equipped with an army." He took his sword and started sharpening it with a sharpening stone. "And Captain, I would say, I am not going to get one. If I brought my army, the sheriff would hang us all."

Jimmy, what would you say? wondered Kevin. *He'd probably growl like* a pirate and say, *'I'll distract him and you hit him when he's not looking.'* "Lord, a lot of good that would do us," muttered Kevin.

Well, it has to be done. Those poor disfigured people behind us— there's so many; I can't ignore them. He put the sharpening stone back in his pocket. *I know Anty you're telling me not go, but Mr. Walsh would never forgive me if I don't. For the sake of poor Liam, someone's got to try. Da, I hope you don't think I'm stupid.* He started to cry. He brushed his forearm across his face. He placed the sling in his pocket and he made sure there were a lot of rocks in his food pouch. Kevin stood up and grabbed the sword in his right hand and the shield and spear with his left.

"Goodbye, Jimmy," he said. "Mam, please take care of Anty."

He carefully followed the long path that led farther up the hill. Kevin thought he heard something move, but he couldn't tell if the sound came from within the treeline or from his loud pulsing heart. *The Púca can become almost anything*, he thought. Kevin looked around slowly and tried to remain still as he listened. He didn't hear anything threatening, so he stalked carefully towards a small opening in the forest. *People say that he can become one of the biggest horses that ever lived. Others say he can sprout wings and fly.* So far Kevin hadn't sensed anything unusual.

He walked to the edge of the opening into the forest. He looked back over his shoulder and then crouched and stared into the black. He didn't hear anything, but wind caressing the canopy above. He put his sword into a sheath, which he strapped across his back. It was unusual for him to put it there, but it was convenient to carry it next to the Gáe Bulgha. He repeatedly reached back and touched his sword hilt. He did this until he was confident he could grab it without thinking. He wrapped his right stocking down, slipped out his dagger from his leg sheath and stepped into the darkness.

As he angled away from the light outside the forest, he tried not to make any noise. There wasn't any sign of tracks of a giant wolf, or a bear-like creature. The forest was quiet and still. He watched for fierce, glaring, eyes or something strange and unknown. The tall trees around were mostly bare except for the canopy far above.

He went deeper into the forest. After passing at least eight trees he planted the spear end of the Gáe Bulgha into the ground, close to the trunk of a tree in front of him. He walked past another two trees and stopped.

From his bag, he removed rocks from his pockets and made rock piles, next to the surrounding trees. He stopped and waited. He still hadn't heard anything.

Kevin knew that when the Púca showed up, he would be fast and stealthy. *I wish there were some birds or something that could give me a warning,* he thought.

He remained sitting against the same tree for the rest of the day. At night, when it became very dark, he became nauseous. *I am unprepared, tired, and I am not well protected,* he thought. *This is crazy.*

About half an hour later he stood up. "Mrs. Walsh I am prepared to fight for you," he mouthed silently. He jabbed his dagger around a few times and sat back down. He put his free hand under his small shield and yawned. About twenty minutes later, he slowly slid down along the tree and fell asleep.

Something snapped. Kevin's eyes flashed open. He was sprawled out on the ground. *Oh my God,* he thought. Kevin froze. The young man crouched back against the tree again and tried not to move for almost another hour and a half.

He heard a series of snaps in the distance and he was jarred to attention.

Lord God Almighty, it's moving through the bush. It's something bigger and heavier than a man. What an absolutely stupid plan. I didn't think this through at all. I'm in the heart of the forest. It's pitch dark at night and I am alone with a monster that tears things apart. It is nice to have my sling, but I can barely see anything and—my legs are stiff. Maybe I should just get out of here.

He heard the creature slow. It was sniffing the air. The creature moved and sounded like it was walking towards his part of the forest.

Kevin slowly got up to stand, but dropped his dagger. He didn't go looking for it. Kevin stepped back and slipped behind the tree. He took a step. It made a crack.

Well, doesn't that just tear it? he thought.

His eyes were adjusting to the darkness, and starlight was visible through breaks in the forest cover. He made out a silhouette distinct from the trees. Kevin crouched and felt around for stashes of rocks with his right hand. Next, he grabbed his sling and checked both ends of it as he stood up.

The beast seemed to sense something and moved towards him. The walk turned into a run.

Kevin's whole body was shaking. *Anty,* he told himself and he glared at the approaching shadow. He stopped shaking. When it got close Kevin wound the sling and let it go.

I'm sure I hit it dead on the head, he thought. He quickly tried to throw another, but it was coming at him too fast. Kevin dropped it and grabbed his sword just in time to swing a slice at the shadow. Something smashed his shield and threw him over a dozen feet away. The back of his ankle smashed a trunk. *God, I hit him with full force and it felt like taking a swipe at a piece of turf.*

Kevin still gripped his sword. He stuck it in the ground by his foot, got up and slung another stone. *I don't know if I hit anything,* he thought. Nothing seemed to move.

Kevin's body shook madly again. He imagined the thing brutally tearing Nick and Liam apart with precision and without effort. *Dear God,* he thought.

He threw again at where he thought it was. Again nothing moved. He loaded again. A form rushed towards him. *It was exactly where I thought it was,* he thought. He lost the sling, lunged out, grabbed his sword and stepped back behind the tree. *Holy Mary, mother of God.* Kevin tried to crush the handle of his sword with his grip, and as the creature came near, Kevin took another swing. It felt like he cut him. The beast twisted and spun around. An enormous hand grabbed the tree trunk that was in front of Kevin. The boy stepped backwards as quickly as he could in the dark. For some reason the thing stopped.

Kevin stared at it but kept backing up. *God Almighty,* he thought. *The Gáe Bulgha. I need the Gáe Bulgha.*

The beast ran at him again. It smashed Kevin. It spun him head over heels in a somersault in what felt like a fatal last breath. The back of his thigh smashed into another tree and the ground pounded his body as it rolled across the forest floor. He tried to breathe as he spit out a mouthful of dirt and needles. "God, it made me wet myself," he muttered. *My sword is gone and my shield is wrecked. Where's the Gáe Bulgha?* he thought. *It's there, there or there. God save us. If I'm wrong, I'm gone.*

Damn, does it climb trees? Damn there aren't any branches.

Kevin crept towards the first tree. *Can't see a damn thing. Maybe it can't either. No way. The damn thing can see in the dark just fine. It's just playing with me. The Gáe Bulgha. I need the Gáe Bulgha.* He touched everywhere around the tree but didn't find it. Kevin ran for the second spot. *Not there,* he thought. *Of course, it is.* He felt around. Kevin imagined the thing stalking Anty. He found the weapon. It was so close to the tree he couldn't make it out. The young man grabbed the weapon, flipped and held it tight as he watched the beast's shadow approaching.

He prepared to ram the horse-like creature with all his might. The creature slowed. Kevin pushed the Gáe Bulgha forcefully into it. The beast stood without moving.

A monstrous voice said, "Boy, what do you think you are doing?"

"Why did you kill Denny's brother Thomas?"

"Of course I didn't."

"You killed the Jeffers, my Anty, my Walsh family and the Browns. You're a maniacal monster. You beast!" Kevin shouted, and he screamed. He pulled and pulled, but the Gáe Bulgha wouldn't come out. The beast kicked Kevin, and he went flying, landing on his back while his sleeve and arm got ripped. He heard something smash against a tree. *He broke my Gáe Bulgha,* he thought. Kevin was shaking madly. He knew he had only seconds before being torn apart. He pulled out a second small dagger from a sheath behind him and ran madly in an attempt to disembowel the monster.

Before he got close, something grabbed his body and twirled him up and out of the forest. Kevin's body smashed against branches near the top of a tree, and his arm got twisted. He tried to grab something to stop his fall backwards, but his arm wasn't able to do anything. His other arm was on the wrong side. *"Ahhh,"* he heard himself scream.

His legs managed to wrap around the small tree trunk top, but as they slipped their grip, the bark and small branches started cutting his legs. When his back smashed the trunk, he was upside down. His good arm managed to get near another branch. His legs weakened, but the slip downwards enabled him to grab a branch. He held the branch as his legs overhead maddeningly let go, causing his body to flip forward. His body smashed into the trunk. He lost his hand grip but wrapped his legs around the enlarging tree trunk. More puncturing broken branches poked into his thighs. The excruciating pain in his dislocated left arm took his mind off the fact that the branch had come very close to impaling his balls. His good hand managed to grab onto another branch. He held on as tightly as he could.

Lord Almighty, I am still not dead. I am here and I am alive, he thought.

A voice from below asked, "Kevin?"

Kevin didn't say anything. He recognized that the voice sounded like Harry Keane's. He hung tightly to the thin, gently moving tree trunk.

"You didn't listen to me before. I didn't harm those people. I expected more of you. Now off with you. I am leaving this place. Maybe forever. If you don't kill yourself on the way down, have a long life," he said.

Kevin heard him rush through the forest towards the mountain. He thought he saw a form of a shadow rise over the treeline, but lost sight of it. Holding on, without moving, made him conscious of the debilitating pain he was suffering from his dislocated arm. *Jesus, have to move or I'll fall off. If I could move my arm, I could put my waistcoat between my legs and slide down, but I can't. Lord Almighty it's a long way down isn't it?*

"Oh, Lord have mercy on our souls. Here goes," he said to himself.

Kevin dug his feet into the side of the tree and let himself slide down. He started to accelerate out of control until he hit a big branch and he bounced. Kevin fell. He grabbed a branch with his good hand but lost his grip. His shoes tightened against the sides of the trunks as he kept sliding. Smaller branches broke. The tree bark scraped into his leg. A big branch smashed his testicles and broke from the force. He yelled, but he landed on a pair of thick branches.

"Oh, my God. Oh, my God. Not moving. Stay right here forever," Kevin muttered. "God in heaven."

He stared into the blackness below. *Still a long way down,* he thought. The pain from his dislocated shoulder was becoming overwhelming. "But got to keep moving," he groaned.

As he stepped down, another branch broke. He fell sideways to the tree until his right foot hit a branch and it almost hit him in the chin. His good right arm steadied him by holding the side of the tree but the friction flaked the skin. His side smashed a thick branch. It broke but slowed his fall to the next one. He rolled off that one, hit the one below and free fell a few feet to the ground below where he smashed his shoulder and his head.

⚯

Kevin slowly tried to force himself to get up but realized that a branch had impaled him in the thigh. "Damn it, Harry."

I can't remove the stick or I'll bleed to death. I can't use my arm to take off my clothes so I can't use my shirt as a bandage. I also can't tighten something on my thigh with only one hand. The ankle of that leg also seems to be broken.

"Oh Lord, I have to move or I will die. Lord God. Kevin Neal, Kevin

Walsh, or whoever you are, walk. Oh my God, Oh my God…"

He hopped on one foot and dragged the other. It was still very dark and his eyes hadn't adjusted. He circled around.

"Branches. I must have knocked branches down," he said. He walked very unsteadily. When he knew there was something there, his eyes helped him make it out. He picked up a long thin bendy branch. He had a problem holding it because the skin of his hand was badly torn. He was disorientated and was suffering excruciating pain. It was difficult for him to move. He had difficulty making out anything around him. He started to panic. He struggled to stay alive, but shock, darkness, excruciating pain, and the inevitability of an impending death caused him to hallucinate.

"I'm tired," Kevin said. "What am I going to do?"

"No," he yelled. He heard his father tell him loudly, *Stay awake.*

Boy, you're fighting for your life. Pain is not the problem, he heard his father tell him. *Boy, go that way.*

Kevin forced himself to move on. He had a bad left arm, a bad left leg, and twisted left ankle. He couldn't put much weight on the stick without it breaking.

"What if I'm not going to get out of here?" he moaned.

Boy, why didn't you take your mother from there? Looking for us was a waste of time. You could have persuaded her and your sister to go home instead of waiting for us. You all knew there was no hope, but stayed. I am ashamed of you, boy. You didn't go home.

"But, father, I did," Kevin said.

Kevin you have to go home.

"I'm sorry, Father. I will go. I will go home," Kevin said. He felt himself slipping and weakening. Every step was taking more out of him. The shock of falling and facing immanent death was making him want to stop and rest. *Those trees. If I touch them, they'll take me,* Kevin thought. "No. Don't," he said. "Don't touch. No, don't touch, Mother. Oh, mother says, 'Don t touch'."

'Hey don't forget me,' he heard Anty say. *'You didn't come for me. You didn't take me home.'*

"Oh, Anty. I'm sorry, but I didn't know."

'Kevin, that's not an excuse. You didn't come for me and you were supposed to. Come and get me.'

As he hobbled on, dim light from occasional starlight enabled him to see lines of trees. They looked like armies of sentinels waiting for him. He stepped over decayed branches, and pieces of deadfall which were scattered everywhere under the spongy mossy floor. Kevin felt like one of them would come and take him.

"Yes, Anty, I'm coming. I'm coming to get you. I have to get over there. There's a place over there. I have to get there."

Kevin was disoriented in the dark and had difficulty traversing the spongy moss covered deadfall. He stumbled a couple of times.

"Anty. Anty are you there? Please, are you there?"

Yes bonehead, you've got to come find me. Stop talking about, how you can't. There are things that only we can do.

"I believe you Anty. Just tired. Got… Yes Anty, I hear you. Anty, you're making so much noise."

"No. Won't," he heard her say.

"Absolutely," Kevin said. He stumbled, but scraped his hand on a branch. He spun to the left and touched a tree.

"It got me. It got me."

"What?" he heard Anty say.

"Ahhh," Kevin screamed. He swung an arm and lightly stamped the air with his bad leg like a frustrated child. He took another step and tumbled to the ground.

The young man was in agony. He felt the ground on his face. "It has got me," he said. "God in heaven above. No, no. No!"

Kevin pushed himself up a little and turned his head. He saw a circle of light and wanted so much to reach for it.

I'm coming home, he thought. With what he thought was the last bit of life, he forced his body up. With his good hand Kevin touched a tree and pulled his body to the opening, and into the light.

PART 4: A Bird Never Flew on One Wing (1810-1811)

We had our differences. I can't do this by myself. I need your help. (Richard Caulfield)

The Red Valley

Kevin stumbled into another world. The reddish brown colour of the rolling open valley was washed by a haunting glow from a huge full moon. To his left he saw the back side rolling outline of Cloroge More. The slopes of the valley in front of him rose higher. The line at the top followed long and higher. The line rose towards the mountain. This place was without sound. The wind didn't blow and nothing moved.

"There he is," he heard Anty say.

"Wha?" mumbled Kevin.

He looked at a stone cottage. It was about a hundred and fifty feet to the right.

"Too far," moaned Kevin. He fell. He felt the ground as he hit and imagined he was becoming part of it. "No, no," he said. "I touched it," he said.

"You're a scoundrel, Kevin. You promised me. I hate you. You're going to leave me," she whined.

"Anty, just another… moment."

"Kevin, don't you dare! I will never talk to you again."

"Promise? All right, I…" He pressed his right hand against the ground.

Kevin tried to push up, but his dislocated arm filled him with terrible, immobilizing pain.

"Damn this," he growled. Kevin grabbed his stick with the other hand and attempted to push himself up. As he got up, the stick broke. He screamed from the horrifying pain.

His stick was gone, and Kevin didn't know where it was. He didn't have the strength to pick it up even if he did. He hopped and waddled his way through the gloomy looking heather scrub. Kevin did his best to meander through the overgrown goat paths.

He reached a wall in front of the stone cottage but couldn't walk any farther or speak and was on the verge of fainting. Everything was spinning. His fingers grabbed some stones from his pocket. He made an underhand toss, but it only went three feet. Kevin made another toss, but it hit the side of the cottage. He threw all he had at the little house, but the last swing brought him to the ground.

Kevin's last words before succumbing to lifelessness was, "Damn birds."

—❦—

"Boy, hey," a voice said. Something kept hitting Kevin in the face.

"Anty, go away."

"Hey, hey wake up," the voice said.

"What?" Kevin moaned.

"I need you awake," said the voice.

Kevin slowly opened his eyes. He saw an old man in his sixties. He had short, messy, white hair, and it didn't look like he smiled a lot. Kevin was lying on a bed of straw in a corner of the cottage. "Are you with me?" he said.

Kevin wanted to ask him where they were going but didn't have the strength. He made a light nod instead.

"Good. You're in my cottage and I've cleaned you up a bit. I need you to be with me. I don't want you to die here. Do you understand?"

Kevin nodded again.

"I'm going to pull the stick out of your leg."

"Oh," groaned Kevin.

The old man's snotty nose dripped onto Kevin's shirt. "Don't leave me, boy. Stay with us. He put a stick in front of his mouth and told him," I want you to bite on this."

On the count of three." He put his hand around the back of Kevin's good but torn hand.

Kevin tightened his hand slightly in acknowledgement.

"One, two…" said the old man, and he pulled the piece of wood out from his wound, and Kevin screamed.

The man put his hand on Kevin's chest to reassure him. "Stay with me, boy. That's the worst part."

The old man used strips from Kevin's torn pant leg to make a temporary tourniquet to control the bleeding on his thigh. He cleaned the wounds with salt water, bandaged him up and washed him down. After removing the tourniquet, he said, "I'll get us some honey for the next time we unwrap your bandages. You know honey does wonders." He poured more water into the bowl and used it to clean his blood-soaked hands.

"You got yourself into quite a spell of trouble. Couldn't you have waited until the morning? Your lips are dry, lad. You need some water. Try to take a sip." The old man poured some water from a bowl and tried to get Kevin to drink it. Most of it spilled over his face. "Sorry about that, boy," said the man as he wiped his face and chest where it spilled. "You'll take what you can, when you can."

Kevin turned his head and relaxed.

"Whoa, boy, we're not done yet. Don't leave me."

Kevin's lips moved to voice a silent complaint.

"I need to fix your shoulder. I am going to turn you onto your good shoulder."

Kevin gave a low groan as he was pushed onto his side.

The man grabbed Kevin's bad arm and stood on his bed above.

"On the count of four. One, two…" and he pulled Kevin's arm to set the shoulder back into place.

Kevin screamed. "You… count… bad," Kevin moaned.

"I bet that feels better. Let's try another bit of water. Good, that is more than last time. As long as your cuts don't get pussy, I think you'll live. Do you hear me, boy? It looks like I'm talking to myself," said the old man as he watched Kevin surrender to sleep. "That's the way it is, around here anyway," he said. "My, my, I wonder if the Púca knows what did this to the young man?"

Kevin opened his eyes to the sunlight coming through a window. He felt something moving on his leg, but was still very tired. He saw a reddish orange chicken walking around his feet. Kevin gave it a kick. "Damned birds," he muttered and fell back to sleep.

The old man entered the cottage and saw Kevin sitting by the hearth fire.

"I hope you don't mind me lighting the fire," said Kevin. "It's getting a bit nippy. It's winter, after all."

"It's about time you got out of bed. You were there for four days. You lost a lot of blood. How's the leg?"

"The ankle isn't in good shape, but I think it's only a bad sprain," answered Kevin. "The thigh is better than it was and I am not complaining about my shoulder."

"I'll bring you some wood and twine, and you can make a brace for your ankle," said the old man. "It's going to take a while for it to heal. There's no need to hurry and run off on my account. If you don't complain about my cooking and you make yourself useful, you can stay until it's healed. I'm Pat Jordan. My Anna passed a few years after '98. She didn't really recover from the loss of our boys. The fighting on the pass on the other side of that hill was terrible. The cost to everyone was dear. She and my boys are buried out back. I like being near them and I never felt the need to leave." He pointed to the table. "Those britches are for you. I set them out. They probably won't fit well, but they're all I can give you. They used to belong to my son."

"Thanks, Pat. Kevin is my name. I'm familiar with these parts, but I've come from a place by the ocean."

"Where would that be, Kevin?"

"Bannow Bay. Have you heard tell of it?"

"I've heard of it but have never been. What's it like living by the water?"

"It's usually a calm place. There's shellfish for the taking. You might not like it, but you get used to it. You don't have to wait for the harvest, and you're not dependent on your food stores, and it's there for the taking during the hungry months of summer. Watching the power of the tides is like feeling the ebb and flow of the wind across the hills and the mountains here. But this place you're in is different. It's got a strange quiet and stillness. The wild goats make their noises, but you can barely hear them. And with the red colour, it's like another world."

"It's different and I like it that way," said Pat. "The landlord knows I'm here, but he doesn't tax me. He doesn't believe the land is worth anything, so he leaves me alone. I trade my sheep, goats and eggs for potatoes and turnips. I set traps for small animals and collect berries and herbs when I find them. This place suits, me and I like keeping the outside world out. I don't like what I've seen out there."

Kevin tried to slide on the britches, but it wasn't working.

"Now tell us, Kevin, how did you end up coming here almost dead?"

"Well, I got lost in the forest. I climbed a tree to figure out where I was, and I got clumsy, and I fell down and nearly killed myself. You know the rest."

"You know, young man that has a very unlikely ring to it. You have your reasons, I suppose. If someone is after you, we don't have to talk about it unless you're a person that means people harm."

Kevin looked the man over cautiously and said, "Pat, I don't mean to cause trouble, but there are people I would rather stay away from. They're the kind of people both of us would definitely not like to see. I've worked as a blacksmith and I've fixed things. Maybe I can gather some things and make us some more traps."

"We'll look at that. For now, I'll have you feed the chickens, the hares, and my lambs. I'll also show you how to finish skins. I trade some of it, but with this bunch I'll get you to make us some blankets. My Anna showed me how."

Kevin accidentally kicked the table, causing him to groan.

"Grab that oak staff leaning in the corner. You'll need it to get around. Until that foot gets better, watch where you put it, Kevin."

"Right, Pat. I got that. You know these trousers don't fit. I need another pair. I know of a tinker that might help me out. When you go to church, would you get the word out to Denny Brien? If anyone can find me a pair, it's him. And tell him that we're interested in hearing more of his stories."

"No bother. I know the man."

Hare Stew

Kevin sat on a stump in front of the stone cottage, cutting a pelt into long strips. He looked up and saw someone come out of the forest.

"Denny," he said to himself and threw him a wave. Kevin hobbled around to the other side of the yard. Pat was on the far side of the valley looking for one of his goats. "He doesn't see me. He's lost in another world," muttered Kevin, as he hobbled back towards the front of the cottage.

"How are yeh? It's Denny, Denny Brien," the visitor said.

He has some grey hairs, and a beard, and walks slower than I remember, thought Kevin. *Years will change a man. He talks like someone that knows how to sell.* "It's Kevin," he replied.

"So you say."

"How's that?" asked Kevin.

"That voice and your look, it's just like Aiden Neal, God rest his soul. Are you related?"

"I'm surprised that you aren't shocked to see me. Most people think I'm dead."

"You're one of the Neal boys?" asked Denny.

"It's Kevin himself."

"And well? The look of him? Little Kevin Neal, all grown up. Aside from the long, upset hair, I see your brother Aiden in you. There's that thoughtful and determined look. I see you've also got yourself banged up. You've a brace on your foot, I see. Fool hardy like Seamus, I'd expect. You know, this is a rough place for a bad foot."

"The last time I saw you was when you were playing outside old man Kavanagh's during his wake."

"I remember it well. It was a terrible loss," Denny said.

"Before that you used to come to our house with your brother Thomas. He used to tell us about the Irish heroes. They were local stories about heroism, brotherhood, righteousness and struggle against adversity at whatever the cost. He's also very much missed."

"So, what are you doing here?"

"It's Caesar Colclough over there that is after my head. He thinks I'm dead and I would like to keep it that way."

"Keeping your head down. I can understand that," said Denny. He stared at the old man in the distance and added, "Pat over there must be asleep."

Pat started waving and Denny responded in kind. He used both arms. "Here we are, just like a pair of sick birds," said Denny.

"If we' had some whisky, we'd have a fitting reason to drink it," added Kevin. "It's a wager whether he'll come back without the goat."

"They're always getting out," said Denny. "He needs a better fence. Forget the goats, fix the fence, I always tell him. He'll probably complain— Well then, the foxes would get them if they couldn't get out. There's no reasoning with him."

"I see you managed to bring the breeches I asked."

"I am a tinker. I told Pat, that pots and scarves and the like, is all that I sell. But I must say he was pretty persuasive at church. He told me you had a terrible accident. 'He lost his trousers,' he said. I see you cut the legs off them, so that was only half true. He told me I had to find a pair because you were scaring the ladies. I told him, Pat there are no ladies up there. It's you he's scaring. We got a big laugh out of it." Denny stared at the bandages around the boy's foot and thigh, and the bad scrapes on his hands and face. "We scraped up a pair of them for you. By the looks of you I'd say Pat was right about the size. Don't worry, we kept your name out of it."

"I'm obliged, Denny. I don't have money on me, but when I get home, I'll have our priest send it to Ballindaggan parish for you. I should be well enough to leave in a few days."

"Pat told me that you are a blacksmith now. My cart needs fixing. We'll take care of that soon enough. Let's put on one of Pat's stews," Denny said with a mischievous grin.

⟡

After the meal, the men grabbed their tobacco pipes. Pat was tall and thin, and his clothes never seemed to fit him. His stockings didn't reach high enough and the drooping waistband was meant for a much heavier man. Denny was tall and had a round face. He kept his hair short and well-trimmed. *He's a fellow that likes to keep himself presentable*, thought Kevin. Pat offered Kevin a pipe, but he refused it. The smell of it reminded him of home and his da.

Denny told them a plethora of stories. When he was done, Kevin pumped him with a long list of questions about the Púca. "He told me he's leaving for America," said Kevin.

Denny looked at Pat. "Oh, so you've met him?"

"I've talked to him a few times over the years," said Kevin.

"I've met with him many times over the years, too, but I wouldn't exactly say I know him," said Denny. "The Púca is a very strange creature."

"You call him a creature. I just refer to him as Harry Keane."

"That's the personal side. He talks to you like he knows you better than yourself. The name is good for that part of him, I suppose."

"I've seen him a lot," said Pat. "He scares off the wild things at night. He told me he's sworn away from human affairs."

"Like the rebellion?" added Kevin.

"All I can say is that when the battles happened at the pass behind us or the one at the other end of the mountain at Newtownbarry, no-one saw him. I asked him why and he told me he couldn't," said Pat. "He's not allowed, he said."

"And who could stop the likes of him from doing whatever he wants?" asked Kevin "I am sure it's not the Sheriff."

"I've asked him that very thing, Kevin, and then he goes off and pretends to do something else," said Pat. "Still, he has never had a problem with scaring bad folks from here. It's hard to understand how he thinks."

"There are many stories of him helping out the less fortunate," said Denny.

"You know it is not in his nature to restrain his disdain for fools and those that take advantage," said Pat. "They usually find he has quite a devilish sense of humour."

"I've noticed he's not comfortable with crowds," said Kevin.

"That's probably true, but it's a positive attribute if you ask me," said Pat. "Kevin, what's your connection with him?"

"I came up here because someone has been blaming him for a lot of nasty things," said Kevin. "There's something out there that's been tearing people up. I've witnessed the bloody results in cottages near Bannow Bay. People told me that the same thing has been happening up here."

"Since '98, I have heard of revenge killings. Recently there have been some horrendous things that have stood out," said Pat. "The household of Martin Bennett was butchered, for example. They lived on the Blacker's Woodbrook estate."

"He may have had his cottage there, but he worked as a foreman for Adam's Caesar in the adjoining parish," said Kevin. "He was responsible for almost getting Nick Walsh killed."

"How's that?" asked Pat.

"He made him work in a thunderstorm and he slipped from a roof. He managed to recover, but his poor health was part of the reason why we had to leave the farm. Anyway, how could something so monstrous happen on the Blacker's estate without someone getting punished?" asked Kevin.

"Well, someone was charged, but it happened again and nothing further was done," said Denny. "People in Darby Brown's and Matthew Whelan's cottages were also killed. The bodies were torn open. The insides were pulled out and blood was splattered all over the place."

"Were any limbs missing or torn or twisted?" asked Kevin.

"As far as I heard, it was just the fronts that were torn," said Denny. "And I heard that one of the men at the Whelan cottage was castrated."

"I only heard about the tearing bit," said Kevin. "There's a real sick bastard out there, isn't there? And this is the first time I heard that a body had been castrated. That is a focused piece of work. It's not something the average beast would waste their time on, don't you think?"

"Even if there was a creature like the Púca that was out of its mind, you'd expect more damage," said Denny. "The doors would be broken and the walls would be smashed. From the people I talked to from Killanne, the inside of the Whelan's house was just messy. I was surprised to hear that none of the stools were broken. The hearth pot was still hung over the fire. You would think that with all the fighting, the place would have caught fire."

"What about the murder at Martin Bennett's cottage?" asked Kevin.

"I don't know anyone who would be interested in having the Blackers know their name," said Pat. "You're not going to run into anyone who knows much about that one."

"There was another man that was hurt bad. Joseph Kavanagh was attacked," said Kevin.

"I heard that Joseph had an accident and that he didn't live long after it," said Pat

These things are repulsive and beneath contempt. Denny and I have talked about this before, and so far those deaths are the only ones that I know of. It's upsetting to hear from you that the killings are still going on."

"Since '98, you said there were other killings. Is there anything that might be connected to this?" asked Kevin.

"For the retribution killings, that I am familiar with, people tend to kill outside so that innocents aren't caught up in the fighting. The beast that's doing this doesn't care. It is an awful creature," said Pat.

"Something awful killed your brother, Thomas. Was it the same thing?"

Denny didn't respond.

"Was it the Púca?" asked Kevin.

"No. He told me that he tried hard to save him but couldn't and I believe him."

"That seems to be a running line with him," muttered Kevin.

"Boy, you told me you knew him." His face started to turn red. "I don't think you know him in any way or you wouldn't talk that way," complained Denny. His expression turned into a scowl.

"The Púca has helped me out a lot. With his help I got a way to take care of myself. Young man, I don't like your tone."

"'You're too close. You're not asking the right questions," said Kevin.

"Why don't you get out of here," grumbled Denny.

"When we met, you told me that you talked to the Púca. Is he the one that did this to you?" asked Pat.

"This thing killed my Anty and my family. Nothing or no-one stops me from killing it."

"You didn't answer me, Kevin," said Pat. "Did you get those wounds from the Púca?"

"No-one stops me from killing the thing that killed my Anty and my family. Not even the Púca. Leave me alone." Kevin stood up.

The other two didn't say a word. Pat's mouth was still open. Denny took out his pipe and bit on it.

"He told me, he didn't do it. I believed him," Kevin said. He hobbled outside. He got beyond the protective wall surrounding the cottage but managed to stub his sprained foot against the bristles of some rough heather. *Damn it. Anty, what am I to do?* he thought. *Why am I here? Why is this happening?*

He looked at the long rolling landscape. He knew there was a way up the Knockroe slopes to the mountain but couldn't see it. *Girl, I can't hear your voice but, damn it, if you could speak I know you'd tell me something.*

He so desperately wanted to walk and get away from the cottage. His foot was sore and the bristles against his braced bare foot reminded him that he wasn't going anywhere. He hated it but knew he was going to have to go back into the cottage. He found himself a rock and sat down and waited for the night sky to show itself.

In the morning, Denny and Pat sat on the wall outside the cottage. "He's a fool. He's hobbling through the thick heather thinking exercise is going to get him out of here quicker," said Pat. "Putting weight on his leg and smashing it is only going to mean he is going to stay longer."

"Well, that wrapping and bracing will help some. He's preparing himself to fight that thing and I know he hasn't figured out how. The only thing he has to fight against is himself. Pat, I don't know about you, but I don't want to give the boy cause."

"Why the confused look on your face?" asked Pat.

"I am just glad I'm not Kevin."

"Fine speech Denny. When you're awake, join me. I'll be checking my traps."

Conversations with the Dead

On his walk up the slopes of Knockroe, the colours became more varied than around Pat's cottage. The slopes were covered with a variety of mossy greens combined with light blond grasses, light to dark browns, and dark reds. As he climbed higher, the dirt patches got darker.

Kevin let his oak staff drop alongside the path. It reminded him of the brace that he tore off before he started. He didn't want to depend on anything or anyone anymore. He followed a trail that led him to a place where his cares were left in a world distant and far below.

From Knockroe, he saw that the mountain range continued its run on each side of him. He stopped and stared at the range on his left that picked up after the pass and went on towards New Ross. The walk that he took that way with his mother and sister, happened so long ago that he didn't remember much of it.

As he headed towards the mountain peak, the air seemed to become more active. He felt and heard it, as the protective valley walls got left behind. After hiking for almost an hour and a half he reached the end of his climb.

The Stua Laighean summit was covered in coloured grasses. Light

-coloured, three-foot-wide rocks lay scattered around as they did on the slopes. From a distance, they still looked like faerie dust against thick underlying reddish brown and blackish brown peat. Torrential rains and wild winds had cut long furrow strips into the peat that flowed down the slope. The stream channels were two to four feet deep. In some places large patches of sod slipped loose from the peat and clumped into small mounds.

The sky was clear and blue. Grey, wispy clouds hugged the farthest reach of the sky while a hazy fog obscured the outline of the horizon. "I know the ocean is there, but I can't see it," he said.

Kevin stopped and glared at the peak of Vinegar Hill. It was about a dozen miles away.

It is easy to blame the monsters and the gods for monstrosities, he thought. *The worst things are done by men. They force us to make awful choices and we're forced to stand by them. They should be accountable and so should we.* Up here, he felt free but vulnerable.

To race, run and fly like a Púca, thought *Kevin. What an amazing thing to imagine.* He opened his arms and slowly twirled around and around. *I am alone at the top of the world and reaching into the sky.* He surrendered himself to the warm sunlight.

I used to look up to the sacred lookout stones wondering about the things that watched over us and protected the land. He looked, at the emptiness, around him. He didn't see the spectres behind the standing stones. "The Tuatha Dé Danann must be gone," he said. "There's just me."

He thought of the look of Anty's dark eyes and shouted, "Hey Anty, I'm here. I made it."

He looked around and said, "No, we made it." He picked up a stone and threw it as far as he could away from the mountain.

"I am going to kill a monster Anty. You'll have to stay up here while I'm gone. Maybe when I'm done, I'll climb up 'and find you."

Kevin walked to the other side of the mountain. "So that's the rest of Ireland," he said. "That's Carlow, and Kilkenny. The land goes out beyond so far and I don't even see the other ocean. There is so much more to see than we've ever dreamed. I could leave Stua Laighean to follow in the footsteps of Fionn McCool, the Red Branch, the Selkie people, the Land of the Giants or I could go to the old rock of Cashel in County Tipperary.

"I have to kill a man, Anty. Sorry, but you'll have to mind this place. Mister Kavanagh will keep you company until we meet again. I am a man without property, or people and I have to go back to meet the living and the condemned. Goodbye, Anty," Kevin turned around and marched back. He stepped through the furrows and headed down to Knockroe Hill.

In spite of the argument we had three days ago, it was strange that both Denny and Pat pretended it never happened, thought Kevin. *There were a lot of questions I was dying to ask, but I played along. I had to walk, again and that was all that mattered. I left without saying goodbye. It might not have been polite, but that's what I needed to do.* As he descended Knockroe hill, he gave a small wave. When he came to his thick oak walking stick, he picked it up again. "This will come in handy for smashing heads. You never know." As he used it to hit the ground a couple of times, he said, "It was strange that Pat Jordan let me have it."

He followed the path down to the valley floor and veered up and went over Cloroge More and down to the main road. The road linked Kiltealy, which guarded the southern mountain pass, to Newtownbarry, which in turn guarded the northern mountain pass. Standing on the road reminded Kevin of the hurling games they used to play on it. He took a couple of swings with his oak staff at an invisible sliotar and then he stopped to assess his options.

You would think that if anyone was cutting the men's distinctive member, it would be a disgruntled woman, Kevin told himself. *Lord Almighty, what an awful thought. No, it's not a woman. She wouldn't have done it as fast and she would have done it differently. The monster is a man and a demented one at that.*

The first terrible killing happened to Thomas Brien. Denny says that the Púca tried to stop it. The next was Martin Bennett on the Blacker estate, followed by Danny Scallan, Darby Brown and Matthew Whelan. The killings moved to the abbey. Although Thomas's killing was grotesque, it was different from the rest. It was more like an animal and less profane and wasteful. Kevin, took a left at the road and started walking north towards Danny Scallan's cottage. *The killer is going to hear I'm asking around. Lord, I have my work cut out, don't I?*

Kevin took a couple of days to talk to people around the cottages of the Scallans, Browns and Whelans. Each night he returned to the Neal property. When he returned the second evening, he felt angry. Most of the stones from his home had been hauled away. He grabbed a block and carried it to a place under a shady tree and sat on it. *Of all the Kellys, Jordans, Murphys, Nevilles, Kavanaghs and Neals that were around the fire of Thomas Brien's last storytelling, there's only me left,* he told himself.

A colt came up close to him. It was probably looking for something to eat. Kevin threw a rock at it. It bolted and ran back. A horse ran towards him. Kevin threw some more stones at it, sat up and yelled, "Not now, Mamma." He growled, "Go away." It was going to take a run at him, but Kevin stared it down. When the landlord's horse and the colt backed away, he sat back.

I guess I could just let them out, he thought. He walked to the front gate and put a stone to stop it from closing and returned to where he was sitting.

"I am not chasing horses too dumb to leave," he muttered. He just stared at the horse that tried to take a run at him earlier. While chewing on grass, she kept an eye on her colt.

Too nice a place to leave; I get it. Kevin grabbed a rock and threw it at the stone boundary wall.

Well, I've talked to a lot of people these last couple of days, thought Kevin. *Ed Williams told me that as soon as Joseph Kavanagh was killed, many of his neighbours were bullied to leave their farms. Liam's friend Johnny Byrne, confirmed that he remembered seeing burn marks on Mr. Kavanagh's assailant's left hand and wrist. The two of them remembered a common brand on each of the horses. It looked like the letter F in a circle. That seems pretty simple to me. Well simple but functional, I suppose.*

Since they knew who I was, I lied to them. "I'm going to Liverpool to get a better job," I said. I don't know if they believed me, but at least they didn't bother me with questions.

They confirmed that Darby Brown and Danny Scallan were castrated. They didn't know that it happened to any of the Whalens. It's not something families would want to talk about. God, and to think that it could have happened to Nick Walsh or Phillip Jeffers. It's the last kind of thing friends or families would want to discuss.

He stood up and gave his father's field a last look over. *The killer is somewhere near Bannow Bay, so I gotta go back. I'll spend the night at the Walsh's place. It'll be warmer there.*

Kevin marched out through the front gate and looked back at the horse. *Not one of them is curious about getting out,* he thought. "Maybe when I'm gone," he said. He picked up a rock, threw it in the air and smashed it with his oak stick down the road. When he saw the Walsh farm, he thought of the landlord's horses. *Who was Nick Walsh talking to before Joseph Kavanagh was murdered? The man who killed Joseph Kavanagh?*

The Return

Kevin took a seat on a stone fence that lined the road that led him back towards Tintern Abbey. He had visited Alistair Alcock's house an hour earlier. He took out some food that the steward had offered to him at the end of his visit. "Thanks, Alistair," he said as he tasted more of the bread and dried apricots.

He remembered how weak the old man appeared. The steward told him that he was recovering from an infection. When Kevin had seen him five years ago, he had used his walking stick as an accessory to a gentleman's clothing, but to-day he depended on it. He didn't seem capable of sitting down or getting up without it. His hair was now more white than grey. He regularly wiped his nose with a handkerchief that he kept in an inside jacket pocket, but his voice wasn't raspy. Kevin, from his last conversation with him, learned to be respectful and careful in what he said. Alistair told him that Harry Keane had asked him about America. "He asked me about a Mr. Ruggles Wright," he said. "The Americans are looking for settlers to build a settlement near Montreal in the Canadas. It's a place in the wilderness where cliffs are surrounded with trees aflame with colour, bound by a circle of waterfalls and cascading rapids. Mr. Keane seemed to like that someone could run for days without meeting anyone. Honestly, I didn't find that much of an attraction," he said.

"Well, he asked me to verify this man's reputation, and I did. The Wrights seem to be men of good character and industriousness. Mr. Keane left the island after our last visit."

"How do you know that?"

Alistair laughed.

Kevin had never seen the man laugh and found the sound of it contagious.

"Well, I couldn't forget because he persuaded me to make a wager. Fortunately, I did, and I managed to make a substantial return on my investment."

"That sounds very out of character for both of you. And what kind of wager was it?"

"Horse racing," said Alistair. "He refused my requests for a follow-up run because he was in a hurry to board a ship." Alistair switched the topic to the current state of Elizabeth and her brother and the conversation quickly became depressing and unsettling.

Kevin, from his seat on the stone fence, looked around at the clear sky and the open road. "Sorry to leave you old man. You deserved much better from me." He felt in his gut that he would never see Alistair again and he felt as if he was still seven years old. He quickly swallowed the last piece of his bread, got up.

I can see why Elizabeth Alcock let herself get locked away. She can't bear letting go of his lordship. Kevin put his pack on.

"He wouldn't want you dead, so fight back, girl," he said as he pounded his stick on the road. "Don't let your brother pull you down. You can't let them win," he told the empty field. "We've work to do. Damnation. Retribution is what we need, girl. It's time to show what we're worth," he said as he restarted his march back to the forge.

To the billowing clouds and a rolling grey and green landscape, he said, "I can't tell if it will storm hell on earth or be a day of sunshine—that's just the way it's in this county and I'm up for it either way."

He passed a raven perched in a tree above a stone wall. It reminded him of Joseph Kavanagh. He stared it in the eye and carefully tapped the last piece of the dried fruit up to it with his oak staff.

A Walk Down a Beaten Path

Before reaching the gate at Tintern, Kevin was confronted by ten men gathered on the road ahead of him. Kevin's hand pushed back his hair and passed through dark brown waves that flowed over his jacket collar.

Half of the young men were circled around Samuel Boyse on the right side of the road. The thin lad had filled out and now he was a pinch taller than Walter. He had new shoes and there weren't any tears on his pants. He still wore the same well patched cap.

The rest of the young men were lined loosely ahead of them on both sides of the road.

Kevin stopped for a moment. "Lord, it's so nice to be wanted," he said in a low voice. He smashed his oak staff on the road and restarted his walk.

"You were told to stay away," snarled big Walter Glascott. To emphasize his square chin he nudged the brim of his cap and *tilted his head slightly back. Hasn't changed much, thought Kevin, and probably never will.*

"So you were expecting me?" asked Kevin. "It was the fella I saw on the horse that passed me back there, was it? He was sure riding in a hurry. I take it, that wasn't his da's horse"

"None of your business, you fool," replied Walter.

"Good day, Richard. Why so quiet?" asked Kevin. Richard tried to push back the long strands of straight hair that flopped at his eyebrow on the right side of his face. He stayed in the background and pretended to ignore him.

"You have no right to be here," taunted big Walter Glascott.

"Not today, Walter. I am in a terrible state. I feel like a bloody raging lunatic. I'm telling you, Walter, it's just not the day for it."

"Watch it lads, he's got a sling," said someone.

"If I was going to use it, I'd have taken your head off," said Kevin.

Kevin noticed that none of them carried sticks. *They are supposed to be working, and they all sneaked out for this meeting,* he thought. *What a bunch they are.*

A few of them headed towards him.

So much for loudmouth ranting, he thought.

"I am coming through and you'll let me be," ordered Kevin.

"I am glad you think so," said Walter.

"Glascott, I'm just not in the mood."

Kevin didn't wait for anyone to try to grab him. Of the three closest to him, he used his oak staff to hit one in the left side of the face, another he taunted with a poke and hit him on the right side of the face, and the one in the centre he made a smashing mess of his nose. He hit each of the other two a couple of more times. The other two stopped in their tracks.

"I told you boys. I am feeling like an absolute raving lunatic today. Can't you see? I went to get a lead on who killed Anty and my family and I'm back. If anyone here's involved, we are going to have a few choice words."

One of the boys, behind the other two, stepped ahead. "Ignore the talk, just take him."

His friend joined him while the other three backed off to observe.

The one who was advancing on him had a knife in his hand. The other followed behind him. Kevin waved the staff towards his face and with all of his weight he poked it hard above his knee. He caught him by surprise, smashed the side and bottom of his jaw and then poked him hard in the chest causing him to fall back. The knife fell to the ground and Kevin used his staff to flick it away.

The other lad stepped back.

"Samuel, are you going to stand there with your hand up your tool or are you going to help me find who did this? Believe me when I say the Púca had nothing to do with it. Well, what do you say?" said Kevin.

"Don't bother with him, boys. He's not worth it. We'll take care of this ourselves," said Samuel dryly.

The other boys let Kevin pass, and Samuel didn't follow.

"Samuel, it is amazing how a nice piece of oak can get a conversation started, isn't it?" Kevin muttered.

Kevin opened the door of his cottage and threw his rabbit skin bag across the floor and started stripping. He quickly lit the hearth fire and then started washing himself.

"God, I reek."

He picked up his clothes and looked them over. *Most of this is beyond repair,* he thought. *Fixing the waistcoat will need an angel's touch. Dear St. Anne, we need an angel's touch.*

Something started smashing on his door.

"Just a minute so I can get respectable."

James Kennedy marched in and asked, "What are you doing that's respectable?"

Kevin did his best to get another pair of trousers on. "I can explain."

"You got yourself in another bender and you're back. Does that mean you're here to do some work?"

"Of course, Mr. Kennedy. The abbey's coming apart and you want me to save it?"

"The likes of you won't save anything. Sevens has taken a bad spell, and the work isn't getting done."

"Is he hurt?"

"He'll recover. You'll find him at the forge. We got a replacement for you, but he made a mess of Mr. Seven's hand. It looks worse than it is, if you ask me. That boy didn't know a coal fire from the back of his arse. If you're not up to it, I'll find a permanent replacement."

"Fine, fine we'll get to it. You know the day is almost over," said Kevin.

"You're going to meet me at the forge," Mr. Kennedy said, "and I am going to show you what you need to do. And you are going to have to figure out how you are going to do four months work in half a fortnight— and if I see you with a bottle while in the forge you're out."

"I'll be right out," Kevin said, as he tried to slip his shoes on and button a shirt at the same time. He grabbed the waistcoat and worn coat he had just taken off and quickly ran after him.

Richard and Samuel, on their walk home, followed behind a sullen Walter.

"Well, weren't you the softy?" said Richard.

"What? What are you going on about," muttered Samuel.

"The long lost comes back and you don't give him the time of day. I think a few knocks to set him right would have been in order."

"Maybe."

"So you don't disagree?" asked Richard.

"It's not about him. He was right. It's been more than a year and we know almost nothing."

"Anty you mean?" said Richard.

"Of course, her. But it's the Jeffers and all of them."

"How can it be that everyone's shut up like a whore's treasure chest?"

"Because they have more to lose?"

"Give me room, why don't you?" replied Samuel. "There's something wrong about the way we're looking at this."

"But…"

"Richard, go loosen some barnacles from Walter there," said Samuel. "There's a pariah back in the village and I don't hear ranting and raving."

"Oh, and of course where's the pity for the likes of poor old Richard here."

"Kiss my boot," joked Samuel as he backed up and pretended to kick Richard's backside.

Richard ran up alongside Walter and asked, "What's got into you? You're like your little sister stuck with her prayers rather than eating her dinner. Are you sick or what?"

From behind him, Samuel said, "That's because we left him back there and this is his long-lost brother."

"Alright. Leave it. I've things to do. I'll see you tomorrow, maybe." Walter gave them both a wave and took a detour across a field.

"That wasn't like him," said Samuel.

"Of course not. Do you think he's depressed because we didn't beat the hell out of Kevin Neal?"

"No. Something's not right. Sick, maybe?"

"Maybe he's dying for Elaine Byrne," said Richard.

"We all are," said Samuel. "Anyway, enough about that."

"I'll tell you," said Richard.

"What? Spit it out."

"Last autumn, I saw a fella in a black coat. Douglas FitzGibbon was his name. He was rough looking. Walter knows him. I opened the door, and there he was. Mam and da and the others were still at church."

"You mean the one responsible for breaking Padraig's arm?"

"Yeh, he's one of those lads," answered Richard. "He's one of Adam's Caesar's men. He just barged in. He wants information. I'm sure he hasn't given Walter any money. He's a bugger, he is. What does he think we are? Dirt?"

"So why didn't you tell me?"

"Makes my skin crawl," answered Richard. "Really, I thought keeping you out was doing you a favour. I think he knows you go into the abbey. I think he was going to try to get me to persuade you to steal stuff. We'd really have to get something worthwhile if we're to risk our necks."

"And you're telling me this now, why?"

"By the way he walks and talks, I think he knows a lot," said Richard.

"What about Walter?"

"Sick maybe," Richard repeated.

"Or Elaine Byrne?" added Samuel.

"Probably, but if he has a secret, like you, he's terrible at it," said Richard. "When he's ready, he'll be back to his usual ranting and raving, and you'll wish he never told us."

"Or Elaine Byrne?"

In unison, the both yelled, **"To Elaine Byrne!"** followed with a cheer.

Loose Ends

Kevin knocked on the door of the Finn's cottage, but no-one answered. He saw a boy wearing a tilted cap who was running on the road. He looked like he was about ten. Kevin went to him and asked, "Have you seen Mrs. Finn around?"

"She's over there on the other side of the fence," said the little boy. "She is supposed to be over there." He pointed to the cottage in front of him.

"How do you know that?" asked Kevin.

"Because she's my mam."

"So Darragh, is it? And you've grown," said Kevin. "I'll be sure to tell her."

Sarah Finn, after giving him a return wave, continued digging in the garden. When Kevin got close, Sarah said, "You look much better than the last time I saw you, Kevin. Your hair though is long and wild looking. We thought you were gone for good."

"I have some unfinished business. How is Jacob?"

"Much better. We get by with hard work, prayer and the passage of time," she said, as she pulled the wood shovel out of a trough and stabbed the top of the potato mound. She walked away from the plot while wiping her dirty hands on her apron.

"Mrs. Finn, I've come back to find who was responsible. Somebody must have learned something since the last time we talked," said Kevin.

"There was another killing, near Newbawn, in November. It was west of here, about five miles," she said as she pointed beyond some trees. "A father and two of his sons were murdered. Most of the men still blame the Púca. They're not going to listen to you."

"Foolishness. The killer is a man. It has nothing to do with a Púca. The superstitious nonsense is just a distraction. I learned some things from people up north. The attacks were quick, precise and without damage to the cottages. So far, I haven't found something that connects the victims."

"How do you stop monsters?"

"Monsters don't need to take the time to castrate. I think, it might just be one man," said Kevin. "And I think we've found an egotistical slip-up."

"The murderer enters the victims' homes and kills everyone. And no-one gets away. Sorry, I don't see how that's possible."

"I don't know how it's done, but people are gutted in the same way each time. All I'm saying is that it is done quickly and there is a consistent style to the work. A bunch of brutes would tend to make a mess of things."

"Whoever is doing this is mad," said Sarah Finn.

"We have to be careful, Mrs. Finn. We can't underestimate his intelligence. He's done this at least half a dozen times. He's quick, efficient and in absolute control, and has likely been going on for years and no-one has been saying anything. I think he's got connections, and I am sure there's people out there that know more than they are saying. Most of the dead are Catholic."

"That's because most of the people in the county are Catholic," said Sarah Finn.

"Well, the Jeffers weren't Catholic and most of the families around here are with the Church of Ireland."

"Maybe, or maybe it's too early to say."

"Enough of that. We have to stop this from happening again. No-one deserves to see what we've seen." Kevin scratched his head and looked away. "Mrs. Finn, do you think Mr. Jeffers knew the man who died in Newbawn?"

"I don't know. Maybe there was a connection during the war. I don't know what to tell you."

"You might have a point. If the parishioners could be convinced that they're only looking for a man, we might get some more clues. I know they're afraid, but if they stand together, they'll feel more confident."

"Kevin, it's good to have you back, but look before you step. None of us wants to go to another funeral."

He looked down at the ground and smiled. "By the way, your son Darragh was asking for you," he said.

"Pay him no mind, Kevin. We let the boys think they have things in hand, but only as long as we have eyes on them. And like I said, watch where your feet take you and we'll work on the rest."

Kevin laughed. It was the first laugh he had in a very long time. *Not since Anty,* he thought. Oddly, it reminded him how empty he had become, and that he recognized that she and Anty shared certain features and expressions, and stubbornness.

⁓◎⁓

"I hear you were looking for me, boy."

Richard turned around and saw Douglas FitzGibbon standing beside a tree he had just passed. He was dressed in black and wore gloves. Richard looked around but didn't see his horse.

"Who, are you calling a boy?" he complained.

"Well?" said Douglas.

"My uncle told me that someone in Newbawn knew where you were," said Richard. "He said he didn't, but you showed up."

"Everyone knows everyone else's business here if you want to look deep enough, they say," said Douglas.

"Walter says you know ways of making some coin."

"For those that can show their worth, are dependable and know how to keep quiet, there might be something," said Douglas.

"Eh, Walter didn't tell me nothing. I just figured things out, that's all."

"How is Walter? He hasn't been in touch. Tell him, I'm feeling lonely."

"He's been really busy on the farm." Richard looked cautiously as Douglas walked closer to him. "And I think he's sick," he added. "What sort of things do you get men to do for you?"

"Kevin Neal didn't get a good beating from you lads in a while? What's up."

Richard spun a white lie, "They felt sorry for him, with him all skinny and wasted away, and everything. He's a miserable sight to behold."

"Back in Tintern again, is he?"

"Uh, probably, but haven't seen him in a long while."

"But Walter would know, wouldn't he?"

"No. He works with his da and can't stand Kevin Neal. I'm sure there's more that know than him."

"Like you of course."

"yeh, I suppose."

"Is Samuel a friend of his?"

Richard hesitated and shuffled his feet as he said, "No, they detest each other. Kevin, tried to steal his girl." With more resolve he said, "He wouldn't mind seeing him taken away."

"Richard, why are you really here?" asked Douglas.

Richard avoided his eyes and grabbed the sides of his waistcoat and said, "I told you, Mr. FitzGibbon, I'm looking for a bit of extra work."

Douglas walked around him.

"The Púca has been making a mess of things, hasn't he?" added Richard.

"It's got people talking, hasn't it?" said Douglas as he encircled like a stalking wolf. It makes people step lightly."

"Do you know anything about him?" asked Richard.

"Him? Who says it's a him? It's a Púca isn't it?"

"Of course," said Richard.

"Why would you say it's not?"

"I didn't. A Púca can be a 'him' right? Otherwise, he'd be an it, right?"

"Whatever you say," said Douglas.

Anyway, I've got to go home," said Richard. "They're waiting for me."

"Tell your parents that they can expect me."

"What? But…"

"There's nothing better than family Richard. Family is at the heart of everything."

"When would that…?" asked Richard.

Douglas ignored him and walked away. He headed beyond the trees towards a huge field.

"Damn," muttered Richard. "This was a really, really dumb idea." He started running. He wasn't sure that once Douglas FitzGibbon got his horse, he wouldn't start chasing him. When he stopped to catch his breath, he remembered the argument he had with Samuel earlier in the morning. *"Wait until the,"* he said. *"Just four more days. We'll both go. Don't be stubborn,"* he said.

"Stupid. Stupid," Richard repeated. *That FitzGibbon knows who's pretending to be the Púca. I'm sure of it. Now that he knows where Kevin Neal is and doesn't trust me he's going to start bothering my family. Poor Walter—it's FitzGibbon that's his problem. Damned. What are we going to do?*

Mr. Pierce Newton King, the former county sheriff, knocked on the front door of Tintern Abbey.

Mr. Stewart answered the door but refused him entry and closed the door.

Mr. King knocked again.

James Kennedy appeared from the side of the building.

"Mr. King, I am told you were asking for me."

"You should have invited me inside. It would have been much more civilized."

"This comes from the man that helped murder the former occupier of this house," replied James. "I heard that your former post of High Sheriff is to be passed on to your cronies. They give that to all sorts, don't they? I'm sure your influence will be put to good use, won't it?"

Mr. King leaned on his oak shillelagh and replied, "Mr. Kennedy, I am a busy man. Adam's Caesar, who provides judicial oversight overseas, is of the opinion that he is legally the guardian of this property. He asked me to review his assets."

"That is a little far-reaching, since the real proprietor of this estate is still fully alive and in a good state of mind. If that is all you have to say for yourself, I will leave you to your coachman. I am sure you know the way out."

"There's a war on and the situation is very fluid. My benefactor, Mr. Colclough, rewards loyal service. Should there be a transition, it is not a foregone certainty that there would need to be a wholesale change of the guard."

"So, why are you really here and what is it, that he wants from me?"

"If you're interested in maintaining your employment here and your connections overseas I suggest you provide us with information as to the whereabouts of Mr. Kevin Neal."

"Why does Mr. Colclough want to find the man?"

"I don't know and I don't care to."

"He was killed on this property. There was a funeral and his gravestone stands in the graveyard."

"Reliable sources have confirmed that he's still very much alive."

"That would be a strange state of affairs, wouldn't it? I'll ask around."

"Please do. Mr. Colclough's consideration of appreciation will not remain open-ended. Mr. Colclough requires results within two days, or stronger measures could be sanctioned."

"So you're giving us until Saturday to do the impossible. To-day is only Thursday you know."

"Don't waste my good will, Mr. Kennedy," said Mr. King.

"I haven't seen Mr. Neal, I tell you. After the Walshes were killed, I was told that someone who bears his description left. I didn't pay attention to the story since I assumed he was dead. No-one knows where this person went. Maybe he went to America. You can ask around and I am sure others will tell you the same, but if Mr. Colclough were to provide us an honorarium, perhaps we could pursue different avenues of investigation."

"I am a busy man and I am disappointed that we haven't resolved the Neal issue. I must warn you Mr. Kennedy, sometimes tragic things happen."

"Like what, for example."

"I couldn't say, but I do hear terrible rumours, as do we all, Mr. Kennedy. Good day." Mr. King readjusted his hat and returned to his coach.

As James watched the coach disappear beyond the trees, he said, "Good riddance, you ignorant buffoon."

⁓◦◉

Kevin walked into the Boyse backyard and yelled, "Samuel Boyse. What are you doing?"

"You can see very well what I'm doing," he yelled back. He was digging a furrow in his father's garden. "What do you want?"

"You know what I want. Where is Anty's murderer?"

"Kevin, leave us alone."

"For Lord's sake, you'd think you'd want to hunt this man down as much as me," said Kevin. "Think of poor Anty, shuddering in her grave."

"It'll be you shuddering in your grave if you don't get out of here. I don't like the thought of anyone seeing me speaking to the likes of you."

"So, you're standing there telling me you're not going to do anything to find the bastard that killed her? You're a poor excuse, for a man."

"Get off. We have our own ways."

"Samuel Boyse, you are a coward and a waste to the human race,"

Kevin complained.

Samuel didn't reply.

"Then stay out of my way," Kevin told him, and marched away.

Kevin walked towards the forge after crossing the bridge into the Tintern estate. James Kennedy, waved him over from the rear of the abbey. When he got close James said, "Kevin, you're in a tough spot. Adam's Caesar knows you're alive and his men are coming for you."

"It's that damn Walter Glascott. Well, it could also be Richard Caulfield. It could also be Samuel Boyse. The truth of it is, there's a long list of possibilities."

"And Pierce Newton King was here," said James as he stared at him firmly in the eye.

"The fellow that set up his Lordship? How long do you figure I have?"

"He said two days, but he's a liar. For all I know, they could be here already. This is what you'll do," James said as he pointed south. "You'll head to New Ross. You'll help bring back supplies for us."

"You mean rum running?"

"Kevin, if you stay here you won't be around long."

Kevin didn't say a word. He turned and looked at the path that led to the bay. "There's a man who is ripping people apart and I need to find him. There are people here that know him. I'm sure of it. Besides, I'm tired of running. When there was a fight to be had, my father and brothers didn't run, did they? They stood their ground."

"But Kevin, you know they're…" James didn't finish the sentence.

"Mr. Kennedy, I'm not blind."

"How about brainless?" added James. "Look here, do you really have any idea who you're dealing with? Pierce Newton King was recently the County High Sheriff and now he's drawing from Colclough's pocket. It will be men of the like that killed poor Mrs. Walsh that will show up at your door and I don't want them at mine."

"Yes, I'd like to take up your offer, but someone has to find the killer. I need to know who it is and stop him. You can't close your eyes to it. If your people are the next to get cut and burnt, could you live with yourself?"

"I understand what you're saying, but until his lordship gets out of jail, we don't have much influence. Young Kevin, I'd like to help you more, but when they come, you're going to be on your own. I doubt very much that the sheriff's men have any interest in taking you back alive." James waved the back of his hand and started walking towards the abbey's servant entrance. "Maybe Mr. Sevens can talk some sense into you," he grumbled.

Mr. Sevens came out of the forge and waved for Kevin to come closer.

"What do you…?"

"Just a minute," said Sevens, as he watched for the front door of the abbey to close. "There's something I have to show you. Follow me it's by the stream behind us." He lead the boy into the tree cover. In front of the stream sprawled out on the ground was a corpse.

"How did that turn up?"

"Your friend Harry Keane, dropped him off. He said you'd probably recognize him."

The shirt was ripped open and the letters "JW" were drawn on a naked chest.

"He's the one that killed Judith Walsh."

"You got that from the initials?"

"I saw him. I saw him kill her. It's him for sure."

"Harry made a point of emphasizing that he didn't kill him. He said he just so happened to be in the right place at the right time."

"That doesn't mean he didn't have a part to play in this."

"What are you going to do?"

"Hang him. What else?"

"That's crazy. You heard what James said."

"I saw him kill her. She was a poor defenceless woman. She was a mother to me. She was more than that to the people that loved her. How could you ever think I'd ever forget what he did? Don't worry. I'll take him from here. It's best that you forget what you saw here."

Kevin waved Sevens off and then muttered, "the priest will hear an earful when I'm done, won't he?" He made the sign of the cross and heaved the body over his shoulder. He carried the body back to his cottage and leaned it against the nearby tree. Mr. Sutcliffe joined him.

"He killed Mrs. Walsh," Kevin said.

"So, he's with that bunch that killed my George?"

"Yes, I believe so," Kevin said. "In case you're wondering I found him this way."

"What are you going to do with him?"

"Well maybe we should hang him."

"But he's already dead."

"That won't be any skin off his nose, will it?"

"No but…"

"Wouldn't be a sin?"

"You mean if he was alive and we hung him, that would be alright but if he's not alive to complain about it, that's not? We'll not get any justice if we take this to any court. The Sheriff and his higher-ups were part of this."

"With no explanation he took off with one of our horses, saying he'll return it tomorrow," said Mr. Stewart. "Sevens, I'm telling you—that boy is up to no good." Both men were headed for Kevin's cottage.

"Well, will you look at that," Sevens said.

Tenants were crowded around in front of Kevin's cottage. There was a corpse leaning against it with a noose around its neck.

"So, what do they expect me to do about it?" muttered a perplexed Mr. Stewart.

"And why are you staring at me?" replied Mr. Sevens.

Kevin reached New Ross in about four hours. Alistair had told him that Harry was going to America. Kevin hoped to reach Harry before he boarded a ship. He knew his chances of finding him were slim but was convinced that he should at least try. He followed the river Barrow on his left to the dockyard. Trees lined his right side and a long forest covered a hill in the distance.

Approaching the walled town made Kevin very nervous. The monsters that he witnessed coming out of this place as a seven-year-old were as horrifying as anything he had fought as an adult. He stopped before going into the town and held the reins tightly. Traumatic images of a child's fears and fleeting nightmares, from twelve years ago came back to him. Approaching the town on horseback helped. He was making an advance on the fortress just like his brother Aiden and Captain Kelly had done a lifetime ago.

I don't know if meeting the Púca again is a good idea. These days I don't know if anything is a good idea. I had to come to this gate some day, I suppose. It might as well be now.

Kevin didn't see anyone around and it was very quiet. Maybe unusually so.

Maybe I should convince him to give me his ticket, Kevin thought and laughed. "No chance of that," he muttered.

"*Where are you going?*" yelled a voice.

Kevin leaned back on his horse and then twisted around. He saw Harry Keane approaching him from behind.

"Looking for you. How did you find me?"

"Now that it is time to go, I've had a lot of distractions. Some of my kind are trying to stop me from leaving. I figured you might show up. More the merrier. I've a sense of things."

"Why not at the docks?"

"You know—I hate crowds; besides I don't see you hurrying to get in."

"No, I suppose not." Kevin changed the subject by saying, "So, you're wearing the coat I gave you? It's missing a couple of buttons. Sorry about that."

Harry grinned.

Kevin held the reins of his horse tighter. "I thought you'd knock my head off the next time I saw you. I wasn't expecting your help."

"Do you think you'd miss it?"

"My head you mean? Probably. Who knows, maybe not."

"I expected better of you," Harry said.

"Things…"

"I have to go," Harry said as he turned to go away but then he hesitated, turned back and said, "Kevin, don't do it alone. You need the others." He turned and ran faster than a man could run. He raced up a rock face into the cover of the forest.

"Good Lord. All this way, and about nothing. Harry, I just wanted to tell you I was sorry, and that I made a mistake and—I was wrong. And I wanted to thank you for—more than I can ever say.

"And I didn't even thank him. Damnation. Harry Keane you're an ass."

Kevin, turned his horse back towards the way home.

"No sailing ticket, and back to a noose. Isn't that a kick in the head?" He petted the horse and gave a light tap with his legs to direct it on.

Kevin arrived back at the stables the next day in the early afternoon. Mr. Stewart followed him to the stables and asked, "Did you find who you were looking for?"

"Yes, I did."

"You were expecting me to clean up after you? What were you thinking about?"

"I didn't mean it that way."

"James and I talked about it. There's a plot in the cemetery. It's not hard to miss. It's yours. You've got some digging to do. By the way your guest is still leaning against your cottage."

"Still? Oh, and thanks, I suppose."

"There's a shovel by your tombstone. You better start digging. Don't do any moving until it's really late, please. And you didn't hear any of this from us. We don't want to have anything more to do with this."

Speculation

The day after Kevin returned—a Sunday—the abbey received an un-expected visitor. Mr. Stewart entered the sitting room and said, "A Mr. Studdard to see you, Mr. Kennedy." A tall, solid, self-confident man followed him into the room. "Sorry, sir, but he was very persistent," he added.

"Sir, I work for Caesar Colclough of Duffry Hall," said Mr. Studdard. "Mr. Newton King on his last visit told you to expect me."

James caught Mr. Stewart's eye and subtly pointed towards the forge. "So, what does he want?" he said.

"He asked you to find Kevin Neal for him. You told him that he left the country."

"That's not exactly what I said."

"I have it on good authority that Neal was seen on this property while you had a conversation with Mr. King."

"I expect that your information was mistaken."

At this point Mr. Stewart slipped out the front door. "Mr. Kennedy, please. My information comes directly from his neighbours. I can be persuasive when I have to, you know."

"Mr. Studdard, I assure you that Mr. Neal is not in the country. I was told that someone fitting his description boarded a ship for America from New Ross. Is there something else I can help you with, Mr. Studdard?"

"Caesar Colclough is also concerned about the poor repair of the estate. He asked me to provide a report."

"Mr. Studdard, you do realize we have met before. You and your colleagues helped me load some of my goods into Mr. Colclough's local stores. Well, walk with me and I will show you how productive our tenants have been." He led Mr. Studdard out the servant's entrance. "I assume you've noticed the slate roofs of the cottages. Quite something, aren't they?" asked Mr. Kennedy. "Our mill is over there across the river." He pointed towards the treeline across the river.

"Your influence seems to have advanced since my last visit," said James Kennedy. "I don't know if you have considered it, but we both of us have much in common. We both manage our situations as we see fit for absentee landlords."

"The influence of Duffry Hall is far reaching, as I am sure Mr. Newton King made clear to you, on his visit," said Mr. Studdard. "We're accountable, and he demands results."

The two men followed the walkway to the mill.

"This is the new mill which I helped design. While members of the family squabble over advantage and assets, we do what it takes to manage the revenue stream. Why don't we retire into the gardens so we might discuss some advantageous business arrangements in private?"

"Mr. Kennedy, you need to direct me to the boy."

―◦◎◦―

"Kevin, what are you doing?" asked Mr. Stewart as he stared at him bashing metal in the forge.

"It's obvious what I am doing. I am hammering this into shape. Why do you have a grim look on your face?"

"The barrister's man is here looking for you. Pierce Newton King knows you're alive, and this lad knows James is lying. This man is here to kill you."

"God," said Kevin. He spun around.

"What are you doing? You need to hide."

"I was looking for something. Sevens, lend me your cap." Kevin grabbed a couple of things.

"Why don't you get one of your own?"

"Thanks," said Kevin.

"What was his name?"

"Who?"

"The man who is trying to kill me, or God's sake."

"Mr. Studdard."

Mr. Stewart followed after Kevin when he left the forge.

"Who is he?" asked Kevin.

"He's one of Mr. Colclough's men."

"Mr. Stewart, you better leave, because I'm going to borrow one of your horses."

"What?"

"Mr. Stewart, didn't you leave already? Some things are best unknown, don't you think?"

Mr. Stewart shuffled away with an irritated perplexed look and headed back to the house.

Kevin hurried towards the woods.

⚮

James Kennedy saw Mr. Stewart come from around the corner to join him at the front of the abbey. After Mr. Studdard mounted his horse James Kennedy told him, "I'll see what I can do about finding the boy, and then we'll talk some more about the other business."

When Mr. Studdard rode off, he didn't say anything further and ignored Mr. Stewart.

As James Kennedy gave the man a farewell wave, Mr. Stewart asked, "Will we be expecting to see more of him?"

"That miserable creature is an opportunity. For a harmless bribe, I made sure he's in my pocket."

"You're paying him?"

"No. He'll get a cut from what Colclough buys from me. Since he's not buying because he is not around, sales are down. Now that there's an incentive I hope we'll get more business. If he thinks he owes me, we might get more information and he might be more discrete on what he tells his landlord."

"And if he does nothing, it might still cost you money," said Mr. Stewart.

If Mr. Pierce Newton King could be persuaded to pay an honorarium for information, it might balance that out, thought James. *...assuming I could trust a slimy snake like Pierce.*

"James, at the moment you haven't given him anything. He's not in your pocket until he does something. I overheard that He knows you lied to him. That man is dangerous. I am sorry to say James, I don't share any of your enthusiasm."

⚜

Sarah and her husband Jacob stood by the entrance door of the Irish Anglican church. They greeted members of the congregation as they went in. Sarah stepped away and walked over to speak with the Boyse and Glascott families who were talking together in a cluster.

"Hello, Mrs. Boyse. Glad to see you at to-day's service," she said.

Sarah stared at Samuel and added, "It was such a terrible thing. We have to catch that man that did it. What do you think Samuel? Are we going to catch him?"

"That man? But people—" said Mrs. Boyse.

"You know people say such nonsense. Isn't that so Samuel?"

"Well, probably."

"I'm sure if you knew something, you'd tell us, wouldn't you?" added

Jacob Finn.

Mr. Boyse stared at Jacob and told him, "You can be sure if any of us hear of something we'll share what we find. You're absolutely right, we need to get to the bottom of this."

"Like Sarah says, it's important that we share what we know and that we stand together. After the service, Sarah is going to say a few words. The Reverend asked me to go up, but I convinced her to. She's so much better with talking than I'll ever be. I'm sure I'd start ranting, and make a fool of myself and they'd all go home."

Sarah gave a wry grin and looked at Mrs. Glascott, and said, "But it's definitely time we spoke up about it. Nothing is getting done. Every once in a while people just need the right kind of reminder to get things going."

"Hello Mrs. Glascott," she added. "Hello Walter. I'm sure if you knew anything, you'd tell us."

"What?" asked Walter.

"The Púcaman killings," answered Samuel Boyse.

"Oh, I suppose so," answered Walter. "But Mrs. Finn, is he someone we should threaten?"

The boy knows something, she realized. *He looks defensive, and he's turned away from Samuel.*

"Walter don't talk like that," Walter's mother said. "Of course, we'd share anything we know."

"That's why as god-fearing people we have to stand together. Isn't that right Samuel?" asked Sarah.

Samuel looked at his parents and said, "I think so. I mean, it's time to go in, isn't it?"

The Reverend opened the door and welcomed the parishioners.

After the Sunday service Mrs. Sarah Finn from the altar steps said, "Thank you Reverend for letting us discuss this to-day. We are here to address a community problem. The murderer of the Jeffers' household is still loose. Another family in Newbawn was desecrated in the same gruesome manner. People are rightfully outraged and terrified. We need to put a stop to this beast before it happens again. Put aside the superstitious nonsense. This was done by a man. This might be a devil of a man, but he doesn't stand a chance against a god-fearing militia." She glared at the men folk seated before her. "I have heard some people say that this might be part of a plan to get retribution against the rebels, but no-one in conscience can defend such barbarous acts. I, for one, will not accept any defence for the cold-blooded murder of the innocent girls in the Jeffers' house that night. We won't get justice from the authorities. The culprit has been getting away with villainy without serious investigation for years. On behalf of the innocents and basic human dignity, please help us put an end to these monstrous killings. There are people in this parish that know more and it is time that we convince them to speak up. I ask you all to stand together. Reverend, would you please lead us in some prayers for deliverance?"

—✺—

"It's one of those days where everything seems to come our way," said Mr. Studdard. He was on horseback. Mr. Studdard took his pistol out of his coat. He double checked his sack of powder and put it back in his coat. *I hate dealing with this FitzGibbon fellow, but he is a necessary irritant. He is effective. This is going to set Mr. Colclough in a most obliging mood,* he thought.

He heard some noise from behind him. He turned around and saw someone on horseback approaching in a hurry. He touched his jacket to confirm where his gun was. Mr. Studdard was a very big man. He wasn't afraid of any man and he didn't restrain himself when he felt lesser men needed to be taught a lesson by their betters.

He looked back again. The horse maintained a steady pace and was gaining. He persuaded his horse to turn around so he could face the man racing towards him. He waited for the rider to slow down, but he didn't. He kept riding on and was riding the horse hard. Mr. Studdard couldn't see his face because the grey cap was pulled down in front and his face was tucked close to the horse's mane. The young man wore a common dark jacket and pants. Mr. Studdard recognized that he was riding a capable gentleman's horse. When the horse passed, he saw that he was seated on a good quality saddle. *One of Tintern Abbey's boys,* he thought. *I wonder where Kennedy has him going in such a hurry?* He moved his hand away from his gun and pulled the reins to direct the horse to turn. When Mr. Studdard faced the line of the road, he was caught off guard. The horse ahead of him had slowed and was turning around.

"Mr. Studdard?" a voice asked.

"Yes, and what do you want?"

"Mr. Kennedy forgot to give you something, Mr. Studdard." The rider headed his way.

"That's close enough. Who are you and what is so important that you had to chase after me?"

"Well, Mr. Studdard…" the young man said and then he swung his arm.

Mr. Studdard felt something hit his head, and he gave a scream as he fell backwards off of his horse. He managed to spin and almost managed to land on his feet. The force caused him to lose his balance, and he banged his knee. The man had a throbbing pain. He felt his head and found it bleeding. Mr. Studdard attempted to get to his feet, but he was dizzy. As his hand reached for a pistol, he heard the stranger say, "Studdard, I am the man you were looking for. I'm Kevin."

"Who?"

"I am the man who killed you."

Before he could pull his pistol out, a dagger pierced his throat.

Kevin stared at the blood pool around the man's head. As he backed up he scouted around to see if anyone was looking. He didn't see anyone. *Dear God, what have I gotten myself into?* he thought. *It's too late now.* He stared back at the blood on the ground. *…going to make a terrible mess of the horse and me, isn't it?* After wiping his blade on the grass, he put it back into his sheath. He rolled the man a couple of times in order to take off his coat, waistcoat and shirt. He cut off the shirt sleeve and with the rest wound it around the man's neck to stop the bleeding. He used the sleeve to try to remove the worst of the blood from his face, hair, coat and vest. It didn't work very well.

Kevin was glad that he had brought a long rope with him. He tied Studdard's hands and pulled his body up across the saddle of his horse. The man was very heavy. He pulled the rope under the belly of the horse and secured the corpse's feet.

He kicked dirt around the pool of blood and tried to disperse it, but he got blood on his shoes. He tried wiping his hands and shoes on the grass but only the worst of it came off.

Kevin rode back to Mrs. Doyle's farm with Studdard's horse in tow. Unfortunately, she was standing in front of the cottage.

"Kevin Neal, what are you doing?" she asked as she walked around his horse to Studdard's horse.

"Mrs. Doyle…"

"Kevin Neal, that man's dead," she said gasped when she saw the blood-soaked bandage at the body's neck.

"Well…"

"You did this?"

"I just need somewhere until it's dark," Kevin said.

"Why don't you take it somewhere?"

"It's in everyone's interest that no-one sees him."

"Mr. Neal this is a shameful thing you've done. You've no idea what's going to come back on the parish."

"Mrs. Doyle, he was here to kill people. I'd rather you didn't know anything about it. I didn't know you would be standing here."

"My Jimmy was always looking for trouble and Kevin… And I thought you would be the one to keep him on the right track. And look at this. Dear Lord, Kevin. If Jimmy comes back, I am going to have to keep him away from you." She whisked her hand and pointed to the back, and muttered, "I don't want to hear anymore about it."

After dark, Kevin led the horse he was riding to Mr. Stewart's barn, and removed the saddle. He led Mr. Studdard's horse, with the body, to the graveyard next to the bay. He cut the ropes, and the corpse tumbled to the ground. The bright moon reflected over Bannow Bay. Lines of waves crashed along the beach, and the air was fresh and sweet. The lack of voices was comforting.

The shovel leaned against the stone where he had left it the day before. "I'm glad I dug it deep yesterday," he told himself. After re-digging the grave he rolled the man into the open grave.

He looked at the body and said, "Mr. Studdard, besides the nice view, you'll be glad to know you have company." He started shovelling dirt on him, and said, "You won't be lonesome but unfortunately it's a tight fit. Where you're going, I'm sure you'll have bigger concerns." He dropped a heavy pile of clay over his face.

When he finished, he stared at the gravestone and said, "My Lord, Kevin Neal, you were a big fella, weren't you? At Sunday Mass we'll say some prayers for you."

Kevin rode Mr. Studdard's horse to the road beyond the gates. He dismounted and scared it off. He walked back to the beach and used a rowboat to get to the peninsula on the other side of the bay. As he rowed across, he stared back at his gravestone by the church near the water.

Now that the job was finished, he allowed himself to feel nervous, afraid and alone. The chilling sea air against his cover of sweat made him shiver.

Dear Lord, I've killed another one. He would have killed me, and probably Mr. Kennedy and Mr. Stewart. Couldn't let him go. It wouldn't have been right, would it?

He looked to the stars above the trees.

Does God really judge what people say is right and what they say you're supposed to do?

"Kevin Neal, how dare you blaspheme," he heard his mother say.

"But Mam…" he said.

He was quiet and kept rowing. Eventually he said an "Our Father" but it didn't seem to be appropriate and it didn't fix anything.

When he arrived at the beach, he pulled the boat into the woods. After setting washed clothes by a small fire to dry, he washed himself in the sea.

Dreaming of Anty made him uncomfortable. *Mrs. Walsh and my family—no it's too hard.* It wasn't possible just to think of her and not of everyone else he had lost. *It's best not to think,* he thought.

He leaned against a tree above the beach and watched the waves crash under the night sky. Something of him had died back at the graveyard and he was at a loss to say anything about it.

Richard Caulfield ran after Walter Glascott who was walking away from Salt Mills. It was almost noon. "Hey Walter," he yelled. "Wait for me. I need to talk to you?" said Richard.

"Not now. I've got to go."

"But…"

"Hello, Walter. Hello Richard," said a voice from behind a tree on their right. "Walter, you know Harold Wheeler of course."

Richard was caught off guard. "Douglas FitzGibbon," he muttered. He spun around to see him. He wore a long black coat with matching dark shirt, scarf, waistcoat and black gloves. Like the last time he saw him, he didn't wear a hat. Recognizing the man gave him a nervous chill.

Harold Wheeler who stood behind him wore a grey tweed coat and brown pants. He's *the one, that broke Padraig Walshes' arm.*

There was another stranger well behind both of them standing on the left side of the road. He was staring away from them. He was tall like the other men, had a noticeable long scar across his right cheek and was dressed in grey tweed. He wore a cap, unlike the others, and had long wavy hair reaching over his collar.

"Who's the other guy?" Richard asked.

"That's Brian Prescott. He's a curious one. He likes to keep an eye on things," said Douglas. He pointed and said, "Richard, I'd like to introduce you to Harold Wheeler." He is a man of few words, but he knows how to get things done. Boys, I am looking for a Mr. Studdard. I know he was here. We had an appointment, today, but he didn't show up. Have you seen him?"

Walter and Richard both shook their heads and shrugged. "I don't know him and I have never heard of him," said Richard.

"Me neither," said Walter. "What does he look like?"

"He is a big fella. Mr. Studdard is twice as heavy as you, Richard, and a foot and a half taller. He doesn't wear a hat, and he's not much on formalities. He manages cleanup jobs for Duffry Hall. On occasion, Mr. Studdard asks for hard-working men to help him out."

"I'm not going to argue with you, Mister. I have to get back to work," said Walter.

I bet either one of these three could kill both of us with their hands tied behind their back, Richard thought. He looked at Walter and then back at Douglas FitzGibbon.

"Well, like I said boys, I know he was around here yesterday," said Douglas. "He would have arrived on horseback. If, you hear anything, I'd appreciate it if you come find us. We'll be around."

"See you, Richard," said Walter.

Richard returned a wave.

"Richard, walk with me," said Douglas, as he pointed down the road that led toward the bridge crossing. "We're going to the Big House."

"Well, I wasn't really going that way," said Richard.

"Learn to be sociable," said Douglas and he waved for Richard to follow.

"Did you find any rebels around the Killoughram Forest?" asked Richard as he followed alongside him back towards the bridge. "That's near the Blacker estate."

"Why do you ask about that?"

"Just making conversation. I heard you were looking for rebels."

"Harold got himself some," said Douglas. "They didn't put up much of a fight, I understand. He put them down when they were sleeping, and Blacker paid well for it. By the way Studdard told me that Kevin Neal was seen around here. Have you seen him?"

"No, sorry I haven't," said Richard.

"I'd say you know better and you shouldn't waste your time with misguided pretense. You know I always get what I want." Douglas slowed his pace to walk alongside him, but he ignored him for most of the walk. After Richard crossed the bridge, he looked back and saw that Harold Wheeler followed quietly behind, but he didn't see Brian Prescott.

When they reached the path that followed the river and led to the abbey, Richard asked, "The Walshes are dead. Do you know anything about it?"

"I heard that the Púca did it. It was a nasty thing wasn't it? People get real torn up with nasty things. It was a shame Nick Walsh was a good lad."

"Why do you say that?"

"I gave him some money once."

"You mean he worked for you?" asked Richard.

"I wouldn't put it quite like that." Douglas stared into the forge as they walked past but saw only Mr. Sevens.

"He reminded me of my father. I must have got hit on the head that night. I gave it to him without asking anything in return. It was an occasion of sheer lunacy." He looked around to see if anyone else was around, but didn't notice anyone. "Harold, would you walk around with Richard and see if you can find Kevin Neal. Mr. Prescott, gets about on his own. We'll all meet up later at the Boyse cottage."

As Richard left, he watched Douglas remove a glove and heard him say, "It's time to have a good cup of tea." Douglas chuckled as he pounded the front door of the abbey with the side of a scarred fist.

"Follow me up this way," said Richard. "How did Douglas get that burn on his hand?"

"Douglas was fourteen, and he got to the barn in Scullabogue when the rebels set it on fire," said Harold. "He managed to drag his sister Evelyn away, but she was in flames. Trying to save her is how his left side got burnt. She might have survived, but men stabbed her to death with pikes. And they stabbed him in the side. The burn marks cover most of his side."

"So, why didn't he die?"

"He's a tough bastard. His older brother found him and told him that the rebels had also killed their parents while running from New Ross. They also destroyed their farm at Three Rocks. The brother drank himself to death and Douglas was left to take care of himself. He keeps reminding me that's where he picked up his charming disposition. You also lost someone at Scullabogue, didn't you?"

"I lost my uncle. He was a tailor. The rebels burnt them alive with more than a hundred others in the barn," said Richard. He pointed to the cottage on his right and said, "That's where the Walshes used to live. Maybe the neighbours know something."

Douglas always wants something, and he only gives a knuckle for our troubles, he thought. He's more trouble than he's worth. I don't like Kevin in the slightest, but there better be something in it for me if there's going to be blood on my hands. That fool Kevin will probably sleepwalk right up to them. Wouldn't that be funny?

Richard showed him where the Walshes were killed.

"Introduce me to the neighbours," Harold ordered.

The door of the abbey opened. Mr. Stewart peeked out. He gave a condescending look and asked, "And who might you be?"

"Would you tell Mr. Kennedy I would like to see him?" said Douglas FitzGibbon. "He'll know who I am. I am sure he's been waiting to see me."

"I am sorry, sir, but Mr. Kennedy is not ready to meet with guests. Perhaps you could come back in a couple of days. Good day, sir," and he proceeded to close the door.

Douglas jammed his foot in the doorway. "Go pour us some whisky,

Mr. Stewart. Oh, and bring us something nice to eat too. Be a good fellow and move along."

Mr. Stewart didn't move. He just stared at his foot.

"Oh, Mr. Stewart," Douglas said as he moved his foot out. He pulled the door towards him a bit and then smashed it back against Mr. Stewart's head. "Oh, how unfortunate."

Mr. Stewart stepped back, and Douglas pushed his way in. "Get us a glass. Go. We don't have all day." He stepped into the sitting room and said, "There you are, James. Stewart wasn't wrong. You definitely are in a bad state." James Kennedy was flopped on the couch. His hand still had a whisky bottle in it. "James, James, James. What are we going to do with you? It is the middle of the day, and you smell like Billy's tavern on a Thursday night. Mr. Stewart, bring us a fresh bottle. His looks abused."

Mr. Stewart came back with a bottle of whisky from the cellar.

"While you were gone, I got a bucket of water and a snack from the kitchen. I don't think you'll mind."

Mr. Stewart saw a full bucket of water set near Mr. Kennedy. He poured Douglas a glass of whisky.

"Leave the bottle, please," Douglas said. "And have a seat. It's time for James to come to life." He gently slapped James on the cheek, and said, "Wakey, wakey."

"Who the hell are you?" James Kennedy muttered.

Douglas took the cold bucket of water and poured it over Mr. Kennedy's head.

"Who the hell are you?" Mr. Kennedy repeated, but more loudly and with more alertness.

Douglas placed the bucket on the table behind him, bent down and hauled James Kennedy up so he was standing. He put his face an inch from James's face and yelled, "Kennedy get your head together or I'll cut off your pizzle."

James eyes lit up. "Don't you dare. No way. Don't you dare." Douglas left him standing and picked up the bucket again and poured the rest of the water down the back of his neck.

"For God's sake, what are you doing?" James yelled. "Who are you and what the hell are you doing in my house?" He meant to push the man away, but Douglas shifted and managed to shove James back down on the couch. "I think we have his attention, Stewart," and he stared back at him.

"Mr. Stewart, please bring me a fresh shirt," said James.

"Mr. Stewart have a seat. There will be plenty of time for that later. Douglas sat down and took a drink from his glass of whisky.

"Mr. Studdard is missing. Where is he?" demanded Douglas.

"Who?" asked a bewildered James.

"He came here yesterday to see you." Douglas got up and put a boot up on the couch next to Mr. Kennedy and leaned closer. "James, can you hear me?" he asked.

"Move off. I can hear you just fine. Give me a moment. I'm trying to focus. Studdard. Mr. Studdard. Yes, now I know who you are talking about. One of the barrister's men. He said he was from Duffry Hall. He said he was looking for somebody and then he left. He didn't tell me where he was going or what he was doing. The last time I saw him was when he rode off through the gate. That was yesterday. I expect he just went home."

Douglas put his face close to James and gave him an icy stare, and then stood up. James stiffened, clenched his fists, and gritted his teeth.

Douglas kicked the bucket out of the way, grabbed his whisky glass and sat down in a chair across from James. He crossed a leg and took a drink.

"What is your name?" asked James.

"You can call me Douglas," he said.

"Douglas, I really don't have a clue what your Mr. Studdard is doing. He wasn't here long, and he didn't say much."

"He did tell you he was meeting someone, didn't he?"

"No, he did not. He also didn't seem to be in a hurry, so I don't know what to tell you. He didn't stay, and I saw him leave. That is all I know."

"Where is Kevin Neal, then?"

"Who?"

"Kevin Neal. Mr. Studdard asked you about him."

"Neal. Oh, Neal. He's the one who got killed. The tenants told me that they buried him in the Catholic cemetery."

"That's where he should be, but I was told he is still pretty limber for someone that is dead," said Douglas.

"I am just telling you what I know. I can ask around and find out if anyone knows anything else."

"I'll come back in a couple of days," said Douglas. "I am sure you will find him by then. By the way, Mr. Pierce Newton King sends his best."

James cringed.

"You have an attractive daughter. Anne is her name, isn't it?"

"Don't you dare mention her name. Don't you even think of it."

Douglas, without looking at him or Mr. Stewart grabbed the bottle and left.

Mr. Stewart threw James one of his clean shirts.

James threw it on the couch and ran past him.

"What on earth," gasped Stewart.

James rushed past the kitchen and dashed outside.

Mr. Stewart followed him and found him on all fours on the ground heaving for all he was worth.

"Dignified or what?" muttered Mr. Stewart. "And this is going to be a noble countenance for the house, is it?"

James came back in, and his face was flushed red. "Don't say another word. I feel like hell, and I am doing my best to pull it together. My eyes are barely in my head."

"Is it your eyes you're waiting to put on or is it your arse? James the tea is coming to a boil. Would you care for some?"

"Yes, of course. What a grim fellow. I must admit, to-day wasn't my best."

A few minutes later, from the kitchen Mr. Stewart asked, "Are you there, James?" He was gathering an assortment of breads, cheeses and fruits.

"Getting washed up helped. ...and it's nice to have a fresh set of clothes. Let me prepare the tea. Would you like some as well, or would you prefer some whisky to take off the edge?"

"Like the stranger said, it's the middle of the day. That's the last thing we need. I don't like what is going on and from what I can see we better fear for our lives and our families." The pot had already boiled, so James poured them both cups of tea.

"You know you were so positive when you said you had Mr. Studdard where you wanted him," said Mr. Stewart as he picked up his teacup. "…it's just this kind that works for Mr. Studdard, and like I told you before it's the likes of them that killed poor Mrs. Walsh."

"I'm not going to pretend I was overly convinced I won Mr. Studdard's confidence. After he left, I came to the conclusion that what you said was right. Lord, I didn't realize how much I miss John Colclough. When he was here, I felt like we could get away with anything. That bastard threatened my family. I'm going to send them to live with our boys, near New Ross. That's what I'm going to do." He took a sip of his tea, as he walked around the kitchen. "…but I really don't feel comfortable doing that."

"You don't trust your boys?" asked Mr. Stewart.

"No. That's not it. I just don't like being so far from Mary and Anne. That's all. In the short term, I am going to try to persuade them to move in here for a spell."

"Are you thinking of leaving us?"

"If I left, who knows what the barrister would do with this place. Honestly, outside of here, I don't know what kind of future any of us would have. Establishing a militia and supplying men with pikes is making people feel more comfortable, but it's not much of a deterrent for the likes of Douglas and a half dozen of his men. Still, we do what we can."

"Douglas wants Kevin. How are you going to handle that?"

"I had a talk with him already and I warned him that this was going to happen. Go find him and tell him to get the hell out of here. Maybe he'll listen to you. If he's smart, he'll leave the country. Remind him that they know where he is and that they want him dead."

"Oh my God," said Kevin as he stretched his arm out wide over his head. "What time of day is it?" He gave a long yawn. He sat up and pushed himself up against a small tree. He saw that the sun was now high in the sky. He was surrounded by shrubs on a peninsula on the far side of Bannow Bay. He had slept under the trees across the bay from the graveyard.

Mr. Sevens is going to want an explanation. Hell, Kennedy doesn't care if I'm at the forge. God, I'm starving. Maybe I can get something from Mr. Sevens. He got up and walked across the peninsula to the side facing the mainland. "Lord, I'm glad the rowboat is still there," he told himself. *Not in the mood for a swim. Wonder what kind of day we're going to have?* he thought as he pushed the boat into the water.

"What is Mr. Stewart doing?" muttered Kevin as he approached the abbey on the footpath that stretched to the beach.

James Kennedy had his head poking out of the servant's entrance and he was saying something. As Mr. Stewart rushed towards Kevin, he pushed the palms of his outstretched arms towards the ground.

Is he telling me to get down? There are trees on my right, but they are way over there? Kevin stopped and looked around to see if he could see anyone else around.

When Mr. Stewart got near he said, "Kevin, an animal by the name of Douglas FitzGibbon came here looking for you and Mr. Studdard. He is connected with Mr. King. At the moment he's a bit preoccupied."

"Is Studdard missing?"

"FitzGibbon complained that he didn't meet him yesterday."

"What were you trying to tell me with the hands?"

"If they see you, they'll kill you. James told me that he wants you to leave."

"I know. I need to find Anty's killer before that."

"Kevin, over there." Mr. Stewart pointed to the trees. "FitzGibbon might still be walking around."

Once behind the cover of the treeline Kevin said, "In the north before these terrible killings started, I saw a couple of ruffians beat up an old man. The men that did that, rode horses that had a common brand. It had a circle with the letter F in it. I was thinking that if I could track them down, I might get a lead on who the madman is that's gutting his victims."

"That doesn't sound very bright. You might as well ask FitzGibbon what he knows. He'll say nothing and then kill you," said Mr. Stewart. "Most large landowners don't use brands. Farmers don't possess good quality horses. Since the big landowners consider themselves above the law, there is not much incentive for anyone to take the risk of stealing from them. A racehorse might be a different concern but from what you told me I don't believe those riders would be men of substance. The owner would issue a brand because they don't trust their more affluent neighbours."

"Something bothered me about the man I'm looking for—Why does he castrate the men?" asked Kevin. "There's a lot of effort to make a mess of their victims and then he goes and does that."

"Why not castrate and rip them?" asked Mr. Stewart. "I expect that lunatics are capable of doing anything."

"If the murderer dealt with just one person, he could afford to waste his time, but he kills everyone in the house. I don't know how he could do it so quickly and without having a single person escaping. He must have done it a lot of times. He has established a process and, so far, it works. He doesn't tie them up. When we enter a house, we find them sprawled around."

"I see your point. It has to be the last thing he does," said Mr. Stewart.

"You know for a sick person you would think it would be first thing they do, but they would do it differently. They would probably tie them up and they wouldn't want to deal with a lot of people. Maybe he likes an audience—but doing this on a continual basis doesn't seem possible."

"I'll bet he's a gelder," said Mr. Stewart. "He uses a crimp for gelding."

"He uses a crimp for cutting it off?" asked Kevin. "Lord almighty. Of all the worst things in the world to get paid for, even if it's for horses. Don't tell me I don't want to know. It sounds disgusting."

"Well, there's an art to it. He probably clips a lot of horses. Landowners pay cash for it and there's a demand for it. He goes in, kills for some premeditated reason, makes a mess of things to scare people and then he does this last thing as a signature, maybe."

"My Lord, what a monster," said Kevin. He looked around to see if anyone that he didn't recognize was looking for him. "Speaking of scoundrels, does the man that's looking for me have a bad burn on his right hand?"

"Yes, he does. How did you know?"

"I didn't," said Kevin.

"Oh, Lord God Almighty, that might be the devil himself," said Mr. Stewart. "What a deranged madman."

"Next time you see him, check the brands on the horses. The other two are likely riding his horses. He must get paid well for what he does."

"You must be out of your mind."

"If he's a gelder, I'd say he's probably the one that killed the Jeffers," said Kevin.

"Or we could all go somewhere and leave the county?" said Mr. Stewart.

"And where would you go? This is your home. Maybe I can convince the others to stand up against him. You'd think it would be simple enough to kill him. But then again, he's a professional killer, has lots of experience and has the support of the most powerful landlords and politicians in Ireland. It does sort of make you pause, doesn't it?"

Mr. Stewart just stared at Kevin. He was at a total loss for words.

"By the way, do you have something to eat? I am starving," said Kevin.

Kevin accepted the bundle of food that was wrapped in a piece of cloth that Mr. Stewart gave him. He headed back to his cottage with it. He didn't see anyone when he passed the front of the abbey. He ran to his cottage door and hurried inside.

When he put the napkin on a table, he heard something push on the door. It smashed open. A huge figure dressed in grey tweed lunged into the room. The man with long wavy blond hair in front of him, had a long scar across his right cheek. Kevin was forced to hop back.

God, he's a foot and a half taller than me and he's built solid like a bull, Kevin thought.

Kevin grabbed a stool and managed to block a knife jab. The man managed to kick Kevin's thigh and try to unsuccessfully grab the chair. Next, he grabbed a bench and smashed Kevin's side and then at his head but Kevin blocked with the stool, which fell apart. Another couple of powerful smashes with the bench caused Kevin to fall back to the floor. The attacker managed to kick him hard in the side.

Kevin tried to get up but was hit so hard by the bench on his shoulders that the bench broke apart. He stumbled to all fours. *He's going to kill me without me even touching him,* Kevin thought. He crawled back away from his opponent. He stared at the far side of the cottage. *My dagger's there,* he thought.

The figure noticed where he was looking and moved back to block his access.

Just a little extra space, that's all I needed, thought Kevin.

Kevin lay flat and stretched both arms ahead of him towards his opponent and sunk his fingers hard and deep into the dirt floor. "Come and get me, you coward," yelled Kevin.

His opponent stepped forward.

Kevin, spun on his side with intention of jumping up. *The knife. Where's his knife?* he considered.

Kevin managed to kick off an initial lunge, but the side of his calf got cut.

From the ground of the cottage, Kevin pulled up the blade of his buried sword. It was an early flawed version of the one he had used against the Púca. He moved his hands to the hilt. Kevin rolled, turned and managed to make a weak cut on the side of the man's lower leg. He jumped up and made a strong swipe across the figure's biceps. Kevin turned again and with all of his might swiped at his neck. As blood spewed out from the cut, as the man tottered. Kevin took another swipe at his neck and the man fell.

He stared at the cut half-way through the man's neck. "Lord, that's a mess," he muttered. "His head didn't come off." *I am definitely no Fionn McCool, or Cú Chulainn,* he thought.

Kevin dropped the sword back in the hole in the ground, covered it again and stamped on the earth. "Can't have Kennedy gnawing at me because he thinks I'm stealing from him," he muttered.

He moved back to lean against the wall to support his aching back. "What am I going to do with him?" he asked, just before he noticed that blood was dripping from the side of his calf.

—❧—

"Yes, I know, Harold. This is where he lives," said Richard.

"Out of the way," Harold demanded and pushed him away from the door.

He saw the outline of a person in the far corner who was lying on straw and covered with blankets. Harold glared at Richard and put a finger to his lips. He crouched low and slowly stepped towards the straw. He pulled the dagger from the sheath and raised it high. He quickly lunged forward and repeatedly stabbed at the figure. The blade and the blanket were covered in blood and he saw the curly hair of the back of a head when the blanket was pulled down to his shoulders.

Harold pulled the shoulders back to see his expression.

"Good God," he yelled.

Richard walked forward. "Did you kill the wrong guy? That's not going to go well."

Harold glared at him and Richard froze as he stared at Harold who threatened to kill him with his bloody knife.

"Hold it Harold," Richard said as he walked closer to the door. "I mean, I'm as shocked about this as you are. I didn't mean anything by it. I mean it's only Kevin Neal we're talking about."

"Caulfield, shut up," Harold yelled. "That damned bastard," he said as he pulled off the blanket.

"It's Brian Prescott. He's definitely had better days," said Richard.

"Caulfield you're damned useless. Get out of here and if I need you, I know where to find you."

The Shadow of the Beast

Kevin hobbled towards Sarah Finn and her young son Darragh who were on the road in front of their cottage. She made the boy drop some stones. She was scolding him for throwing a rock at a bird. Kevin couldn't make out what she was saying, but it reminded him of a similar conversation between him and his mother.

Kevin froze next to a tree. He saw someone riding a horse. When he was sure he couldn't be seen by the rider, he kept walking towards the Finns.

When he got close enough Sarah asked, "Kevin, what happened to you?"

"Look Mam, his pants are covered in blood."

Kevin put a hand on it, and said, "It's just fine." He looked at Sarah and then back at the boy and said, "Maybe I should have a word with your mam."

"What about?" "About you terrorizing the birds, and what to do with you—If you don't mind."

Sarah pointed to the door. "Let's have a look at that. Here, put your hand on my shoulder."

She turned back and looked at her son and told him, "You're not to wander off. I need to know where you are, do you hear?"

"Yes, Mam," he said as he wandered off."

Once inside Kevin said, "Sarah, it's not as bad as that. Most of the blood's not mine."

"Uhh, is this you, Richard and Samuel at it again?" she said as she poured warm water into a bowl.

"This time? No. Not at all."

"All angels, you are?"

"I wouldn't go that far."

"And that's a terrible-looking bandage. You're supposed to wrap it around your leg, not your trousers. What on earth were you up to?"

"I was in a hurry," he said.

"Boys, usually are," she said as she waved her son back towards their garden.

Once inside, she heated up a pot of water, and said, "Kevin, take the trousers off and put your leg up on the stool."

"Mrs. Finn…"

"There's a blanket there in the corner to cover yourself up."

He wondered if she'd slap him if he didn't.

She returned a few minutes later with scraps of cloth.

Kevin noticed he was missing a button on his jacket. "There's lots to be fixed." Kevin was holding an ill-fitting bandage on his bare leg. When she removed it to clean it he gave a groan because it pulled on some dried blood.

"Don't complain to me like a baby. All this talk about you wanting to take on the world. Oh my, that it is a mess, isn't it? It'll be alright. Needs a good cleaning. You can't just throw a rag on it and expect it will just be fine. So again, tell me what this was all about."

She put on a salt mixture which made him cringe.

"I had a serious conversation with an eejit that was trying to do me serious harm."

"And which of you got the worst of it?" she asked, as she wrapped a new bandage around his calf.

"I'm here, aren't I?"

"Maybe."

The cottage door swung open, and Kevin instinctively pulled away from Sarah.

"What's going on. I heard sounds," Sarah's young son said.

"There's a bit of bread over there," she said as she pointed to it. She looked back at Kevin and said, "I'm trying to do this and you're not helping. You're a pair you are."

Kevin put his leg back up on the stool so she could finish.

Sarah readjusted the pad over the wound and re-wrapped it with a bandage.

"Darragh, he has a cut," she answered. "Now take the bread and let me finish this, please. And don't forget to close the door."

After her son went outside, Sarah pulled the new wrapped bandage tight causing Kevin to groan.

"Are you fixing it or are you punishing me for my sins?"

Her son didn't close the door, so Sarah got up and closed it. She picked up Kevin's trouser's and looked them over. "There's quite a tear, and that's quite a mess of a stain," she said.

"Sarah, no," Kevin yelled as she dipped his pants into a bowl of water.

"You can't go out with this," she said as she brought the bowl towards Kevin. Make us some tea while I get the worst of the stains out," she ordered. "We'll dry it by the fire when we're done."

"Really, I can't. I can't stay. I have to go. They're looking for me."

"That's what I figured. There's always trouble following you. Should I be concerned?"

"Well…" said Kevin.

"And who's looking for you?"

He threw some more peat onto the fire and said "Adam's Caesar's boys are behind it." Kevin poured some more water into the pot. He re-wrapped his blanket around him as it almost slipped off and he returned to his seat.

"Maybe I should go fetch my son," Mrs. Finn said.

"You'll all be fine I'm sure," he said as he brushed an itchy nose. "No-one knows where I am. More importantly, I think I figured out who killed Anty," Kevin said.

"I'm not convinced by your confidence," she said as she checked the door.

"Like I said, your son will be fine," said Kevin.

"Well, don't sit there like you're waiting for the grim reaper, get on with it. I'm listening."

"Douglas FitzGibbon is his name. When I lived near the mountain, I saw him and another man beat up a neighbour. I recognized the burn mark on his arm. I'm sure he was working for the landlords as he is now. It was years ago and just before the disembowelling started. He's here and his lads are trying to cut me up."

"He did this?"

"No. One of his men."

"So, he knows you're alive."

"He won't be a problem."

"You can't say that?"

"Not if I'm somewhere else."

"Oh," she said. "And if he's not following you."

"It's not like that," he said.

"Then I won't ask," she said as she crossed her legs to the other side. She squeezed the trouser leg and then got up and started flapping the pants in the air. "Not all the blood is going to come out, but I've got the worst of it," she said.

"Mr. Stewart convinced me that the murderer is a gelder, so I need to prove FitzGibbon is the one. So far I have no idea why these people are being killed."

"Maybe he's just crazy?" she said.

"Maybe. Don't know."

"Well, he's got to be brought to justice," demanded Sarah as she sat down and prepared to sew the tear in his pants.

"Justice? The sheriffs and the courts are under the thumb of the landlords. Pierce Newton King, who's a former County Sheriff, oversees

FitzGibbon's work. We can only rely on ourselves."

"My husband, Jacob, is in the militia, and pretty well everyone has fought in the rebellion."

"You're right there. Mr. Stewart is organizing and we've given them pikes. They're going to need some training. Once we've identified the next house that's going to be attacked, they'll need to be ready."

She hung the trousers next to the fire, and looked back at Kevin and asked, "What are you looking at?"

"Just don't want my pants to catch fire. That's all."

"Have patience."

Kevin stared at the door. *How will we explain this when her husband walks in?* he wondered.

"You said that FitzGibbon is working for Adam's Caesar. Why does Caesar Colclough want you dead?"

"I know he's linked to John Colclough's murder, his brother's imprisonment and that he's trying to steal the Tintern estates. He doesn't like loose ends."

"We're in interesting times," she said.

"By the way, have you heard anything from Samuel Boyse?" Kevin asked.

"No, I haven't. Why?"

"Nothing. Just wondering."

"But I believe Walter Glascott knows something," said Sarah.

"Why?"

"I talked to him at church on Sunday. I think he knows something about these people"

"How was the sermon?"

"It's the first time people got talking as a group. Everyone is afraid. Some got childishly boisterous. When people hear the talk publicly, they start realizing how ridiculous the Púca stories are. I think we're going to get more support for the militia. By the way most of them liked my speech."

"I thought your husband was going to give it."

"He's not much for getting up in front of crowds," she said and passed him a bowl of tea.

Kevin readjusted his blanket, drank the tea and nervously stared at the door.

Sarah sewed a button on Kevin's jacket as he pulled on his dried pants.

Sarah's husband and son barged in from outside.

Jacob Finn looked like a large, powerful ox of a man.

"What may I ask are you doing?" asked her husband, Jacob.

"He didn't have any pants on," his son said.

"Jacob, I can explain."

"And how did you do that?" Jacob Finn asked.

"What?" responded Kevin.

"Darragh told me that Sarah was fixing a nasty cut."

"Jacob, it was one of Colclough's boys. Do you really want to know?" Sarah said.

"I probably shouldn't, but in the name of heaven I'll ask, anyways."

"They want my head for warning poor John. I was jumped in my own cottage, if you can imagine. I'm telling you, they've no respect."

"Should we expect them here?"

"That last one has been taken care of," Kevin said.

Jacob looked at the bandage and said, "I see. You're right, maybe I shouldn't have asked. By the way, did Sarah tell you about the stellar job she did at the church on Sunday? Fear of God was in their souls if you can imagine. It definitely has people talking now."

"I really have to go," Kevin said as he hobbled over to grab his pants. "I am really impressed," he said as he tried to slip on his pants without losing the blanket.

"Mr. Finn, if I find out where this madman is going to attack next, will the militia be ready to back me up?"

"We have our work cut out for us, but I'm sure we'll be there, Kevin."

"And please get the militia to ask around about Douglas FitzGibbon. People know more than they're saying." Kevin dropped the blanket on a stool and patted their son on the back. "Sorry, I have to go," he said.

As Kevin opened the door Sarah said, "Kevin Neal, don't forget your jacket," and she tossed it to him. "Keep alert and don't get yourself killed."

"So what's been bothering you?" asked Samuel as he looked down at Walter who was busy digging a ditch near his parents' cottage.

"I have to get this done," replied Walter. He pulled the brim of his cap down and scratched his cheek and said, "If you want to talk, then grab a shovel and help me. Well, what are you doing? Wash off the look of an idler. Come on."

Samuel picked up the wooden shovel and started digging up a run about eight feet away from his friend.

"yeh, so like I asked, what's been bothering you?"

"So now you're asking about things you didn't want to know," said Walter. "You didn't have a problem with me arranging to have someone teach Padraig a lesson, so long as I didn't tell you the details."

"Distraction and you know it. What's going on with you?"

"Well, it's about my baby brother and Edith—your sister," said Walter and he remained quiet as he aggressively did some more digging.

"And…" asked Samuel.

"And the killings," replied Walter.

A couple of hours after Walter Glascott and Samuel talked, Douglas FitzGibbon rode up to the cottage. Walter left his shovel and walked out to meet him. "Mr. FitzGibbon, what do you want?" asked Walter.

"Have you seen Kevin Neal around?"

"You asked me that before. The answer is still no."

Douglas dismounted and walked up close to Walter. He stared at him with stern unforgiving eyes. "Where does Mike Nolan live?"

"I told that to Harold already."

"I'm asking. Where does he live?"

"I know someone that's a friend of his children. Why are you asking about him?"

"That's none of your concern. Who are you protecting? Harold told me that you had a baby brother."

"I have a brother. You wouldn't!"

"Who?"

"Samuel Boyse's sister. She is always there."

"Tell me where he lives."

Walter gave him the directions he asked for. The Nolans lived near the Boyse's cottage.

"James Kennedy has a house around here. Where is it?"

"Why do you want to know?"

"Tell me where he lives. Now, don't waste our time."

"But—" Walter complained. "Someone's going to hear."

"Would it be easier for you to answer if we go inside?" asked Douglas.

"No. No. Stop." Walter gave him the directions to the Kennedy's cottage.

"Are you sure?"

"Yes. Yes I'm sure," Walter replied.

"Is there anyone home other than his wife and daughter?"

"No. There is no-one else."

"How old is the daughter?" asked Douglas.

"Fourteen, I think."

"Have you been talking to anyone about me?"

"No, of course not," said Walter. He tried to look him in the eyes, but the man scared him.

Douglas sensed his fear, and it was easy to see he was sweating.

"So you haven't told anyone about the Wexford Púcaman?"

"No. No. Please. I just want to go," pleaded Walter.

Douglas glared at the man who was shivering with fear.

"You're right Walter."

"I'm right about what?"

"This is really not the place for talking about such things. I hope you'll forgive me. Sometimes I get so caught up with my work and I forget my manners. I'm going to take you to the beach."

"But my da wants this done and—"

"That will have to wait, Walter," Douglas said. He remounted his horse and helped Walter climb up behind him.

After dismounting at the beach, Douglas said, "This is a nice place. I like the sound of the waves. Don't you? The crashing and rolling is soothing. Don't you think?"

"Well…" said Walter.

Douglas took out a long, sharp surgical spike-like tool and tapped it against Walter's side. "You told me that you didn't tell anyone about me?"

"No-one knows you're Wexford's Púcaman," said Walter.

"You know, Walter, you are a terrible liar. Why are they thinking it's me and not the Púca?" He stared at Walter and watched him shiver.

He put his nose half an inch from Walter's and said, "When I went into the Jeffers' cottage. Anastasia Kelly wasn't there. I heard that you warned her away." He watched Walter try to look away.

"No, why would I do that?"

"Who was the other girl?"

"What other girl?"

"There was another girl there. Green skirt and a ribbon in her hair."

"Good God."

Douglas raised a knife sideways between Walter's eyes and slipped it up and down between his thumb and fingers.

"It was Elaine Byrne. I know her. She was a good friend of Anastasia and Eileen Jeffers. She was from Newbawn. Oh, my God. She ran away from home because her father would beat her when he got drunk. I didn't know she'd go there. I swear." Tears poured down Walter's face. "What do you want from me?" he moaned.

Douglas didn't say anything.

"Who told you I knew?"

"How do you know her?"

"We lived in Newbawn before we moved here," said Walter.

Douglas stuck the knife hard into Walter's side and he began to scream.

"If I move to one side, the pain will increase dramatically. Like this."

Walter was going to fall to his knees, but he froze to avoid the pain getting worse.

"Where's Anastasia Kelly?"

"What are you talking about? How would I know? I thought she was dead. Everyone thought she was dead."

"Maybe she went to visit her sister," he whispered. "Elaine told me that she got a letter from someone that knew where her sister was."

Douglas twisted his blade and Walter screamed in agony.

"Liverpool. I believe it's Liverpool," he groaned. In truth Elaine hadn't told him where she was. She had only told him that Anty had received a letter from her.

"Elaine was my friend and I …I liked her. Why?" He was physically shaking.

"I bet you did," said Douglas as he looked Walter up and down as he continued to shake.

"And Anty was Samuel Boyse's sweetheart. How could you?"

"Miss Kelly's sister's name and address, please," demanded Douglas.

"I don't know," whimpered Walter.

Douglas retrieved a crimp from an inside pocket of his jacket. He pushed down on the knife in his side and order him to display an open hand.

"No," whined Walter. He gave a made up address when Douglas threatened to remove a ring finger.

"Are you sure that's correct?" Douglas asked.

Walter said it was, but Douglas removed a baby finger, causing him to scream. He didn't flinch because Douglas continued to press down on the knife in his side. "Don't lie to me Walter," Douglas said. "I guess we'll have to remove the thumb."

Walter gave him another street address and began to fall backwards.

Douglas grabbed him, slapped his face and asked, "Who else knows?"

Walter froze and was almost oblivious to the question.

"You made that up," whispered Walter.

"About somebody squealing? yeh, and I wasn't even sure that the girl wasn't the Kelly girl. Elaine didn't look like Kevin Neal's type that's all. … didn't even know people thought she was there until I heard a rumour."

As he put the crimp around Walter's right thumb, he told him, "But I'm not fooling about this. Who else knows?" Douglas twisted the knife slightly again.

Walter replied, "Maybe Kevin Neal."

"So, what did you tell him?" asked Douglas.

"You have a list of names of people that you're going to kill," moaned Walter.

"I need dependability and consistency, Walter." Douglas removed the crimp and put it back in his jacket pocket and backed away a few inches from Walter's face and said, "So you think I kill people?" Douglas asked.

Walter stared at the man's cruel, cold face, but his tears blurred out what he saw.

"You know, Walter, unfortunately it's true." Douglas twisted and opened the cut so Walter bled out. The roar of the waves drowned the sounds of Walter's dying moans. Douglas grabbed the back of Walter's shirt and hauled him towards a row boat. He picked him up and flopped him into the boat and then pushed it into the bay. Douglas took out the knife that he had stuck in him and put it back into a sheath strapped at his waist. He rowed it out and said, "Walter I'm fortunate that the tide is going out. I don't think they'll find you. The fish will get to you first."

When Douglas felt he was far enough out he pulled Walter up and leaned him over the side. Walter I don't know why you went to so much trouble for the Kelly girl. She's a papist after all. With a second knife Douglas cut Walter's throat and then pushed the body into the sea. He sat back and relaxed as he washed his knife in the water. He looked at his reflection on the blade and spat on it and then wiped it on his pants. He admired the clean reflection and then put it back into the sheath that was strapped to his leg.

—◈—

Richard waved at Samuel Boyse who stood in front of the family cottage. Richard was heading home to get something to eat, but he needed to talk to Samuel. "I talked with Walter. I know what was bothering him," he said.

"Douglas FitzGibbon?"

"No doubt about it," Richard replied.

"A couple of days ago, you said you were sure he knew who's behind the Púca killings."

"Oh, it's more than that. He's the man himself," said Richard.

"So Walter knew."

"Yeh, but don't be harsh, FitzGibbon is a devil of a man," said Richard. "I've seen him and he's not a raving lunatic. He's without fear, ruthless and unforgiving when he doesn't get what he wants. Walter told me that they threatened to kill his baby brother. He's also threatened my family. We're going to need help," said Samuel.

"You know it's the former sheriff that pays him on behalf of the landlords," said Richard. "It's old Pierce King."

"So we kill them and the crown strings us up? You remember what happened to John Colclough," says Samuel.

"You know if we tell anyone, they're going to kill us?" said Richard. "By the way, FitzGibbon and his men are around. I saw them a couple of hours ago."

"Well, isn't that a pleasant bit of news? Do we know anything about him? I mean does Douglas just wander around and beat people up?"

"He made money castrating."

"You mean he works as a gelder?" added Samuel.

"yeh. He does that for horses. He keeps his horses near Newbawn and he travels a lot. I liked the idea of blaming Neal for something," said Richard, "but honestly this Douglas FitzGibbon is a terrible bit of work.

Someone should deliver him to the gates of hell where he belongs."

"Newbawn is near Scullabogue. That's where twenty people from our parish were burnt alive," said Samuel.

"Yes, the very same place. That's where I lost my uncle. Douglas got those terrible burns on his arm in the fire. He keeps it covered, but you can see it if you watch for it. Walter told me that he made up a list of rebels that were at the barn burning. Douglas used the Púca killings as a ruse to get Colclough to pay him for enacting his revenge. Douglas forced Walter to tell him where some of them lived."

"The Jeffers," said Samuel with a gasp.

"You have to understand that the man that guts his victims was threatening him and his family," said Richard. "Oh, and I forgot to tell you something. One of Douglas's men asked me about Mike Nolan."

"He's after Mike Nolan?" asked Samuel. "My God. They live next door to us and my sister Edith cares for his mother. God Almighty, does he know where they live?"

"If they don't, it'll be easy to find them," replied Richard.

"Damnation," said Samuel.

"Anyway, this morning they had me walking around with them. We were looking for Kevin Neal. It was a really strange thing. I'm being dragged around by this lad named Harold into Kevin's cottage and he madly stabs what he thinks is Kevin in his bed. Low and behold he finds out that he's chopping up his good friend Brian Prescott. I'm telling you, if things weren't so desperate I would have rolled laughing on the ground all the way to the bay."

"Jesus," said Samuel. "It's definitely not what you'd expect."

"The thing to keep to heart is that Harold Wheeler and Douglas are now in a really foul mood," said Richard. "If you see them, run. Run really fast. Harold thinks he owns me. I think he wants me to do something. FitzGibbon, besides being a lunatic and a monster is a miserly bastard. He has never offered to pay me for anything and I think that might be the same for Walter."

"I'm going to have my da talk with the militia," said Samuel.

"I'm going home to make sure they aren't bothering my family," said Richard. He turned to leave, but he said, "Samuel we've got guests."

A rider on horseback approached.

When he got close he said, "So you must be Samuel Boyse."

"Samuel, this is Harold," said Richard.

"Douglas wants both of you to help out tonight."

"But we're busy," said Samuel. "Can't tonight. Maybe tomorrow."

"I'm not asking for to-night. We're going now," He leaned forward and smiled. "Samuel, I'd hate to tell Douglas to do the asking."

"If Douglas is paying, I'm sure there won't be a problem," Richard said. "Who are we looking for?"

"Let's go and I'll tell you on the way," Harold said.

When Kevin entered the forge Mr. Sevens said, "Now that you're here, maybe your lordship will get back to work. Mr. Kennedy has given me a long list. Why he didn't get a replacement for you is beyond me. It's not like people haven't been offering."

"Please not now, Mr. Sevens. Who's looking for me?"

"A couple of mean looking types were around. They didn't ask anything. They just kept showing their ugly faces. It was hard to get anything done. The look of them could spoil milk. I expect they're the ones that are looking for you. Are they Colclough's men?"

"There's nothing going to get by you, is there?" Kevin said, as he sifted through containers of clutter. He found some red buttons. He put a couple of them in his pocket. Harry could use those, he thought. He kept sorting through the stuff.

"What are you looking for in such a hurry?"

"It's here somewhere," Kevin replied.

"Just don't make a mess."

Kevin showed him the sheath he was looking for. He put his knife in it. "Sorry Mr. Sevens, but I can't stay."

"Well, look who came home," said a voice from outside the forge.

"Caulfield. Richard Caulfield," replied Kevin. "Another something that washed up on the beach. Richard, what are you doing here?"

"Nothing, I'm just waking the dead. That's all," he said.

"Richard, out of here," ordered Mr. Sevens. "You're not wanted here."

"No. Just a minute" said Kevin, as he stepped away from the forge. "Caulfield. The man with the burnt hand where is he?"

"Now calm down," said Richard. "You're going to split your pants if you keep that up."

Kevin clenched his fist, and his face started to turn red. He looked around to see if Richard had brought anyone with him."

"Kevin, I can't talk to you like this. We're going to be seen."

"So?"

"So, if Harold Wheeler or Douglas FitzGibbon talks to anyone that sees us, the bunch of us will be prayed over on Sunday morning."

"Over there in the trees then," said Kevin.

"If there's any trouble, the two of you take it away from here, do you hear?" said Mr. Sevens.

"Yeh, I'll be fine and thank you very much for your concern," said Kevin as he checked back at the forge.

Once behind the cover of trees Richard said, "Neal, I tried to steer Harold in the wrong direction, but he's very persuasive when he gets impatient. A little boy almost lost his hand. Anyway, Harold found your guest. It was quite a sight. If you move back in, I suggest you set the place on fire first. You know it really reeks."

"I get your meaning. And you're telling me this to let me know they're close and that you're glad they know where to find me."

"No. Not really. We've had our differences, but this bunch is really beyond the pale. I can't do this by myself. I need your help."

"How does that follow? You'd do anything to get rid of another papist."

"Knocking sense into you is one thing, but I'm telling you, this is a whole different thing."

"Sure. Right as rain, you are," said Kevin as he looked away from Richard and out towards the forge.

"Neal, just shut up and listen. It's Douglas FitzGibbon that killed the Walshes and Jeffers."

"The man that guts his victims? Is he a gelder?" asked Kevin.

"Yes, he is. How did you know?"

"I pieced it together."

"I don't have a lot of time."

"You're one to talk. Look at me," said Kevin.

Richard ignored him and said, "Harold stopped me on my way home. He told me that I have to help them find someone near the north shore of Bannow Bay," said Richard. I think they want to kill him."

"Do you know him?"

"No, but I know people who might."

"What's in it for you?"

"Nothing." Richard looked at Kevin's face and repeated, "There's nothing in it for me and sure as hell I'd rather have nothing to do with them. They threatened to kill Walter's brother," said Richard. "And they were serious."

"Walter's baby brother? He's only seven. Terrible bastards, aren't they?"

"I don't want to think of what FitzGibbon might do to my family," said Richard. "It scares the hell out of me." Richard moved outside of the tree cover and looked around and returned to Kevin. "Didn't see anyone, but I don't have much time before I have to go."

"So you're telling this all to me why?"

"They are either going to attack someone on the other side of the bay or Mike Nolan who lives not far from Samuel's cottage."

"I know the Nolans. Why them?"

"FitzGibbon has a list of names he is trying to cross off. Samuel's sister stays with them.

"I thought maybe we could meet up at the black castle. I'll tell you what I found out and if I find out they're going to attack tonight, you can go back and bring help. Do you know where it is?"

"There's a bunch of old ruins there, said Kevin. The Black Castle is the old Fitzhenry's tower house in Clonmines." Kevin stared at Richard in the eyes. "Jimmy referred to it as the Black Tower. It's pretty isolated and it's a fine place for a trap."

"I swear to you on the life of my family, it's not," said Richard. "I know we don't trust each other but…"

Kevin interrupted him and added, "…sometimes there are things that need to be done that you can't do alone. I'm just repeating something that a friend told me once. Alright, but Richard if you double-cross me on this, you will pay dearly, do you hear me?"

"Neal, when it comes to this we're on the same side."

"I hope so," replied Kevin.

"Oh, one more thing," said Richard. "FitzGibbon told me something strange. While we were walking by the forge over there, he told me that he lent your foster father some money."

"That doesn't make any sense."

"Take it with a grain of salt. I'm just repeating what he told me."

"He said Mr. Walsh reminded him of his father," said Richard. "They got drinking and Mr. Walsh wanted to put some money down on a race and he gave it to him. He told Mr. Walsh that he didn't owe him anything for the money. He seemed to go out, of his way to say he wasn't conning him."

"Yeh, right. He rips apart his boy and does the same to him and he's telling us he is a man with a soul," said Kevin. "Let's kill him so he can burn in hell. He's worse than the devil himself. I'd like to kill him with my bare hands."

"Look at yourself and think before you breathe," said Richard.

Harry Keane was right, Kevin thought. *"Don't do it on your own,"* he said.

"FitzGibbon's probably the most dangerous man in the county and so far no-one's survived. He's in the killing business and he is good at what he does. If he baits you, it'll be your blood on the ground and he'll get away and do it again. Anyway, I have to go. I'll see you tonight and you're going to get us help. Right?" said Richard before moving off.

"At the Black Tower, in Clonmines an hour before dark," repeated Kevin.

As Richard walked into the light, he said, "Neal, I still think you're an ass, but that was some trick getting Prescott. You're a real John Kelly."

"Yes, but he died," muttered Kevin. *I suppose that was his point.*

Clonmines Ruins

Kevin walked past a line of trees that were strung inland as far as the horizon on his left. Ahead of him were the ruins of two Norman tower houses, two churches and a priory that were loosely sprawled along the western shoreline of Bannow Bay. They were on a flat, open meadow that spread out ahead of him and to his left for miles. The ruins were surrounded with lots of grazing sheep. He caught the sweet smell of seaweed, the sound of constant flapping waves, and the sight of free flying sea birds. From the vantage point over the ruins near the treeline, the flat openness of the land and the pastoral setting had a calming effect.

He walked another two hundred feet to the first tower. A long shadow stretched towards the water. It reminded him to be cautious.

The last one—the Black Tower, which was tall, thin, and almost square, was another two hundred feet away, and less than a hundred feet from the water. There wasn't any tree cover for a very long way in the other directions. *It looks like it's an excellent place for a trap*, he thought. *There's no mountain and no forest to run to for protection. There is just a thin line of bushes near the water, and there's no-one around for miles. God, this place is dangerous and strange.*

"And why didn't I take one of Mr. Stewart's horses?" he asked.

Douglas FitzGibbon told Richard a story about Nick Walsh as they were passing the forge, he thought. *He pretended to be good with Nick and then killed him. Douglas must have known I worked there, so maybe he thought he was speaking to me directly. He's either a shortsighted, impulsive fool or he is playing with me. No, he definitely is no fool, though he must be a lunatic.*

"This doesn't feel right," he softly whispered as he approached the tower. "Hard to believe Richard was lying." Kevin looked around and didn't see or hear anyone else. *Maybe I am just being a coward. Cowards need a place to hide and are afraid of the dark. But, then again, Richard called me another John Kelly and John Kelly's dead. Damn, maybe Richard was trying to warn me.* Kevin walked around to the wooden doorway on the side farthest away from the water.

He pulled his knife from his sheath and opened the door. It creaked a little when he pushed it. It was dark inside. Kevin stopped and listened, but he didn't hear anything. He didn't go into the room until his eyes had adjusted to the dark. He could make out the outline of a stone step which appeared to jut out from a wall.

It's a stairwell, he thought. There was a bit of light shining from what seemed to be the top of the wall. He heard the sound of a voice upstairs, so he cautiously climbed the stone stairs. As he stepped on the last stair, the sound of broken glass made a loud crackle. Before he could step back, his head was hit hard with something and he lost consciousness.

When Kevin opened his eyes, he found himself in a bad way. His wrists were securely tied and his arms were drawn upright to a supporting beam above him. The pain in his shoulders was excruciating, and the ropes tore into his wrists. There was a throbbing pain from the back of his head. He had difficulty breathing and was forced to balance on his toes. His chest was bare. Someone had taken his shirt, coat and vest.

He recognized his oak staff lying on the floor next to the opposite wall. A ball of a black form shifted near it. The room in the stone keep was small and felt claustrophobic and smelled like a latrine. The black form in front of him moved. Kevin made out the bottom of a boot under it. From under the black form, he recognized a pool of blood slowly expanding towards him across the stone floor. There were some other colours in the mix. The red sticky stuff slipped off the sole of the boot. Kevin was shivering. It was getting colder. He didn't see his boots or stockings anywhere. Kevin felt like he was going to throw up.

The figure moved. It was the back of a man's black coat he was staring at. A face looked back at him and said, "Be patient lad, all things come in good time. We'll be with you soon enough." Kevin heard a muffled groan. When the man in black re-positioned himself to the right he saw the outline of another man spread out on the floor. Kevin saw that he was gagged, had a long thick rope wrapped around his wrists, and his bare chest was cut open. It made Kevin even more nauseous.

He must have been strung up like me, he thought. *It's monstrous! It must be the poor fella from this side of the bay, that Richard told me about.*

The man in the black coat stood up. As he stepped back Kevin watched him pull the body's insides out across the floor. Kevin's body prepared to throw up. Kevin tightened his grasp on the rope he was hanging from, as his terror making him drip with sweat caused him to shiver more.

Kevin watched the man untie the rope from the man's wrists. He undid the gag and wound the rope into a tidy circle. He secured the rope bundle with the gag cloth. He wiped a couple of blades on a rag and put them back into a leather wrap, which contained an assortment of other blades. He wrapped the bundle up and slipped it into an inside jacket pocket.

Well, isn't he an orderly piece of shit? thought Kevin. *He didn't take his shirt off like me. He just undid the buttons. I wonder what that's all about?*

Kevin almost lost his footing on the cold floor as he back-stepped too far and started to swing, putting more stress on his outstretched arms. The man got up, threw the rope bundle across the room towards the door opening and walked towards him.

"Well, if it isn't himself, Douglas FitzGibbon," Kevin said, as he tried to crush the rope in his grip above him. The man wasn't wearing a scarf or gloves. Kevin wondered if he had the strength to strangle him with his feet.

"And if it isn't Kevin Neal. He's just the man I need to see. How are you feeling?"

"Better than a kick in the arse, thank you," replied Kevin. "If you're afraid, maybe you could go home and we could talk about this in the morning."

Douglas smiled. He grabbed the loose end of the rope that tied Kevin to the beam above him. He pulled it across the beam, and tied it securely so that it was far out of Kevin's reach. Kevin noticed that the right hand of the man on the ground responded with a nervous twitch.

"Who's that?" Kevin asked.

"Frankly, I don't have a clue—a straggler. Couldn't have him around. Unfortunate, don't you think?" Douglas drew a long, thin dagger from a sheath strapped to his calf and walked over to Kevin. He stopped in front of him. His pupils were contracted and his red eyes were watery like his nose. Douglas pushed Kevin's belly with his left hand and he started to swing back. Kevin's toes madly danced to acquire a perch to control his stance. The dagger remained in Douglas's right hand.

"I take it you're not popular with girls?" asked Kevin. He couldn't stop shivering.

"I like the ladies. I just do what I have to do." He wiped his runny nose on his sleeve. "It's nice to get paid, you know. Nothing personal."

"I take it you really like your work," said Kevin.

"I am well paid for what I do and they are glad to pay. Unfortunately, they always expect a little more. 'Make sure your work doesn't come back on us,' they say. That requires a little extra tearing, flair and rumours about the Púca—people are such fools."

"Have you ever thought of retiring? I hear that Australia is a nice place."

"Kevin, you know that for the likes of us, they'll never let us go. Colclough, Annesley or Loftus—they're the real monsters."

"How is it that you never got caught or no-one stopped you? You must have had an army to dispose of them all."

Kevin heard someone groan behind him and noticed that the sound got Douglas's attention.

"I got myself some concentrated opium from England," said Douglas. "When I first started this, I gave it to all of my victims. It made them very manageable but unpredictable. But it was too expensive, and we weren't making any money, so I stopped giving it to them."

"You kept it for yourself. You don't look right," said Kevin. "You look sick."

"Don't insult me, boy," said Douglas, and he pushed the end of his blade against his throat.

"Douglas, hold on. I didn't mean anything by it. I'm just saying."

Douglas took the blade away from his throat. He stepped back and walked behind him. Kevin twisted around carefully on his toes. *Dear God! It's Richard hanging there,* he thought. He was hanging from a joist, just like Kevin was. He could see that Richard was still breathing, but his head was down and his legs were almost bent. His shirt was open, and a hole in his side was bleeding out. *Douglas has been torturing him,* he thought.

"Why, did you beat up Richard? I thought he was a friend of yours?"

"That was unfortunate," answered Douglas. "He was a little overly talkative." He wiped the snot that was dripping out of his nose on his sleeve and told him, "There was something about letting people know and things that got a little out of hand."

This man isn't behaving like the disciplined killer that I imagined, Kevin thought. *He's really disoriented. The other side of him must have been as sharp as a knife—quick, articulate, knowledgeable and very disciplined.*

"So you like horses?" said Kevin. "I hear you sell the horse meat. Do you get a good price?"

"Go on with you," Douglas said. He drew a long, thin knife out of a sheath. "Wouldn't think of it." He walked closer to Kevin. He stared at him and took a moment to focus his eyes.

"The young lad there told me that you were wondering why I snipped people," Douglas said as he caressed the blade he was holding.

"To sign your work?" said Kevin.

"What?" Douglas asked. "Oh, smart lad, Kevin. It keeps the process focused, you know."

"Uh. No. Not really. Uh."

"When I was younger, I worked as a butcher for a landlord. It helped control a bad disposition."

Kevin thought to say something sarcastic, but the sharp knife in Douglas's hand made him hesitate.

As Douglas put the knife back into its sheath he looked around the room and started checking his pockets.

"So, Nick Walsh wasn't around to help his friend Joseph Kavanagh because he had some drinks with you," rambled Kevin.

Douglas just smiled and looked at the door.

"How did Nick Walsh get to know you?"

Douglas ignored him and walked over to look at Richard.

"Richard told me that you wanted to tell me something about him," Kevin said.

"He does like to tell tales doesn't he?" Douglas said.

"Mr. Walsh?"

"No," replied Douglas as he stared at Richard.

"I saw you on the road with him afterwards," said Kevin.

"He told you about it, did he?"

Kevin replied with a lie. "Of course, he did," he said.

"Nick Walsh sort of helped me get started. Did he tell you that? No, I guess he didn't. He couldn't have known." Douglas slowly walked towards Kevin and told him, "Martin Bennett was a supervisor for Caesar Colclough and almost got Nick killed. Nick knew that Martin was one of the rebels that set the barn on fire at Scullabogue in '98. He told me that Martin Bennett could get me a list of rebels who took part in my sister's murder. For the favour, I put off a visit to one of Nick's neighbours."

"By the neighbour, you mean Joseph Kavanagh?"

Douglas nodded. He was looking slightly away from Kevin and he started reaching for something that wasn't there and tottered slightly on his feet. Douglas looked back at Kevin, wiped his nose and said, "Bennett was very familiar with my work. He did not take it well, when I paid him a visit.

"So why did you kill him?" asked Kevin.

"Martin Bennett?"

"No, Mr. Kavanagh."

"I roughed him up a little, that's all," said Douglas and he stared at Kevin's feet. He was still trying to balance his weight on his toes.

"You didn't go back a second time and finish him off?"

"I only had to scare him off. No, that wasn't me."

Douglas marched back to Richard.

To distract him, Kevin said, "You know, when faced with death, most people will tell you anything they think you want," said Kevin. "He could have made it all up. You might be killing the wrong people. Have you considered that?"

Douglas took the long sharp knife out again, and said, "Trust me, Kevin. I am very good at what I do. You have to choose where you're going in life and be determined." He approached Richard and pressed his left forefinger up under his chin to raise his head.

"You said Nick Walsh didn't owe you anything for the money you lent him. You told Richard that he reminded you of your father. So why would you kill him and his son?"

"My father is dead." He wiped his dripping nose. "He left me. Besides, it was business. ...And you were warned about what the Púca can bring, but none of you listened."

For a moment, Kevin's eyes looked down and muttered, "...the Browns, and the Whalens..."

"He shouldn't have stayed. He should have taken you all away. Anyways, when you work with the powerful, you have to do what you're told," said Douglas. They don't let you go soft."

"But you didn't give them opium."

Douglas ignored him and stared at Richard. "Sorry, Kevin, but there's work to do."

Kevin's arms and torso muscles were strained from bearing most of his weight. Awkwardly balancing on the ends of his toes wasn't helping much.

I've got to do something, he thought. *That beast killed Anty, the Walshes… He killed them. Richard, what am I going to do?* Kevin stared up at the beam over his head. *I can't get a hand free because I can't get the rope to loosen and my hands can't grab anything,* he thought. *I can swing, but it's too high to get my feet on the beam and I don't have enough strength. Even if I had strength to swing, Richard is way over there and I'm here. There must be a way. There must be something… Lord God, what am I going to do?*

Kevin saw Douglas slice the skin on Richard's stomach.

Richard awoke and moaned in agony.

"Hey! Stop it! Stop it!," screamed Kevin. "He was your friend. You don't do that to your friends." Kevin started bouncing on his toes trying to rip his hands out of the wrapped ropes, but he wasn't getting enough height. Kevin was powerless, sore, weak and completely defenceless.

Douglas drove the blade deeply into Richard's stomach. Douglas stopped for a moment, and said, "I don't have friends. That's not what I do."

"That's insane. Douglas, stop."

Douglas continued cutting as Richard's body writhed about. Blood poured as he ripped up towards his chest.

"No, don't. You can't. Stop, you insane bastard. He doesn't deserve it. No-one deserves it," yelled Kevin. "Why aren't you satisfied with just me? No-one is paying you for Richard. It's not in your contract."

Douglas kept cutting and slicing Richard's chest so that soon organs were visible.

"Why do you kill the loyal and the innocent?" yelled Kevin.

Douglas ignored him.

"Why do you go in and kill everyone that's there?" yelled Kevin.

"I'm sorry about that, Kevin, but I'm trying not to make this personal.

Caesar Colclough is the one who wants you dead. Even if I was willing to avoid this, Colclough represents the law of the land and his friends control and own everything. To stay alive, you have to choose sides. Consider yourself fortunate, Kevin. I never discuss my work with anyone and I don't expect I ever will again."

Richard's screams were short-lived. The devil in front of him started disembowelling him. Kevin could still hear him breathing and he thought he heard his heart still beating or maybe it was his own. He saw the intestines fall out. Douglas grabbed them and pulled them out, across the room.

"A Púca's work is never done," Douglas said, and he went back and started pulling out other organs. When he untied the rope from the wall, Richard's body fell to the floor. He removed the rope from his wrists and wound and secured it into a neat roll and threw it by the other one near the stairs.

"Because Nick Walsh reminded you of your father," said Kevin.

"What?" asked Douglas, as he wiped the blood off his blade on Richard's shirt.

"You're telling me this because Nick Walsh reminds you of your father. I recognize that scar on your neck. It was a terrible cut and you are definitely that boy. I remember it from a very long time ago. You probably don't remember it, but we met just after you got it. You were being chased."

"When was that?" Douglas said as he got up and walked towards Kevin.

"At New Ross. The soldiers were chasing us. You rescued me, but you left me."

"They didn't know who I was. Now they do."

"You ran off to chase after your family. That's where I lost my family. I remember them calling your name. 'Douglas,' they said."

"And they deserved it," said Douglas and he stabbed Kevin in the side.

Kevin screamed.

Douglas saw that although Kevin's hands were tied, he pulled himself up.

"You smashed my hand that day. That old lady with the bloody hands. I remember that," said Douglas. "You refused to go." Douglas put the knife back in his sheath.

"I'll be back," he said. "Forgot something."

"Imeacht gan teacht ort!," groaned Kevin.

"Bugger off, to you too. Oíche mhaith!" replied Douglas. "And besides, no-one is innocent."

—ა-©ల

Samuel Boyse came rushing from the stairs a couple of minutes after Douglas left.

"Bastard. Is it your turn?" gnarled Kevin.

"Save it, you fool. We have to get you out of here before he gets back."

"You knew…" said Kevin.

"What the hell?" said Samuel, as he saw the disembowelled remains of what used to be his friend Richard. "Oh dear God, what a monster." He rushed over to Kevin and started untying the rope holding him up. "I heard that he killed people in the north," Samuel said. Once Kevin fell, Samuel started cutting the rope around his ankles. "I didn't know that he was killing innocents. I came to understand what kind of animal he was, when he threatened to kill my sister and Walter's brother. I know he's willing to hurt them whether he's helped or not, and what has happened to Richard is unspeakable." He froze.

"Samuel," muttered Kevin. "We can't stay."

"Hurry up, your shirt is on the floor, grab it, and roll it up for a pad. Put the pad on the wound and I'll tie it up with my shirt." Samuel took his shirt off.

"What are you doing?"

"Kevin, shut up," Samuel said as he finished tying his shirt around Kevin's waist. "I'm trying to save your damned useless life. We don't have any time. He's gone to the church ruins where he left his horse. It's only about five hundred feet from here. There's only the one horse here. I'm supposed to be minding it. He's going to come back in a hell of a fury. Now, get up you bum. We've got to get out of here or we're both going to die."

Both of the young men shook with fear. Kevin had his arm around Samuel to bear weight. "God," he moaned as he prepared to leave. Samuel leaned down and grabbed his coat and Kevin groaned. "Let's go," he said, and they quickly shuffled down the narrow stone stairwell.

"My shoes," said Kevin.

"Too late, we don't have time. Keep moving or I'll leave you here," said Samuel.

"Forgot your vest, eh?" Kevin said as they raced across the darkened main floor.

"Kevin, shut up."

At the entrance door, Samuel said, "We are going to run to the bushes near the water. It is the only place with cover." Samuel opened the door slightly. He didn't see Douglas anywhere. Samuel opened the door the rest of the way and stepped out. He still didn't see Douglas anywhere. He stepped back to the door, pulled on Kevin's arm, and ordered, "Now, move!" Samuel closed the door behind and put his arm around Kevin again to support him. They rushed for the bushes by the bay, but Kevin moved too slowly. Samuel grabbed him, put him over his shoulder and carried him another forty feet to the dry ditch. It was overgrown with six-foot-tall shrub-like trees which formed a thick bushy line along the river bank.

Kevin moaned when Samuel dropped him.

"Quiet!" ordered Samuel. "His horse is in the priory. He went to get something."

"He forgot his crimp tool," Kevin said. "Fortunately for me, the man is drugged out of his mind."

Samuel stared at him.

"Forget it. You don't want to know."

"Ready for a swim?" asked Samuel.

"We won't make it," said Kevin. "The water is too shallow. He will follow us and bring his horse."

"If we stay here, he'll find us," said Samuel. He saw that Kevin was shaking.

"He'll catch us in the water and there's no cover on the other side, so you have to take his horse," Kevin said.

"We're going to go to the end of this old moat," Samuel said. "It goes as far as the next tower. He kept the horse in the ruin by the treeline. When he comes back and enters the tower, I'll run to the church and get his horse. I'll pick you up at the end of this ditch, down there." Samuel pointed to the ruins and the end of the ditch wasn't far from it. "I hope, he doesn't carry a pistol."

They started moving along the ditch, but they both froze when they heard Douglas ride out from the ruins with his horse.

"Damn you, Samuel," yelled Douglas as he mounted his horse and rode back to the tower from which they had just escaped.

Kevin pointed to the horse and then the abbey and then a sign to screw off which was intended to mean that if Samuel couldn't get to him he was to keep going.

Samuel quickly passed Kevin his jacket and followed the ditch back to where it was closer to the Black Tower.

Douglas quickly dismounted. He had the metal crimps in hand. When the entrance door on the other side of the tower closed, Samuel quickly ran towards his horse. It was grazing by the door. It wasn't tied up and backed away as Samuel approached it. Samuel slowed his approach. He heard Douglas scream something from within the tower. Samuel picked up his pace and managed to grab the horse's reins before it bolted. Samuel quickly mounted it and managed to get the horse to turn.

"You miserable…" yelled Douglas as he thundered out the tower door. He ran madly after Samuel and almost reached his horse's tail.

"yeh," Samuel screamed, as he whipped the reins and tightened his feet on the horse's ribs. The horse felt his fear and picked up into a gallop. Samuel's grip on the reins loosened, and he gave a loud scream. He fell forward, and the pain got worse.

Kevin saw a knife in Samuel's bare upper back.

Samuel managed to tighten his hold on the reins and stiffened his resolve to get away.

"Oh, good God! We're not going to do this," Kevin muttered. Although Samuel was in agony, Kevin managed to get the horse to slow down. He saw that Douglas was running after them with all his might. Although they were both in agony, Kevin managed to get up front with Samuel's help.

"Time to fly, let's go," Samuel said as he put his arms around Kevin. The horse sensed their fear and didn't need much persuasion to keep running.

When the horse slowed down to a trot, Kevin said, "It's going to take both of us to get where we are going, if we are going to warn anyone. The abbey is about five miles away. I don't know how we are going to last. I'd like to stop and pull the knife out, but if we get off I don't think either one of us is getting back on and neither of us wants to share our last moments with the likes of FitzGibbon."

"Keep going, Kevin," said Samuel. "There is a place where we can stop about half way there."

"When the horse steps, it feels like it is pulling on my wound. It must be worse for you," said Kevin.

"Talk about something else, Walsh."

"It's Neal."

"No matter."

Samuel had his arms around Kevin's waist, but his grip was loosening.

"Damn it, Samuel. Maybe I should take that knife and pin your sleeves together. You have to hold on. I don't have the strength and I feel dizzy. We need each other."

"Need you like a hole in the head."

"How about a hole in the back?"

"Maybe a trade," Samuel said.

"I can see the turn in the road ahead. Where is this house that we're going to?"

"…plague burial ground."

"Now, really? Now I know we have our troubles, but if we're going to fall down and die, why not roll over here?"

"No. Támhlacht is an old name. It's safe there."

"Samuel, you're repeating yourself. Támhlacht is Irish for plague burial ground."

"It's Taulaght House now. We're their cousins. Road winds right, turns left and straightens towards the abbey," said Samuel. "Long line of trees in front of Taulaght House. Crossroads after is too far; then I'll take the knife out …kill you."

"Horse, do you hear that? Sam will be very upset if we don't find the trees," mumbled Kevin.

"Samuel, don't fall asleep. It's your turn to talk to the horse."

"Kevin, I'm sorry."

"For what?"

"FitzGibbon came here because of me. When Anty died, I wasn't thinking right. Maybe I was just as insane."

"No-one is as insane as he is. Well, that's a kick in the gut isn't it?"

He felt Samuel loosen his grip.

"Hey, Samuel, wake up! It's not time yet. Anyway, take it from me, I was there, and it was the same for me. I had to get away. I did the same thing to someone else."

"What?"

"I got my ass kicked, and he threw me at a tree."

Samuel's grip continued to loosen.

"Damn it, I wish I had a rope. Samuel, I need you to hold on to my bandage so I don't leak out."

"We're almost there," said Samuel

"To the grave?"

"I don't know."

"Why are we going there?"

"They know me."

"You mean like FitzGibbon?"

"No."

"Samuel about Anty," said Kevin.

"No."

There was quiet between them for a few minutes.

"Move," said Samuel. "Promise—save my sister. Kevin, promise."

"I promise."

"Going to kill Edith and the Nolans. He's going to kill them all."

"I know. Richard told me. I told Mr. Stewart. He'll tell Kennedy. They'll be safe."

"Him too," muttered Samuel.

"What?"

"FitzGibbon said he would."

"Just a little farther, Samuel."

Samuel leaned on Kevin and weighed against the wound on his side. Kevin had to let go of Samuel's hand and brace it against his thigh in order not to fall off.

"Samuel, I can see the trees. We're almost there." Kevin shifted slightly and Samuel rolled off his back and off the horse.

"My God, Samuel. Samuel. No. Good God," Kevin muttered. He didn't turn. He was afraid of falling off. "Going to get help," he muttered.

Kevin kept riding. On the property he thought he would call for help, but no sound came from his lips. He felt the world spinning, and sensed he was flying through the air. His left hand was caught in the reins and initially stopped his fall. His wrist slipped out and his right foot touched the ground, but he fell and landed on his back. His head and back were sore, and he remained unmoving, staring at a blue sky. "Douglas. Samuel. Edith. Got to…" Kevin mumbled. He put his hand on his sore wound. Kevin looked at blood leaking around his fingers. He got up and staggered up a long driveway to the front of the Boyse Big House. Every time his bare feet scratched against a stone he'd swear saying "Damn Douglas. Damn you!"

When he reached the stairs that led to the front door, he fell into a sitting position. A man came out the front door. Kevin raised the bloody hand that was covering his wound and said as he pointed, "Samuel. Get. Now." Kevin stared at him and said, "Please."

The man nodded and Kevin lost consciousness.

When Kevin opened his eyes, he felt tired and miserably in pain. His head, neck and shoulder were as sore as his side. There was a bandage around his head. The jacket was off and a young man about his own age was washing his face. Kevin found himself lying on a couch in the sitting room of an elegant Big House. An older woman brought over a cup. The man took it and offered it to him.

"Drink this," he said. "I did my best to clean the wound and wrap bandages. That wound is an ugly one. You've lost a lot of blood. I don't know how long you've been riding. You've been asleep for hours. You're going to need some rest if you're ever going to recover."

Kevin tried to say something, but the man said he couldn't hear him.

He got closer and Kevin repeated, "Have to save Edith Boyse—your cousin. Have to save James Kennedy."

"You're not going to go anywhere."

"Samuel?"

"Not now, Thomas," said the older lady.

"Man did this. ...man who stabbed Samuel... kill Edith, ...James. Have to stop..." Kevin lifted his hand and pointed towards a window, pointed and said, "Tintern Abbey." He rolled off the couch.

"Good Lord," said the woman. "Poor Edith."

"Coach, please," said Kevin.

"Stay down," said the man. "Mother, call the servants. I'll make this man a stretcher. The servants will carry him to the cart.

About twenty minutes later Thomas Boyse said, "Kevin, we're going to lift you and carry you to the cart."

"No," said Kevin. "Samuel isn't here?"

"His wounds are severe, and he's lost too much blood. There's not much more that we can do."

"Knife, please."

Thomas retrieved Douglas's knife from the table. He unwrapped the cloth around it and handed it to the patient on the couch. Kevin took it and placed it in his sheath. "Thomas—have to go. Have to find Edith," he whispered. "Douglas FitzGibbon is a monster."

Thomas Boyse sat on one side of Kevin in the back of the cart and a servant sat on the other. About ten minutes into the journey the servant said, "You better ask him now, Mr. Boyse. He might not make it."

"Kevin, where do we find her and who is doing this?"

"Ride to the abbey. Mr. Stewart or Mr. Kennedy will help. Sarah Finn will help. Thomas, did you hear me?"

"Mr. Kennedy?" said Thomas.

"No, Mrs. Sarah Finn. Lots of men. Weapons. Sarah Finn."

"I got that."

"Douglas FitzGibbon is with Harold Wheeler. He'll kill you. …need Mrs. Sarah Finn."

"Yes, I understand. Try to rest. I will let you know when we get close. I know James Kennedy. John Colclough and I were very good friends. Losing John was a terrible, terrible loss."

In spite of bumps and shakes, Kevin relaxed and fell asleep.

Twenty minutes later a stranger, on horseback approached them. As he passed, Thomas noticed that he ignored the driver.

He said, "Hello, your Lordship, I hope you're doing well," and stared at the body in between them.

"Don't recognize the man, sir. Frankly, he doesn't look like the kind of man you would want to know," whispered his servant.

Thomas didn't reply. He just stared at the rider's back.

The man was Harold Wheeler.

Exchange of Harsh Words

Harold rode round a bend and looked down a line of road that faced the bay. It had been quite a lonely ride. It was hours after sunset. It was late, and he was tired. There wasn't quite a full moon in the sky, but with the reflection on the water he could see a figure on the shoreline. He was rocking He looked like a boy. The straight run of road led towards him. When it came time to make the turn to the left, he heard the figure mumbling something. *What's the fool saying,* Harold wondered as he scratched the right side of his thick wiry beard. *Oh Hell, the figure's just lost and worth nothing.* Harold kept riding around the corner and headed towards the Clonmines ruins.

"Wheeler, is your arse up your nose or are you dead and you don't know it?"

Harold looked back and yelled, "Damn it, FitzGibbon." He turned his horse around and headed towards Douglas FitzGibbon.

No wonder I didn't recognize him, Harold thought. *Rocking back and forth and he's clear out of his head again. The fool. He's going to get us killed. He's too unpredictable. Anything is possible, and that's a very bad thing. If he didn't pay well, I'd leave.*

"And why the hell are you wasting your time here," yelled Harold. "You were supposed to have left hours ago. You're lucky I didn't wait until morning"

"Boyse lied to me," said Douglas, as he wiped his dripping nose on his sleeve again. "I didn't think he had the guts to betray me. I thought he hated Kevin Neal."

"You can't trust anyone, Douglas," Harold said as he rode alongside him. "You can't trust people; they'll always let you down."

"Can I trust you?" replied his partner who stared up at him from his place on the grass.

"Douglas, I'm always here for you, as long as you have the money," said Harold from his horse. "You know that. I mean, who would do what we do if it weren't for the money, right?" Harold stared at the bloodstains on Douglas's jacket, knees, right stocking and wet shoes.

"I had a word with that Kevin Neal. Well, I did after smashing him with his own piece of oak. What a fool, he was. I have him where I want him and he greets me like I'm a long-lost friend, wanting to share a pint. 'It's Kevin Neal,' he says."

Harold stared down at him, but Douglas avoided looking at him.

"No, he's made himself a new man. He steps through life on his own terms. He said no to Colclough, Pierce Newton King and all of them. He's a tough fella he is."

"The boy—like you? You think he's a tough fella, like you? Douglas, you really are gone. He's just a boy. The man I used to know wouldn't give an inch of ground for the likes of him. Pull yourself together."

"Don't trip over yourself Harold. Relax. Enjoy the view. I suppose I do have a terrible way, but most of it's just the job and we do have to make a living. Still, the lad's got the spirit I thought I had."

Douglas took a suck on his pipe.

"You don't need that. Throw the damn thing away," demanded Harold. "What's wrong with you?"

"Harold don't. Just don't," ordered Douglas and he took another drag from the pipe. After a couple of minutes, he clasped his hands together, and asked, "What would you do if I just went home?"

"What? Douglas now you're starting to act stupid. Why don't you go and hang yourself?"

"I could take out something inside and you wouldn't even know it was me that was there."

"FitzGibbon, don't you dare threaten me. Not in a joke. Not in anything. I'm only here for the money you promised me, do you understand?"

"Don't let the crickets crawl up your trousers." Douglas got up off the ground, put the pipe in his shoulder sack and started walking towards the trail.

Harold voiced a couple of clicks to tell his horse to follow and when alongside Douglas asked, "Where are we going?"

"I have another job to get out of the way."

"Where's Caulfield?"

"I don't know. Maybe he went home early."

"You were supposed to take care of Neal. Did you run into anyone else here?"

"Just those two. Samuel stole my horse."

"How did you let that happen?" Harold said as he straightened up. He was revolted by Douglas's blood-stained shoes. *He has killed Richard and now he's lying to me about it,* he thought. One hand held the reins, but both of them closed to make fists.

"Well, I got a knife in both of them," replied Douglas. "They're probably dead. You must have passed them. Did you see my horse?"

Harold hurried to match Douglas's pace. "Douglas where are you walking to in such a hurry? They're miles from here. And no, I didn't see your horse, but I did pass a cart," he said. "There was someone lying in the back. A gentleman sat on one side and a servant on the other. It looked odd. Maybe that was one of them. I didn't get a look at the person in the middle and I don't know if he was living or dead."

"If it was a dead man, his lordship wouldn't sit in the back with him. I'd say the one in the back is alive but in bad shape. If the other was alive, you would have seen him there too.

"And what about the man on the north shore that Richard was supposed to have tracked down?" asked Harold.

"No. we'll leave that for another day. There's two paying contracts left."

"Kennedy and Norton?"

"No. It's for Kennedy and Kevin Neal. I am sure it was him in the cart. Kevin was in better shape and I doubt they would have taken Samuel with them at this time of night. Kevin is a stubborn fellow. If we kill Kennedy & Neal, we'll be well paid. You'd like that wouldn't you Harold?"

"Lord, Douglas. You're a strange one. You're a big fan of Neal one minute and then you're itching to cut his throat the next."

"It's just work. I happen to be good at it. If it wasn't for the work, I don't know what I'd do."

"Look at your hands, they're shaking. Every time I see you, you're getting worse."

"Are you sure you're going to be in shape to…?" asked Harold

Douglas raised his right hand. Harold cautiously stared at the dried blood spattered on Douglas's raised hand and sleeve. Douglas grabbed the back of Harold's jacket and swung up behind him. Douglas sat tall and his hands gripped the loose sides of Harold's coat as Harold, with a click directed the horse to move away from the bay. Harold checked the unloaded pistols by his chest but refrained from drawing attention to his knife which was near Douglas's right hand.

The trail leading to the abbey was dark, isolated, and crossed with weak starlit shadows.

For a very long time the two didn't talk. For part of that time Douglas fell forward and leaned on Harold. He was sure his partner had fallen asleep, and he was sure he was going to fall off. *He's going to break his skull and sure we'll both be better for it,* thought Harold.

A turn in the road pointed them into a wind blowing across the bay.

"Not far from the abbey," said Harold.

"What?"

"Nothing," Harold replied. He was surprised the man was awake. He felt a tug on his open coat. He didn't like it that Douglas's right hand was so close to his knife.

"It wasn't nothing," said the voice behind him.

"What were you going to tell Kevin Neal about the Walshes? I mean no good could come from it."

After a couple of minutes of silence, Harold said, "Are you still there?"

"If I was going to tell you, I'd tell you in my own time, wouldn't I?"

Harold shifted in the saddle and brushed his elbow against his knife sheath.

Douglas told him, "Relax," and seemed to let go of his coat. He took a breath of sea air and said, "Give me a minute."

Harold was sorry he asked and wished the man would just get away from him.

"It was at Billy's public house," Douglas said. "I was having another mug and Martin Bennett started tearing into me. 'Caesar Colclough won't wait,' he yells. 'He wants to see you now. So I tell him to go back to his mother. That really set him off. I think I would have puked on him before I had a chance to kill him, but I was really lost in another place." Douglas let out a spit. "It was the strangest thing. Nick Walsh appears and tells Bennett to bugger off.

"I didn't know whether to laugh or cry about this fella coming to my rescue, so I treated him to a couple of drinks. Apparently, he hated Bennett as much as I did and he hated Caesar Colclough even more.

"Lord I must have really been out of it that night."

"And you think you're right now?" said Harold.

"He told me that he was there because he was afraid he was losing his boy. Padraig I think his name was. He lost his baby girl, and it was stopping him from loving the boy. His story had a tragic sound to it and I gave him a glass, and then another and another.

"Well, Nick Walsh got me talking about me losing my sister, and my brother. I didn't tell him about my da not waiting for me because it really wasn't right."

"So, Walsh reminded you of your da."

"Not exactly. This man realized he'd made a mistake and I could see that he could fix things."

"And if he didn't make the right choice you would have killed him right?"

"Harold, I'll admit I'm not perfect and sometimes I can get carried away.

The man is crazy, thought Harold. *He's telling me about a heartfelt conversation about a man and his son and not too much later has no problem ripping them apart. 'It's just business,' he'll say. He's totally mad.*

"Nick Walsh was an imperfect man, but he meant right for his family," said Douglas. "I mean if you don't have family, what have you?"

Harold came to a turnoff away from the route to the abbey. They followed a trail towards the bay which wound around to the Salt Mill's bridge crossing. "God help us," Harold muttered.

"Relying on prayers won't help. I gave that up long ago. And can you believe it, Nick Walsh was in a bad spot and I gave him money."

"You mean he asked you for a loan?"

"No, he didn't ask for anything. I am telling you I must have really been out of my head. That night, I must have got hit by a horse or something. It was the strangest thing—it's not something I'd ever do. I had just paid the last of what I owed to get my father's farm back, and I still had money in my pocket. He had his eye on this particular race, but he had nothing to put down on the bet. It was old man Kavanagh that put him onto it. I went outside to have a piss, and I stared up at the moon. Just as sure as spit, I got hit by a fart from the heavens and I went back in and I lay down some coins. That night he was so adamant that he was going to win. There was something about his conviction. 'Take the money and you don't have to give it back,' I told him. 'You're going to do it and you're going to stick to it and your life is going to turn around.' All he had to do for the winnings was to pour me another shot of whisky."

Harold heard Douglas make another spit, and then he slipped off the horse.

Harold stopped his horse, and when he turned around, he could barely make him out. "So, why did you give him the money?" asked Harold.

"I made a lot of money doing something I didn't want to do. It is funny how life works out," Douglas said as he walked past him.

Harold had his horse follow alongside him and asked, "Did he win?"

"Yes, he did, but he never collected."

"But…"

"Killing old man Kavanagh wasn't part of the job," said Douglas. "We had them squeezed. They were going to leave anyways.

"You've never cared about nobody. Why are you going on about this?"

Douglas spat on the ground.

"Get your head together, FitzGibbon.

"I know what you're saying, Harold. It's a tough world we live in. But you know there are rules. There has to be rules. So why did you kill old man Kavanagh?" said Douglas.

"You're being stupid." said Harold.

"I guess I could have put pressure on them that needed to pay."

"From what I remember, you got distracted with Bennett's list," said Harold.

"I went to Nick's house before we went Kavanaghs. I stopped in to see if the race panned out. I showed up as a sober, more formal version of myself, and he got quite defensive. He must have thought I was going to take back their winnings. Maybe I could have forced him to tell me who he was dealing with, and then I could have helped."

"Colclough wanted the farmers out," said Harold. "It wasn't just your complete lack of social skills that made him want to close the door."

"Well, trying to do something good just got away from me. I thought I could make my way back to my da's farm, but I saw then that it wasn't going to happen."

"What does giving coins to a bum have to do with building yourself a cottage in the middle of nowhere?" Harold asked.

"Wheeler, just shut up."

"Well, at least you're awake."

"Fool, I'll make sure you're not. I'll walk from here," Douglas said. "I need to exercise my limbs."

"Where are we going? To the abbey or Salt Mills?"

"Tie up the horse on the far shore on the other side of the bridge. I'll meet you on the other side."

Harold watched Douglas staring into an open view of the bay, which was similar to the one where he had picked him up. Harold could taste the sweet fresh air from the Celtic sea. After all these years of working together, he's acknowledging that we no longer trust each other. He grabbed the reins with both hands and galloped across the remaining quarter mile to the Salt Mills bridge.

⁕

"Mary, that miserable Stewart was supposed to bring you back hours ago," yelled James Kennedy, as he escorted his wife and daughter up the path that followed the river towards the abbey. "Anne, keep ahead. Mary are you with us?"

"My, aren't you the concerned mother hen tonight?" answered his wife Mary.

"I'll have you know I can crow like the best of them. Really, I have a feeling about to-night. I don't know what's to become of this place. Things have got so vile and ugly."

"I am sure you don't worry about such things when you're in France."

"Mary, I don't hear you complain when I bring home fine fabrics for your new Sunday frock. Or what about the perfumes and chocolates?"

"James, I'm just teasing you. Calm down."

"Before we go, in I'd like to check on the young blacksmith," said James. He took a left from the abbey and knocked and then opened Kevin's door. "Kevin, are you awake?" he asked. The room was dark. With a bright moon a weak light came through a window. "I can see you there, Kevin. Are you all right?" He meant to touch his shoulder. He recoiled in horror when he felt the clear sensation of dried blood. "Mary, light a lamp. There should be one by the door. Something is terribly wrong."

Mary found the lamp on the ground. After lighting it, her daughter said, "Good Lord."

"What is it?" Mary asked. "Oh, my God."

"Kevin's dead," answered her husband. "The bastards have killed him." He picked up a leg of a broken chair and pressed it against the man's shoulder and he turned him over. "Good gracious! Who in Lord's Holy name is that?"

"Dear Lord, he stinks," Anne said.

"Young lady, don't you use the Lord's name in vain or I'll…"

James laughed nervously in spite of the gruesome sight. "Dear heavens, I have no idea who this is, but obviously someone tried to chop him up. I am telling you this is awful, but it's the strangest thing."

"James lets get out of here. This is ghastly."

"…and stinks terribly," added Anne.

"Yes, we heard that already. If we ever see Kevin again, I'll have your mother tell him to clean it up."

⁓◦◉ɔ

"We're at the abbey, sir," said the driver.

"Should we wake him up?" asked Thomas's servant.

"No. Let him rest," said Thomas. "Both of you wait for me. I'll talk to the others before we decide what to do."

When he returned, he was accompanied by James Kennedy, and Mr. Stewart.

"I'm sorry for the loss of your cousin, Thomas," said Mr. Kennedy.

"Tell me again what you know?" asked James.

"The young men were seriously wounded from an attack. Apparently by a Douglas FitzGibbon. They say he is going to try to kill you and a Mr. Nolan. Mr. Kennedy, I'm sure I won't have a problem locating the Nolans.

Your directions were very clear."

"God speed. I pray you'll find your niece safe and well."

"Mr. Boyse, when I finish here, I'll notify the militia," said Mr. Stewart.

"Mr. Boyse's men wrapped Kevin in the blankets that Mr. Stewart had brought. The others moved near him.

"Be careful with him," said Mr. Boyse. "He has a bad wound in his side."

Mr. Kennedy and Stewart with the help of Boyse's two men lifted Kevin out of the wagon. He opened his eyes, as he was being jostled about. When he saw James Kennedy's face near him he said, "You're not dead yet."

"I hope not," answered James.

Once inside, Kevin was placed on the sofa in the sitting room. "I don't believe you want to share your bed with your house guest at the cottage, so you'll have to bear with us for now," said James Kennedy. "Well, that got a smile from him, didn't it?"

James' wife, Mary, and his daughter, Anne, sat on chairs across from Kevin.

"Mary, this is Kevin. He has had quite an adventure and you can see he's not the better for it. Mary, would you have a look at his wounds, please?"

"I can help," said his daughter Anne.

"You most certainly will not. Stay away from this one. He's that kind of trouble."

"Father, I'm fourteen."

"And that's why you have better things to do."

"Anne, find me some clean rags, and bring us some more water," ordered her mother.

"Sarah Finn..." said Kevin to Mr. Stewart.

"I hear you, Kevin," he replied.

"What's that about?" asked James.

"I'm not sure, but I'll look into it," replied Mr. Stewart.

"Edith, …hurry," Kevin said.

Mr. Stewart gave him an irritated look and proceeded to escort Boyse's men outside. On his way out the front door, James handed him an extra flask of powder for Thomas Boyse's pistol.

"Mary and Anne, I want you to stay here," said James. "You're not to open the door for anyone unless it is me. If anyone else comes, hide upstairs until we get back. The man that did this to Kevin and Samuel is a madman. At no time do you answer the door. Do you all hear me?"

"Anne, bring the water for your mother, please," repeated Mrs. Kennedy.

"Mr. Kennedy," said Kevin.

"Kevin, I have to go." He came back to the sofa to hear him.

"Put thatch in the house and burn him. Use the lanterns."

"You're in a fair and forgiving mood today aren't you," said James.

"Mr. Kennedy," said Kevin as he raised a hand.

"Kevin, what else?"

"Pikes," he said and pointed under the couch.

When Douglas approached the bridge below Salt Mills, he didn't see Harold. The slopes above the shoreline on the Salt Mills side was dark and tree covered. Here, like the bay, the air was sweet and cool. He couldn't see the moon because the sky was becoming overcast. The clouds moving in were gradually covering the few remaining stars.

"It's a nice night to get to work," Douglas said to himself.

As he walked across the bridge with the aide of the last of the starlight, he could see that the tide was out, and most of the riverbed was dry. He could still make out algae, and seaweed in the mud. There wasn't any light coming from the cottages ahead or any sign of people. It wasn't until he had almost reached the end of the bridge that he saw Harold. He was next to his horse, loading a pistol.

"On my account is it?" muttered Douglas. "Tsk, tsk." Once he crossed the bridge, he kept marching up the hill. He heard Harold cursing as he ran after him.

"FitzGibbon, you arrogant fool," grumbled Harold when he got close. "Tell me what you're doing. At this rate we'll never get out of here."

"Shh," Douglas said. "You'll wake up the dead."

"I'll wake you up," Harold said. As he walked up the hill, he loaded a second pistol with powder from his gunpowder pouch.

Douglas wandered ahead, but kept a close eye on his partner. By the time he made his final approach towards the Kennedy's cottage, Harold had caught up to him.

"Are you in any shape to do this?" asked Harold.

"Of course I am," Douglas replied. "I'm always ready. But you know it was strange; I forgot my crimps to-day. It was the first time. I never forget them. I mean never."

"You're getting sloppy. We can't afford that. Am I your mama now?"

"Don't be rude, Mr. Wheeler. It's not helpful. Maybe I'll introduce you to my crimps and show you how inappropriate that is." With a hand he made a cutting motion with two fingers.

"Do you have your wrap with all of your knives?" asked Harold.

"Of course," answered Douglas and he patted the left side of his coat. "It's in there," he said. "Here's the introductory fish cutter blade," said Douglas as he pulled the long knife from a sheaf strapped to his waist belt and waved it at him.

"You better put that away before you lose it," Harold said as he looked around nervously to see if anyone else was around.

Douglas put the knife away and waved him off. "You better get back Harold. You don't want to get caught up in this." He started walking towards the house. Lights shone from both front windows. Douglas took a deep breath and made himself tall. He widened his arms and legs and started to walk like a large monstrous animal. "It's good to have work. It's even better when you're good at what you do," he said. As he walked towards the entrance of James Kennedy's house, he saw a pair of pikes move in the trees to his left. When he looked to his right, there seemed to be an outline of another on the ground. He stared at the door. "Nick Walsh, is it time?" he asked. "Let's go in then," he said.

Harold ran back to Douglas and whispered, "They know you're here, you've got to go."

"Don't worry, lad, don't worry. I'll be fine."

Harold hurried away.

"I see it is just the two of us," said Douglas. "It will be fine Nick. Don't worry. It's just the work." He opened the door and closed it behind.

⸻◦◦◉)

The man's a lunatic. Now he's talking to himself, thought Harold. *I know Douglas knows they're hiding in the bushes. If there were only two of them, I would have cut their throats. I know there are more of them. I can feel it.*

Harold carefully moved back towards the river where he had left his horse. From a place behind tree cover he saw at least a dozen men with long pikes crowd around the front of the house. A man walked towards the door with a block of wood. Another carried an axe and some large spikes.

Douglas will probably do his business and pull himself up through the thatch roof. The ignorant farmers won't even see him leave. They'll think he was a ghost. They're just a bunch of simple-minded fools. The lunatic might even be mad enough to come back and kill the lot of them. And then, for no good reason, come after me.

He saw some figures on the road and he quickly slipped behind some tree cover. Harold recognized Mr. Stewart standing beside a woman and two men. He heard him say, "Mrs. Finn, I'm glad we got here in time. I have to leave because I need to be with the Kennedys." He watched him leave the Finn woman and head downhill towards the bridge.

"Well, damn it. Douglas, what the hell are you doing in an empty house? What an ass," he muttered. Harold slipped down the cliff through some trees.

He saw James Kennedy come across the bridge on horseback from the Abbey side of the river. *Damn, Douglas, you didn't even get Kennedy. What were you thinking?* Harold, in the dark, stepped carefully toward the bridge from the shoreline.

"Where were you?" yelled James Kennedy.

"I'm sorry, but it took an enormous effort to get all the men to come," said Mr. Stewart as he walked towards him. "Mrs. Finn, though, was very persuasive. We filled the house with thatch bundles. Once he enters the house, he won't have a chance."

"You might have got my Anne and Mary killed. Did anyone see him? I better get over there before they set my house on fire."

A two-foot-high wall followed the bridge road. To step from the beach over the wall to the bridge was only a height of three feet. Harold stepped over the wall onto the bridge and fired his pistol at Mr. Stewart's head. The body spiralled to the ground. James's horse reared up, but he hung on. He managed to turn it back towards the abbey. Harold raised a second pistol and took aim. James' horse took off at a gallop, but Harold managed to take a shot. James recoiled and almost fell. He was shot in the lower back on his right side. He leaned forward, and the horse kept running.

Harold ran back to get his horse from the beach where he had tied it to a tree. *Our contract is to make sure James Kennedy is dead. If Douglas isn't up to the job, I'm sure his lordship won't mind if I take care of it.*

He followed James across the bridge to the front of the abbey. He dismounted and tied his horse to a tree. He loaded his first pistol and put it in the back of his pants. He loaded the other one and kept it in his hand as he approached the abbey's front door.

—◦◉◦—

Douglas scanned the room. There were raw thatch bundles aligned against all the walls.

"Nick, you said you were afraid your wife wouldn't forgive you. It was a terrible thing. 'She thinks I forgot my son', you said. You lost your daughter. Oh, Nick, it was so tragic. They stabbed her and did such terrible things. They were such monsters. Thinking about her hurt you so much, you forgot your boy. 'Douglas,' you told me, 'I couldn't let anyone think that I would ever forget my boy. No, I'll never forget my boy,' you said. 'I have to go back and let him know.' And you did, Nick. It was a remarkable thing. You're a good man."

Something was bashing on the front door. Douglas turned and saw nails coming through. There was some more bashing and more nails appeared higher up.

"Why are we here, you're asking? It's my job."

The men outside smashed the door some more.

"Nick, did you know that it was the Púca that gave me the idea for my work. It was before I had a talk with Joseph Kavanagh, and it was even before I met you Nick. I got myself a little drunk, and I ended up sleeping next to a forested stream near Kavanagh's. Screaming woke me up, and I followed the sound to where I saw a truly unnatural sight. There was something that looked like a wolf but it was much, much bigger. I saw it rip apart and then devour a man—bones and all. It was a very messy eater. It left some loose bits around. I followed it as it ran away from the stream into a field on the other side of the main road. It didn't get far as it tried to race across the open field. A devil of a bird-like creature descended from the heavens and reformed into something like a man as it tore through the gardens. The two beasts of hell had a most fearsome battle. At the beginning of the fight I was sure the wolf-like beast had the advantage. I mean, look at its nasty jaws and powerful limbs. The Púca though, was a wiry and determined adversary. With strength of will it was able to smash its nemesis with a most furious vengeance. It pummelled the beast mercilessly until it no longer breathed. After the Púca regained its strength, it grabbed the corpse by the neck and hauled it back into the forest. I imagine that it was being taken back to its lair for a proper butchering. I enacted my work, in a small way, to commemorate homage to the strength and flare of the Púcaman."

Something came in through the back window. The bottle smashed against the bottom of the front wall. Flames followed a spill of oil across the floor. The dry thatch bundles at the back wall caught fire. A second bottle smashed through a front window. Douglas started coughing and had difficulty breathing.

"My daddy left me," mumbled Douglas. "Soldiers chased me and my daddy left me. Nick, why would someone do that?"

His coughing became worse, and the smoke caused Douglas to stumble to his knees. Another bottle came in through another window and exploded near him.

It's like the flames of hell, he thought. "Forgive me, Evelyn," he moaned. The flames from the nearby canister caused his clothes to burst into flame.

"This is how I come home, Da."

In a dying haunted breath he screamed "Father!"

The fire consuming everything in the house, rose through the thatched roof and illuminated the miserable dark clouds above. The light shone through much of southern Wexford.

Harold tried to open the abbey door, but he found it locked. He tried kicking it open, but the lock didn't break. He shot at it and then kicked the door open. He swapped the empty pistol for the loaded one. He didn't see anyone in the sitting room. Harold heard the sound of a girl's voice upstairs. He marched down the hallway and slowly and cautiously turned to the staircase to make his way up to the next floor.

Kevin held a dagger in his right hand as he moved out from behind the couch. From under it he grabbed a pike. The man turned and Kevin threw his dagger at his head but missed. It stuck in the wall near the foot of the staircase.

"Damned," Kevin said.

Harold turned, fired at Kevin and missed. "I don't have time for this," he said and marched back up the staircase.

Kevin, with a pike in hand, followed him to the staircase. He pulled the knife from the wall and hurried up the stairs hoping to reach the man before he reloaded the pistol.

Harold turned, put the pistol, in his belt, and attempted to grab the pike as Kevin jabbed at his legs. Kevin saw Mrs. Kennedy drag a heavy metal statue across the floor to the top of the stairs. Harold heard the noise as well and tried to check back, but Kevin managed to jab his thigh. When Kevin jabbed a second time Harold managed to grab the pike and tell him, "You're really starting to bother me, boy."

Mrs. Kennedy heaved the statue, and it hit Harold's upper back. Harold groaned as he stumbled forward. Kevin pulled the pike out of Harold's grip and he drove it into his belly.

Harold quickly grabbed the pike with both hands. Kevin stared fearfully at Harold's blood drenched hands. He tried to drive the pike in deeper, but couldn't. Kevin realized that if Harold's hands reached him, he'd be dead. Kevin didn't have enough strength.

"You should have run away while you had a chance," taunted Harold. He slowly started pushing Kevin back down the staircase and Kevin stumbled. Harold stepped back and gave a loud groan as he pulled the pike blade away from his stomach. It hadn't gone all the way through. Harold held the end of the pike to his side with one hand and the other was covering his stomach.

Kevin took a swipe at the man's thigh with the knife, but Harold managed to sidestep him. Kevin saw Mrs. Kennedy's head appear at the top of the stairs again. Harold backed up a stair and then kicked Kevin in the face, causing Kevin to drop the knife and stumble back down the staircase. The knife followed him down. He picked it up and retreated into the hallway in the direction of the sitting room.

When Harold reached the hallway, he tossed the pike away. "What did you say to Douglas that made him lose himself?" he asked.

"Nothing he didn't want to tell me," Kevin told him.

Harold kicked over an end table and a vase smashed into pieces across the floor.

"He didn't like to talk to you much did he?" Kevin said and then threw the knife at Harold's face. Harold moved out of the way. He started reloading his pistol as he followed Kevin into the sitting room.

"Why did you kill Mr. Kavanagh?"

"Harold stopped pouring the powder, and said," The old man and the woman? Maybe because Douglas told me not to. I didn't need to give a reason to him and I certainly don't need to give a reason to the likes of you."

Kevin threw a lit candle, but again missed him. "And you killed Anty," Kevin yelled.

"Who?" asked Harold. He focused on his pistol.

Kevin stepped back across the room, grabbed an oil lantern, rushed at Harold and threw it at his belt. The powder ignited and Harold exploded into a bright light and Kevin felt himself blown across the room.

When Kevin opened his eyes, he lay on his back and found himself too weak to move. He felt pieces of pottery cutting into his legs. He heard women upstairs yelling.

He remembered looking through branches during the battle of New Ross, into a time and place he didn't want to remember. He saw the women around Mrs. Sinnott. Their blood sprayed like fire. And protecting him from the cruelty was a brave and affirming Mrs. Sinnott. As he stared he saw in the height of the flames—Kathleen. And behind her was the many feet and many arms of an approaching monster.

The monster in the room in front of him was also on fire and hell was turning it to black. The many parts of monsters that he remembered were now limited to a single writhing unburnt arm which was extended from the pyre. The flames quickly consumed the mortified unclenched hand and the Abbey's wooden staircase behind.

A voice upstairs yelled to someone, "We're going out the back way."

"They're safe. My God. They're safe," he said, and he started coughing as the surrounding smoke thickened. He was too weak to move and was finding it hard to breathe.

"Anty, please forgive me, for not coming back for you. The fires of hell are taking me," he murmured as he felt the smoke trying to suffocate him. He closed his eyes for what he thought was the last time.

—◦◦◉◦—

Kevin was jarred by something hitting him on the face.

"Wake up," she yelled. "Don't leave us. Come on."

"Is he gone?" he heard, someone else say

Kevin's eyes opened, and he saw a woman's eyes and her wavy hanging curl. He kept looking and noticed buxom cleavage.

"That's quite enough Anne," said Mr. Kennedy. Sevens will take it from here.

As Mr. Kennedy's daughter backed away, Kevin found that he was wrapped in a blanket, lying on the grass in front of the abbey. Mr. Kennedy was lying next to him and Mr. Sevens seemed to be treating his wounds. There was a lot of hysteria as a long line of people passed buckets into the abbey. Mrs. Kennedy approached them from the bucket line.

"Nice throw," said Kevin.

"What was that about?" whispered Mr. Kennedy.

"Not important, James," she said.

"What happened to Mr. Kennedy?" Kevin asked Mr. Sevens.

"The man that tried to kill you, shot him in the side, and he killed poor Mr. Stewart.

"Harold got what he deserved," Kevin said. "He's gone to hell, where he belongs."

"Anne, go help with the water brigade. We have this under control."

"But Mam…" Anne complained.

Her mother pointed to the river. "If the abbey burns, your father will be out of work, now hurry," she said.

"I managed to get most of the pieces out, but he's lost a lot of blood," said Mr. Sevens.

"Thanks, Mr. Sevens but I'll take over from here," Mrs. Kennedy said.

"It will take an awful lot of work to repair the abbey. It's going to be in very bad shape," said Mr. Sevens. "…but we'll find our way. We always do."

"My cottage is available," said Kevin.

"Thanks," replied James. "By the way, whose body is in your bed?"

Kevin closed his eyes. He focused on the loss of Mr. Stewart. He couldn't believe that he was dead and that he wouldn't see him anymore.

"The boy better recover quickly. There's a lot of work to do," said Sevens.

"No, he has to leave. He doesn't have a choice. Colclough still wants him dead."

The wounded slept in rooms at the rear of the abbey that were untouched by the fire. Four days had passed. Mary Kennedy watched her husband who was covered in blankets on a couch. Her daughter gave a last goodbye kiss and hug.

"Give my love to your brothers, Anne," said James.

"Come on, Anne," called her mother. "We have to go."

From the next room, she heard men carrying Kevin out to the waiting carriage. "Boys, careful with him," said Mr. Sevens. "Watch that side of his. Get him in. I don't want him bleeding on the seats. We have got to get him out of here."

"Anne carried a bag and ran past her mother to get in the coach before

Mr. Sevens closed the door." Anne you keep an eye on his bandages," said Mr. Sevens.

"No, Mister that will be my job," said Mrs. Kennedy as she followed her daughter inside. After settling in, she moved Kevin's hand to reposition a bandage.

"Father should be coming with us, but he's so adamant about staying."

"Anne, settle down," Mrs. Kennedy said. "It is going to be a long trip to New Ross." She wiped Kevin's head, and called to the coachman, "The boy is burning up. He's not in any shape to travel."

"We don't have any choice, Ma'am," said Mr. Sevens. "We have to keep on, no matter what."

Kevin opened his eyes. "What the hell?" He found himself in a bunk, but he was tied up. "Where am I? On a ship? What am I doing on a ship?" He was surrounded, by lots of other bunks with people in them. He could feel the ship slowly rolling with the waves. It was listing at an angle that made him feel disoriented.

He tried to undo the rope, but he balked at the terrible pain in his side. He just flopped back and looked at the wood of the bunk above him. He was on the bottom bunk and the next one was about two and a half feet from his face. He felt he was losing consciousness again.

"I didn't think this was what happened when you die. Strange," he muttered as he slipped away from reality.

"There you are. Lad, I'm glad to see you with eyes in your head."

"Who are you?"

"I work with the cook. You survived the fever. You were lucky. It didn't look good at all. I tied you in because I didn't want you falling out. You would have died, for sure."

"Uh, thanks. It's good not to be dead."

"Now, let me look at that wound." He cleaned the wound and changed the bandages. "I don't see any puss, which is good, but you're not moving anywhere for a while. Your chamber pot is there. You can untie yourself, but you've got to keep yourself tied up when you're sleeping. You can't lie here indefinitely. When you're able to stand, you'll start earning your keep in the kitchen. Mr. Kennedy told me to tell you that Colclough knows you're alive, but from what I heard, you probably already know that."

Kevin eventually got out of bed and he was put to work in the kitchen the following day. After a couple of months, he became a deckhand. He worked at sea into the next year and deliberated on a future. Kennedy's smuggling runs continued to be lucrative.

Kevin was seated around a table below deck, with five of his shipmates. As Kevin took a first drink from his bottle of whisky, he watched the cards being dealt out.

Alistair Alcock told me that Harry Keane left Ireland for a wild country, Kevin thought. *'...where cliffs are surrounded by trees aflame with colour, bound by a circle of waterfalls and cascading rapids. And where someone could run for days without meeting anyone.' Sounds like the Púca has gone to heaven. Like an exotic wine, it might not be everyone's taste.* Twenty-year-old Kevin took another sip.

Kevin passed his hand through his short black hair. He had cut off his long mane and stubble and made himself look more like his brother Aiden. He caressed his chin and his cheek and got the impression that he had the face of a proper gentleman. Being clean-shaven and having his hair trimmed reminded him of Douglas FitzGibbon, or at least what he could have been. The greasy hair, enlarged pupils, red eyes, and blatant cruelty of what he had recently seen obviously lessened the man, but he had definitely made himself into a force to be reckoned with, through considerable determination.

If Douglas FitzGibbon had taken me with him after my mother died what would have happened? Maybe it's not important. Killing Studdard, and Prescott came too easy. I mean it didn't bother me that much. Bashing Glascott and Harry Keane was thoughtless and unwarranted. Maybe we are already too much alike, he thought. He took another drink.

No. I'm not him. I could never be him. Mr. Kavanagh, the Walshes, the people of the abbey and Anty, have given me a better self. He savoured another drink.

But being without Anty, maybe I'm condemned to mull over only the worst of myself. He put the cork back in the bottle, and thought, *I've stepped across a clochán on the waters of life, and damnation, it's taken me here …to the middle of a sea. What's next? Ireland or America? America is expensive, and both places are filled with risk. Wherever I go, the priests will know where to contact me.*

He looked at his shipmates positioned around the table again and rechecked his cards. He weighed more than the value of his hand.

"I'll raise the pot a pound," he said.

The man with a devilish grin on his left upped his bid.

CONCLUSION (1812)

Choose where you're going in life, and be determined. (Douglas FitzGibbon)

"…she resided at the top of another mountain far away on the other side of the island. She was a defiant warrior princess who would not…" (*Legends of Mount Leinster*, Harry Whitney, (1855), *Evenings in the Duffry*, Patrick Kennedy, (1869))

"Aye, hell. No way. Hold on girl, I'm coming.…" (Kevin Neal)

Twists and Turns

Kevin, from the deck of the ship, stared at the rest of the kitchen's crew following the passengers along the gangplank down to the New Ross docks. They all were eager to get ashore, but Kevin was reluctant. The last time he had looked at the walls of the town was when he had said farewell to Harry Keane. He didn't know what to expect.

The shops and houses beyond didn't look foreboding. Without the pyres and soldiers, the people on shore looked like the people of Tintern, and those leaving the ship.

"Oíche mhaith agus codladh sámh," he said, as his focus was drawn closer to the ship. Staring at a coach at the end of the dock, he whispered, "He's brought the old man's fiddle."

When Kevin re-opened his eyes, he thought he was looking at an angel. She tenderly caressed his forehead and hummed softly.

Terrible pain in his head and body confirmed that he was still alive. When his eyes refocused, he stared at the wrinkled face of an old woman who still had a couple of teeth showing when she grinned. He recoiled when he saw the putrid cloth she was washing him with.

"Thanks Missus. I'm fine. No. No. That will be fine," he said as he tried to push the rag away without touching it. He tried to get up, but groaned when he moved.

"We thought we lost you, when they threw you down the stairs," she said. "A nasty bash, yeh have. The rolling seas are bad and you hit your head and coming down the stairs. I think your shoulder took the worst of it. They brought you down and tossed you onto your bunk. You've only been out a short while."

"I'll be fine. Thank you, ma'am." he said. "I just need to rest." He tried to roll on his side, but a sour shoulder prevented him. He felt the fiddle in his pack by his left leg. Kevin felt relieved enough to want to relax. He stared at the deck above.

I really must have had a lot to drink last night. I must have really got into a tear with the lads up top. That's a pity.

And I do remember Mr. Kennedy telling me some things. And that Samuel Boyse... He's not dead. Of all the miracles... Him fixing Denny's wagon wheel—I mean can you believe it? His honour, the gentleman farmer—I didn't know he was good for anything but shovelling and rescuing the likes of me. And Denny took him on a run across the mountains to Kilkenny. Lord knows what you'll see in this life. Thought he'd live and die back there.

And Mr. Kennedy sending me off to the Canadas. Just like Harry Keane. 'A good place for lunatics,' he says. He gave me a letter from Padraig to his mother—so what am I supposed to tell him?

At that Kevin let the waves rock him back to sleep.

⚜

In another few days Kevin managed to make his way to the bow of the ship next to the anchor. He was extra cautious, at not banging his head on the way out. *That tumble would have really set old man Kavanagh letting into me, wouldn't it?* He pushed the hair off his forehead to feel the wind. The sea on all sides blended into lightly clouded skies.

A deckhand who was tightening up lines to the mast, returned a stare. The figure lumbered towards him. "I told you to stay below," the able seaman bellowed. "You've been trouble ever since you joined us in the inn last night. And you know, no drinking on ship. Like I said, 'twas Captain's orders."

"When you took it, you didn't throw it away. You owe me. And when smelly tried to steal coins, you joined in."

"That's Smiley, and he says you cheated him last night."

"That's what losers say when they don't want to pay up. Hitting me from behind and throwing me down the ladder wasn't gentleman-like was it? The bash on the head was your doing."

"You've still got some coins, don't you?"

Kevin smirked and turned away.

"You don't belong here. Get below."

"I…"

"Don't give me that. Passengers stay below. Look at the sky. Don't ask me how I know, but there's a storm coming."

"There's always a storm coming, and those aren't Captain's orders. You're making that up."

"Don't. Now do what I say and get below, or I'll not be so obliging."

Kevin looked ahead and watched the other deckhands scrubbing decks. "I know you're supposed to be scrubbing with the rest and this little visit is your way of getting out of it. Tell the Captain you're teaching me the ways of seaman life and I'll help with the scrubbing. Less work for you maybe. Get me into the next game of cards and I'll split my winnings for my first two hands. In turn you give me your next rum ration."

"You are a determined little prick aren't you." Staring back at the others, he said, "Well maybe. Not giving you my rum, and it'll be first three winning hands and if you lose, you give me two pence. I know you have it because I saw it."

"First three winning hands, half the next ration and nothing more,"

Kevin countered.

A figure from the bow of the ship waved back menacingly.

"Better get on. Boss there is impatient."

The seaman looked him up and down. "Better move it before I change my mind."

"So Andrew, do we have a deal?"

"Kevin, show me the winnings," Andrew replied.

At the next game, Kevin lost the first hand but won the next two. The game broke up because the others complained that he was cheating. Kevin shared the next rum ration and talked Andrew into sharing from his personal store. The ship's company, however, never had a follow-up card game.

On the next day, black anvil shaped thunder clouds moved in and forced out the remains of a clear sky. As the day got darker, a building wind reshaped waves into rolling hills, and the seamen madly tried to secure the rigging and bring down the sails.

Kevin pulled up the collar of his coarse woollen jacket, as the waves got rough and the rise and fall of the deck became more pronounced. When the ship sailed into the dark curtain of the storm, a downpour of howling rains accompanied a shroud of fearsome darkness. As the ship crashed and pounded into rising, rolling crests, it seemed that the driving rains were pulling the clouds down and the ocean was rising up to meet it. As the waves got larger, the ship took on a steeper pitch. Kevin lost his footing on the slippery deck—only his hands held him in place.

The stern seemed to get lower, after each attempt to rise over the next swell. The bow plowed its way up and over. Kevin watched the waves tumble with force along the ship's sides. The helmsman tried to angle the ship into the oncoming swells.

The sea will tear me away if I stay here, Kevin thought. Waves washed over the ship. He grabbed at a line to save himself as the ocean tried to pull him out. He was left soaked and cold.

When the ship reached the peak of the swell, he watched more waves rising up like rows of mountains, blocking the horizon.

The ship slid down from the crest towards the trough. Kevin stared at the mountain of water that was heading for them. He laughed. *It's just like being home*, he thought. He laughed again. The wall of water continued to rise. Instead of climbing, the ship veered along the trough. Kevin looked left. The wall on the port side kept growing in size. *My God, the wave is going to devour us. I'm going to drown. I won't be able to breathe.* He pictured himself suffocating and sinking into the black.

Kevin looked back at the helmsman, then stared way upwards. A portion of the fore top gallant sail was loose. The ship was listing towards the starboard side. *We're not going to be able to sail across the oncoming wave*, thought Kevin.

Seamen were frantically trying to adjust rigging from the deck. Two men were climbing the rigging to get to the sail. One of them was Andrew Collins. Kevin left his hiding spot at the bow, to slide back down towards the sailors. Another huge wave washed over the ship. It washed Kevin off the deck, but he managed to lock an arm and a leg round a line to the forward mast.

He saw that the men above were still climbing. The ship got pounded again in a change of wind, and one of the men was blown off into the wake of the ship.

Kevin confirmed that he still had a knife at his waist. He saw the look of terror on the helmsman's face. Kevin stared at the man above him. The mast was shaking wildly.

"If the sea is going to plough us into the abyss, then that's where I am going to be," he told himself.

He ran to the main sail mast, stepped up on the gunwale and with a twist grabbed onto the shroud that secured the mast. When he reached fifteen feet up, another tumultuous wave almost washed him away. Both hands were torn from their grip but a bent knee against a cross rope again kept him in place.

"You don't make it easy, do you Anty?" he groaned as he struggled to get hold of the ropes again. Whether it was tears or just the sea in his eyes, he told it to "get back." With frozen hands, he grabbed the cold swaying rigging, pounded ratlines with his soaked feet, as he forced his way up the mast against the howling storm.

"Aye, Hell. No way… Hold on girl, I'm coming."

Beyond the Shadow of Death

As he sank into the abyss, Kevin dimly remembered Andrew repeatedly calling, "Hold on. Hold on. Don't let go." Now his weak outstretched arms and legs had nothing to grab on to. After he had heard what he thought was the sound of a seabird, Kevin remembered hearing whispering that was less audible than the ripples around the timber. "Stand alive," he heard. Another time a voice said, "There."

"No. No," his dried salt-caked lips answered back, fearing death was calling, as his arms let the wood go.

Sinking and succumbing towards eternal blackness he imagined the world of light above leaving, and Kevin was disappearing. With the glimmers almost gone in the drowned cold, he sensed himself fading into numbing quiet.

The surrender was interrupted by a memory of someone trying to say something. The word was, "find..."

In between never and there, Kevin remembered Andrew repeating "don't let go." Kevin felt a presence in the stillness observing him. What will you do? What can be done? It was waiting. "What?" asked Kevin.

In the stillness of everything, he was aware there was nowhere to go and nowhere to hide. Kevin remembered his story but saw new things. He saw Aiden complaining about how his father died, saw how the FitzGibbons were chased from their farm, saw his mother's reluctance of leaving her boys on the battlefield, saw why Mrs. Walsh chose her husband and saw how Douglas FitzGibbon came to choose to enter a stone pyre with Mr. Walsh. *In seeing these impossible things, can I possibly forgive him?* wondered Kevin. *I mean, there's Anty, The Walshes, Richard, Walter and even Joseph Kavanagh. It was for selfishness, wasn't it?*

He saw how Douglas as a boy, tried to keep his sister alive. Kevin saw his own sister and her friend in blood and fire surrounded by souls whisking around in madness and terror.

He let his thoughts hover in the solitude.

Kevin reached out. The hands of Douglas FitzGibbon formed.

In all honesty, I can't forgive. I know I should. A better man than me I'm sure could. I'm sure would. I believe there's a process and yes in time I believe I could because it's a right thing. I mean it's something I have to do. I don't want to repeat the story of the first Irish sorrow. I know it stops with me. Kevin was prepared to wait until he could find his way through. With this, existence returned to stillness.

The stillness of the next life was disrupted. The word "find" echoed and formed a vortex. Kevin felt its existence first as a premonition, followed by something like a touch of a feather almost against the back of his neck. He felt a current pull.

No. No. It's not supposed to… Kevin thought as he was drawn away from the inevitable. He imagined being sent back towards the light but he lost consciousness.

When Kevin awoke, he felt himself throwing up in a smelly boat and surrounded by a cackle of voices. He heard himself breathe and sensed the sweet smell of seaweed and hot sun. Eventually, they carried him on a blanket. His baked eyelids squinted as he passed the outline of a leaning tombstone on a rocky hill.

A woman's voice said, "he's better off than the one he keeps calling for."

"Another clochán," Kevin Neal whispered and lost consciousness again.

⌇

When Kevin opened his eyes again, he saw an old woman with a cloth. When she went to wipe his face again, he tried to push away.

"Good to see there some life to you still," she said. Behind her was a hearth fire blazing and a warm wind was blowing in from an open cottage door. The rag didn't look as vile as it did last time. He realized he was somewhere else, other than a ship.

"You've been out for a long while," she said. "The fever almost took you. Are you up for a taste of soup?"

Kevin nodded.

She came back with a bowl and patiently spooned him sips.

"America?" Kevin asked.

"Turned around are yeh?" she replied. "No. Just Dingle."

"What?" Kevin whispered.

She wiped his mouth with a rag. Some soup had dribbled on his chin.

"It's County Kerry. You know—it's in Ireland. Where you from?"

She gave him another spoonful of soup.

Kevin didn't answer her.

"I was just making conversation. I know you're from County Wexford."

"Andrew?"

"I heard you were asking when they brought you in. No, he's not here. You were alone out there, I'm afraid. It's that fellow you need to thank."

Kevin squinted to make out a black silhouette in the doorway.

"Harry," he whispered. "It's Harry Keane. Well if it isn't the devil himself." Kevin sensed his wry grin even if he couldn't see it.

When Harry came in he was followed by two men.

"Those are my boys," Charlie and Arthur," she said. "It was Mr. Keane that brought them to you," she said. "They thought he was a madman."

"No, didn't doubt him for a minute," said Charlie.

"It was coin that changed your mind," she said.

"He brought you from the sea," Charlie said.

"Anyway it was a miracle finding the young lad," said Arthur. "Harry here seemed to know exactly where you were. It was the strangest thing."

"I think that's enough for one day. Kevin can barely keep his eyes open. Everyone out now and let him rest."

Two days later Kevin was much recovered. For the first time, he took a walk along the beach searching for what the sea had to offer. He was confused about what he'd heard in his dreams.

Was it Andrew's voice or my own? he wondered. *Andrew was a stubborn, belligerent, cantankerous bastard but his harassing had kept him going. Was it him or just the memory of his eternal pestering to not let go that I heard?* he wondered. *If I'd been more responsive, maybe he'd be here too.*

But then again, maybe it wasn't him at all. He wasn't part of any of my story and there were a lot of things I've never seen myself. I know I could have guessed how some things looked like because I found out later but still some of those memories seemed so clear.

He stared back at the smoke rising from the cottage's hearth fire. *I heard the prodding and I assume it was Andrew. He was going after me so steadily, I just assumed it was him.*

Harry. There's no understanding Harry. Scooping me up from the dead. There's no understanding the nature of a Púca, but the command to find could only have come from Douglas FitzGibbon himself. There was no stopping that one when he put his mind to it. The Púca pulled me out of the water, Andrew helped me to hold on, but Douglas FitzGibbon is the one that saved me.

"Are you ready to go?" echoed a voice behind him.

"Harry, you startled me." Looking around, he asked, "where did you come from?"

"Are you ready?"

"Ready for what?" Kevin asked.

"We're supposed to be going to America?"

"I thought you went already."

He opened his arms and replied, "I'm still here."

"Yeh, I can see."

"The crown still has a bounty on your head, you know. You would be wise to make yourself scarce."

"I don't have a ticket and all I have is what I'm wearing. I don't even have a set of boots."

"We'll work something out. We've got to get on a ship at Cork."

"You're going to work something out?" Kevin repeated.

"I've made some investments that paid off," Harry said.

"We need to leave in about two hours."

"I'm still a bit weak and I still need to get some boots."

"I bought a pair from Arthur. You go talk to him about it. If they're on the large size, ask his mother if she has some stitching supplies. To get your strength back you need to walk and why not walk there than around here? Anyway, hurry up about it. We don't want to be late."

Kevin stared at the ocean and tried to focus his thoughts. When he looked back, he noticed Harry was gone. "What's going on?" he asked himself.

After getting and making minor adjustments to his shoes Kevin returned to the beach. They were a larger size. He made himself a leather sock insert to accommodate the difference.

Harry, in the distance, waved for Kevin to join him. Kevin rushed to keep up.

"Did you say your goodbyes?" asked Kevin.

"Yes, before I talked to you."

"You really are in a rush, aren't you? How did you know our ship went down? How did you even know where to look?"

"Uh, I guess I just had a sense. Lucky guess perhaps."

"And you just happened to be nearby?"

Harry didn't answer. He quickened his pace.

After Kevin caught up to him he said, "Alistair Alcock, said he placed a wager on you."

"It was a few. 'twas private off-track betting. The crown was quite restrictive at the time."

"Was Mr. Kavanagh, involved?" Kevin asked.

"I can't say for sure."

"You mean you won't. You know just before Mr. Kavanagh was killed, he and Nick Walsh won a wager as well."

Kevin stared up at Harry Keane.

"Well, I wouldn't know anything about that," he said.

Kevin laughed. "You know by inheritance, that comes to me."

"Well, maybe when we get to Cork, we could spare you a ticket," he said. "What do you think about that?"

"And I hope you're planning to eat. It's a long ways."

Harry picked up his pace again.

Kevin wasn't in shape for running. He bent over, took some big breaths and hobbled after him again. He noticed that Harry Keane tended to slow down when he brought up something new.

"What happened to Thomas?" Kevin asked.

Harry kept walking.

"But he was killed by a monster," Kevin said.

"I didn't know that Thomas was attacked, until months later."

"In a dream, I was told that you killed it," said Kevin.

"The wolf, you mean," said Harry.

"A giant one—if that is what it was," said Kevin.

"We guard places where the boundaries between places are weak. They hunt on the other side."

"We?" asked Kevin.

"A few of us were left around. The wolves aren't supposed to cross. And Kevin Neal, as I told you before, no, I didn't kill him. Some just prefer to see what they want to believe."

"Mr. Keane, I'm not inferring…"

From his pocket, he threw Kevin a piece of bread

With a stunned look on his face, Kevin caught it.

You didn't eat it after you had your soup," Harry Keane said.

"The wolf and I had a few harsh moments but he made it back alive. It was fortunate for me that he didn't have company. But I must say, the poor thing was in a really bad way. He suffered from something like rabies.

"The border breaches had been happening too often. From before the Rebellion is when it started. I'll have you know that there's more than a few realms on the other side. And one of them, like this one, was also tossed on its' head. And at the same time, my people had an exchange of differences. It was a woefully difficult time."

"So the wolf getting loose wasn't an accident?"

"Too many to be a coincidence. And thet happened at the same time. 'Keep out of sight. Don't interfere,' I was told. Still something was going about its business and it wasn't bound by the same restrictions. Looking back, I should have asked for help."

"You mean—like helping Captain Kelly?"

"No, I mean—from my kind. And now that someone in America is calling for me, I'm leaving."

"Isn't that going to be a problem?"

"Probably, but I've got a new coat and it's time for a change, don't you think?"

"I suppose," Kevin said.

Harry tossed him another piece of brad.

"Anyway, it was getting too risky for Thomas and his brother to be near me. I used to think that if I kept them close, I could have protected them from the worst of the war, but things got difficult to manage, I had to tell Thomas to keep away."

"If you explained what was going on, it might have saved his life."

"As I said, it was a difficult time."

"So why are you telling me this and why didn't you leave when I saw you in New Ross?" asked Kevin.

"When I last talked to John Kelly, he asked me to keep you safe, and I have promises to keep."

"Promises?" Kevin, repeated.

"A little boy asked me to find someone. It took a long time but I did."

"Find?" Kevin repeated.

Harry picked up his pace again. "Hurry, you don't want to miss Red Carrauntoohil."

"What?"

"The mountain is between us and Bantry. It's the tallest on the island. Hurry up. And then we're going to the New found land. But you know why."

"I do?"

"That's where your Miss Anastasia Kelly is."

"What? But I thought…"

"She acquired a lead from someone in England that knew where her sister was. Douglas FitzGibbon, unfortunately, killed someone else. Aren't you lucky you're coming along with me?"

"Alive. She's alive?" Kevin felt stunned. He stared at Harry who was getting ahead of him.

"And I guess, somehow, I did but was afraid to confess it."

"Stop mumbling and come on," Harry said.

"Anyway, I thought you were going to America?" Kevin asked as he picked up his pace.

"Well, the New found land is pretty close, don't you think?"

"I wouldn't know?"

"One other thing. Caesar Colclough is there as well."

"Colclough?"

"Colclough is the chief justice for the colony. He has the power to do pretty well whatever, and he knows where she is. He is the law of the land. Coming?"

"How do you know?"

"Connections, Kevin. You know, I have connections. Besides if you don't keep up I'll have to go ahead on my own. I have other commitments."

"Commitments?" repeated Kevin.

"Na soilse ó thuaidh."

"The Northern Lights."

"Soilse."

Kevin looked at him blankly.

"Soilse na súl."

"Hard on the eyes? You're going to see a woman?"

"No."

"A Púca?"

He gave a small grin and picked up speed as he followed the path up a rocky hill.

"So Púca's have… You're going to… I thought you had business in…"

"There are things that I have to do, but there can be more than one reason to leave."

"Soilse?" repeated Kevin.

"Na soilse," corrected Harry. She's one of a kind. She's like a flash of lightning, but so much more."

"Soilse na súl. She must be something-for a Púca, I mean."

"For you too. She can be trouble."

"What?"

"Kevin, keep up."

So much for having a choice, Kevin thought. *And Her name is Soilse.*

So that's how it happened. Harry knew where I was because he sailed with us.

As the slope steepened, Kevin was left behind. He couldn't believe that Anty was so far away and still in danger. Harry beckoned for him to catch up.

Looking at the silhouette ahead reminded him of the last time he watched him run away. He was racing up a hill like this near New Ross. Kevin raced faster than any man alive and then he seemed to fly into a cover of trees. It seemed nonsensical at the time but at the moment he wasn't so sure. He, needed to catch up before the Púca left the ground— and left Anty and himself behind.

The young man hurrying towards the light, yearned for breath.

Terms

Anty Kelly is not a Russian name that was arbitrarily dragged in. "Anty," which is short for Anastasia, appears quite often in local surveys of the mountain people in ~1830's (Tithe Survey) and 1850's (Griffith Survey). The Neal spelling was how the name was commonly written in those same books.

Clochán is an Irish stepping stone that is set in place to enable a river crossing. In the middle ages, monks applied the word to their round igloo-like houses made of blocks of stone. They expected that stone houses of prayer could serve as stepping stones for souls to cross over to the next life.

Denis Brien is an historical character. Although the Wexford folklorist Patrick Kennedy in his books (Legends of Mount Leinster, Evenings in the Duffry, Banks of the Boro), used the Denis spelling, I have written the name as Denny because that is how the Irish would have pronounced it. Much of what is known about Irish folklore (esp. The Púca), comes from stories repeated by Denis Brien to Patrick Kennedy in the 1820's.

Ratlines, are lengths of thin line tied between the shrouds of a sailing ship to form a ladder.

Seanachaí, is a bearer of "old lore" (i.e.. storyteller/historian). Long folkloric lyric poems were traditionally recited.

Shrouds, on a sailing ship, are pieces of standing rigging on each side of a mast. They stretch from chain plates tied to the hull each side up to partway up the mast. There can be multiple stretches of shroud up the mast. The last stretches to the top of the mast. The lines of shrouds on each side of the ship hold a mast in place. The ratline cross pieces (lines or wooden) enable sailors climb a ladder like structure to configure rigging and sails.

Tintern Abbey de Voto (Tintern of the Vow), was founded in c.120 by William Marshal, Earl of Pembroke, as the result of a vow he had mad when his boat was caught in a storm nearby. Once established, the abbe was colonized by monks from the Cistercian abbey at Tintern i Monmouthshire, Wales, of which Marshal was also patron. To distinguis the two, the mother house in Wales was sometimes known as "Tinter Major" and the abbey in Ireland as "Tintern de Voto" (Tintern of the vow. After the Dissolution of the Monasteries the abbey and its grounds we granted firstly to Sir James Croft, and then in 1575 to Anthony Colcloug of Staffordshire, a soldier of Henry VIII. (sour https://en.wikipedia.org/wiki/Tintern_Abbey)

County Wexford Map

https://www.lawrenceobrien.ca/
https://www.facebook.com/LawrencePOBrienCA

For News And Behind the Scenes Look at Stories:
https://www.lawrenceobrien.ca/newsletter/

Thank you for you curiosity and perseverance.

And please leave a review. I would appreciate to see what you have taken away from your read of **CLOCHÁN**

Amazon	https://www.amazon.com/CLOCHAN-Lawrence-Patrick-OBrien/dp/1777815509
Goodreads	https://www.goodreads.com/book/show/59610337-clochan
Kobo:	https://www.kobo.com/ca/en/ebook/clochan
Smashwords:	https://www.smashwords.com/books/1107044